ONE SWEET KISS

Cosima took Benedict's face in both hands and kissed his mouth hard.

"Do you still think I'm mocking you?" she asked softly. Her eyes were half-closed.

He slipped his hand behind her neck and kissed her mouth softly. Cosima was startled. Men usually attacked her if given half a chance. This was not an attack, but a lingering caress and she didn't quite know how to take it. He seemed to be savoring her mouth slowly and gently. Now why would he do that? As far as she knew, men only kissed women to distract them from what their hands were trying to do lower down. *He* seemed to be in no hurry to get on with it at all.

"I could kiss you all day," he murmured. "You taste like apples. Green apples."

"I made a tart this morning," she explained.

He kissed her again in the same style. His tongue felt clean and cool in her mouth. Her senses began to stir and quicken as she breathed in his scent. It really was as if he meant to go on kissing her all day, slowly and steadily. . . .

Books by Tamara Lejeune

SIMPLY SCANDALOUS

SURRENDER TO SIN

RULES FOR BEING A MISTRESS

Published by Zebra Books

RULES FOR BEING A MISTRESS

TAMARA LEJEUNE

ZEBRA BOOKS
Kensington Publishing Corp.
www.kensingtonbooks.com

ZEBRA BOOKS are published by

Kensington Publishing Corp.
850 Third Avenue
New York, NY 10022

All Kensington titles, imprints, and distributed lines are available at special quantity discounts for bulk purchases for sales promotion, premiums, fund-raising, educational, or institutional use.

Special book excerpts or customized printings can also be created to fit specific needs. For details, write or phone the office of the Kensington Special Sales Manager: Attn.: Special Sales Department. Kensington Publishing Corp., 850 Third Avenue, New York, NY 10022. Phone: 1-800-221-2647.

Zebra and the Z logo Reg. U.S. Pat. & TM Off.

ISBN-13: 978-1-4201-0129-4
ISBN-10: 1-4201-0129-3

First Printing: May 2008
10 9 8 7 6 5 4 3 2 1

Printed in the United States of America

Chapter 1

Despite all rumors to the contrary, Sir Benedict Wayborn had not been born with a cast-iron poker lodged up his bum. He simply had excellent posture. Even while traveling alone, as he was now, in a hired carriage miles away from his own county, the baronet sat up straight, as stiff and unyielding in private as he was in public. His face might have been carved from marble as he considered his lack of progress in securing a wife.

He was on his way to Bath. A hard rain continued to fall as night closed in, but Benedict ordered the coachman to drive on. From Chippenham they advanced at a snail's pace until, about four miles from Bath, they stopped altogether. A vehicle was foundering in the road, its wheels lodged a foot deep in mud. As servants worked to move it, a gentleman and a young lady watched from beneath a single umbrella.

Having lost half of his right arm as a boy after being mauled by a dog, Benedict was never eager for the company of strangers, but he civilly instructed his driver to invite the Fitzwilliams to share his carriage for the rest of the journey.

Smelling strongly of cheap tobacco and French musk, the gentleman climbed into the carriage first. He scarcely looked old enough to be the uncle of the well-dressed young lady who jumped up after him, but that was his claim. Benedict kept his cynical suspicions to himself, and the carriage resumed its slow crawl toward Bath. The lady's maid sat outside on the box with the driver, but the Fitzwilliams' other servants were left to extract the gig from the mud.

Benedict had just begun to hope that his guests were as unsociable and taciturn as himself when the young man suddenly exclaimed, "Why, it's Sir Benedict Wayborn! Forgive my silence, sir. I did not know you were anyone."

If the baronet forgave, he did so silently.

"I daresay you don't remember me; I'm Roger Fitzwilliam. My brother Henry is married to the Duke of Auckland's sister. Now that your own charming sister is safely buckled to His Grace, you and I are brothers-in-law, are we not?" Having established this tenuous connection, Mr. Fitzwilliam ventured headlong into intimacy. "How *is* the dear duchess? Breeding, I trust?"

"I have not heard from my sister since she left England on her wedding trip," Benedict replied, fumbling for his black silk handkerchief. He sneezed into it violently.

"Must you wear so much scent, Uncle?" hissed the young lady, embarrassed.

The Earl of Matlock's daughter was a pretty girl of seventeen. Unfortunately, the purity of her skin was lost in the gloom, along with the brilliance of her dark eyes and the luster of her expertly curled chestnut hair. Her worst defect, however, was glaringly apparent: a wide space between her two front teeth. She looked as though she had not fared well in the boxing saloon.

"We waltzed together once at Almack's, Sir Benedict, but you neglected to call on me the next day," Rose accused. "All my other partners called in person, except my Lord Redfylde, but *he* at least sent tulips—and he is a marquess!"

Try as he might, Benedict could not remember dancing with her. She was just the sort of insipid, yet insufferably vain, debutante that had forced him to abandon London.

"Don't annoy the gentleman," Fitzwilliam admonished his niece. "As I was saying: what a good thing you were passing,

Sir Benedict. We actually sank in the mud, by Jove! I blame Rose: five enormous trunks full of frills and furbelows!"

"It would be a very strange thing if I had fewer than five trunks," Rose protested. "You men may wear the same thing three days running if it pleases you, but a lady must change her dress at least three times a day, *and* she must never be seen wearing the same thing twice."

"Poor Rose! Only seven hundred pounds a year on clothes. How *do* you survive?"

Rose did not choose to respond to her uncle's impertinence.

"I daresay we will have less competition in Bath," Fitzwilliam went on. "Eh, Sir Benedict? Little Bath is not so crowded as mighty London. Cheaper, too, if that matters to you."

Benedict merely eyed him with chilling scorn.

"I did not get on at all," Fitzwilliam complained. "London ladies all think themselves too smart to be vicars' wives, I can tell you! If the Marquess of Redfylde would only make up his mind, we poor bachelors might get on, but, as it is, all the girls have set their caps at him."

"We are not all mercenary, Uncle," Rose said hotly.

Fitzwilliam's smile was pained. "You must understand, Sir Benedict, that my niece's season has been scrapped for a complete disaster. I am conducting her to her mama in disgrace. Lady Matlock will be able to puff her off in Bath, I daresay. The place is full of gouty old men on the lookout for something young and warm. Present company excluded, of course, Sir Benedict," he added unctuously as Rose fought back sudden tears.

Fitzwilliam patted her hand. "There, there, pet. It was not *your* fault Westlands did not propose. You did everything you could. What did his lordship mean, taking her out driving in the park every day, waltzing with her at Almack's, and then haring off to Derbyshire without proposing?" he demanded, apparently of Benedict. "You know Westlands, of course, Sir Benedict: Lord Wayborn's son. Why, you must be cousins."

"The connection is very distant, I assure you," Benedict said coolly.

"She might have had Redfylde himself, poor child, if Lord Westlands's attentions had not been so marked. She might as well be used goods! I've a mind to call him out, the rascal."

Rose said maliciously, "You forget, Uncle, that Westlands is an excellent shot."

"So am I an excellent shot!" cried Fitzwilliam, and the pair fell to arguing over which gentleman would most likely be killed in the hypothetical duel: the viscount or the vicar.

Benedict took the opportunity to blow his nose. Perhaps it was selfish, but he did not care if Lady Rose Fitzwilliam died an old maid. He did not care if his distant cousin Lord Westlands had behaved like a cad. He did not care if Westlands and Fitzwilliam killed one another in a pointless duel. He wished he could set the Fitzwilliams down in the road and leave them to their fate, but, sadly, one was bound by a code of civility.

He pretended to fall asleep. Fitzwilliam soon slept in earnest, but Rose, bored, drummed on her jewel box with her gloved fingertips. "You can stop pretending now, Sir Benedict," she said, pouncing onto the seat next to him. "We must have *some* conversation, or I shall go mad!"

He opened his eyes. "Kindly return to your seat, Lady Rose."

"You're *only* number fifty-six on my aunt's list of eligible bachelors," she sniffed angrily. "Aunt Maria says you're too stuffy and dignified to run after girls half your age, but I've noticed that you dye your hair black in an effort to appear younger."

Benedict could not be goaded so easily. He simply closed his eyes again. To his relief, Rose returned to her seat and did not speak again until they reached her mother's house in the Royal Crescent of Bath, and there she only thanked him haughtily as she quit his carriage.

Lord Matlock had not joined his countess in Bath. Therefore, his lordship's youngest brother was obliged to put up in the York House Hotel in George Street. Fitzwilliam jumped out into the hotel yard, grumbling about the expense, and releasing such potent waves of French musk that Benedict was obliged to step out of the carriage until he stopped sneezing. Reluctant to return to the noisome, confined space, the baronet paid the coachman and dismissed him.

The house he had leased from Lord Skeldings stood at a distance from York House, but Benedict had strong legs and an excellent umbrella. For sixpence a boy from the hotel agreed to carry his valise. Declining both Fitzwilliam's offer of a late supper, and the landlord's offer of a sedan chair, he gave the boy the address, and they set off on foot. The rain, which had almost stopped, seemed to pick up again as they climbed up Lansdown Road to Camden Place.

By no means as famed as the Royal Crescent or the Circus, Camden Place was still one of the most exclusive neighborhoods in Bath. Benedict had chosen it for its remoteness. The long, steep walk up Lansdown Road did not trouble him in the least. He liked to walk.

On a night like this, Benedict's valet would usually greet his master at the door with a hot brandy, but, oddly, there was no sign of Pickering as they walked up to No. 6 Camden Place. More puzzled than annoyed by his manservant's absence, Benedict paid the boy from the hotel his sixpence and rang the bell. When no one answered, Benedict became concerned.

He could not possibly have guessed that the storm had played a cruel trick on him. This was not No. 6 at all. It was No. 9. The violent storm had pulled the brass number loose at the top, spinning it around and around until it finally came to rest upside down. Pickering was waiting up for his master across the street. In fact, had it not been for the long, narrow park that ran down the middle of Camden Place, Pickering would have been able to see his master from where he stood looking out of the window, and Benedict would have been able to see him.

Benedict took out the key that his landlord, Lord Skeldings, had given him. His handicap obliged him to close his umbrella and wedge it between his knees first, which made it a wet and awkward operation. To make matters worse, a sudden gust of wind sheered his hat from his head and tossed it over the iron railings of the park. Benedict scarcely noticed the loss, having just discovered a greater calamity: his latchkey did not fit.

"Perfect!" he muttered. *Now* he was annoyed. Cursing under his breath, he began to bang on the door with his umbrella.

Miss Cosy Vaughn gasped as her naked feet slapped the floor of her bedroom. The bare floorboards were so cold that, for a moment, she forgot why she was getting out of bed in the middle of the night. A rhythmic banging from downstairs soon restored her memory, however: some nameless fool was pounding on the front door, and if she didn't put a stop to it, the noise would wake up her mother, if it hadn't already. Fumbling for the candle on her bedside table, she lit it, savoring its warmth as she pulled on her dressing gown.

There was no fire in her room because the coal was running out, and the collier, who could roast in the hot coals of hell for all she cared, had declined to extend the Vaughns any more credit. Cosy had gone to bed bundled in a shawl, with woolly socks on her feet. The socks had itched so badly that she had peeled them off in the dark, but now, still half asleep, she searched for them, her teeth chattering.

The windows of her bedroom faced the street, but with the rain coming down in sheets, she could see nothing when she looked through the dark glass. As the knocking continued, she hurried to check on her mother and sister, who were sharing a bed in the next room to conserve fuel. Warmed by "logs" painstakingly crafted from tightly rolled overdue bills, the room was blazing hot. Lady Agatha, propped in a sitting position so as not to disturb the cold cream on her pockmarked face, snored peacefully while nine-year-old Allegra had flung the bedclothes off and was hanging half out of her mother's bed, her mop of pale, straight hair almost grazing the floor.

"Who is he at all, Miss Cosy? Sure he knocks like a bailiff."

Nora Murphy had come down from the attic with a shawl thrown over her nightgown, scraping her wiry, grizzled hair into a bun as she hurried down the hall.

"A bailiff wouldn't trouble himself in such weather," Cosy shrewdly pointed out. "It must be a messenger," she added, crossing herself in a quick prayer.

Nora's beady eyes bulged in terror. "Is it our Dan?"

Dan was Cosy's brother. Lieutenant Dante Vaughn had recently sailed out of Tilbury on his way to join their father, Colonel Vaughn, who was stationed with his regiment in India.

Fearing everything from shipwreck to cannibals, Cosy ran back to her own room with Nora at her heels. Opening the window, Cosy leaned out. Rain blurred her vision, but she could just make out the shape of a man. "He's left-handed," she reported, having absorbed in childhood the Irish superstition that left-handed people are an unlucky breed.

"A *ciotog*," Nora cried, crossing herself. "Sure the left-handed are the Devil's own."

Ashamed that she had yielded even briefly to a silly old superstition, Cosy pushed her head out of the window again. "What is your message, sir?" she called down, shouting over the roar of the streaming gutters. Her voice was instantly carried off by the wind, and she was obliged to scream at the top of her voice: "WHAT DO YOU WANT?"

Benedict had rented a house complete with staff. "Let me in!" he roared, incensed that one he took for a servant was not already downstairs waiting on him hand and foot.

"WHAT?" Cosy shrieked, shielding her face from the rain with one arm.

"LET ME IN. I AM SIR BENEDICT. I'VE BEEN GIVEN THE WRONG KEY."

"It's not a messenger, thanks be to God!" said Cosy, pulling her head in out of the rain. "He says he's Sir Benedict. He's locked out of his house, poor man."

"I don't care if it's *Saint* Benedict he is," Nora declared stoutly. "You can't be letting in strange men in the middle of the night, Miss Cosy. You're not in Ireland anymore."

Cosy stuck her head back out and howled, "I'LL COME DOWN."

"You're too kind," Benedict muttered, shivering, as she slammed the window shut.

Wet to the waist, Cosy ran to her wardrobe and opened the doors, her teeth chattering. "You'd not want to be left out in the rain yourself, Nora Murphy," she snapped in response to Nora's silent disapproval. "I daresay none of his *English* neighbors would let him in."

"I'll wake Jackson," said Nora, naming the only other servant in the house.

"You will not," Cosy said, toweling her hair into a damp, tangled mess. "He's stocious, and I'll not have Sir Benedict thinking all Irishmen are drunkards! Go and let his lordship in while I get dressed." She threw off her dressing gown and pawed through the clothes in the wardrobe in search of something warm and modest to put on.

"I'll not be seen by an Englishman in me shift," Nora declared, shocked. "And a *ciotog* on top of it! He'll be apt to make an atrocity out of me. You'd better go yourself, Miss Cosy."

Cosy gurgled with laughter. "Ha! And be made an atrocity of?"

"Sure they never interfere with the gentlewomen," Nora explained, pulling her shawl tightly around her crooked, spare body. "But he'd ravish *me* quick enough, and I am only a servant."

Cosy grabbed an old riding skirt and pulled it on over her

nightgown. The nightgown was of the finest French silk, but the skirt was of cheap green baize, the felt-like material used to cover gaming tables. Hardly fashionable; she usually wore it with a matching jacket when she cleaned house. "Let him in, you old wagon," she insisted, hastily tucking her nightgown inside the skirt, "or I'll tell Father Mallone of your un-Christianlike behavior!"

The threat had its effect on Nora. "I will, Miss Cosy," she intoned in her sepulchral voice, her ropy limbs taut with offended dignity. "But when the *ciotog* murders us all, don't come crying to me."

Nora swept out, leaving her young lady to finish dressing in the dark. Downstairs, she opened the door so suddenly that she almost received a rap on the nose from the gentleman's umbrella. "Good evening," he said with crushing dignity. "How awfully kind of you to let me in. I do hope it wasn't too much trouble."

He held out his umbrella to the little hunchback, but, to his astonishment, she let out a shriek and ran away. "Sure Miss Cosy will be down in a squeeze, your honor!" she squeaked as she ran. "'Tis only after jumping into her clothes she is!"

She took the candle with her.

Presumably, "Miss Cosy" was the housekeeper, probably the woman who had shouted at him from the window. Benedict disliked her already. Needless to say, he was not accustomed to being kept waiting in a cold, dark hall while the housekeeper *jumped* into her clothes. And why was she a *Miss* Cosy, anyway? Married or not, most housekeepers assumed the honorific of "Mrs." when they achieved the rank of an upper servant. Obviously, Miss Cosy wanted every man she met to think of her as marriageable!

After pushing his valise inside the house with his foot, the baronet closed the door against the wind and the rain and wiped his wet face with his sleeve.

Where the devil was Pickering? he thought angrily.

Since losing his right hand, he had learned to do everything with his left. Taking out his silver cheroot case, he lit a match, striking it on the underside of the hall table. After lighting the candles in a nearby sconce, he was able to see his surroundings a little better. The damask-covered walls and gilded sconces were in keeping with the elegance one expected from a Camden Place address, but the cheap tallow candles in the sconces cast a dirty, orange stain over everything. Benedict preferred the clean, white light of beeswax, a fact well-known to Pickering. Seriously displeased, he placed his umbrella in the stand just as a figure in skirts appeared at the top of the stairs. "Ah. Miss Cosy, I presume?"

Her Christian name was Cosima, but, as no one but her mother had ever called her that in her life, she saw nothing odd in this form of address. "Aye," she answered, coming down the steps. "You said you were given the wrong key, Sir Benedict? You're locked out?"

Miss Cosy was Irish, but, although she was obviously more genteel than the other servant, she made no attempt to speak with an English accent. "I rang the bell," he complained.

"Ah, sure, we disconnected that jangly old bell," she explained cheerfully.

"Indeed! Help me out of my coat," he commanded brusquely, putting his back to her. As he turned, Cosy caught sight of his right side. His right arm ended abruptly at the elbow, and his coat sleeve had been pinned up. Poor man! He really was a *ciotog. He must be a war hero,* thought the colonel's daughter, instantly claiming the stranger for the Army.

"I will, sir," she said in a tone of great respect. Descending on him in a rush, she peeled the fine black wool from his shoulders. Wet through, the fabric stank of tobacco and perfume, which could only remind her of her own father, except that, being an incorrigible drunkard as well as a remorseless philanderer, Colonel Vaughn usually stank of whiskey, too. "I'll hang it to dry in the kitchen, Sir Benedict," she offered courteously.

"Certainly not," he said harshly. "I won't have my coat smelling of cooking."

Cosy thought the smell of her cooking would have improved his musky coat, but she held her tongue. "I'll hang it here so," she said cheerfully, finding a hook for it above his umbrella.

"You will give my coat to Pickering, of course. Where in damnation *is* he, anyway?" Reserved with his own class, the baronet gave his irritation full reign with her. "I sent him ahead of me. I hate being looked after by strangers. This is an unforgivable lapse."

A sheltered young lady might have been shocked and intimidated by his anger, but Cosy was used to the rough ways of fighting men. Her father and brothers all drank and smoked and swore routinely in her presence. Compared to them, Sir Benedict was the consummate gentleman. She went to the table and fumbled in the drawer for matches. "That's the trouble with sending a man ahead of you," she said in her creamy Irish voice. "Sure they don't always wait for you to catch up."

Benedict preferred to be served in silent awe by his subordinates. "I sent my valet ahead of me to Bath with my baggage," he explained coldly and ponderously, as if addressing an idiot. "I take it he has not yet arrived in Camden Place. He must have been delayed by the weather."

Miss Cosy's cheekiness was not quelled in the least. "You weren't delayed yourself," she pointed out as she lit the three candles in a branched candlestick. "If he left before you, and he's going at the same rate, I'd say your man is in Bristol this night."

She held the candlestick up and, for the first time, he saw her face.

His worst fear was confirmed in spades. Miss Cosy was a stunning beauty. *How men must fawn over you,* he thought. In the dull, orange light he could not tell the true color of her eyes or hair, but there was no denying that satiny smooth skin, that heart-shaped face, that cupid's bow mouth. True, her nose was a trifle short, but this only served to take the edge off a beauty that might otherwise have been intimidating.

Benedict searched in vain for some other flaw that might give him a disgust for her. Her impertinent little chin had a hint of a cleft in it, but he liked that. Her breasts were small, but, unfortunately, he had always preferred females with light, youthful figures, while at the same time deploring the light, youthful minds that usually went with such females. In desperation, he noted that her hair was a tangled mess, carroty in the candlelight, but who knew what color in the sunlight; her clothes were ugly, cheap, and wrinkled and she looked like an unmade bed.

Ah, bed . . . What would it be like to share the bed of a beautiful young woman? To kiss that plump, saucy, little mouth, to feel those long silken legs wrapped around one's waist, and to hear that soft, creamy voice sighing exquisite nothings in one's ear?

One was appalled by one's thoughts. One savagely set them aside.

Housekeeper, my arse, he thought. She looks more like a homewrecker.

Miss Cosy, if that was her real name, would have to be dismissed, of course. His sole purpose in coming to Bath was to make a respectable marriage. There could be no convincing the rude minds of the polite world that the ravishing Miss Cosy was not warming his bed as well as ordering his coal, and the inevitable gossip could only have a dampening effect on his marital aspirations, to say the least.

She would have to go, but how the devil was he supposed to get rid of her? Technically, she was Lord Skeldings's servant, and his lordship now lived in London.

During this prolonged scrutiny, Cosy had been staring at him with ever-widening eyes. Finally, it was too much. "I'm sorry, sir," she cried, fighting back a disrespectful giggle. "But your hair tonic is running down your face in black bars. You look like you're in gaol."

Humiliated, Benedict allowed her to **lead him** to the cupboard under the stairs.

When he came out with a clean face and **neatly** combed black hair, Cosy was pleasantly surprised. **He was** younger and better looking than she had expected. **Naturally,** she would have preferred a younger man with a spectacular **phy**sique, but he was taller than herself in an age when few me**n** were. *'Tis always easier,* she thought forgivingly, *to fatten a man up than it is to slim him down.* She didn't mind **the scars** on his right cheek at all and the cold, penetrating **unfriendlin**ess of his light gray eyes actually sent a pleasurable **shiver** down her spine. Of course! He was a battle-hardened officer. Her pulse quickened as she imagined him, gray-eyed and black-haired, mounted on a white steed, in the midst of an internecine battle, issuing his commands no one would dare disobey with cold, ruthless precision.

She had fetched his valise while he was in the cupboard washing up.

"Is there no manservant to take my bag?" he inquired angrily.

She looked surprised. Evidently, men were supposed to take one look at her and turn into spineless jellies. That most men probably did just that was completely beside the point.

"There's Jackson," she answered, "but I gave him leave to attend a funeral this morning, and the result is, he's no use to anyone tonight. It's nice and warm in the kitchen, though, if you'll follow me."

"No, indeed! Be good enough to light a fire in the drawing-room." Benedict brushed past her toward the stairs. Startled, Cosy dropped his bag and caught at his arm without thinking, taking hold of his empty right sleeve. Instantly, he pulled away from her, and, instantly, she released his sleeve.

"I beg your pardon, sir," she stammered, truly horrified. "I meant no offense. There's not enough coal for a fire in the drawing-room, I'm sorry to say."

"Nonsense, Miss Cosy," he said sharply. "I'm a member of

Parliament. If there were a shortage of coal, I would have heard of it."

It occurred to her that his severity might be masking a dry sense of humor. "I didn't think to report it to the government, sir," she said. "I didn't think Lord Liverpool would be interested in the state of my coal scuttle," she added, naming the prime minister.

Miss Cosy would have few options when she lost her position here, he was thinking. She belonged to the class meant to scurry about in the background, silent and invisible. *She* could never be invisible, not with that outlandishly lovely face. No sensible lady would hire her, and, if a gentleman lost his head and did so, the result would be only misery and disgrace, for what man could resist the constant temptation of sharing a house with such a beauty?

It would be wrong to dismiss her simply because she was young and beautiful.

And yet, she could not remain under his roof because she was young and beautiful.

Only one reasonable solution to this ethical dilemma presented itself. He could, of course, move her to a furnished apartment in London in the usual way, thereby averting any hint of scandal here in Bath. A charming mistress could only be an asset to him in his political career. In fact, if he meant to get on in politics, a charming mistress would be quite as necessary to him as a dull, respectable wife.

"You mean you failed to order enough coal," he said aloud.

"I suppose I did bungle it," she said. "I'm used to the turf we have at home, you see."

"Home?" he repeated absently. "Oh, yes, of course; you're Irish."

"Don't worry, sir," she told him impishly. "I haven't come to blow up Parliament."

"I am glad to hear it," he replied without a trace of humor.

Cosy gave him up as a lost cause. On the battlefield, he might well be a hero, but as a ladies' man, he was a pure failure. "Will you come down to the kitchen, sir? It's where the cat sleeps," she added persuasively. "So you know it's nice and warm."

She started down the hall with his bag in one hand, the candlestick in the other.

As he followed her, Benedict could not help observing that her undergarments were of very fine silk, in marked contrast to the cheap baize of her skirt and jacket. He was able to make this observation because the back of her skirt had been tucked into its waistband. Giving her the benefit of the doubt, he chose to believe this had happened accidentally, no doubt while she was *jumping* into her clothes. Rather than call the faux pas to her attention, which would have embarrassed them both, he reached out and corrected the problem with a sharp, decisive tug.

Cosy whirled around. "What do you think you're doing?" she demanded.

Benedict showed her only boredom and a slight, puzzled frown. "I beg your pardon?"

His unruffled calm succeeded in confusing her. "I thought—I thought I felt something brushing against me," she said uncertainly.

"Oh? I daresay it was a draft."

Evidently judging it best to keep an eye on him, she backed through the swinging door that led into the servants' part of the house. After a short flight of stairs leading down, Benedict found himself, for the first time in his life, standing in a kitchen.

Chapter 2

Unlike the cold, dark hall upstairs, the kitchen was warm and inviting. Cosy dropped his bag next to the huge brick chimneypiece, placed the branch of candles on the big work table, and invited him to sit down. Though shabby and thread-bare, the two chairs beside the fire were upholstered in bro-cade and must have graced a drawing-room at some point in their careers. As promised, a tortoiseshell cat was curled up in one of them. Benedict took the other.

Miss Cosy's easy manners seemed better suited to the kitchen. He felt that he was now in her domain and that she, and not he, was in charge. Briskly, she stirred up the small banked fire with the poker, adding a few broken bits of wood to it. Then she stood on tiptoe to retrieve the whiskey bottle from its niche in the chimneypiece. She poured a generous measure into a glass.

"Get this in you quick as you can," she said, holding it out to him.

He raised a brow. "You keep the brandy in the chimney, do you?"

Her eyes twinkled at him. They were green as the sea. He was less sure about the color of her hair. In this light, it looked more yellow than orange. "There's no brandy in this chimney," she told him. "It's whiskey. And it's doing you no good this side of your tonsils."

Leaving him to it, she took the kettle into the scullery to fill it from the pump. "He'll spoil the milk if he stays," Nora warned her, taking the kettle from her.

Cosy was not surprised to find Nora hiding or, rather, spying, in the scullery.

"That is an ignorant superstition, Nora Murphy," she said angrily. "Anyway, he can't help being left-handed, poor man. He's an amputee."

"I had the notion he was foreign the moment I clapped eyes on him," Nora said darkly.

"Aren't you ashamed to be so ignorant?" Cosy scolded her. "He's had his right arm amputated at the elbow, Nora. That means it was cut off by the surgeon. Now, go and make up the fire in my room before I lose my temper."

Nora was shocked. "Your room, Miss Cosy!"

Cosy blushed. "I'll be sleeping with *you* in the attic, of course," she snapped.

When she returned to the kitchen with the kettle, the Englishman was sitting as straight as a ramrod in his chair, but he had finished his whiskey like a man. Encouraged by his thirst, Cosy set the kettle on the hook, swung the arm into the fire, and then refilled his glass. Not a word of thanks did he utter. She could only suppose that extreme privation had made him forget his manners. And, of course, being English, he had little manners to begin with.

She tied on her apron. "You're hungry, of course," she said brightly. "And if there's anything I won't stand for, it's a hungry man in my kitchen."

"No, thank you," he replied.

"It's no trouble," she assured him.

Incredibly, he claimed not to be hungry.

"Are you sick?" she demanded.

"Certainly not," he said coldly.

"Would you not have something?" she pleaded. "Even if it's only bread and jam."

Benedict sipped his second whiskey, accustoming himself to the smoky flavor. "You seemed to be having trouble hearing me, Miss Cosy," he said. "I am not hungry."

The sad fact was, she had little in the house to tempt a man's appetite.

"You should have been here last week, sir," she sighed. "The scallops were so nice. You wouldn't have said no to them. God forgive me; I nearly forgot the pear! With a drop of honey, it'll make you a nice tart."

She looked at him hopefully, but he was unmoved. "I dined earlier in Chippenham."

She retreated reluctantly. "If you're sure you're not hungry . . ."

"I am!" he told her curtly.

"Oh, you *are* hungry," she cried, delighted. "Will it be the tart, then?"

"No, I'm *not* hungry," he said, cutting short her pleasure. "I am absolutely certain of it."

He sipped his whiskey.

"Sure that pear was bruised anyway," she said, rallying. "Is it a pipe you smoke, Sir Benedict? I could fill it for you. My own father smokes a pipe, and, ever since I was a young girl, I'd always fill it for him, so it's no trouble."

"I don't smoke," he said.

She smiled incredulously. "*You* don't smoke?"

"Not anymore," he said with more accuracy. "The tax has become so impertinent, I have decided to give it up for a bad habit."

"In that case, I'd say your coat's been sneaking a few behind your back." She laughed.

Benedict was horrified. "That is not the scent of *my* tobacco," he said quickly. "I was obliged to take up some stranded people on the road. The gentleman smelled of cheap tobacco—and perfume, unfortunately. The carriage was utterly polluted. But I had no choice. In good conscience, I could not have left them out in the rain."

"'Tis such a bother, indeed, taking in strangers on a cold, wet night," she gravely agreed. "Sure they're more trouble than they're worth, them strangers, and never a word of thanks!"

"Quite," he answered, in no way connecting her remarks to his own situation. "But one must always be charitable to those in need. I apologize if the odor offends you."

"Ah, no. It's myself that owes you an apology," she said, sitting down on the brick step with her back to the fire. "Here I thought you'd been out all night, smoking and womanizing, like a proper gentleman!" Her green eyes danced.

Benedict could not believe the woman had sat down in his presence. Usually, his reserved manner was enough to curtail all such impudence. "No, indeed, Miss Cosy," he said stiffly. "I told you I no longer smoke."

She laughed out loud. "Just the womanizing then?"

Benedict stared at her. The women of his own class, ladies, never laughed with their mouths open. It was considered vulgar, but, perhaps more important, few women of this age had better than tolerable teeth. So, instead of laughing out loud, they smirked, they tittered, and they giggled behind their gloved fingertips or their fans.

He ought to have been disgusted by this vulgar, laughing Irish girl. Instead, inexplicably, her laughter aroused him. He suddenly wanted to make love to her right there, right where the cat sleeps. It was an irrational impulse, of course, like all sexual attraction, but to deny it would have been even more irrational, and, where irrationality could not be avoided, Benedict liked to keep it to a minimum. Recognizing the attraction was the first step in controlling it.

"I am too old for such exercise, Miss Cosy," he said firmly.

"Ah, no. Your hair is still black, and your back is still straight. Why, you couldn't be more than a hundred and ten."

"Miss Cosy!" he said sharply. "Are you flirting with me?"

"Only for about the past *five* hours," she said with mock exasperation.

"I am thirty-eight," he said indignantly. "You cannot be more than twenty-two."

The kettle whistled, and she jumped up to take it off the hook. "Are you sure you won't have a cup, Sir Benedict?" she asked. "No sense wasting a boiling kettle, is there?"

"No; I thank you. One is obliged to drink so much tea in society that I never drink it in private life." He held out his glass. "Whiskey will suffice, I think."

Cosy hesitated. Having learned from bitter experience that a third glass of whiskey could turn even the most respectable man into a thorough blackguard, she had decided to cut him off at two. "That would be your third, sir," she reminded him gently. "You might want to slow down."

"Why?" he said sharply. "Is there something wrong with your whiskey?"

She stared at him blankly for a moment, then, for no reason he could detect, burst out laughing. Again, her laughter had its unsettling effect on his physiology. With tears in her eyes, she uncorked the bottle. "You've earned your third glass, so you have. 'Is there something wrong with your whiskey?'" she repeated as she poured it out.

She sat down on the step again and wiped her streaming eyes with the corner of her apron. "It's just the sort of thing Sandy would say, to get a third glass out of me. He could always make me laugh, Sandy. God forgive me, he's the one I miss the most."

Benedict felt absurdly jealous of the unknown Sandy.

"I've three brothers altogether," Cosy said, after a moment, persevering in the face of his apparent indifference. The man had a face like carved marble. "*They* appreciated my cooking," she added, giving him a look of strong reproach. "Of course, they'd eat their own fists if I let them, so it's hardly a compliment."

Benedict was pleased. "I see. Sandy is your brother?"

"One of three," she reiterated.

The possibility of three Irishmen running tame in his house, eating their own fists, did not appeal to Benedict at all. "Are they in Ireland?" he asked, concerned.

"They are not. Larry's in hell, of course," she said matter-of-factly, "but there's hope for Sandy, I'm thinking. I'm on my knees for him, anyway. They served in the Fifty-fourth, the Duke of Kellynch's Own Regiment of Foot. Do you know it?"

He spoke gravely. "Yes, of course. Only four men survived the Waterloo action."

She nodded. "My father was one. He's in India now, with two hundred fresh recruits. Larry and Sandy were not so fortunate. They died there in Belgium, like so many."

"I'm sorry," he said gravely. "Especially in regards to poor Larry."

"They were fighting men," she said simply. "Were you at Waterloo?"

"Only as an observer." Benedict held up his glass. "To the fighting Kellynch."

The toast earned him an unprecedented fourth glass of whiskey. The drink seemed to be loosening his tongue, which pleased her. She thought he was the most interesting man she had ever met. She could have talked to him all night. She never wanted to go to bed.

"You said you had three brothers."

"My youngest brother is on his way to India now," she told him. "That's Dan. He's only eighteen, the lamb. When you knocked, I was afraid you might be bringing me bad news."

Reassured that her father and brothers were all out of the way, he had no further interest in her family. "How long have you been acquainted with Lord Skeldings?" he asked abruptly.

"Skeldings?" she repeated in surprise. "Which one is he?"

"How many have there been?" he wanted to know.

"Too many," she said frankly. "One more lordship, and I'm off to America."

He frowned at her. "Lord Skeldings is the owner of this house, Miss Cosy."

"Is he so? It was all handled by agents," she explained. "I asked only for a nice, quiet place in a respectable street. So I did all right for myself, I think?"

"Certainly Camden Place is respectable enough for anyone," he said.

She wrinkled up her forehead. "Pretty steep, though, I'm thinking?"

"Yes; but walking uphill is good exercise."

"No; I meant the rent." She laughed. "Don't you think it's exorbitant? Sure England is a dear place; everything is exorbitant."

"Not everything, surely," he murmured.

By strict definition, it was impossible for *everything* to be exorbitant, of course, but Miss Cosy did not seem to concern herself with definitions, strict or otherwise. Her fondness for the word "nice," for example, almost amounted to a speech impediment. "Aye; everything!" she insisted. "I've not had a nice joint of beef these three weeks together. *Eleven*·pence a pound! And now it's Lent, and I couldn't have it, even if I could afford it."

He looked at her thoughtfully. If Miss Cosy was to be his mistress, she would have to learn to be more precise in her choice of words, and to elevate her conversation above these mundane matters in which he had no interest. To that end, he would recommend books for her, to improve her mind and refine her tongue. Her soft, creamy voice would remain unchanged. He didn't even mind her Irish accent. It occurred to him suddenly that she might not be able to read at all; reading was widespread among women of the upper and middle classes, but most of the lower orders, both male and female, usually were illiterate. This was especially true in Ireland.

"What do your friends call you?" she asked him suddenly. "Benny? Or Dick?"

He was appalled. "Neither, I trust!"

"They can't call you *Sir Benedict*," she pressed him. "It's unnatural."

"It is not unnatural," he said stiffly. "It is my name. My brother and, occasionally, my sister, call me Ben," he added reluctantly. "I don't encourage it. I believe nicknames are a form of degradation."

"It's a form of affection," she argued, laughing. "Ben. I like it."

Rather to his own surprise, he made no objection to this form of degradation.

She leaned toward him. "Did you know that, in the Italian language, 'ben' is an endearment?" she asked him.

He shook his head. To his astonishment, she began to sing to him softly in Italian.

> *"Caro mio ben,*
> *credimi almen,*
> *senza di te*
> *languisce il cor."*

He had not been sung to by a woman since his nursery days. Her voice was light and pleasing, though by no means perfect. As she sang, she moved her fingers along her knee as if she were playing the melody on a pianoforte. The simple, plaintive melody tugged at him, body and soul. Without understanding a word of Italian, he was seduced.

She translated. "My dear beloved, believe me at least. In want of you, my heart languishes." She laughed at his amazement. "Sure, I'm Italian in my heart."

"You should have lessons."

"Is it as bad as that?"

"I didn't mean—" he began quickly, but she waved him off.

"It's true, I'm no singer. All the lessons in the world won't change that."

"But you've had some education," he said cautiously.

"Now *that* would be grievously overstating the matter! I'll say this for my father: if ever any of his children wanted to learn something, he made it possible. Fortunately, hooligans like ourselves never do want to learn much."

He frowned. "Why do you say 'fortunately'?"

"We never had much money," she explained without hesitation. "What we had, my father, in his wisdom, gambled away. He'd have been overwhelmed, poor man, if the five of us had been scholars! I remember, once it was so bad, we had to sell everything in the house, except for my pianoforte, and we ate our dinners off it because we had no table."

"Oh?" he said. "You play the pianoforte?"

"At least as well as I sing," she said. "My father won the pianoforte at cards when I was five. There was money then. I had lessons. It was the only thing he ever gave me that didn't end up under the auctioneer's hammer. Do you like music?"

"Very much," he said, but with the air of one closing a subject. "Miss Cosy, shall we speak plainly?"

She looked at him in surprise. "Are we not speaking plainly now, Ben?"

"I have enjoyed our conversation very much," he began, looking at her directly. "You know, of course, that I'm an amputee. Tell me now if it disgusts you. I will not be offended."

For a moment she was too startled to answer, but her gaze did not falter. She said firmly, in a voice that rang true, "It does not disgust me, Ben. Why would you think so?"

"Some females do find it rather off-putting. I don't blame them."

"Then they don't deserve the pleasure of your company," she said indignantly.

"I'm a single man," he went on, encouraged, "and, like all single men of property, I must marry. I've come to Bath to find a wife, in fact."

"Then it's London you want, not Bath," she said knowledgeably. "From what I hear, all the English girls go to

London on purpose to find husbands. So they're halfway to the altar already, right? And you, with your good looks, and your fine, dry wit, you'd slay them."

"I've tried London," he said, a little disconcerted by this advice. "My plan in coming to Bath was to find some plain, dull, respectable woman to be my wife. She needn't even be pretty. She could have a hump for all I care. All I ask is that she be young enough to give me a son, and sensible enough to leave me alone after that."

Cosy burst out laughing. "Plain, dull, respectable, with a hump! Where exactly do you plan on finding this dream girl?"

"It is no laughing matter," he said coldly, which only made her laugh more. "For myself, I wouldn't marry at all, but there's the baronetcy to consider, and the electorate. They will expect me to marry an unexceptional woman. The moment I saw you, Miss Cosy, I knew that all my carefully laid plans were in jeopardy. To put it bluntly, you are too beautiful."

"Ben!" she said, hitting him on the knee. "Are you flirting with me?"

"I never flirt," he said curtly. "I am perfectly serious. Your presence here can only mean trouble for me—trouble I can ill afford. How am I supposed to pursue a marriage with some dreary, good woman when you're here? You look like bloody Venus!" he accused.

She laughed. "You've met Venus? What was she like? Was she as tall as me?"

"The point is," he said sternly, "any woman I court would suspect me of harboring some secret, passionate regard for you. There would be gossip. I'm a respectable man, Miss Cosy. The last thing I need is gossip. That being the case, I have no choice but to make you an offer. I don't like it; it is not the way I hoped to start things off here in Bath. But I have considered the matter very carefully, and it is the only logical thing to do."

Her eyes were round. Hastily, she held up both hands. "I'm

going to have to stop you right there, Ben, before this becomes awkward."

He scarcely paused. "Obviously, you are a very desirable female. I am prepared to offer you generous terms. You would want for nothing for the rest of your life."

He realized that he sounded rather like a corporation attorney but he couldn't help that. To fly off into romantic rhapsodies would have been so out of character for him that it would have amounted to a form of deception, and, if she was to share his bed, Miss Cosy deserved to know his true character. He was neither passionate nor romantic.

"If it is the thought of intimacy that repels you, let me reassure you on that score. I would not presume to enjoy relations with you more than, say, twice a week. Twice a week is not unreasonable, surely, for a woman of your age."

"No," she was obliged to admit. She had already remarked the sad lack of children in the city of Bath; now she understood why it should be so. Where the adults came from remained a mystery to her. "Do you think you might be a wee bit drunk, Ben?" she asked him gently.

"I am not drunk," he said, annoyed. "Consider this: if you accept me, it will be in my power to present you to a better class of gentlemen than you are likely to meet with in Bath. Nothing would be beyond your reach in London. I certainly wouldn't stand in your way if you got a better offer and decided to leave me."

Cosy was on her feet. "I'm afraid, sir," she said indignantly, "that in Ireland we take marriage rather more seriously than this! Why, in God's name, would *I* marry a man who couldn't be bothered to stand in my way?"

Benedict blinked at her. "Who said anything about marriage?" he demanded.

"You did! Didn't you?"

"I wasn't asking you to marry me," he said vehemently. "Do you think me a fool?"

Cosy was flabbergasted. "Well, I don't know you very well, do I?" she retorted.

His eyes narrowed. "You may be a little piece of heaven, my girl, but I am not so bowled over by your beautiful eyes that I forget myself!" he said angrily. "I am a gentleman. Gentlemen don't marry women like you. It would be a highly reprehensible connection, degrading to us both. I'd be a laughingstock. My career in Parliament would be over. I couldn't very well present *you* to my family and friends, now, could I?"

"Oh!" was all she could say.

"Let there be no pretense between us, madam," he said. "You know perfectly well I was asking you to be my mistress. Don't become the outraged innocent with me!" he went on as Cosy choked on her own fury. "I am prepared to offer you a thousand pounds if you will come away with me tomorrow. The rest can be negotiated when we get to London. We'll be drawing up papers, of course. You can have an attorney, if you like."

"Papers! Attorney!" she spat.

"Of course. I suppose in Ireland things are not so civilized?"

Cosy pulled herself together. He had reminded her that she represented Ireland in this sordid little conflict. She must not allow him to get the better of her. "No, indeed," she said coldly. "We're savages!"

He shook his head. "I suspected as much. Rest assured, *we* will have a legally binding contract, Miss Cosy. It is as much for your protection as it is for mine. If I should fail to meet my obligations, you will have recourse under the law. And vice versa."

"How nice for us! How civilized!"

"Yes. You will come to London with me for a thousand pounds."

It was not a question. The Englishman really assumed that, for a mere thousand pounds, she would gladly leave her home and her family to become nothing more than his whore. He might say "mistress," but that was just perfume. Nothing could disguise the stench.

For this insult, he deserved to suffer the worst humiliation of his life.

"Not so fast there, darling," she said sweetly, her pleasant voice masking her anger. "I'll have to see the goods first, you understand. How do I know you're bona fide?"

Secretly, Benedict was disappointed by her cold, calculated response to his offer, but, without a change of expression, he reached inside his coat for his wallet. "I'm glad you mean to be reasonable, my dear. I am not entertained in the least by feminine hysterics. It is essentially a business arrangement, and I prefer to conduct my business without emotion."

He took out a thousand pound note.

Cosy looked at it, her fury hardening like hot steel plunged into icy water. "That is not what I meant, sir," she said, smiling angelically.

"Naturally, I am not adverse to establishing my good faith," he said. "Forgive me! I do not have the pleasure of understanding you. What is it you want of me? As fetching as you are, Miss Cosy, you can not expect to receive a larger sum."

"Money's a fine thing, sir," she observed, "but I'll not be shagging your wallet, now, will I? No, 'tis your naked body I'll be laboring like a slave to please. I'd be a fool, wouldn't I, if I didn't take a long, hard look at your dangler before I commit myself to such an arrangement?"

The crudity of her language shocked him. "You certainly are a soldier's daughter!"

"Did you mistake me for a fine lady?" she returned coolly. "I wouldn't buy a horse without looking it in the mouth, and I won't take a man to my bed unless he passes inspection."

"You expect me to—to *undress*?" he said incredulously. "Here in the kitchen?"

"It's the warmest spot in the house," she pointed out. "We could even do the deed here, if you like," she added, her sweet, lazy smile at odds with the breathtaking naughtiness of what she was suggesting. "Sure! We'll pile the cushions on the floor, and you can mount me any way you please, for I'm not at all particular, not when I like a fellow as much as I like you."

She had gone too far; with his scarred face and his amputated arm, he knew he was no young girl's dream. "Let us not be ridiculous, Miss Cosy."

She looked down at her hands. "For all I know, you're covered in sores. If I went to London with you, only to find out you're scabrous—!" She shuddered delicately. "I'd be stuck in London with a scabby man, now, wouldn't I?"

"I am *not* covered in sores, you hussy," he snapped.

"Good," she said. "Then you won't mind proving it. You don't plan on coming to my bed all buttoned up, with your boots on, I hope?" she added impatiently. "So I'll be seeing you in the flesh anyway. Right?"

Her request, while startling, was not unreasonable, he reflected. After all, a lady entertaining an offer of marriage had the right to know the character of her future husband before she accepted him. Did it not follow that a woman in Miss Cosy's position had the right to know that her future lover was physically sound before she threw herself into his power?

As incredible as it seemed, he was actually considering displaying his nude body to a strange female in a kitchen.

"Is it as bad as that, sir?" she said pityingly. "Is it scales? *Carbuncles*?"

Benedict abruptly stood up and began to struggle out of his coat. "There is absolutely nothing wrong with my body— apart from its obvious defect, that is."

He threw his coat down, and stood in his waistcoat and shirt sleeves. The right sleeve of his finely pleated linen shirt had been cut short at the elbow and neatly hemmed, unlike his coat, which was tailored in the usual way.

"Of course, if you'd rather not," she said quickly, "I'll understand!"

"No. I insist. You are perfectly right to safeguard your

health by making certain of mine," he said, unbuttoning his waistcoat.

"You can keep your shirt on if you prefer."

His lip curled. "I would not have you treat me any differently than you would your other lovers!" he said coldly. "You will find nothing wrong with me, however."

Loosening his cravat, he tore off his collar and pulled his shirt off over his head.

She stared at him in dismay. While he was not covered in sores, the thick, bristling, black hair that covered his torso was scarcely more attractive to her than a nasty rash would have been. On his chest it grew in ugly, black whorls, and, on his belly, deep, thick chevrons plunged downward to his loins. She hardly looked at his amputated limb. *That,* at least, she thought, a little irrationally, *is not his fault.*

"There," he said, slapping his belly proudly. "That, madam, is all muscle. I walk four miles a day without fail. I am as fit as a fiddle."

A hairy fiddle! she thought with ill-concealed disgust.

In a few minutes more, after an embarrassing struggle with his boots, he was standing before her naked as the day he was born. As always, his posture was excellent. The hair at the joining of his thighs was especially bushy, and the pale flesh of his manhood retreated into it like a little bird into a nest. It was so ugly it was almost fascinating.

"You know," she said thoughtfully. "You don't look like the sort of man who'd be all furry under his clothes. I thought you'd be smoother."

"As you can see, madam, there is nothing the matter with my private parts," he said, taking himself in hand. "Normal in size and color. Scrupulously clean. Free of all disease."

Cosy tried to look knowledgeable and interested. "Could you turn around please?" she asked. Her voice squeaked, and she cleared her throat to regain some control over it.

"Certainly."

"Hmmm," she said thoughtfully, as she considered what to

do next. If she hit him on the head with the poker, there would be the danger of killing him, while the bellows might not be heavy enough to knock him out completely. It was a difficult choice. Meanwhile, the back side of the man was not unworthy of a glance. His shoulders, back, and buttocks were smooth and white. His muscular legs were as much like carved marble as she could wish. There was only a little hair on the back of his calves. If only the front of him matched the back!

"Well?" Benedict said.

"Hush, man! The angels are singing," she said, stalling for time. Her eye went to the bottle of whiskey. That would knock him out as well as the poker, she reasoned, without breaking his skull. Perfect! "Shall we drink on it, sir?" she asked brightly, jumping up to pour him a glass. When he turned around, she saw with some surprise, that her disgust of him was not as strong as it had been. There was something odd and fascinating about his hairy body, now that she had seen his naked back. He was like a god and a beast joined into one being.

"There are better ways of sealing a bargain such as this," Benedict grumbled. He was cold, and the cold had caused his manly flesh to shrink. Too proud to offer excuses for his poor showing, he was more eager than ever to give her a practical proof of his fitness.

"To Ireland!" she insisted. "You'll not refuse to drink to *Ireland*?"

"To Ireland," he agreed irritably. He wanted her so badly, he would have toasted France. Against his better judgment, he then drank to Father Murphy, who died for Ireland, and, then to the Boys of Wexford, who also, apparently, died for Ireland. Each time he drank, his glass was refilled as if by magic. She was amazed he was still on his feet.

"To Lord Edward Fitzgerald!" she said, finally, in desperation.

Benedict felt queasy, and the room seemed to be in motion

around him. "Did this Lord Edward die for Ireland, too?" he asked suspiciously.

"He did!"

"Excellent," he said. He drank, and then asked with disarmingly simple innocence, "What happens now? Do we go to bed?"

"Darling," she said, "you'd never make it."

The room began to spin around him like a carousel. "I see what you mean," he mumbled as he slipped painlessly to the floor. "Let's do it right here, where the cat sleeps."

"Sleep well, *caro mio ben,*" she said, kicking him to make sure he was unconscious. "What kept you?" she demanded as Nora belatedly came flying out of the scullery brandishing a frying pan.

"I thought you liked him," said Nora, staring at the man. "You sang to him and all."

Cosima's eyes blazed. "I did no such shameless thing!" she cried. "And if you tell anyone, old woman, I'll kill you."

Nora was a little near-sighted. "'Tis a good thing you threw that old carriage rug over him, the naked hoor."

"I've got news for you, Nora," Cosy retorted. "That's no carriage rug!"

Chapter 3

"Is it murder?" Ajax Jackson wanted to know.

The two women had awakened the manservant with a bucket of cold water. The massive, wall-eyed Irishman was not entirely sober, but neither was he entirely drunk. His iron-gray hair hung down his back in rivulets. Fortunately, he had fallen asleep in his clothes.

"Murder, indeed!" Nora Murphy scoffed. "And ourselves without a bog handy?"

"There's a river, woman," he told Nora. "A river's as good as a bog."

Nora rolled her eyes. "The Avon River is not the sort of river you can just toss a body in whenever it suits you. It's not the Liffey! Sure the people would take notice of a corpse splashing around in the Avon River."

"Just get him out of here, please," Cosy said wearily. She stood at a distance, holding the cat in her arms. The naked Englishman looked so harmless in his sleep that she wasn't even sure she was still angry. She was beginning to think this was all her fault. Perhaps she had flirted with him just a little too hard, given him too much to drink. She knew she had been showing off for him, singing in Italian like a hussy! What was he supposed to think, the poor man, when she turned on the charm like that? If they didn't get him out of her kitchen soon, she would be down on her knees, waking him up to beg his pardon. Unthinkable!

"We'll hand him a nice beating first, of course," Nora said eagerly.

"While he's drunk?" Jackson sneered. "He'd think it was patty fingers with all the blood running in his eyes. Now, if your brothers were here to defend you, Miss Cosy, they'd geld him for your sake, and he'd wake up with his cullions in his mouth."

"Ugh!" said Cosy, revolted.

"Too much blood," said practical Nora. "We could tar and feather him, I suppose."

"And ourselves without any tar? We could bridle him," Jackson suggested.

Cosy looked interested. "Bridle him? I never heard of that."

"May God preserve your innocence, child," said Nora. "You force the iron bit of a bridle into the unsavory mouth of him. That way his tongue may acquire a touch of civility."

That sounded like a fair compromise. "Have we got a bridle?" Cosy asked.

"We have not," Jackson said angrily. "And, if you are determined to spare him, Cosy Vaughn, then there's nothing to do but take him to the middle of nowhere, and leave him there to die like the low-down, dirty blackguard that he is."

"And where are we supposed to find the middle of nowhere in this Godforsaken place?" Nora wanted to know. "Sure the English are packed in Bath city like seeds in a sunflower."

"There's the park," Cosy suggested. "No one ever goes there but ourselves."

"Sure the English do prefer promenading themselves in the Pump Room," Nora sniffed.

"The park!" Jackson cried in disgust. "Sure the Watch would find your man safe and sound in the morning, if that matters to you! You might as well tuck him up in bed like a baby!"

"I don't like it any more than you do!" Cosy said crossly.

"If we were at home, he'd go straight into the bog, but we're not at home, and he can't stay here."

Although it was but a paltry vengeance in his opinion, Jackson obediently carried the baronet out by the tradesman's door, and returned from the park not twenty minutes later. To his surprise, the young lady was still up, pacing the kitchen and wringing her hands.

"Did you tie him up, nice and tight, to a tree?" she asked anxiously.

"I did not," he replied, highly pleased with himself. "With a bit of luck, he'll wake up and go traipsing through the streets of Bath crying for his mother in his shameless nudity. 'Tis how Ned Foley met his end in Drogheda. Drunk as he was, he never saw the cart coming, and the next thing he knew, he was under the hooves of it, trampled like the grapes of wrath."

"Are you mad, you bollocks? Go and tie him up at once before he wanders off and does himself a harm," Cosy angrily commanded.

"Is it sweet on him she is?" Jackson grumbled as she swept off to bed.

"Sweet on him?" cried Nora. "And he offering to ravish her twice a week, poor child!"

"Twice a week is not very affectionate," Jackson observed. "She'd have the right to expect more attention, even if he *is* a cold fish of an Englishman. Mind you, that's an easy class of husband, and that's five nights' rest she'd not be getting if she married with an Irishman."

"He wasn't after asking her to marry him!"

"Poor lass! Did she want to marry him as much as that?" he asked curiously.

"And if you think so, Ajax Jackson, you know nothing of women!" Nora cried.

"I may know nothing of women, Nora," he replied. "But I know a fair amount on the subject of men. Sure I happen to be one! He'll be back," he said confidently. "And I wouldn't want to be in Cosy Vaughn's shoes when he does."

"He'll leave town, surely, and never come back," said Nora nervously.

Jackson laughed. "And if you think so, Nora, me darling, 'tis yourself that knows nothing of men."

Leaving her open-mouthed, he went to find a bit of rope.

Sir Benedict's valet saw no reason to alter the morning routine simply because his master had been brought home by the Watch naked and quite insensibly drunk. It was not about punishing the delinquent baronet. It was about maintaining a high standard of service. At precisely six-thirty that same morning, therefore, Pickering entered his master's room and flung open the bed curtains. Never having suffered the ill effects of a night of drinking himself, he was startled when a small china ornament smashed against the wall, narrowly missing his head.

"Sir Benedict!" he cried in amazement.

"*Must* you be so loud?" Benedict demanded, sitting up in the big four-poster bed.

Sitting up was the worst mistake he could have made. A threshing machine inside his head was instantly set in motion. Its razor-sharp blades began making hay of his brain. Certain that he was dying, though not quickly enough, Benedict fell back in bed and lay paralyzed.

"Good morning, Sir Benedict," Pickering said sunnily.

Benedict winced. To his sensitive ears, his valet's voice sounded like the voice of an angry God. The threshing blades in his head rattled violently. He did not dare move, but the desire to be released from his present torment was so strong that he risked speaking again.

"Pickering," he whispered, scarcely opening his lips. "My will is with my attorney in London. You have much to gain if you kill me. Kill me now, I beg of you." He burrowed down into the bedclothes and rode the gently lapping waves of nausea back to deep sleep.

Pickering returned late in the evening and lit some candles. Benedict complained that the light hurt his eyes, but, after a little cajoling, he was able to sit up and drink a cup of beef tea. "What happened to me, Pickering?" he asked presently. "Everything is all jumbled in my head. There was— Was there a woman?"

"Yes, Sir Benedict," Pickering grimly replied. "I'm sorry, sir."

Benedict sank into the pillows. "Don't be. She was very beautiful. She liked me enormously, I think. We forged a bond that few can boast. Pickering, I love her."

Somehow Pickering managed to overcome the strong urge to roll his eyes. "Yes, sir. I'm sure you do, sir. Would you care to bring charges against her?"

"Now, what was her name?" Benedict mused.

A few seconds passed before he exclaimed, "Charges! What do you mean?"

With unwholesome relish, Pickering explained that the beautiful woman had *not* liked him enormously, or even a little. In fact, as proof of her contempt, she had robbed him of everything, including his clothes, and then had left him tied to a tree in the park, innocent of all clothing, for the Watch to find. Most likely, she was part of a gang of vicious robbers. She had only pretended to like him so that she and her accomplices could rob him.

According to the constable of the Watch, a very knowledgeable and zealous custodian of the law, it was the oldest trick in the book. It was called "The Honey Trap."

At first, Benedict did not believe a word of it.

"I haven't been robbed," he scoffed. "What's-her-name would never do such a thing. You don't know her as I do, Pickering. And I think," he added acidly, "one would remember if one had been tied to a tree."

"The constable has reconstructed your movements of last night," Pickering informed him. "Evidently, you left a Mr.

Fitzwilliam at the York House Hotel, then you walked to Camden Place. Most unwise, Sir Benedict; you ought to have taken a chair. You were an obvious prey for streetwalkers. The woman you met deceived you shamelessly."

"Streetwalker! She's the housekeeper here. Red hair? Bit of a dish? Miss Cosy is her name," he added, suddenly remembering.

Pickering was revolted. "Miss Cozen, more like! The woman was a thief."

"I don't believe it," said Benedict. He suddenly felt naked and betrayed and just a tiny bit foolish. "She seemed so warm, so open, so friendly."

"Yes, sir," Pickering said dryly. "It must be necessary in her . . . line of work to look like the innocent flower, but be the serpent under it."

Benedict groaned. "Was she not the housekeeper?"

Pickering shook his head. "There are no female servants here. I dismissed them all. You were discovered just before dawn by the Watch. The thieves had stripped you of everything. They even took the ring from your hand."

Benedict looked at his hand, almost spilling his tea in the process. His signet ring was indeed gone. He remembered everything up until the moment he had drunk to the Boys of Wexford, who were probably her gang. After that, Miss Cosy, the beautiful, warm, and friendly Irish housekeeper who sang to him in Italian, vanished from his memory like a ghost in sunlight.

"Needless to say, I paid the constable well for his discretion."

"What? Er . . . oh, yes. Well done," Benedict said absently. His thoughts were elsewhere. He hadn't been beaten and robbed. The little rogue had gotten him drunk, and talked him out of his clothes! He had actually *given* her everything he had. Worse yet, he had wanted to give her more. "Damn," he said through clenched teeth. "I must have walked right into her trap like a mewling lamb to the slaughter! And, like a lamb, she fleeced me, did she not?"

"Yes, sir. Though she must have had help tying you up."

"Yes, of course she had help," he snapped. "I should have known it was all too good to be true! My watch! My ring! I had a thousand pounds in my wallet—but never mind that! Are *you* all right, my old friend?" he asked Pickering. "You seem unharmed."

Pickering was surprised, and touched. It was just like his master to think of others at a time when he might be excused for wallowing in their own misfortunes. He could almost forgive Sir Benedict for fouling up so spectacularly. "I was a trifle shaken up, Sir Benedict, of course, but my nerves are holding up very well. I thank you."

Benedict looked around the bedroom. It seemed amply filled with silver candlesticks and there were no blank squares on the walls where paintings had once been. "They did not burglarize the house at all?" he asked, showing a belated concern for Lord Skeldings's property.

"Oh, no, Sir Benedict," Pickering assured him. "The house was quite untouched."

"The other servants? All well? No one hurt?"

"Some shock more easily than others, but, all in all, fine."

Benedict sighed with relief. "I am glad. If I had been the means of injuring his lordship's property or his servants, I would have been grieved, indeed. For myself, I am resigned never to see my thousand pounds again, and, I daresay, all my clothes will find their way to a secondhand shop. However, it may be possible to recover my ring, and my watch, too," he went on thoughtfully. "It would be more profitable for the thieves to sell them back to me, rather than take the trouble of melting down my ring for its gold content or rubbing out the inscription on my watch. I shall offer a reward. 'Gentleman seeking lost property. No questions asked.' One sees such items in the newspapers from time to time. See to the advertisement, Pickering. And let us never mention this regrettable matter again."

"Oh, Sir Benedict!"

Benedict looked at him in astonishment. "Pickering! You are not *crying*?"

Taking out his handkerchief, the manservant blew his nose. "It is all my fault," was his anguished cry. "I am to blame!"

"You, Pickering? How so?"

"I have neglected your loins quite shamefully," Pickering explained, his long nose quivering with emotion. "Can you ever forgive me?"

"My dear fellow! Neglect them all you like. In fact, I prefer it."

"No! They have been neglected too long, Sir Benedict," said Pickering firmly. "They demand immediate attention."

"No, they don't."

"You need relief, Sir Benedict!" Pickering insisted. "When a gentleman is reduced to applying to streetwalkers for the fulfillment of his carnal needs—!"

"She was not a streetwalker!" Benedict objected. For some reason it disturbed him to hear that conniving little minx maligned in any way. "She was a thief, Pickering, and a good one. She had beauty and charm, and she knew how to use them to her advantage. I thought I was past the weaknesses of my youth. She made me feel young and stupid again. You've no idea how much I *hate* feeling young," he added bitterly. "That *bitch!*"

"She ought to be hanged, if you ask me," Pickering sniffed.

Benedict scowled. "No one *is* asking you. Now, be good enough to ready me a hot bath. After such an adventure, one feels ever so slightly redolent."

As far as Benedict was concerned, the subject was closed.

Pickering obediently went to draw his master's bath. When he returned to the bedroom, Benedict was sitting on the edge of the bed with his bare feet on the floor. Pickering considered this progress. Now, if he could just get his master to see reason.

"Mortification of the flesh is all very well, Sir Benedict," he said severely, "but the only real way to be free of temptation is to give in to it."

Benedict groaned. "Yes, that *is* what the Church of England teaches us."

Pickering was unperturbed; his master had never shown anything but the most cursory interest in what the Church of England taught. "This will come as a shock to you, Sir Benedict—it certainly shocked me! But there is a class of woman that we can employ to help us to purge ourselves of these . . . inconvenient humors. I have learned that a Mrs. Price in the Registry Office here in Bath has a number of Prime Articles in her keeping."

By all outward appearances, the Registry Office in Gay Street was a respectable employment agency. Pickering had learned of Mrs. Price's less than respectable activities only a few hours before, from the constable of the Watch, who received a small stipend from the aforementioned for sending customers her way. "Needless to say, her clients are all gentlemen of the highest character. She doesn't waste her time on the riffraff. And the girls are very high quality. As good as anything one can get in London, I am persuaded. I beg of you, sir, for the sake of your health, let me make an appointment for you."

Benedict answered him with a look of strong disapproval. "Pickering, you astonish me. Do you mean *prostitutes*?"

Pickering's face fell. "You've heard about them already?"

"Pickering! You are addressing a member of British Parliament!"

"Of course, Sir Benedict," Pickering said contritely. "Didn't it help at all?"

Benedict was indignant. "For the love of God! After slavery, prostitution may be the greatest social evil of our time. In fact, it *is* a form of slavery, a particularly disgusting form of slavery, in which a woman, unable to support herself by any other means, is forced to sell her body to strangers. A gentleman, Pickering, does not use prostitutes. A gentleman," he said piously, "keeps a mistress. You see the difference. How could you possibly think that I would be interested in such a thing? I am deeply offended!"

"Mrs. Price's girls are not *all* prostitutes, if that is what troubles you," Pickering assured him. "I have had a long conversation with the footman about it. Some of them are quite respectable married women from the counties. They just do it to make a little money from time to time. There's nothing wrong with *that*, is there?"

"Oh, my God," Benedict said violently.

Pickering tried a new tact. "If you will not do it for yourself, think of your poor wife. I believe it was Aristotle who said that a man should approach his wife discreetly, lest the pleasure of being fondled too passionately should transport the poor creature beyond the bounds of reason. You do not want to take her ladyship by storm, after all. Better to get it out of your system *now*."

"Have you been drinking?" Benedict demanded.

Pickering went on doggedly. "If it is your health that concerns you, Mrs. Price's girls will not infect you with a social disease. They won't rob you or blackmail you. That's the Price guarantee: honest girls at an honest price. She can get you any kind of female you would like."

This elicited something between a snarl of pain and an explosion of derisive mirth from the baronet. "Is that so, Pickering? Can she get me . . . I don't know . . . a tall, slender Irish girl with tangled red hair, green eyes, perfect skin, good teeth, small, high breasts, and a laughing mouth?"

"I don't see why not, sir."

"While you're at it, have her sing to me in Italian! Can your Mrs. Price find me a girl like that?" Laboriously, he climbed to his feet. The room tilted and swayed around him. "No, don't help me," he said sharply as his valet started toward him.

"I can prepare you a cure, if you like," Pickering offered as his master limped past him into his dressing room. "My father's recipe."

"No," Benedict said firmly. "I drank my bottle, and now I must suffer for it." He looked around him in distaste. The dressing room was a six-sided chamber with a mirrored door set into every wall. He had come through the first door. Four of the other doors concealed closets while behind the fifth a steaming Roman-style bathing pool awaited him. Lord Skeldings, apparently, had spared no expense on his Bath home. The bathing chamber was equipped with up-to-date plumbing, with hot water piped in.

"Cover these mirrors," Benedict uttered in distaste. The last thing he wanted was six full-length views of his mortal body. He walked through to the bathroom.

After his bath, he was able to sit next to the fire for a few hours. His entire body ached. For dinner he managed to eat a plate of the injustly famous Bath olivers. The oliver was a dry digestive biscuit developed by Bath's own celebrated Dr. Oliver. Perhaps they tasted better when washed down with the foul-tasting water on offer in the Pump Room.

Pickering brought him the Bath papers, neatly folded into small sections, which made it easier for Benedict to manage the flimsy newsprint with his one hand. Ordinarily, he never glanced into the society columns, but, then, ordinarily, he was not on the lookout for a wife. The sooner he got married, the better. Then he could go back to his happy way of life, which did not include reading the society columns.

He found himself wondering what Miss Cosy might be doing at that moment. Certainly not reading the society columns! Probably, she was enjoying her portion of his thousand pounds. He hoped that her accomplices, whom he imagined to be big, burly men, had not cheated her of her fair share. She had earned it. He did not expect ever to see her again.

"She's probably halfway to London by now." He sighed.

"Sir?" Engaged in spreading a shawl over his gentleman's knees, Pickering looked up.

"I was thinking about the unfortunate young woman who robbed me," Benedict explained. "She must have been forced by extreme poverty into a life of crime. I have often thought it is a great pity that, outside of marriage, the women of our society have few options in life, other than thievery or, God forbid, prostitution. I would rather she steal from me a little than sell her body to countless men. In her place, I might have done the same."

"Oh, sir!" said Pickering, appalled. "Not one of your crusades?"

Benedict smiled ruefully. "I have but one crusade in Bath, and that is to find a wife."

"I have informed myself on the Bath social calendar," Pickering said eagerly. His interest in who would become Lady Wayborn was, if anything, keener than his master's. After all, her ladyship would set the tone at Wayborn Hall in the years to come. Pickering hoped she would be kind and beautiful; Sir Benedict would need someone to soften him around the edges. "There is a lecture on the growing threat of Atheism in the Upper Rooms tonight."

"God, no," said Benedict, with unintentional irony. "I couldn't possibly go out tonight. Besides, such a subject would be highly unlikely to attract marriageable young ladies," Benedict pointed out. "I believe the most prudent course of action would be to retire early, get a good night's rest, and begin afresh tomorrow."

With his little silver pencil he began circling the names of promising females in the newspaper column on the table before him. Any name prefaced by a "Miss" received an equal share of his attention.

Chapter 4

As usual, Lady Dalrymple had positioned herself with a commanding view of the entrance to the Pump Room. "Sir Benedict Wayborn!" she exclaimed, putting up her quizzing glass to inspect the new arrival. "He'll do for you, Millicent. About three thousand a year."

"But, Mama!" her daughter cried in alarm. Recently, Miss Carteret's spots had cleared up, and a special preparation had carried off the fuzz on her upper lip. She certainly did not intend to throw herself away on a mere baronet, and a one-armed, middle-aged baronet at that.

"I know, my love," said the viscountess with a sigh. "Not to mention: he is one of these dreadful reformers. Why, if he had his way, your poor brother would actually have to stand in an *election* for his seat in Commons. One shudders to think what would become of England if the common man had his way. But I hope I am not so stupid as to turn my nose up at three thousand a year simply because I disagree with the man and everything he stands for!"

Benedict gazed around the room in dismay. Crotchety-looking, elderly females abounded, but, none of them, it seemed, had brought along a nubile young dogsbody who would jump at the chance to marry anybody kind enough to ask. There were no desperate damsels in brown bombazine casting him hopeful glances. Not even one.

Mr. King, the master of ceremonies, hurried over to him. Bath was no longer the fashionable resort it had been during the war. Nowadays, the rich and privileged were flocking to the playgrounds of continental Europe, which had been closed to them for so long while the war raged on. It was all Mr. King could do to scrape together a few dozen couples for his cotillions on Thursday. After a few oily pleasantries, he offered to introduce the baronet to anyone he liked.

"I am looking for a wife," said Benedict. "Have you got anything under thirty-five?"

Mr. King had been master of ceremonies in Bath for twenty years. The baronet's request did not shock him in the least. "You are in luck, Sir Benedict. Lady Dalrymple is in Bath with her amiable daughter, Miss Carteret. If you are indifferent to fortune, perhaps Miss Vaughn can tempt you. She is not a rich young lady, like Miss Carteret, but beauty is not an unworthy dowry, when accompanied by good birth. Do you not agree?"

"I know of no marriages that fail sooner than those based on the beauty of the lady," Benedict replied curtly. "We do not marry to please ourselves, Mr. King."

"Er, yes. Lady Rose Fitzwilliam has only just arrived in Bath. This young lady is sure to melt your heart, for she joins in one person the virtues of birth, beauty, fortune, and youth."

"Only *three* young ladies of the class?"

Mr. King forced a smile. "It will be more difficult than the Judgment of Paris."

Benedict scowled. "What are the French up to now?"

Mr. King looked pained. "I was not referring to the events in France, Sir Benedict. You will have a more difficult time, I think, choosing between Miss Carteret, Miss Vaughn, and Lady Rose than Prince Paris had choosing between Venus, Juno, and Minerva."

"Ah," said Benedict. "Present me to Miss Carteret, then."

Benedict knew the viscountess slightly, but he had never had the opportunity to meet the amiable daughter. This being the case, he did not know how improved Miss Carteret was. Nor was he aware that her bonnet, an absurd construction with a cylindrical crown and a huge poke, was in the first stare of fashion. The mean little face surrounded by this pink monstrosity reminded him of a garden mole digging its way out of a subterranean den.

Lady Dalrymple whipped open her large painted fan as the gentlemen approached. "Shoulders back, Millie!" she hissed. "Uncross your eyes! He is not very handsome, perhaps, but he is rich!"

Almost in the same breath, she swept aside Mr. King's attempt at an introduction.

"But Sir Benedict requires no introduction! We are dear old friends. His aunt, Lady Elkins, and I have been bosom bows all our lives."

Benedict bowed. "You were missed at the funeral, Lady Dalrymple."

"Did she die?" cried Lady Dalrymple, clutching at her daughter's hand for support. Millicent obligingly rummaged in her reticule for a handkerchief, which she applied to her mama's dry eyes. "Oh, my poor, dear Amelia! Why did no one tell me?"

"Elinor," Benedict quietly corrected her.

Lady Dalrymple was startled out of her lamentations. "I am so distraught I do not know what I am saying," she exclaimed. "Dear *Elinor,* of course! I wish I had known she was dead. I should have been only too pleased to have attended the funeral. You remember Lady Elkins, Millicent. She had the house in Park Lane with the apricot saloon. So elegant!"

"I have painted the saloon black, I'm afraid," said Benedict.

"Oh," said Lady Dalrymple, batting her eyes at him. "Did you inherit?"

"Yes. My sister and my brother both having married so

well, my aunt took pity on me and left me all her estate, including the house in Park Lane."

"Did you hear that, Millicent?" Lady Dalrymple exclaimed. "My dear friend, Lady Elkins, has died and left this gentleman all her estate. Say hello to Sir Benedict."

But Millicent's attention was riveted elsewhere. A tall, young gentleman in a blue coat had just entered the room. In addition to nice blue eyes and an estate so large that one hardly noticed his harelip, the young Earl of Ludham had a perfect halo of crimped brown hair.

"Millicent was a great favorite of your Aunt Imogen," Lady Dalrymple said quickly.

"Elinor," Benedict corrected her patiently.

"*Dear* Elinor. She quite doted on the child, but, then, Millicent is so easy to love. Was there no mention of her in your aunt's will?"

"None."

Lady Dalrymple blinked rapidly. "Curious! She did not leave my daughter *any* token of her affection? I am sure no one was more devoted to Lady Elkins than my Millicent. Could there have been a secret codicil or something?"

"My aunt's chief occupation in life was keeping her will up to date. Her wishes could not have been plainer."

"Such a delightful woman," Lady Dalrymple murmured. "She was forever hinting that she meant to leave her rubies to dear Millie in her will." She sighed breezily. "But, I daresay, her ladyship was only teasing. I expect those rubies will go to Lady Wayborn—and so they should, even though Lady Elkins promised them to Millicent."

"I do not like rubies," said Millicent.

Meanwhile, Lord Ludham stood almost in the center of the room, looking about him searchingly. His eyes fell on Millicent's bright pink bonnet, then withdrew hastily. He spoke briefly to Mr. King, then left.

"No, don't go!" Millicent cried softly, the words slipping from her lips.

"Millie! You are too modest," protested her exasperated mother. "You *know* that nothing suits you better than the fiery brilliance of the Elkins' rubies. She is too modest, Sir Benedict. So the Duchess of Auckland has the rubies now, does she? Well, well. I hope it does not trouble Her Grace to wear them, when they were *promised to another.*"

Mr. King hurried over to them. "That was Lord Ludham," he said. "His lordship has asked that I add the waltz to the dance program! A *waltz,* in the Upper Rooms!"

"Scandalous," Lady Dalrymple barked. "It will never catch on!"

"The waltz is danced in London, even at Almack's," said Benedict. "For myself, I prefer it to the cotillion. It is easier to remember three steps than a thousand, and, best of all, it only lasts a few minutes. One can endure anything for five minutes, I think. The cotillion is half an hour at least. Too long!"

Mr. King's eyes popped. "But the waltz, Sir Benedict, is *fast!*"

"It is certainly brief," Benedict agreed. "That is what I like about it."

"But the lady is carried about the room, as if by storm, in the male embrace!" protested Mr. King. "Whenever I think of it, I am reminded of the Rape of the Sabine Women."

Benedict arched his brows. "In that case, I hope you do not think of it often, Mr. King."

"My dear Lady Dalrymple," said Mr. King, turning to that lady with an unctuous smile. "Rest assured there will be no waltzing in the Upper Rooms. I do hope that you and your amiable daughter will be with us at Thursday's assembly. Miss Carteret is a great favorite with the gentlemen. They would all want to dance with her, I am persuaded, if she did attend."

"Of course," the mama assured him.

"And, if I could persuade you to chaperone your young friend, Miss Vaughn?" he went on smoothly. "As you know,

Lady Agatha is too ill to attend parties and assemblies. On Monday, at the dress ball, all I heard from the gentlemen was 'Where is Miss Vaughn?'"

Lady Dalrymple said frostily, "Miss Vaughn? I do not know a Miss Vaughn."

Mr. King was startled. "But—but I had thought your ladyship and Lady Agatha Vaughn were the dearest of friends!"

"Oh, *those* Vaughns," her ladyship sniffed. "We were obliged to stay with them in Ireland last summer, when I turned my ankle and could not move for a month. Unfortunately, the poor, desperate creatures followed us here, Mr. King. I am sorry to hear that Miss Vaughn has been so unprincipled as to drop my name. She means to advance herself in society, I collect."

Mr. King was distressed. "That is most unfortunate, my lady. Lord Ludham has begged me to present him to Miss Vaughn as a desirable partner."

Lady Dalrymple became shrill. "Miss Vaughn is not a fit partner for Lord Ludham or anyone else! Miss Vaughn is a penniless Irish upstart. I would not do his lordship the disservice of presenting him to such a person. Millicent has twenty thousand pounds, and she is quite as handsome as Miss Vaughn."

Benedict suddenly smelled a strong odor of tobacco and perfume. In the next moment, the Honorable Mr. Roger Fitzwilliam was bearing down on them. Lady Dalrymple suddenly remembered that she needed to change a book in Meyler's Library. Snapping her fingers for her footman, she departed, dragging Millicent with her.

"Mr. Fitzwilliam is a younger son," she explained to her child when they were safely away. "We are not *quite* desperate just yet, I think. We have a little money left."

"There goes Miss Carteret and her twenty thousand pounds," Mr. Fitzwilliam said wistfully. "She's a bit long in the tooth to be turning her nose up at you, Sir Benedict."

"Excuse me," Benedict said coldly, and walked away.

Fitzwilliam fell into step with him. "You're welcome to Miss Carteret," he said generously, "for I have found something better. Lady Serena Calverstock is no longer young, but she's a damned fine female all the same. I don't mind mutton, if there's no lamb to be had. King has promised to present me at the cotillion tomorrow. You do not dance the cotillion, I collect?"

"Why wouldn't I?" said Benedict, bristling. "I am not an invalid."

Fitzwilliam frowned. "You wouldn't poach, would you? I saw Lady Serena first. She's ripe for the plucking, too! Now that her sister, Lady Redfylde, is dead, Serena can no longer live with her brother-in-law, you know. She has been cast out into the cold, cruel world."

Benedict snorted. "Lady Serena is perfectly able to keep her own house. And it would hardly be proper for her to live with Lord Redfylde now that he is a widower."

"You *know* her ladyship?" Fitzwilliam said jealously.

"She was my sister's matron of honor. I have known her for years. And she is possessed of a pretty independence. If she marries, it will not be in desperation, Mr. Fitzwilliam."

"Setting up house is a most tedious undertaking for a single lady," Fitzwilliam argued. "Even a wealthy woman will resent having to spend her own money on necessities when she never had to before. The more she spends on food and rent, the less there is for clothes and jewels and carriages. I doubt Lady Serena has ever had to pay a butcher's bill in all her life. And tradesmen always *do* cheat a woman, if they can. Depend on it: right now Lady Serena is feeling all the disadvantages of spinsterhood."

Benedict looked at Fitzwilliam thoughtfully.

"It would be remiss of me not to pay my respects," he said.

Although she was a near-total invalid, Lady Agatha Vaughn still took interest in society when she felt up to it.

Today she felt up to it, and, as she was eating a meager breakfast of biscuits and beef tea, her eldest daughter dutifully read the society columns to her. Cosy was continually amazed by how many people her mother still knew, even though she had been out of society for decades.

"Did you say Sir Benedict *Wayborn,* my dear?"

Cosy blanched. Her mother had been a Wayborn before her marriage. Now, as it turns out, the devil who had propositioned her in the kitchen was a Wayborn, too. "He's not one of your brothers, is he, ma'am?" she asked anxiously. How nasty it would be if he turned out to be my uncle, she thought.

But, fortunately, Lady Agatha had no brother by that name. Cosy sighed with relief.

"I wonder! Could he be one of the Surrey Wayborns?" Lady Agatha mused. "How long does he mean to stay in Bath? Is he ill? Is he a knight or a baronet? Is he married?"

"It doesn't say, Mother. Probably he's no relation to us at all."

Lady Agatha finished her tea. "I think I will be well enough to get up tomorrow."

When Lady Agatha felt well enough to get up, she would put on her auburn wig and paint her face with white lead. She had been badly scarred by smallpox as a child, and she never allowed anyone but her family and her maid, Nora, to see her without her face on, as she put it. She had no idea that the deadly poison was slowly killing her.

"Perhaps Lady Dalrymple will visit us again."

Cosy silently cursed Lady Dalrymple. It had been Lady Dalrymple who had first put the idea of coming to Bath into Lady Agatha's head. Then the old witch had dropped her mother like a hot potato when she found out the Vaughns had lost all their money. The woman, and her son, and her daughter, had spent three months with the Vaughns in Ireland, eating them out of house and home, but now, apparently, they couldn't be bothered to maintain the "friendship."

"Perhaps," she said, turning over to the personal advertisements. She had placed an advertisement in the paper a week ago herself, in the hopes of earning a little money by giving piano lessons, but there had been no response. Yesterday, she had finally sold the beautiful Erard pianoforte she had dragged, at great expense, all the way from Ireland, in order to pay the chemist for her mother's medications. She had hoped the sale would fetch enough for her to buy her mother a Bath-chair, but that had not been the case. Today was the last day that the fruitless, yet not inexpensive, advertisement would run. It would be the height of irony if today's paper contained a response, and she dearly needed a laugh.

There was no response today either, but, halfway down the page, an interesting item caught her eye. "Sizeable reward," she read aloud. "For the return of a gentleman's property. No questions asked." A watch and a ring were described in detail. The ring she was certain of instantly, but she had to go down to the kitchen and take the watch out of the man's valise to be sure. Opening it, she saw the inscription: "To my son, B. R. W. Tempus Fugit."

She had no idea what "Tempus Fugit" meant, if anything, but that would not prevent her from claiming the sizeable reward. How sizeable? she wondered greedily. Twenty pounds would be enough to buy a Bath-chair secondhand. A hundred pounds, and she could put her sister back in that snooty English school. A hundred pounds was a sum that took her breath away.

Ajax Jackson walked in just as she was pocketing the watch and the ring.

"There's a reward offered!" She showed him the newspaper, forgetting in her excitement that he could not read. "Sizeable, it says. I think I'll go over and collect it. There's his direction. Number Six, Camden Place. Right across the street. I'll be back in a flash with the cash."

Giddy with excitement, she put on her bonnet and ran out of the house. Pausing in the park between Upper and Lower Camden, she pulled the layers of her veil over her face. She would have to disguise her voice, too, she decided. Her Irish accent might give her away to the servants. Fortunately, her mother was English; she could do a fair imitation of a hoity-toity English lady. She went confidently up the steps, and rang the bell.

The door opened, and a portly man of middle years stood before her. He was elegantly dressed in knee breeches and buckled shoes. His head looked like an egg with a face drawn on it. She guessed he was the butler. Pickering would have been insulted. He was not a butler. He was a gentleman's gentleman.

"Mrs. Price?" he whispered, looking both ways down the street. Distracted by his furtive manner, Cosy looked up and down the street, too, but saw no one. Apparently satisfied, the servant pulled her inside and closed the door. "In here, Mrs. Price, if you please."

Of course, she ought to have corrected the man's mistake at once, but his manner was so strange that curiosity got the better of her. Who was Mrs. Price? And why would a married lady be visiting Sir Benedict's butler in the middle of the day? Or maybe she was visiting Sir Benedict himself. A married woman!

That man is a menace, she thought.

Pickering put her in the study.

A generous fire crackled in the handsome fireplace of carved marble, drawing her to it. She warmed her hands and looked around. The beveled glass doors of the bookshelves gleamed as if teams of slaves had been polishing them all night. The walls were paneled in green damask. A huge desk of carved walnut, for heavy thinkers only, dominated one end of the room. Grouped at the fireside were a sofa, two chairs, and an ottoman, all upholstered in a green and gold striped brocade. The closed curtains on the two tall windows matched the upholstery. It was a man's room, and she felt like an interloper.

Then again, interloping was a good way to get to know someone.

She strolled to the desk, but there were no incriminating

letters to Mrs. Price left out on the blotter, just a bill from the wine merchant. The man had paid sixty pounds for his port, and a hundred pounds for a case of brandy! The rest of the desk was taken up by a display of classical marbles and bronzes, a veritable Pantheon of gods and goddesses. And a big box of chased silver. Sea nymphs writhed on the lid, and the key was in the lock, just tempting her to open it.

Twenty pounds, she realized, would be nothing to the man who lived here. Not if he was in the habit of paying out a thousand pounds to this girl and that. A thousand pounds! Now, *that* would be sizeable. With a thousand pounds, she wouldn't have to worry about money for years.

"Don't touch that!" Pickering cried angrily.

Bustling over to her, he slapped her hand away. She yelped in rage.

"Where is Sir Benedict?" she demanded. "I have private business with him."

Taking out his handkerchief, he began to polish the ornaments on the desk.

"My master," he said coolly, "has entrusted me with the task of making the appointment. I can tell you precisely what sort of woman he desires you to send."

Behind her veil, Cosy's eyebrows touched her hairline. "Your master, Sir Benedict Wayborn, wants me, Mrs. Price, to *send him a woman*?" she repeated carefully.

"Yes, of course, a woman," Pickering snapped. "What are you implying?"

"Nothing," she said quickly. "Please go on! You were saying?"

"My master desires you to send an Irish girl; tall, slender, with perfect skin, red hair, and green eyes. He wants her to sing to him in Italian, but, between you and me, my master doesn't speak Italian, so, really, she could just improvise. He won't know the difference." He stopped, peered at her through the layers of her veil. "Aren't you going to write any of this down?"

"I have an excellent memory," she assured him in a clipped

English falsetto. "Are you quite sure he wants *red* hair? It's been my experience that gentlemen prefer blondes."

Pickering drew himself up to his full height. "If my master has a lech for an Irish girl with red hair, who are you to question his taste? You forget yourself, Mrs. Price."

"Sorry," she said quickly. "I didn't mean to forget myself."

"You almost made me forget about the breasts," he whined. "Sir Benedict prefers a small, high bosom."

"Oh, he does, does he?" she said tartly. "Anything else?"

"I should warn you not to send a squeamish young woman. My master's right arm was amputated some years ago. He doesn't like people to feel sorry for him, of course, but an expression of shock and horror would scarcely bolster his confidence. Other than that, he is a perfectly healthy specimen, I assure you. A little shy, perhaps."

"Shy!"

Pickering sighed. "I'll be frank with you, Mrs. Price. Sir Benedict's loins are in a dreadful state. If my master doesn't bed a woman soon, I fear he might explode. Of course, it's my fault completely. For years, I have drawn his baths, darned his stockings, boiled his shirts, pressed his suits, and starched his collars, but I never once thought to get him a woman."

"You were busy," she said charitably. "Stockings don't darn themselves, you know."

"How soon can you get the girl?" he asked eagerly.

"I'll see what I can do," said the imposter. "In the meantime, I understand that ice baths can be most efficacious in cooling an overheated body. Or you could try putting saltpeter in his food. They use it in the Army when the men get a little too randy for their own good."

Cosy left the interview with a feeling of accomplishment. As she went down the front steps, she saw a veiled woman coming up the street. Her suspicion that *this* was the real Mrs. Price was borne out almost at once as the other woman walked up to the gate.

The two veiled ladies looked at each other angrily.

"Mrs. Price?" Cosy said coldly and imperiously.

"Who wants to know?"

Cosy threw back her veil. Her green eyes glittered dangerously. "I am Lady Wayborn," she said with cool dignity. "If you ever come near my husband again, I will tear out your liver and feed it to my dogs. I will laugh while you die, and I will dance on your grave. Are we clear, Mrs. Price?"

The other woman gasped, sucking in her veil. "Yes, Lady Wayborn," she said meekly.

Lady Matlock no longer lived with her husband. Having provided her lord and master with two healthy sons as well as one superfluous daughter, the countess was now free to enjoy the ill health she had always complained about. Deeply engrossed in the pursuit of Parisian actresses, Lord Matlock had offered no resistance when his lady removed to Bath.

Lady Rose, their only daughter, had been brought up in the country by a governess, then brought out in Town by an obliging aunt. The return of Rose to her mother's bosom had forced the invalid to make a remarkable recovery, but it was very tiring to be well again. Society expected so much of one when one was well.

"Are you or are you not pregnant?" Lady Matlock snarled as she neared the end of a long, uncomfortable interview with Rose. She was no closer to understanding Lord Westlands's odd behavior toward her daughter than she had been the day before, and her delicate nerves were completely frayed. *I am too young,* she raged inside, *to have a grown-up daughter.* "If you are increasing, he will have to marry you. We will *make* him marry you."

Rose was curled up in the window seat, scornful and sullen. Her eyes were red from crying, but she was all cried out now. "I am not increasing," she howled.

"Then you will have to marry someone else," said her

parent, exasperated. "You can't stay here. I'm too ill." Opening her daughter's wardrobe, Lady Matlock began pulling out the gowns Rose's maid had so carefully put away the day before. "And no wonder!" she exclaimed in disgust. "You will never catch a husband dressed so modest. I was practically *naked* when I met your father. Fardle! Fardle!"

Rose's maid, who had been banished to the privy closet for the mother-daughter interview, reentered the room. "Yes, my lady?"

"Here is a shocking piece of intelligence for you, Fardle," said her ladyship. "Men like looking at bosoms! Lower the bodices of the ballgowns by three inches, and the day dresses by two inches. That ought to do the trick." She looked angrily at her daughter. "I expect you to *try*, Rose. For *my* sake. You will find little competition here. There is a Miss Vaughn that all the men are in love with, but she's poor, and half-Irish, so I do not take their love for her seriously. Better to be rich than pretty, I always say, and you, my dear, are both!"

"I should like to meet her," Rose said eagerly.

"Who? Miss Vaughn? What on earth for?"

"She is Lord Wayborn's niece, Mama. That makes her Westlands's cousin."

"Then, for all we know, *she* is the reason Westlands jilted you," snapped Lady Matlock. "Though, I daresay, if she is poor, Lord Wayborn would never approve the match."

"Westlands did not jilt me," Rose protested for the hundredth time. "There was never any understanding between us, Mama. We are friends, that is all."

"Men and women cannot be friends. For one thing, their parts don't match. Aye, me!" Exhausted by her exertions, Lady Matlock sank down into a chair.

"Couldn't I stay here with you, Mama?" Rose begged. "I could help look after you. I could bring you your hartshorn as well as any nurse. I need not go to balls. I need not marry."

Lady Matlock rallied. "My daughter? A nurse? No, indeed! You are the daughter of an earl. Your duty is to make us all proud, and marry well. Honestly, Rose, with this ungrateful attitude, I am tempted to marry you off to the first gentleman who asks for you!"

Rose suddenly shrieked in alarm. Kneeling up in the window seat, she pressed her nose against the glass. "Oh, no! It is Sir Benedict Wayborn! He is coming here!"

Instantly, Lady Matlock was on her feet, marshaling her forces like a general. "The nice gentleman who found you in the road and brought you home? Yes, I think he will do *very* nicely. Don't just sit there, child! Go and wash your face. Put on your blue gown. Hurry!"

"No, Mama, please!" begged Rose. "He's so old. And I am sure he does not like me." She looked out the window again. The baronet had stopped at another door. "He has stopped two—no, three—doors down. Who lives there?"

Lady Matlock was furious. "Serena! He ought to have called on *me* first. *She* may be the daughter of an earl, but *I* am a countess. More to the point, he spent four hours in a closed carriage with my daughter—and I am not even acquainted with him! He has a duty to call on me first! But that is how it is." She sniffed. "No one has any manners anymore."

"Perhaps he will marry Serena," Rose suggested happily. "She is *quite* as old as he is!"

"If not older," said Lady Matlock, but that was only spite. Anyone who possessed a copy of the Peerage could easily discover that Lady Serena Calverstock was only thirty.

Lady Serena received Benedict graciously in her elegant drawing room. She was just emerging from mourning for her sister, Lady Redfylde, and she looked charming in a lavender gown with a jabot of black lace at her throat. Her black hair was worn in a topknot with a frisette of glossy ringlets on her brow. As a debutante, her ivory pallor, raven tresses, and cool violet eyes had made her portrait one of the most admired in the National Gallery, and she was still considered one of the handsomest women in England.

They exchanged the usual pleasantries over strong black China tea.

"What brings you to Bath, Sir Benedict?" she smiled.

"Duty, I'm afraid," he admitted ruefully. "My brother has managed to get himself elevated to the peerage, leaving my little baronetcy quite without an heir. Suddenly, I find myself in want of a wife, Lady Serena."

Serena inclined her head. "I saw your brother's name in the List of Honors. Tell me, does his lordship mean to build a fort somewhere with archers on the battlements, or will he be content to live in London as a man of fashion?"

Benedict suppressed a shudder of revulsion. "It is a bought title, of course. A wedding gift from his father-in-law. A Glaswegian whiskey merchant, and the girl's not even pretty."

"You wrong Lady Kensington," Serena chided him. "Heiresses are always beautiful, or didn't you know that?"

He smiled briefly. "I am glad my brother married money, at least. I was terrified he'd make some disastrous love match with an actress, like your poor cousin, Lord Ludham."

"Lady Ludham was an opera dancer," she corrected him without rancor. "*Pamela* was the creature's name, if you please!" She laughed discreetly.

"How relieved you must have been when the divorce petition sailed through Lords."

Her violet eyes widened. "I, Sir Benedict? Why should I be relieved?"

"It cannot have been easy watching an opera dancer take your mother's place," he said quietly. "Forgive me. It must be a painful subject. I should not have mentioned it."

"I never met the famous Pamela. I spared myself the degradation of curtseying to *her ladyship*. As you know, I had no brother, so Felix inherited. I went to live with my sister and her husband immediately after my father's funeral. Isn't it curious? When Papa died, I lost my father and my home all in one day. Likewise, when Caroline died, I lost my sister and my home in one fell swoop. It seems to be my lot that, whenever there is a death in the family, I lose . . . everything."

"It must be something of an adjustment to live alone," he hinted blandly.

She replied, "It must be something of an adjustment to find yourself without an heir."

"I mean to marry as soon as possible," he said. "I might advise your ladyship to do the same. Then you would not have to adjust to living alone."

She looked down at her hands. "But I have been single so long that no one thinks of me! I can not compete with these seventeen- and eighteen-year-old debutantes. They seem to be getting younger every year."

"Quite," said Benedict.

"I understand you rescued Lady Matlock's daughter on the road from Chippenham," she said, smiling. "Naturally, everyone is dying to wish you joy. A very pretty girl, but so young! Too young, I think, to be pitchforked into society. But . . . very pretty, I grant you."

"You are wrong when you say that no one thinks of you," said Benedict.

Serena blushed.

So Fitzwilliam was right, he thought. *The lady is on the market.*

He stayed with her only twenty minutes, the prescribed time for a social visit. In his view, the call went very smoothly. The ice was broken, at any rate.

Chapter 5

Wednesday passed with nothing more interesting to report than a stroll in the Sydney Gardens, but Benedict began Thursday with a feeling of complacency. If tonight's ball concluded on a note of accord between himself and Lady Serena, he saw no reason why he could not propose to her on Friday. It was a little soon, perhaps, but not, he thought, too soon for propriety's sake. After all, he had known Serena before he ever set foot in Bath.

Most of the morning was taken up in grooming. Benedict sat in his black dressing gown wanting a cheroot as his hair was cut and his sideburns were trimmed. His fingernails were trimmed and buffed to a high sheen, and, even though no one but Pickering was going to see them, so were his toenails. Usually Benedict paid little attention to Pickering as he fussed about, but today he watched him like a hawk.

He startled Pickering by suddenly demanding, "*What* is that foul concoction?"

Pickering had been humming a cheerful little tune as he applied the special nourishing hair tonic to the roots of his master's luxuriant black hair. It died now. Sir Benedict had never questioned him before. It was disconcerting to hear the special nourishing hair tonic described as a "foul concoction."

"Foul concoction?" Pickering echoed tremulously.

"You're *dyeing* my hair!" Benedict roared the accusation. "Pickering, how *could* you?"

Pickering clutched the black bottle to his breast protectively. "Now, Sir Benedict," he said soothingly. "Everyone does it."

"How long have you been doing this to me?" Benedict demanded furiously.

"I don't recall the particulars—"

"Damn the particulars! How long?"

Pickering's memory improved. "It was about the time that Master Cary disobeyed you, and enlisted in the Army as a private, Sir Benedict. You began to go gray at the temples—quite prematurely, of course."

"Good God!" said Benedict. "I wasn't even thirty when my brother went to Spain. That was nearly ten years ago! You have been dyeing my hair black for *ten years*?"

"Master Cary would give anyone gray hairs."

"You will stop dyeing my hair at once, Pickering," Benedict commanded, getting up from his chair. "Only fops and old women dye their hair. I am neither, I trust."

Pickering was apologetic but firm. "It would be most unwise to stop now, Sir Benedict. Your roots are already beginning to show," he gently explained. "It will be so very noticeable when you bow to the ladies. Not at all the thing when one is looking for a wife. One never gets a second chance to make a first impression, you know."

"Pickering, I could *kill* you!"

"You will thank me for this when you are married, Sir Benedict. Ladies always say *nay* to Mr. Gray. Mr. Gray, go away, they say. Come back, Mr. Black."

"Oh, shut up!"

Pickering shut up.

Unable to watch the rest of the demoralizing operation, Benedict leaned back in his chair and closed his eyes. "I'm too old for this," he muttered. "I should have lived in the

Middle Ages. I could have traded a few cows for my neighbor's daughter."

"You are *not* too old for Lady Serena," Pickering assured him. "Why, she's thirty, if she's a day, and clinging to it like a burr. And if that black hair is her own, then I'm the King of France! I've seen her maid in the apothecary's shop."

"Are you saying that Lady Serena dyes her hair?"

"Not only that, sir, but I have seen her maid buying white lead and belladonna drops."

"But those are poisons, surely."

"They are only poisonous if one ingests them, sir," Pickering said confidently. "Ladies—and some gentlemen—routinely paint their faces with white lead. It's perfectly safe. As for the belladonna, a few drops in the eye enlarge the pupil, for a more speaking glance."

Benedict shook his head in amazement. "What else do women do for the sake of beauty? Clean their teeth with bluing?"

"Certainly. And they bleach their skins, too."

Benedict looked at himself in the mirror. "You haven't been bleaching *me,* have you?"

"No, indeed, Sir Benedict," Pickering assured him. "Fortunately, you are naturally pale, like all true English gentlemen. No one would ever mistake you for a laborer."

"Heaven forbid," said Benedict.

The ballroom presided over by Mr. King was one hundred feet in length, supported by Corinthian columns and decorated with neoclassical friezes. Five enormous glass chandeliers hung from gilded compartments in the ceiling, the brilliance of their white candles reflected and magnified by the enormous mirrors at either end of the room.

The right sleeve of his dress coat had been neatly pinned back, and he disdained to wear a glove on his remaining hand, but other than that, he was in correct evening dress.

The musicians had already assembled in the gallery when Benedict arrived, but Mr. King had not yet given the signal to begin.

"You will dance with Sir Benedict if he asks you, Millicent," Lady Dalrymple hissed.

Miss Carteret's headdress of saffron-colored plumes towered over her mother, and, indeed, over her brother. She had worn her canary yellow satin gown specifically to seduce Lord Ludham. She had no intention of wasting it on the amputee. "Sir Benedict makes one queasy, Mama," she protested. "That nasty stump! I'll be sick, I know it."

"Hush! He will hear you."

Benedict had excellent hearing, but he gave no sign that he had heard this exchange.

"Here he is, Millie," cried Lady Dalrymple, seizing him by the arm as he tried to slip past. "She is longing to dance with you, Sir Benedict. My son Frederick you know. Freddie holds the seat for Little Wicking, of course, in Cumberland. Why, you must see one another all the time in Parliament."

Freddie Carteret, who spent as little time in the House of Commons as possible, and even less than that with his constituents in Cumberland, bowed. Lady Dalrymple's youngest son was good-looking in a harmless, silly way. He was blind as a mole, but too vain to wear spectacles. He bumped into people constantly, especially buxom young women.

"Ah! The famous Sir Benedict Wayborn, champion of the common man," he said, baring his yellow teeth in an ironic smile. "I have heard you described as the New Cicero . . . but you have never yet won an argument over *me*, sir!"

"Arguing with you would be a complete waste of my time," Benedict agreed.

These pleasantries had scarcely been exchanged, and, what with this and that, Sir Benedict had not yet been prevailed upon to ask Miss Carteret to dance when Mr. King and Lord Ludham came bustling up to them. "Lady Dalrymple, his lordship has expressed a desire to be acquainted with your amiable daughter. May I present the Earl of Ludham to you?"

Miss Carteret's moment had come at last, and she made the most of it, throwing her shoulders back and smiling as well as she could without revealing her less than perfect teeth.

Benedict recognized Serena's cousin as the gentleman in the blue coat from the Pump Room. As before, Lord Ludham seemed to be in search of an elusive someone, and, even as he said everything a gentleman ought to say to the viscountess and her daughter, his blue eyes scanned the crowd eagerly.

"Do you dance, my lord?" Millicent asked him breathlessly, not willing to leave the matter entirely to chance. The question came perilously close to soliciting the gentleman, but it was still within the bounds of propriety—just.

"I *do* dance, Miss Carteret," his lordship replied. Miss Carteret's lips puckered in a smile, but her delight was soon replaced by less agreeable feelings, as his lordship continued, "And, if Miss Vaughn will be attending tonight's ball, I shall ask her for the honor, for she is the most beautiful creature I ever saw! I understand she is a great friend of yours, Miss Carteret. How fortunate you are in your acquaintance! I intend to ask her for the first dance. I would dance them both with her, but, I understand, that is not at all the thing."

Lady Dalrymple pretended to misunderstand his lordship's meaning. She was all smiles. "Of course, my lord. Millicent will be delighted to give you the first dance."

"Indeed, my lord," cried Millicent, blinking rapidly.

"I'd ask you, Miss Carteret," Ludham replied, "but I must keep myself free, in case Miss Vaughn arrives late. Indeed, I came here tonight with no other purpose but to dance with your good friend. Is she coming, do you know?"

Lady Dalrymple glared at Mr. King.

Mr. King said hastily, "I *did* try to tell his lordship that your ladyship and Miss Carteret are not acquainted with Miss Vaughn. However—"

Ludham laughed. "Of course they are acquainted, King,"

he scoffed. "I have *seen* Miss Carteret and Miss Vaughn walking together, in Milsom Street, arm and arm."

"Oh, Miss *Vaughn*!" cried Lady Dalrymple. "I thought you said Miss Fawn! Miss Vaughn, of course, is Millicent's dearest friend. They have been knowing one another forever. We stayed with the Vaughns in Ireland for two months last summer. Such delightful people! The mother is English, of course, which helps. The girls became friends at once, but then, Millicent has such a sweet and generous nature. She makes friends wherever she goes. Why, they were Christian-naming one another within three days."

"What is her Christian name?" Lord Ludham asked.

Lady Dalrymple batted her eyes. "Why, Millicent, of course. We call her Millie."

"What an extraordinary coincidence!" exclaimed Ludham. "Miss Vaughn and your daughter having the same name."

"Oh, was it Miss Vaughn you meant?" Lady Dalrymple sniffed. "She has a very silly name, I'm afraid. Cosima. It's too ridiculous for words. Poor Miss Vaughn! She has never been presented, you know, and I daresay she never will be. Not our sort, really. But we *quite charitably* took her under our wing."

Benedict made no comment; after all, it was a woman's prerogative to change her mind. Lady Dalrymple was well within her rights to deny this Miss Vaughn one day and claim her the next. It was no concern of his.

"Cosima," Lord Ludham said, pleased. "I've never met a Cosima in the whole course of my life. It's Italian, isn't it?"

"Such pretentious people, I know," said Lady Dalrymple. She placed her fan on Ludham's arm. "But I do pity them. The mother, Lady Agatha, as she calls herself, is ill, which prevents poor Miss Vaughn from going anywhere much. The father, Colonel Vaughn, has deserted them completely. Gambling debts, I'm afraid. Miss Vaughn and her sister are as good as portionless, and all they have to live on is Lady Agatha's tiny little annuity. They have lost everything."

Lord Ludham did not seem to find anything disagreeable with this picture. "Oh, she has a sister, has she?" he said eagerly.

"A mere child," Lady Dalrymple sniffed. "Wilful and wild. Lady Agatha can do nothing with her, and there is no money for a governess. I daresay Miss Vaughn will make someone an adequate governess herself, when the mother goes, and she is forced to earn her bread. When the time comes, I shall be more than happy to find her a place in some respectable household."

"I am glad to hear that the Vaughns are not without friends," Benedict said dryly.

Lady Dalrymple had forgotten that Sir Benedict had been present in the Pump Room when she had denied knowing the Vaughns. She remembered now, horribly, but there was nothing she could do about it. "I consider it my Christian duty to help the Miss Vaughns of the world," she said sweepingly. "It is especially hard on the pretty ones, I think. Their vanity leads them so quickly down the wrong path, if they have no money."

Millicent could no longer contain her spite. "They are so poor, my lord, that they have *no credit* in any of the shops in town. Miss Vaughn is obliged to pay in cash wherever she goes! You mentioned Milsom Street, my lord. Well, it was very shocking for me to see Miss Vaughn actually *pay* for her ribbons. I have not seen her since; I daresay she is too ashamed to see me."

"I don't care if a girl has twenty thousand pounds or twenty," said Ludham. "I'm a simple man. I like Miss Vaughn, and I want to dance with her. I am not mercenary."

"No!" cried Lady Dalrymple. "Nor am I! What I cannot bear is being deceived!"

A slight frown appeared in Ludham's eyes. He was not the cleverest of men, and, this being the case, he had been deceived often enough to know that he disliked it as much as Lady Dalrymple did. "Deceived, madam? In what way were you deceived?"

"The Heiress of Castle Argent, they called her in Dublin!" Lady Dalrymple complained bitterly. "Anyone would think she was fabulously wealthy the way they talk about her over there. Anyone would think she was the Queen of Ireland."

Ludham was instantly diverted. "Does she really live in a castle?" he cried.

"Castle? A farmhouse with battlements!" Lady Dalrymple squawked. "When I think of how I suffered there—! Such cramped quarters! Such indifferent servants! Such noise from that enormous hell-hound of a dog! And, then, when my ankle healed at last, what should happen, but I should fall on the stairs and hurt myself again! I thought we would never leave!"

"A sentiment shared, no doubt, by the Vaughns," Benedict murmured.

"What?" Lady Dalrymple snapped.

"It must have cost the Vaughns a great deal of money to entertain you for over two months," Benedict pointed out.

"That is quite their own fault," the viscountess returned frostily, "for pretending to be rich! I was never so deceived in my life!"

"What about *me*?" cried Mr. Carteret. "I asked the girl to marry me! I'd be in the basket now if she'd said yes."

"Good God, so would I!" exclaimed Ludham.

"Depend on it, my lord: Miss Vaughn is a fortune hunter!" cried Lady Dalrymple, abandoning the subtle approach completely.

"How fortunate then that she refused to marry your son, madam," said Benedict.

"Yes," Lord Ludham agreed. "If she is a fortune hunter, she ought to marry someone with—well, with a *fortune,* you know. Will you tell her, Miss Carteret—since you are such good friends—that my income is ten thousand a year? Well, strictly speaking—I don't want to deceive anyone—it is nine thousand, seven hundred-odd, you know." He shrugged helplessly. "My man can get the exact figure."

Benedict looked at him incredulously. Serena was right to

worry about her cousin, he reflected. The young man seemed to have learned nothing from the fiasco with his opera dancer.

"She has the face of an angel," Ludham sighed blissfully.

"Yes, indeed," Lady Dalrymple agreed warmly. "Millicent is admired wherever she goes, and, of course, she has twenty thousand pounds . . . or so my Lord Dalrymple tells me," she hastily added. "I never concern myself with money, you understand. Nor does Millie, not like some young ladies who must scrape as they can, and calculate as they go. I am but a bird-witted female, my lord, and I don't pretend to be otherwise."

"Excuse me," said Benedict, abruptly, unable to bear any more machinations that were, at least to him, transparent. "I must pay my respects to Lady Serena."

"What a rude man he is!" cried Lady Dalrymple as he strode off. "He did not even ask Millicent to dance."

Lord Ludham mumbled some excuse about paying his respects to Lady Serena as well, and scampered off. Lady Dalrymple sighed. Sometimes, even though one did all one can do, things did not turn out as one had hoped. "It will have to be Fitzwilliam, after all," she said, raising her lorgnette.

"I do not like the Church," said Millicent. "And he smells bad. I want to be a countess."

"If Lord Matlock and his two sons should die, you will be," said her mama. "One never knows. Ah, Mr. Fitzwilliam! Poor Millicent has been longing to see you this age!"

"I daresay Lady Dalrymple thought I was talking about her daughter," Ludham said when he had caught up with Benedict. "But, really, I was talking of Miss Vaughn."

"I had guessed as much," Benedict said politely. "From what I can tell, your lordship speaks of nothing and no one else."

Ludham took this for an invitation to expand on his favorite subject. "The first time I ever saw Miss Vaughn was in the rain. Naturally, I offered her my umbrella. I told her she was like Venus washed ashore, but I daresay she did not understand me. She told me to go away."

As Lady Serena regally inclined her head to him, Benedict

could not help but notice how black her hair was, the same improbable black as his own. Her beautiful face was painted, too. Her maid was such an artist that it was only detectable in the wrinkles at the corners of her eyes and mouth, but, now that he was looking for it, he noticed it. As ever, she was elegantly and simply dressed, neither addicted to the latest fashions nor aloof to them. While the other unmarried women seemed to be coming out of their clothes, Serena's neckline showed only a modest hint of bosom.

"I see you have met my foolish cousin, Sir Benedict," Serena said. "Now, Felix, you must not rattle on about the beautiful Miss Vaughn. You will give the unfortunate young lady a reputation before she ever enters society. Ah, Lady Matlock!"

"Serena!" Lady Matlock sailed through the crowd, which parted around her and her daughter like the Red Sea in deference to her exalted rank. The ladies kissed the air around each other's faces. "You remember Rose, of course."

Rose was trying to hide behind her mother, but the countess pushed her forward. Obviously uncomfortable in her low-cut gown of dampened muslin, she tried to cover herself with her lace fan, but her mama snatched it away, and all she could do was toy nervously with the pearls at her throat.

Benedict suppressed his burning desire to take off his coat and wrap the half-naked child up in it. He had once been the guardian of a much younger sister. Not in a hundred years would he have permitted Miss Juliet Wayborn to make such a spectacle of herself. Lady Matlock would be fortunate if her daughter did not contract pneumonia, rather than a husband.

Lady Matlock herself was dressed warmly in a garnet-colored velvet gown and a massive brown wig. Numerous chains of gold hung from the precipice of her bosom, twisted together in a hopeless tangle. "Do you dance, Ludham?" she demanded, attacking that gentleman first, by order of precedence.

"I do dance, Lady Matlock," he answered. "And if I could

ever be introduced to Miss Vaughn, what's more, I *would* dance!"

"Miss Vaughn?" cried Rose eagerly. "Is she here, my lord? I would so like to meet her! Indeed, I have heard so much about her from Lord Westlands that I feel I know her already."

"Does this Lord Westlands know Miss Vaughn?" Lord Ludham demanded jealously.

"He is her cousin," replied Rose. "They have known each other all their lives."

"Is he here? Can he not introduce me?"

"He is back in London now, I believe," replied Rose. "But we need not apply to him. Here is *another* of the lady's cousins. Surely, Sir Benedict can introduce us."

"I, Lady Rose?" Benedict protested. "I never heard of the Vaughns."

Rose looked scandalized. "You deny them because they are Irish? That is very bad of you, Sir Benedict! In any case, Lady Agatha Vaughn is not Irish. She is Lord Wayborn's elder sister, and *your* cousin."

"I've never been introduced to Lady Agatha," said Benedict. "The Derbyshire Wayborns have little to do with humble Surrey Wayborns like myself. I assure you, I had no idea of these ladies being related to me in any way."

Serena laughed behind her fan. "I should have thought that *all* the Wayborns, both Derbyshire and Surrey, were in St. George's Church when Miss Juliet Wayborn married the Duke of Auckland."

Benedict smiled. "Lord Wayborn even disputed my right to walk my sister down the aisle. He wished to do it himself. There were no Vaughns in evidence, however."

"There was a rift between brother and sister some years ago," said Rose. "Westlands did not know all the particulars, but he said that Lady Agatha and her daughters must suffer for it all their lives. His father's resentment, once aroused, is implacable. It's up to you to help them, Sir Benedict."

Benedict lifted his brows. "I?"

"Yes! You are her nearest male relative, so you must help her. *And,* as Lady Agatha is too sick to come to you, you must go to her. It is not fair that Miss Vaughn can never go anywhere simply because her mother is ill."

"Lady Rose is perfectly right," said Ludham. "You must bring her to balls, Sir Benedict, so that I can dance with her."

"They live at Number Nine, Upper Camden Place," Rose said eagerly. "I wanted to visit them myself, but Mama said I may not."

"That is right across the park from me," Benedict remarked in surprise.

"Then you have no excuse not to visit!" said Rose.

Lady Matlock changed the subject abruptly. "It was so very kind of you, Sir Benedict, to rescue my daughter when she was stranded. Sir Benedict happened to be passing by when Rose's carriage got stuck in the mud," she explained to Serena, who showed an expression of polite inquiry. "It was fate, I am persuaded. I have been urging Rose to dance. Everyone has asked her, but she says she will only dance with you, Sir Benedict. You are her hero."

The gentleman did not seize the hint, but Lady Matlock persevered. "It would be very strange indeed if my daughter did not fancy herself in love with you, Sir Benedict. You are her knight in shining armor. Pray, for the sake of my nerves, take her away and dance with her. She will sulk all night if you do not ask her."

"Thank you, my lady," he said, "but I have hopes of soliciting Lady Serena for the first cotillion, and I am engaged to Miss Carteret for the second."

Serena declined to rescue him, however.

"Thank you, Sir Benedict, but I do not mean to dance," she said firmly. "As you can see, my skirts are too long."

"I can pin up your demi-train for you, Lady Serena," Rose said quickly.

Lady Serena demurred. "Pins in my lavender crepe? I think not. No; dancing is an amusement for young ladies, I think."

"You are still young, my lady," cried Rose. "Indeed, you look *much* younger than you are! No one would ever guess you were thirty!"

"Thank you, child," Serena said coldly. "What a pretty compliment."

"The set is forming, Sir Benedict," Lady Matlock said threateningly.

"Lady Serena is not dancing," said Benedict. "I am pledged to keep her company."

"I will sit with Serena for the first dance," Ludham said generously. "What's more, I will dance the second with Lady Rose, if I may."

"Certainly, my lord!" cried Lady Matlock in triumph. "Hurry! The set is forming."

"Mother, please!" cried Rose, clearly horrified by the prospect of standing up with the baronet. "He's old enough to be my father, for heaven's sake."

Lady Matlock stabbed her daughter in the back with the sticks of her fan. "Thank the gentleman for asking you," she insisted, quite forgetting that Benedict had done no such thing.

"I thank you, sir," said Lady Rose, regarding Benedict with revulsion.

"Indeed, I am in your debt, Lady Rose," he replied.

"Hurry, my dears. The set is formed! The musicians are tuning up!"

Exhausted, Lady Matlock sat down to fan herself. "Thank heavens there are only two cotillions performed in an evening," she confided to Serena. "If this new waltzing catches on, there will be *so* many partners to get."

"I don't like this Sir Benedict sniffing around you, Serena," Ludham said darkly.

Serena lit up. "Felix! Are you jealous?"

His face turned red. "Don't be daft! He's probably a fortune hunter, that's all. We're cousins, and we have to look out for one another."

"Are you implying that a man can't find me attractive?" she snapped.

"No, of course not," he said. "Just be careful, that's all."

"I'm not the one who needs to be careful," she said, still angry.

Rose Fitzwilliam did not believe in mincing her words. "I am not in love with you, sir," she told Benedict, on the very first occasion when the dance brought them close enough for such an intimate disclosure.

"How very kind of you to put me on my guard," he answered as they parted.

"If you ask me to marry you, I shall kill myself," was her next tragic communication.

"You mean to flatter me, I see."

"You are old enough to be my father!" she snapped, nettled by his cool reply.

"Fortunately, however, I am no such thing," he said pleasantly.

"I wish you *were* my father! Then you could not ask me to marry you!"

"No," he agreed, "but I could take away your pin money, and you wouldn't like that."

Tears pricked her eyes. "I think you are hateful and odious," she declared. "I wish you had left me in the mud! I was happier then!"

At the end of this delightful exercise, Benedict conducted his partner back to her mama, and the tea interval was announced. Lady Matlock claimed the right to leave the ballroom first, before the crush of the crowd, but Lady Dalrymple and her daughter were not far behind her to the first table.

Lord Ludham had gone to the card room. Lady Dalrymple took advantage of the earl's absence to warn Serena that Miss Vaughn had designs on him.

"I do not believe she is a fortune hunter!" Rose hotly declared. "She may be poor, and she may wish to marry, but that does not make her a fortune hunter."

Lady Dalrymple had not expected to find Miss Vaughn so well defended. "How innocent you are, my dear," she murmured. "You will understand when you are older."

"But not everyone can afford to marry for love," Benedict pointed out, annoyed by the woman's self-righteousness. "In our society, a poor woman can only better herself through marriage. What would you have poor women do, Lady Dalrymple? Starve?"

Lady Dalrymple glared at him. "In our society, Sir Benedict? You make us sound like savages! Is there anything you *like* about England? Is there anything you would *not* change?"

Benedict saw that he had spoken too seriously for his company. He smiled ruefully. "The weather, my lady. I would not change good English weather for the world."

Puzzled silence. No one seemed to realize the gentleman was making a joke.

Nothing could prevail on Benedict to stand up with anyone else for the second cotillion, and he spent the last half hour of the ball pleasantly engaged in conversation with Lady Serena while Ludham danced with Lady Rose.

"Now *that* would be an equal match," said Benedict.

"She is absurdly young," said Serena. "But, I daresay, so is Miss Vaughn!"

"You should encourage him to return to London," Benedict suggested. "He would soon forget Miss Vaughn in London, I am persuaded."

Serena sighed. "He cannot go to London, Sir Benedict. They have published the letters! The entire body of criminal correspondence between that wretched Pamela and her Frenchman! I have not seen it, of course, but I understand it is perfectly unexpurgated."

"Ah," said Benedict.

"So embarrassing for poor Felix. Besides which, London

is full of opera dancers! At least I can keep my eye on him here in Bath. In London . . . !"

"Quite," said Benedict.

"It would be just like Felix to rush headlong into another disastrous marriage. He is so susceptible to a pretty face, and so blind to everything else. I don't wish Miss Vaughn ill, of course, but . . ." She shrugged her shoulders helplessly. "It would be as much a mistake for *her* as for him."

"Someone should explain to Miss Vaughn the evils of an unequal marriage."

"I say! That's a good idea. As her cousin, Sir Benedict, you must be able to exert some influence over her. You can see I have no influence over *my* cousin," she added ruefully, "but *he* is a man. Any assistance you can offer me in this matter would be most gratefully received," she added persuasively.

"I will call on Lady Agatha tomorrow," he promised. "And then, I would like to call on *you,* if I may, Serena. Would one o'clock be convenient for a private interview?"

"A private interview to discuss Felix and Miss Vaughn?"

"You must know I am going to make you an offer of marriage," he said impatiently.

She smiled. "I believe you just did, Sir Benedict!"

The ball ended punctually at eleven o'clock, and the doors of the ballroom were thrown open to admit the chairmen, who strode right into the ballroom with their sedan chairs. Owing to the steepness of Bath's streets, carriages were rarely used.

Benedict commandeered a chair for Lady Serena, bade her good night, then walked alone up to Beechen Cliff. He sat down on the damp ground, took out his cheroot case, and lit up.

Chapter 6

The big brass numeral on Lady Agatha's front door looked like a six. The nail at the top had come loose, allowing the number to swing into the upside down position. As he waited for the servant to answer the bell, Benedict flicked it with his finger. The number spun around, still attached by a single brass nail at the bottom. This sort of thing could lead to postal errors, he thought with annoyance. These people might be getting his mail, and vice versa.

"I have been ringing the bell for some time," Benedict said coldly when, at last, the door was opened by a massive, gray-haired manservant dressed in rusty black. He looked seedy and he smelled of whiskey. He looked at Benedict in surprise. Then a twinkle appeared in his eye.

"Ah, sure, didn't we disconnect that bell?" he said in a careless Irish drawl. "And very noisy it was, too. I was just going out to post a letter for Herself, or I'd never have known you were here at all, at all."

An odd feeling came over Benedict as he stepped into the hall. The place seemed familiar to him, even though he was certain he had never been here before.

"You really should do something about the number on your door," he said, taking out his card. "It has come loose at the top. It looks like a six."

"So it does," the Irishman said agreeably. He winked at Benedict.

Benedict glared at him. "Will you kindly take my card up to Lady Agatha."

Benedict waited in the hall while the man went up, chuckling to himself. Doors opened and closed on the floor above in a flurry of activity, then the house fell silent, and the manservant returned, still laughing. "She'll be down in a minute," he said. "She's after putting on her best dress for you, but you didn't hear that from me."

He went out by the front door, not the usual way for servants to come and go, but this, evidently, was an unusual household.

Presently, a slim young woman came down the stairs. Her best dress was a cream-colored cambric striped with blue. It looked unfortunately like mattress ticking. As she stopped on the landing, the morning sun shot through the fanlight over the door and fell directly on her.

"You!" he said, thunderstruck.

She stared back at him. Her least favorite person looked none the worse for his adventure in the park. In fact, the man was infuriatingly perfect. His hair was so perfect it looked like carved ebony. His patrician face might have been carved of marble. His light gray eyes were hard and brilliant. And his clothes were gorgeously tailored. He looked lean and fit. His shoes were polished to a high sheen. He didn't look seedy at all. He looked dead aristocratic.

Fleecing him was going to be a delight and a pleasure.

"You yourself!" she snapped. "You've a bloody cheek showing your face here after what you did to me. If my brothers were here to defend me, you'd be a dead man."

"My God, it *is* you," Benedict said, as if she had not said a word. "You look different. Your hair— You've changed your hair."

Her hands went to her hair. She had braided it tightly and

pinned it up as she always did. She thought it looked nice.
"What about my hair?" she demanded.

"It looked orange in the candlelight," he said. "I thought—"

"Oh, you thought I was a redhead," she murmured. "That
explains it."

She had been wondering why he didn't ask Mrs. Price for
a blond girl.

Benedict, meanwhile, had pieced it all together. Obviously,
he had come to the wrong house on the night he arrived in
Bath. Obviously he had behaved very badly. Of course, she
had overreacted to his bad behavior, but there was no denying that he had behaved very badly indeed. He was mortified.
It was one thing to try to seduce one's own housekeeper, and
quite another to try to seduce someone else's. He could only
hope that Miss Cosy had not reported his faux pas to her em-
ployer. A scandal like that could ruin his reputation.

"I suppose," she said, "you've come to collect your things.
They're in the kitchen where you left them. I'll fetch them
for you."

"Thank you," he said. "I was just going to pay my respects
to Lady Agatha."

She frowned. She didn't want him anywhere near her
mother and sister, but Lady Agatha knew he was here, and
she was beside herself with joy at the thought of having a visitor. "All right," she said reluctantly. "But be quick about it.
She's a delicacy, so don't say anything stupid to upset her."

Benedict started up the steps to her. She waited on the
landing, her hand on the railing.

"You haven't told her anything, have you?" he asked
anxiously.

"Of course not," she said scornfully.

"There's no reason, after all," he said, looking into her
green eyes, "for Lady Agatha to know. She would be very
angry with you, I'm sure."

"With me!" she said. He moved closer to her, but she did
not move away.

"Yes, with you," he said softly. "It is most unfair, I know, but, in such cases as these, the woman is always blamed. She might even turn you out of the house. Have you thought of that? A beautiful girl like you? On your own in this cold, cruel world?"

He traced his finger along her jaw. Her eyes widened but she did not flinch.

"Of course, *I* am to blame," he said. "My behavior was atrocious. I was not a gentleman. Forgive me?" He moved his lips to hers, and, when she still not flinch, he kissed her. It was a chaste, quiet kiss. "Am I forgiven, Miss Cosy?"

He kissed her again. Her mouth tasted clean and tart, like a green apple. He wanted more of it. He wished she might kiss him back, but he supposed that was out of the question. A housekeeper could lose her place if she was caught in such a compromising position.

"Come away with me," he whispered. "Let me be your protector. Let me take you away from a life of drudgery and care. You'll never have to work again in your life. You've no idea how boring my life was before I met you. Say something, my angel."

She stepped back from him and touched her mouth. She looked quite surprised.

"Are you trying to seduce me?" she demanded.

"Oh, yes."

"You devil! Meet me in the kitchen in five minutes," she said. "You can shag the fanny off me then, if you like."

He smiled. He was a young man when he smiled. "Make it twenty, you little beauty. I have to go up to the drawing-room now and make nice with bloody Lady Agatha. But then . . ." His eyes glowed. "Oh, then, my angel, my dove, my sweet, sweet honey, I shall ravish you to your heart's content."

She pushed him away and smoothed down her dress. "Keep your breeches on, lover," she said. "You still have to make nice with Lady Agatha. I'll take you up now."

"A pox," he said, "on Lady Agatha. Lead on, bright star. Take me anywhere you like."

She turned smartly and started up the next flight of stairs. It was all he could do not to run a hand over those slim, young haunches. She looked back over her shoulder at him and plucked his heart out with a smile.

"After you," she said softly at the drawing-room door, and, very deliberately, he brushed the front of his body against hers as he went in. He was looking forward to the next twenty minutes of pleasurable agony, to be followed by twenty minutes of agonizing pleasure in the kitchen.

But first . . . the social niceties must be observed with the mistress of the house. In the drawing-room, a frail woman of uncertain age and a robust child were sitting in front of a small fire. The older woman, presumably Lady Agatha, was disposed on the sofa, bundled in a shawl, with a rug over her knees and a cap over her frizzy red hair, while the child, a girl of perhaps nine years of age, was draped across a chair, rapidly and noisily shifting the tiles of a fifteen puzzle. She was wearing an ugly pinafore dress of brown bombazine. She had flaxen hair and green eyes, just like the delectable Miss Cosy.

That struck Benedict as rather odd. After all, green eyes and flaxen hair were not all that common outside of the Scandinavian countries.

The room was cold.

"Mother?" Cosy said softly.

The lady on the sofa gave a start and looked around, confused.

Benedict knew just how the poor woman felt.

"Mother, this is Sir Benedict. Sir Benedict, this is my mother, Lady Agatha Vaughn."

"Ah," said Benedict.

"Sir Benedict has come for a nice long visit. Isn't that nice of him?"

She sat down on the sofa and arranged her striped skirts.

Benedict looked at her without expression for a moment, then turned to her mother.

Lady Agatha was not, Benedict realized instantly, a fashionable hypochondriac like Lady Matlock. Cosmetics could not hide her ravaged complexion. She was tiny and frail. She breathed wheezily. Benedict seized on the excuse to beat a hasty retreat. "Perhaps I should call when her ladyship is feeling better," he offered.

To his horror, Lady Agatha burst into tears. "It's the light," she sobbed. "The morning sun is not kind to a woman of my years."

Cosy looked daggers at Benedict. "Nice!" she snarled at him before turning to her mother. "You look beautiful, Mother," she said soothingly. "I'm sure he didn't mean it like that!" She took out her handkerchief and carefully dried her mother's face. "Allie, go and draw the curtains!" she snapped.

"I'm working my puzzle," the younger girl snarled.

Muttering unladylike imprecations under her breath, the elder girl went to the windows and closed the curtains herself.

"Of course," said Benedict, "I did not mean to insult your ladyship. I was told that you were very ill, Lady Agatha. I simply do not wish to intrude if you would rather be resting. That is all."

"Mother's having one of her good days," Cosy said as Benedict's eyes adjusted to the darkness. "Aren't you, Mother?"

"I feel quite like my old self," wheezed Lady Agatha.

Good God, Benedict thought.

Cosy lit a branch of tallow candles standing on a pedestal in one corner of the room. The candlelight cast an orange stain over parts of the room, casting black and umber shadows over the rest of it. "We're glad of the company," Cosy said. "We don't know very many people here." She looked at him angrily. "Well? Aren't you going to sit down and make nice?"

"I wasn't asked to sit down," he retorted. "Miss Cosy," he added irritably. "Or should I say *Miss Vaughn*?"

"Will you sit down," she said. It was not a request. Almost in the same breath she barked, "Allie! Take that clackering over to the window; you'll ruin your eyes."

Benedict sat down and the child took her fifteen puzzle to the window seat.

Cosy sat down next to her mother again. Lady Agatha had withdrawn as far as she could into the shadows. The gentleman had made her feel self-conscious about her looks.

Benedict said, "Please forgive me for presenting myself to you unannounced, Lady Agatha, but I understand that your ladyship rarely ventures out into society. I am a little acquainted with your brother, Lord Wayborn," he added.

"That's society for you," Cosy murmured. "Everybody knows everybody."

Lady Agatha's voice quivered. "Did my brother send you, Sir Benjamin?"

"It's Benedict, Mother. Like the saint," Cosy said maliciously.

"Oh, I beg your pardon," said Lady Agatha. "Did my brother send you, Sir Benedict?"

"No, my lady. But I felt it was only right that I pay my respects when I discovered that his sister was in Bath. In point of fact, I am a distant relation. Mine is the Surrey branch of the Wayborn family. My sister, Juliet, married a duke last summer. You may have read about it in the papers. The wedding party lasted a month. I had many conversations with your brother."

"We were still in Ireland last summer," said Lady Agatha. "It's so difficult to get proper news in Ireland," she complained. "We are much better off here. Cosima, ring the bell for tea."

"Sir Benedict doesn't like tea," said Cosy. "And besides, Nora's gone to the market. There's no one in the kitchen at all, at all."

Benedict glared at her.

"I do wish you wouldn't speak in that dreadful brogue," said Lady Agatha, wincing. "What will the gentleman think?"

"The gentleman," said Miss Vaughn, "can think whatever he likes."

"It is so nice to have a visitor," said Lady Agatha hastily. "Lady Dalrymple used to visit us when we first came to Bath. And her son, Mr. Carteret, was very much in love with my daughter, but then we got that awful letter from the bank—"

"And so the love dried up," Cosy said with a short laugh.

"Cosima," Benedict said, looking at her.

She looked at him, startled.

"You have an unusual and lovely name, Miss Vaughn. It is Italian, I believe?"

"All my children have Italian names," Lady Agatha said. "Colonel Vaughn and I honeymooned in Italy, you know. Of course, he was only a captain then. All the children are like him, as tall and blond as Vikings. No one would ever guess they were half-Irish."

Benedict looked at Cosima. "Larry? Sandy? And Dan, I think it was?"

"Lorenzo, Alessandro, and Dante," she replied.

"Of course. And your father is the colonel of the regiment?"

"Aye. And that changeling in the window is my sister, Allegra."

"My Italian is not very good," said Benedict. "But I think that means 'lively'?"

"And doesn't she look lively too!" Cosima snorted. "Have you even *looked* at your lessons today, Allie?"

Miss Allegra Vaughn was outraged. "I'm doing my fifteen puzzle!"

"You're going to be the most ignorant girl in that school," Cosy warned. "Sure, the English girls will all be laughing at you and your fifteen puzzle."

Allie scowled. "I don't care what you say! I'm not going back to there."

Cosima laughed mirthlessly. "My sister was enrolled at

Miss Bulstrode's Seminary for Young Ladies, Sir Benedict, but we had a tiny little problem with the fee."

"We couldn't pay it," Allie explained. "And so Miss Bulstrode turfed me out. We still can't afford it," she said happily.

"Oh, didn't I tell you?" said Cosima. "We've come into some money. Sir Benedict has agreed to pay all your school fees. Now, isn't that nice of him?"

"I beg your pardon!" said Benedict in a cold and withdrawn voice.

"I know you wanted to keep it a secret," she said. "But I don't keep secrets from my family. Besides, my mother would worry if I suddenly turned up with, say, a thousand pounds?"

Benedict glared at her. He understood that he was receiving a veiled threat. If he didn't pay Miss Vaughn what she wanted, there was going to be a scandal the likes of which Bath had not seen since Miss Linley ran off with Mr. Sheridan. He would have to pay, too; she was so lovely anything she said would be instantly believed. It was blackmail, pure and simple.

"Of course," he said coldly. "We would not want your mother to worry."

Snakes and bastards, she thought. *I should have asked for more money.*

"I am sure, Sir Benedict," said Lady Agatha, "that you could not ask for a better wife than Cosima. Not only is she the prettiest girl you will ever see, but she is the dearest, kindest girl, with the sweetest disposition I ever met with."

"Indeed!" said the gentleman, indulging himself in a short laugh.

Miss Allegra looked up from her puzzle game. "You're getting married?"

Cosy felt her cheeks go hot. "Of course not! Mother, you misunderstand. Sir Benedict doesn't want anything in return for his benevolence. Besides, he's too old for me," she said brutally. "What on earth would we have to talk about in the evenings?"

"I was on the ark with Noah," Benedict said grimly. "I could tell you all about it."

"But, dearest, we can't accept money from a stranger," Lady Agatha protested weakly. "Not unless he marries you, Cosima. It wouldn't be proper."

"If you were her husband, you could beat her," Allegra offered enticingly.

"I could indeed, Miss Allegra."

"And he could beat *you,* too, miss," Cosy snapped. "Or send you to the North Pole. *And* he could put Mother in the hospital or God knows where. So be careful what you wish for."

"Oh, no!" wheezed Lady Agatha.

"He wouldn't do that to *us,*" said Allegra. "He likes *us.*"

"Nobody's getting married," said Cosy.

"Then we really shouldn't take the money, my dear," said Lady Agatha. "I may be poor, Sir Benedict, but I don't like charity."

"He's a relative, Mother," Cosy said patiently. "There's no harm in taking assistance from a relative, is there? Besides, he's stinking rich. He'll never miss it."

Lady Agatha giggled suddenly like a schoolgirl. Her scruples vanished without a trace. "A thousand pounds," she cried. "Sir! How can we ever thank you? That would just about set us up for life! You can get your pianoforte back now, Cosima! I was so sorry for her, Sir Benedict, when we had to sell it. If only you'd come last week."

Cosy frowned. She did not want the odious Sir Benedict to know that she had been obliged to sell her precious piano. Somehow, his knowing just how miserable poor they were spoiled the triumph of having lifted a thousand pounds from him.

"That old thing," she sneered. "Sure it was so old and cranky and slow there was no playing it anyway. My father won it at cards. I've my eye on a sweet new Clementi with *eight* octaves."

"I want a French lady's maid and a pony," said Allegra. "And all new clothes."

"You do, do you?" her sister retorted.

"You must let us do something to show our appreciation. Could we not invite Sir Benedict to dine, Cosima?" Lady Agatha pleaded. "Cosima is an excellent cook, Sir Benedict."

"Miss Vaughn does the cooking?" he said, startled.

"Why?" Cosy said angrily. "Don't your English girls cook?"

"My sister, the duchess, used to make a sort of salmon mayonnaise," he said. "Her adventures in the kitchen were never due to necessity, however. We always had more servants than we knew what to do with at Wayborn Hall."

"Good for you."

"We were obliged to dismiss all the servants here except for Nora and Jackson when the letter came from the bank," Lady Agatha said.

"You were?" he said frowning. "Usually these houses come with servants in place. The landlord pays their wages."

"You mean we might have kept our servants?" Allie said furiously. "You had me in the kitchen scrubbing pots like a slavey!" she accused her sister.

"Well," said Benedict. "It would hardly be gallant of me to accept an invitation to dine. That would only make more work for Miss Vaughn and Miss Allegra."

"How very thoughtful of you," Cosy said, gritting her teeth.

"They are ruining their hands in the kitchen, I know it," cried Lady Agatha. "How are they going to find husbands with burned and calloused hands?"

"It's a kitchen, Mother. Not a smithy."

"I wish with all my heart that Cosima could go out and enjoy herself, Sir Benedict. It's no life for a young girl to be trapped indoors all day looking after a stupid old woman."

"It wasn't so bad when Lady Dalrymple finally left us," Cosy said, trying to laugh.

"I meant *myself*, dearest," Lady Agatha said earnestly. "Our subscription to the Upper Rooms is paid, Sir Benedict, but Mr. King told Cosima she could not go to any of the balls without a chaperone. And I am simply too ill to accompany her. No sooner do I go out, but my knees shake, and the world swims before my eyes. Do you think it would be all right if I used some of the money to hire a chaperone?"

"That won't be necessary, ma'am. As a relative, it would be my honor to escort Miss Vaughn to the various entertainments."

Cosima glared at him suspiciously.

"Yes, my dear, you must go!" cried Lady Agatha with growing excitement. "You must have all new gowns. You must go to all the balls, and dance with all the young men. Who knows but that one of them will marry you, and then you will be settled and secure. I worry about my girls so, Sir Benedict."

"Why does she get new gowns?" cried Allie. "What about me?"

"I couldn't leave you here on your own, Mother," Cosy objected.

"Nonsense," said Lady Agatha. "Nora will be here, and I can send Jackson to fetch you home at once should anything serious take place. Do it for me, Cosima. I hate to see you wasting the best years of your life in the sickroom. The subscription is paid. It's only going to waste. Mr. King won't give us our money back. Please, dearest. For me?"

Cosy chewed her bottom lip for a moment. True, he was an untrustworthy bastard but, after all, there was no such thing as a perfect man. If she sat around waiting for Mr. Perfect to come along and escort her to the Upper Rooms, she'd never go anywhere. It would be a waste of money hiring a chaperone, when she could get one for free.

"No balls," she said firmly.

"Excuse me?" said Benedict.

"I'd like to go to the concert on Tuesday, but I've no interest in balls," she explained.

"But you love to dance," said Lady Agatha.

"*Irish* balls are an entirely different matter. English balls are all about pomp and circumstance, but Irish balls are fun."

"Tuesday?" said Benedict. "Some songs in Italian, I believe."

"You are always saying that you are Italian in your heart, my dear," said Lady Agatha.

"I've never said that in my life," Cosy muttered, embarrassed.

"What about me?" Allegra Vaughn demanded angrily. "May I go to the concert, Mama?"

"It is not an entertainment for young people," Benedict told her. "You would not want to sit still for two hours and listen to a large woman singing in a foreign language."

"I would not," she admitted. "I want to go up in a balloon and see fireworks. Also, acrobats on the high tropics."

"Trapeze. You will have to go to London for that, I'm afraid," he replied.

"Will you take me to London?" Allie demanded.

"Certainly not!" said Cosy and Benedict at once.

"London," Cosy added severely, "is a black den of iniquity."

Glancing up at the clock on the mantel, Benedict was startled to discover that he had been sitting with them for four hours. Then he realized the clock had stopped. He stood up.

Allegra Vaughn let out a gasp. When he had come into the room, she had been engrossed with her puzzle. She had not noticed that their visitor was an amputee.

"What happened to your arm?" she blurted out.

"Allie!" Cosy gasped, appalled.

Benedict was startled by the direct question, but not offended. "It's quite all right."

"I'm sure Sir Benedict doesn't like to talk about the war," said Cosy, glaring at her sister.

"The war?" he repeated, puzzled.

"You said you were at Waterloo," Cosy reminded him.

"As an observer." It dawned on him suddenly that she must

think he had lost his arm in battle. "I am not a war hero, Miss Vaughn, if that is what you think."

"Oh! You were in the Navy, then?" she said, sniffing.

"No, I was not in the Navy, Miss Vaughn," he said irritably. "I was attacked by a dog when I was about your sister's age."

Cosy and Allie spoke at once. "What did you do to the dog?"

Benedict sighed. "The dog had to be destroyed, of course."

"No! What did you do to the dog to make it attack you? Dogs don't just attack people."

"Did you poke its eye out with a stick?" Allie asked eagerly.

There was a slight pause as Benedict gave Lady Agatha the opportunity to constrain her curious daughters. But her ladyship seemed to have drifted off to sleep. "Certainly not," he said. "The dog was attacking someone else, and I intervened."

"Were you awake when they cut it off?"

"That's enough, Allie!" Cosy said firmly. "I think Mother's had enough excitement for one day. She needs her rest. I'll walk you out, Sir Benedict."

"This is blackmail, of course," he murmured as she walked him down the stairs to the front hall. "I realize you are poor, but that is no excuse."

"Blackmail? Is that what you call it in England? In Ireland we call it fair play."

"Fair play?" he repeated in astonishment as they reached the bottom of the stairs. "You took everything I had, including the clothes off my back. Was that also fair play?"

"You had it coming," said Cosima. "You said yourself your behavior was atrocious."

"When I woke up I thought I had been robbed!"

"So you would have been," she said primly, "if *I* hadn't taken everything."

"Oh, yes?"

"For safekeeping!" she clarified. "You should be thanking me."

The gentleman did not share her opinion. "Thanking you! And, I suppose, I should also thank you for tying me to a tree!"

"Aye. You were drunk, and in no condition to be staggering around town."

His mouth twitched. "So that was for safekeeping also?"

"You made it home all right, didn't you?"

"The Watch brought me home!"

"So what are you complaining about?"

"And now you are blackmailing me for a thousand pounds!" he accused her.

"I am not blackmailing you," she said, annoyed. "You offered a reward. I'm just collecting it."

He stopped and stared at her. "I offered no reward."

"Didn't you?" Marching down the hall, she threw open the door to a small book room with flowered chintz curtains. Benedict followed her.

Picking up a newspaper from the small writing desk, she showed it to him. "Did you not put this advertisement in the paper?" she demanded.

"My father gave me that watch," he said furiously. "That was his ring."

"Then it's a good thing I took them for safekeeping!"

"It does not say a thousand pounds," he pointed out. "It says: sizeable."

"I'd say a thousand pounds is sizeable, wouldn't you?"

"You could have had more than a thousand pounds, you know," Benedict said. "You had the winning hand, but you frittered it away for a mere thousand pounds."

Her eyes narrowed. "What do you mean?"

"If your mother knew everything, Miss Vaughn, I would have to marry you to avoid a scandal. You would have had considerably more than a thousand pounds at your disposal."

"Oh!" she said. "Now you want to marry me? You were singing a different tune in my kitchen, as I recall. I wouldn't consent to be your mistress for a thousand pounds," she reminded him. "What makes you think I'd *ever* consent to be shackled to you for life?"

"I don't want to marry you," he said angrily. "I consider that I've had a lucky escape."

"You don't want to marry me?" she said in amazement.

"No!"

"I suppose you don't want to shag me either."

"I don't," he said airily, "even know what that word means."

"But . . . what about the sweet love you made to me on the stairs?" she protested. "I felt something there. Were you only trifling with me, *caro mio* Ben?"

He glared at her. "Miss Vaughn," he said coldly. "I am perfectly aware that you are mocking me."

"I wouldn't do that," she said softly, moving closer to him. "*It tuo fedel sospira ognor,*" she murmured in Italian. "*Cessa crudel tanto rigor.*" She sighed. "You're not a cruel man, are you, I hope? You won't leave me suffering, surely?"

She took his face in both hands and kissed his mouth hard.

"Do you still think I'm mocking you?" she asked softly. Her eyes were half-closed.

He slipped his hand behind her neck and kissed her mouth softly. Cosima was startled. Men usually attacked her if given half a chance. This was not an attack, but a lingering caress, and she didn't quite know how to take it. He seemed to be savoring her mouth slowly and gently. *Now why would he do that?* she wondered. As far as she knew, men only kissed women to distract them from what their hands were trying to do lower down. *He* seemed to be in no hurry to get on with it at all.

"I could kiss you all day," he murmured. "You taste like apples. Green apples."

"I made a tart this morning," she explained.

He kissed her again in the same style. His tongue felt clean and cool in her mouth. Her senses began to stir and quicken as she breathed in his scent. It really was as if he meant to go on kissing her all day, slowly and steadily.

"I think," he said slowly, "we should be married at once."

She blinked at him. "Who said anything about marriage?" she said.

"What?" Benedict said sharply. He controlled his temper with difficulty. "You kissed me, Miss Vaughn. It is the height of impropriety for a woman to kiss a man she does not mean to marry."

"It was only a kiss. Nothing to get excited about. We do it all the time in Ireland," she lied. "It doesn't mean anything."

"Doesn't mean anything!"

"It wasn't even that good of a kiss, I'm afraid. It was sort of like kissing a newel post."

"I see," he said quietly. "You were mocking me, of course." She shrugged. "Of course."

His gray eyes suddenly blazed. "You, Miss Vaughn, are a nasty piece of work!"

"I'm sorry you think so," she answered. "As you know, I think the world of you."

"There was a thousand pounds in my wallet," he said after a pause.

"Then there still is," she said coldly. "I'm not a thief."

"No; a blackmailer!" he retorted. "Take it. I'll send a servant for my bag. I'd like my watch and my ring now, if you don't mind."

"Here." She took his watch and his ring out of her pocket and gave them to him.

"Good-bye, Miss Vaughn."

"Not good-bye, surely, but *au revoir,*" she said sweetly, opening the door for him.

He looked at her incredulously.

"I'll be seeing you Tuesday evening for the concert, right?" she said.

He looked at her incredulously. "The concert!"

"You are a man of your word, are you not?"

Benedict eyed her with loathing. Miss Vaughn smiled angelically.

"Until Tuesday, madam!" he snapped. "Enjoy your ill-gotten gains!"

"I will, Sir Benedict," she replied.

Chapter 7

Benedict had never been so angry in his life.

Lady Serena took one look at his face and ordered her butler to leave the room. The baronet strode up and down for a moment, his face dark with fury.

"What on earth is the matter, Sir Benedict?"

"I have met Miss Vaughn!"

"Is it as bad as that?"

Benedict ground to a halt. "I don't want to talk about Miss Vaughn, if you don't mind. Miss Vaughn is the most insolent, unscrupulous, vulgar female I have ever had the misfortune to know. She is an ill-mannered, insufferable brute!"

Serena clutched her pearls. "Poor Felix! I must do all I can to keep them apart."

Benedict laughed harshly. "On the contrary, the sooner they meet the better! Believe me, twenty minutes in the company of *that female* will be enough to cure your cousin of his ridiculous infatuation. I will be bringing her to the concert on Tuesday," he added. "By Wednesday morning, I assure you, everyone in Bath will have a disgust for her."

"But is she beautiful?" Serena inquired eagerly.

"Oh, an angel!" he replied. "She is the most beautiful girl I ever saw. But underneath all that beauty beats the heart of a ruthless buccaneer!"

Bejeweled rings flashed on Serena's fingers as she massaged her temples. "She will not show that side of her character to Felix. He will see only her beauty."

Benedict smiled grimly. "Miss Vaughn is so vain she won't even *try* to conceal her less amiable qualities. She thinks her beauty conquers all, I daresay!"

"Do please sit down, Sir Benedict," she said graciously. "I was just about to have tea." He took the seat she offered. "I did not come here to talk about Miss Vaughn," he said presently. "My task is much more agreeable. I have come to make you an offer of marriage. I daresay, you must have known my intentions the moment I walked into your drawing-room."

"I did not suspect you were trifling with me," she admitted.

"No, indeed! Serena, will you marry me?"

Serena put his brusqueness down to nerves. She chose her words carefully. "It would be my honor to consider your proposal, Sir Benedict. At my age, I had all but given up hope of marrying."

"At *my* age, I would be a fool to marry out of the schoolroom."

"Quite," said Serena. "In light of your declaration, I do not think it would be improper for us to be seen together in public. You will not find Bath lacking in entertainment, I assure you. If you would bespeak a box at the theater tomorrow, I should be pleased to see the play."

"Certainly."

"There will be other members to our party, of course," she said demurely. "It would not do for us to be seen as a *couple* so soon after your arrival in Bath. It would look so particular. You know how people love to talk. They might even say you had pursued me here."

"Invite anyone you please," he said carelessly. "I believe you have a fair idea of my income. . . . My position in society. You have seen my estate in Surrey, and I believe you visited my aunt in the London house. I should be happy to send you any other information you might require as you consider the matter."

"Thank you, Sir Benedict," said Serena gratefully. "It is an important decision. Indeed, it is the most important decision of a woman's life. I would be remiss if I did not consider the matter very carefully before I agreed to become engaged to you. I shall need time."

He bit back his annoyance. "How much time?"

"Oh, not long," she assured him. "Perhaps a month or two. Three, at most. One wishes to be certain before one commits oneself, naturally."

"Naturally!"

"Do you think me unreasonable?" asked the lady. " I mean to be conscientious."

"I should think three days would be conscientious enough for anyone."

"Three days?" she repeated incredulously. "That is scarcely enough time for me to choose a new gown!"

"Indeed," he said. "However! Three months seems a trifle . . . ungenerous."

"You men are so impatient," Serena chided him. Her voice was low and teasing. "Do not think to bullock me into giving you an answer before I have had time to think, Sir Benedict! I am only asking for the opportunity to know you better," she pointed out gently.

Benedict was silent.

"Come now, Sir Benedict! You have asked me to be your wife. You can have no objection, surely, to *knowing* me a little better?"

"No."

Lady Serena consulted her engagement book. "It's Friday. I usually play cards on Friday evening. Tonight, I see that Lady Matlock has the honor of hosting us at whist. May I expect you to partner me, Sir Benedict?"

"It would be my pleasure."

"Saturday is the theater, of course. Sunday I attend services at the Octagon Chapel. Monday is the dress-ball in the Upper Rooms. Tuesdays we have our concerts. Wednesdays . . ."

As she recited this unexciting schedule, Benedict saw his days stretching out before him, days of boredom with no relief in sight but a Tuesday night musicale or a Friday night card game. *This was not courtship,* he thought angrily. *This was indentured servitude. This was limbo.*

The only thing worse would be having to start all over with some other woman.

"A veritable whirlwind of activity!" he said, forcing a smile. "I quite look forward to it."

After cards at Lady Matlock's, he walked up to Beechen Cliff and sat for half an hour, enjoying a taste of solitude and freedom. The night was clear, cold, and fine. He lay on his back and looked up at the stars. It was well after midnight when he returned to Camden Place.

Pickering was waiting at the door to take his coat and hat. "I trust you had a pleasant evening, Sir Benedict."

"No, Pickering, I did not," Benedict replied. It was his first opportunity of the night to be honest with a fellow human being, and he took full advantage of it. "I had a damned boring evening. I played cards with a bunch of damned boring hypocrites and cheats, and I wasn't even allowed to keep my winnings because my partner was a *lady.*"

"I am very sorry to hear that, Sir Benedict," Pickering said soothingly. "However, the night is still young, and there is someone here to see you."

Benedict frowned. "It's late, Pickering. Who is it?"

"She did not give a name, sir, and I did not inquire."

"She!"

"Mrs. Price sent her," Pickering explained. "I put her in the study."

"WHAT?" Benedict thundered but, then, thinking better of

the noise, he began again in a whisper. "What? Pickering, are you telling me that there is a *woman* in my study?"

"There is indeed, sir," Pickering said proudly. "A *femme de nuit*. A *fille de joie*. A woman of pleasure."

"Good God! I certainly hope she's not sitting on the furniture," said Benedict, revolted. "The furniture doesn't even belong to me. Get rid of her, Pickering."

The valet blinked. "But, sir! She's just what you wanted."

"What I wanted?" Benedict repeated, aghast. "I don't want anything. After the day I've had, I'm off women forever. I certainly don't want a *prostitute*. The last the thing I need is to contract syphilis. That would certainly put a period to my hopes of marrying well!"

Pickering drew upon his reservoirs of patience. "Sir Benedict, I realize how nervous you must be, but you *did* ask me to find you an Irish girl with tangled red hair, green eyes, a small, high bosom, perfect skin, and so forth. I did not, of course, inspect her skin—I leave that to you—but she did sing me a pretty little Italian song."

"I'll bet she did! Get rid of her," Benedict said harshly. "Get rid of her now."

Pickering coughed gently. "You will hurt her feelings, Sir Benedict. Just because men pay her to pleasure them doesn't mean the poor girl has no feelings. And, may I point out, you will have to pay her even if you don't use her. Time is money in the skin trade."

"Did you learn that from your friend the constable?"

"Yes, sir."

Benedict strode across the hall and placed his hand on the study door handle. "I am going to get rid of this doxy, Pickering, and then I am going to kill you."

"I'm only trying to help you, sir!" Pickering said, hurt.

Benedict went into the study and closed the door sharply. A girl with an unruly nest of bright red hair was sitting with her feet up on his desk. She was wearing a dark cloak over her clothes, but this had parted at the bottom to reveal the high-heeled black slippers on her feet and white silk stockings on her long shapely legs. Her slim ankles were crossed.

"Kindly get your feet off my desk," he snapped.

"Sorry," she answered, not moving. "I thought you might want to look at my legs."

She was Irish.

"I'm not sure I can afford it," he answered coldly. "Look here, miss! There's been an awful mistake. I've had a long hard day, and I'm not in the mood for . . . *this*. You'll have to go."

Slowly the girl uncrossed her ankles, then crossed them again, this time with the other ankle on top. "What sort of an awful mistake?" she asked curiously.

"Damn," he murmured in dismay. To his chagrin, he was experiencing the first stirring of male excitement. Rationally, he knew that this was not his fault. It was merely a physical response to being alone with a disreputable female, a female who had come here to pleasure him.

She stood up and pulled the strings of her cloak and let it fall to the ground. He stared at her, unable to help himself. The simple white garment she wore fitted her tightly in the bodice but hung loosely about her legs. His eyes made the pleasant journey from her shapely ankles to her heart-shaped face. Incredibly, Pickering had got it exactly right. Then his whole body recoiled in shock as he recognized the cool green eyes of Miss Vaughn.

She had taken great pains to disguise herself. She had painted her face with white lead and put on a long, tangled red wig. He guessed it was her mother's. Her lips and cheeks were heavily rouged. Her eyelashes and brows had been darkened inexpertly with kohl. She looked like a badly painted doll, but it was not enough of a disguise to fool him. He would have known those green eyes anywhere.

"What are you doing here, Miss Vaughn?" he said angrily. "Have you lost your reason?"

Cosima's heart skipped a beat. He could not *possibly* recognize her! The last time she had looked in the mirror, she had not recognized herself. Evidently, she looked more like herself than she had realized. Sobering thought!

"Do you need money as badly as this?" he said a little more calmly.

"I'm not Miss Vaughn," she said, scowling. "I'm her sister. But I was born on the wrong side of the blanket, so I'm not acknowledged in the eyes of the world. They keep me locked in the attic by day. I'm the dark secret of the family."

He didn't seem to give her story any credence, however.

"I see," he said. "You're the illegitimate half-sister. Of course you are."

"I prefer the term *love child,* if you don't mind."

"Would you excuse me for a moment?" Benedict went to the door and opened it so unexpectedly that Pickering almost fell into the room. "Pickering, you may retire for the evening," his master said coldly. "I shan't need you anymore tonight."

He closed the door in Pickering's face. After pausing to collect himself, he turned to face his uninvited guest. The right thing to do, of course, would be to end this ridiculous charade at once, snatch that repulsive wig from her head, spank her, and send her home with tears carving lines into her painted cheeks. To do anything else would be stupid and irrational, not to mention immoral and illegal.

"I'm afraid I'm not being much of a host," he said clearly. "Please, sit down. May I offer you a little brandy? Or sherry, perhaps?" He was already walking toward the liquor cabinet.

"Are you trying to get me drunk?" she asked suspiciously.

"Certainly not," he said, pouring out the brandy for himself with a steady hand that belied his jumping nerves. He downed it in one gulp and quickly poured out another.

"Please, sit down, Miss—?"

"Cherry," she answered promptly.

"What an unusual name," he said. "Short for Charity, I suppose?"

"No," she said impatiently. "It's because of my hair."

"Of course. Please sit down, Miss Cherry."

She thought about it. After a moment, she walked around to the front of the sofa, flounced her skirts, and seated herself with her ankles crossed and her knees clamped together. He sat down in one of the chairs and took a sip of brandy.

"Now, then, my dear," he said in his best avuncular tone. "As I was saying, there's been a dreadful mistake. My man-servant got it completely wrong, I'm afraid."

Her green eyes narrowed. "Oh? You *didn't* order a girl to warm your bed for the night?"

"God, no! What do you think I am? A dirty old goat? I would *never* do anything so crass as to hire a woman for im-moral purposes. I'm simply not that sort of man. Not that there's anything wrong with being a prostitute," he added quickly. "Some very nice people *are* prostitutes, or so I un-derstand. *You* seem very nice, and I'm sure you're very good at whatever it is you do. Please don't take it personally."

Cosy glared at him.

"I don't happen to regard women as disposable com-modities, that's all," he said piously. "How exactly did you come across Mrs. Price, being locked up in the attic all day, as you are?"

"I want to earn enough money to go to America," she ex-plained. "So I snuck out of the house and went to see Mrs. Price for a job. And she sent me here. You're my first job. She said you were a rich bastard, and you'd pay me a king's ransom for the jewel of my innocence, so how could I resist?"

"Good heavens!" said Benedict. "Here I thought I was hiring a—a respectable, hard-working young woman to work for me. How could Mrs. Price have got it so wrong?"

"Oh? Was it a *servant* you were after hiring?" she said, fold-ing her arms under her small breasts, her skepticism apparent. "Someone to tidy up? Starting with your *dangler,* I suppose!"

"My what?" he asked, apparently puzzled.

"Your affair," she clarified. "Your yard-arm. Your love-dart. Your *thing,* man!"

"Oh, my *thing*," he said, understanding her at last. "It's very kind of you to offer, Miss Cherry, but I am perfectly capable of tidying up my own dangler. I wanted you for something else. Something completely different." He sipped his brandy as he tried to think of what that something else might be. "Something perfectly respectable. Some honest employment that would require you to visit me alone late at night . . . I just can't seem to remember at the moment what it might be, but it has absolutely nothing to do with the jewel of your innocence."

"Let me guess," she said helpfully. "You're an *artist,* and you want me to model for you in the nude for your latest masterpiece. Am I getting close?"

"Alas, I am not artistic. You could pose for me in the nude all night, but I fear the result would not be a masterpiece. I don't even sketch."

"Why can't you just admit it?" she demanded crossly. "You want a girl in your bed, and you're willing to pay for it. You want *me.*"

"You do seem to possess all the necessary qualifications," he admitted. "However, I *don't* want to take you to bed. For one thing, I'm much too old for you."

"Then why didn't you ask for an old woman?"

"Because I needed a young woman for the job."

"Which is?"

His eyes roamed over the book-lined room, searching for inspiration. "Well, Miss Cherry, I am glad you ask. I'm no longer young, and my eyes are tired. I can no longer read into the night as I used to, which is fairly devastating, as I love a good book. I thought I might employ someone with young eyes to read to me."

Her painted mouth twitched as she fought back the sudden urge to giggle. There was nothing wrong with the man's eyesight. He had recognized her immediately.

"Someone? An Irish girl with red hair, green eyes, and a small bosom, for example?"

"Yes, exactly. You see, when I was a boy, I had an Irish

governess. She used to read to me at night. I found her voice very soothing. She had red hair, green eyes, and, ahem, a small bosom. She was almost like a mother to me, really."

"What part of Ireland?" she demanded.

"Beg pardon?"

"What part of Ireland was she from, your governess? It's a simple question."

"Oranmore. I have cousins there."

"You're Irish?" she said, startled.

"No, of course not," he said irritably. "I have cousins there, that's all."

"Have you tried spectacles?" she inquired politely. "For the reading?"

"I'm too vain to wear spectacles," he explained. "Even when I'm alone, I like to feel handsome. You might not think it to look at me, but I'm completely eaten up with pride."

She sniffed.

"Now, perhaps, we should agree on a price for your services," he suggested.

Her green eyes snapped. "What?" she said sharply.

"For reading to me," he said mildly. "Penny a page? You *do* read, don't you?"

"Of course!" she said indignantly. "Tuppence a page. Take it or leave it."

"I think," he said, "I will take it."

She pursed her lips. "Are you sure you wouldn't rather just get another girl?" she said.

"Quite sure."

"And what will I be reading to you, then? Some dirty book, I suppose?"

"My old governess would never approve of *that*," he said mildly. "I always try to read something edifying before I go to sleep. Keeps the old brain sharp." He went to his desk and picked up a book. "Right now I am reading this," he said, bringing it to her.

"*The Subjection of Women,* by Mr. John Stuart Mill." She looked up at him in astonishment. "You dirty fecker!"

"The author is not in favor of it," he quickly explained. "Neither am I, really. In case you wondered. Shall we begin? Have you got enough light there?" Without waiting for a reply, he got up and placed another branch of candles on the table behind her.

"Thank you." She opened the book on her lap. "And, just so you know, I *wasn't* going to sleep with you. I was going to blackmail you, but that's all."

Benedict returned to his chair. "I am glad to hear it, Miss Cherry. I'd hate to think you were the kind of girl who would yield up the jewel of her innocence for a king's ransom."

She looked grave, cleared her throat, moistened her lips, and began to read:

> "The object of this Essay is to explain as clearly as I am able grounds of an opinion which I have held from the very earliest period when I had formed any opinions at all on social political matters, and which, instead of being weakened or modified, has been constantly growing stronger by the progressive reflection and the experience of life. That the principle which regulates the existing social relations between the two sexes—the legal subordination of one sex to the other—is wrong itself, and now one of the chief hindrances to human improvement; and that it ought to be replaced by a principle of perfect equality, admitting no power or privilege on the one side, nor disability on the other."

About halfway through the first sentence, she lost her Irish accent and began to read in a pompous English accent. He supposed she was imitating him, and he supposed correctly. She broke off abruptly as he suddenly crossed the distance between them and sat beside her on the sofa. "Hello!" she said. "Were you not comfortable in your chair?"

"Excessively comfortable, but I was having just a little trouble hearing you over there."

"I can speak up, but it'll cost you," she offered.

"Wouldn't do any good," he replied. "I've become quite hard of hearing in my old age."

"Deaf *and* blind? Poor man," she murmured, clicking her tongue. "I almost feel guilty making you pay for it, but I'm not running a charity, you know."

"Please go on, Miss Cherry," he said crisply. "Exciting stuff, is it not? This notion of perfect equality between men and women?"

"I never met a man who was my equal," she answered scornfully. "And I never met a man who thought *I* was *his*."

"I should have thought the subject would be of great interest to you," he said, surprised.

Jumping up from the sofa, she threw open the beveled glass doors of one of the bookshelves. "Look at all these gorgeous books! They can't *all* be dry as shite!"

"By all means, choose something more congenial to your taste," he said. "What sort of books do you like to read? Novels, I suppose?"

"Too long," she complained. "Too many characters. Too many things to remember. Sure I can't be bothered with all that. Have you got anything funny? I love a good laugh."

Benedict consulted the shelves for something in the humorous vein and finally pulled down a dusty green book. "Miss Cherry" took it from him, opened it to the title page, and read:

"GULLIVER REVIVED;

"OR, THE VICE OF LYING PROPERLY EXPOSED: CONTAINING SINGULAR TRAVELS, CAMPAIGNS, VOYAGES AND ADVENTURES IN RUSSIA, THE CASPIAN SEA, ICELAND, TURKEY, EGYPT, GIBRALTAR, UP THE MEDITERRANEAN, ON THE AT-

LANTIC OCEAN, AND THROUGH THE CENTRE OF MOUNT
AETNA, INTO THE SOUTH SEA.
                    "Also,
"An Account of a Voyage into the Moon and Dog-star,
with many extraordinary particulars relating to the cook-
ing animals in those planets, which are there called the
Human Species.
            "By BARON MUNCHAUSEN."

She looked at him and laughed.

The next morning the baronet ate his breakfast with un-
common gusto, slathering his digestive biscuits with shocking amounts of marmalade.

"You appear to be in good spirits this morning, Sir Benedict," Pickering remarked smugly. After all, it had been his
initiative that had brought about the happy event.

"I am in excellent spirits, thank you, Pickering," Benedict
replied.

"And may I say, sir, you look ten years younger. Your company obviously agrees with you. Will your special guest be
visiting us again any time soon?"

"Yes," Benedict answered. "Tonight. I've given . . . my
friend . . . a key, so you needn't wait up. But I should like to
offer her some refreshment."

"A key, sir?" Pickering was alarmed. "Do you think that wise?"

Benedict glared at him. "As I was saying, I would like to
offer my friend some refreshment. Nothing too heavy."

"Strawberries and champagne?"

"Perfect! We'll have a picnic on the rug. I am attending the
theater tonight, but I shall be home by eleven-thirty. See that
everything is ready for us in the study."

Pickering was enthusiastic. "Very good, Sir Benedict."

* * *

That night, he left the Theatre Royal with a spring in his step. He **had p**aid only scant attention to his company, even less to the **play**. Miss Cherry reading Munchausen in an outrageous **German** accent was more entertaining than anything Bath had **to offer,** he was sure.

He **ha**d enjoyed every moment spent with her, even if it was **o**nly reading, and, he believed, she had enjoyed his com**pany as** well. Was she already in his study, waiting for him? He **imag**ined her sitting on the sofa, her white skirts spread, **her eyes** on the door in anticipation of his arrival, her plump lips **sligh**tly parted. He became sharply aroused just thinking of her.

He let himself into the quiet house. To his disappointment, "Miss Cherry" had not yet arrived, but it was only a little after eleven. She was not so very late. He could be patient.

A bottle of champagne was in the ice bucket on the liquor cabinet. A blue and white china bowl full of hothouse strawberries sat on a silver tray on the ottoman.

At half past eleven, he dug out his watch and checked it against the clock on the mantel. Both the clock and his watch seemed to be keeping excellent time. She had promised to read to him again tonight, but, it seemed, she had decided to break her promise.

Time and again he fell for her tricks and, each time, she was only mocking him.

Furious, he dug out his silver cheroot case. It was better this way, he decided, as his anger cooled. Let it end before it begins. He was glad she did not come, he told himself. True, she had amused him last night, but he would soon find something else to amuse him. He could even ask Mrs. Price to send him another girl, if he chose.

He did not care if he ever saw Miss Cherry again. If he did, he would probably strangle her. Miss Cherry indeed! No one outside of a playhouse was ever named that. Did she think he was an idiot?

A little after midnight, he put out his cheroot and stood up to go to bed. At almost the same moment, the door opened, and Miss Cherry, dressed in an unattractive green baize jacket and skirt, slipped into the room. Cold air swirled into the room with her. She ran to the window and, without so much as a word to him, twitched the curtain aside and looked out.

"You're late," he said sternly.

"I know!" she whispered. She sounded frantic. She was out of breath, as if she had been running. "I'm sorry! I couldn't get away sooner, with that fecking dirty constable of the Watch lingering in the street like a bleeding vagrant!" She let the curtain fall closed. "I don't think he saw me, the bollocks."

Benedict felt a stab of guilt. He had never given a single thought about the risk she was taking in coming here. It was scarcely a hundred yards from his door to hers, but for a young woman it was as fraught with danger as the Silk Road. He shuddered to think what would have happened to her if the constable had caught her.

She took a deep breath and smiled at him. She had not bothered to paint her face tonight, and her red hair was tied back neatly with a ribbon. On her feet were sturdy boots; walking the steep, slippery paths of the cold, dark park in high heels on the previous night had not been such a delightful experience that she wanted to repeat it.

"Smoking, Ben? You said you gave it up," she teased him. "Did they repeal the iniquitous tax on tobacco?"

"I decided it was not fair to punish the British merchant for the stupidity of his government. I didn't think you were coming," he added stiffly.

"Honestly, I couldn't get away sooner," she said. "I was afraid you'd gone to bed already. But I decided to risk it, in case you hadn't. Shall we get started, then?"

Not waiting for an answer, she sat down on the sofa and picked up the small green book from the table. She had marked her place with the ribbon attached to the book's spine. "I think we'd made it to Chapter Five: 'A favorite hound described, which pups while pursuing a hare; the hare also litters while pursued by the hound—'"

He sat down next to her on the sofa, turned her face to his, and kissed her.

Chapter 8

He tasted of warm brandy. Dropping the book, she slipped both arms around his neck and gave her mouth to him completely. He was pulled down to the sofa, and somehow ended up crouched over her, kissing her. Her mouth clung to his. His hand slipped to her breast, cradling it in the curve of his palm. He could feel her heart beating in wild measures. The roughness of her clothing annoyed him. Hoping that underneath the coarse fabric she would be wearing the silk and lace of the night before, he began to unbutton the jacket.

Cosima froze. She had welcomed his kiss, and she did not really object to being caressed over the protection of her clothing, but she was not ready for this. She was deeply insulted that he would think she would permit such an invasion. He knew perfectly well that she was no woman of easy virtue. Or did he?

He felt her shrink from him, and he drew away from her. She sat up on the sofa and put one hand up to her wig to make sure it was still in place. She had pinned it on securely, but she had not bargained on being mauled. He had been nothing but respectful on the previous night. "It's so nice," she said coldly, "to be with a man who doesn't take insufferable liberties!"

"I beg your pardon, Miss Cherry," he said, getting up from the sofa.

"I am not," she said angrily, "jumping into bed with you just because—" She broke off in confusion and buttoned her jacket. "Well, I'm just not, that's all! If it's a harlot you want, I recommend you go back to Mrs. Price and ask for somebody else!"

"I don't want anybody else," he said quietly.

"Well, you can't have *me!* I'm not for sale."

He sat down in the chair opposite the sofa. "I still don't want anybody else."

She felt absurdly pleased. He was a hard man to read, but she thought she detected suffering in his cold gray eyes. "I'll read to you, but that's all I'm doing," she said primly.

"Of course. Please forgive me. I was a brute."

She picked up the book again and found her place. She liked kissing him but, obviously, anything more was completely out of the question. She had not meant to shut him down completely but, she supposed, it would hardly be fair to start him up again when she had no intention of coming across. He wouldn't be satisfied with just kissing, and she absolutely would not give him anything more.

Unless they married, of course, in which case she would have to let him do as he liked, whether she wanted to or not. The thought of marrying anyone threw her into a blind panic. She certainly didn't want to marry a man who was in the habit of hiring prostitutes and making indecent proposals to innocent young women, even if he thought they were only housekeepers.

But what a kiss! Her mouth felt lonely without it. So that, she thought, is what brandy tastes like. The men in her family were not brandy drinkers. Sir Benedict, obviously, was a bit more sophisticated than her rough-and-tumble brothers.

"Was it like kissing a newel post?" he asked.

"What?"

"I have been told," he said, "that kissing me is like kissing a newel post."

"Who would say such a terrible thing?" she said softly.

"And you such a lovely, lovely man? She must have been a terrible girl. Could be she has no talent for it herself so she doesn't recognize it in you."

"That must be it. Would you care for a strawberry?"

She frowned, and he was suddenly quite ashamed of his blatant attempt to seduce the girl. Such a cliché, too. Strawberries and champagne, indeed. Pickering really had no imagination. "It's after midnight," she pointed out. "I have Mass in the morning."

He didn't see the connection.

"I have to be in a state of grace to receive the body of Christ," she explained. "I can't eat until after Mass."

"I'll put them away," he offered.

"No need," she said. "I can exercise self-restraint, you know."

"I suppose champagne is out of the question," he murmured.

"I should really do my reading," she said taking up the book. "You'll not be able to hear me over there," she said as she found the ribbon marking her place. "I'd only be wasting my voice. Are you so senile in your old age that you've forgotten that you're deaf?"

Benedict had assumed he was to be banished from the sofa, but he was not slow in joining her.

"Now, put your hand on my knee," she instructed when he was beside her.

He looked at her in surprise.

"Put your hand on my knee," she repeated firmly. "I don't trust you," she explained. "Obviously, I won't be able to keep an eye on you while I'm reading, but this way I'll know where your hand is at all times. Go on," she commanded.

He leaned forward a little and claimed her knee.

"That doesn't look comfortable," she observed.

"It isn't. Why don't I put my hand here instead?" Leaning back, he placed his left arm across her back and cupped her shoulder with his palm. "Consider the benefits of this position.

I will be close enough to hear you even if you should whisper. You will know where my hand is at all times. And, I think, it is a comfortable position for us both."

"Aye," she agreed. His nearness made her skin tingle, and his hand felt hot through the green baize of her jacket. "Would it be an insufferable liberty," she asked, "if I were to rest my head on your shoulder like so?"

"Not at all."

Nestled against him, then, she began to read in an outrageous German accent: "All these narrow and lucky escapes, gentlemen, were chances turned to advantage by presence of mind and vigorous exertions . . ."

In the morning, Pickering was astonished to find the strawberries uneaten and the champagne still corked. Still more puzzling was the fact that his master did not seem unhappy in the least. Quite the opposite, in fact.

"Will your friend be coming again tonight?" he asked hopefully.

"Not tonight," Benedict replied.

Pickering was crushed. He felt like a dismal failure.

The clock on the mantel was quietly striking midnight when she arrived the following night. "Good evening, Miss Cherry," Benedict said, climbing to his feet.

He was surprised to see her.

Cosy stared at him in dismay. He was dressed for bed, a black brocade dressing gown loosely belted over his snowy white nightshirt. On his feet were embroidered velvet slippers. Thick black hair filled the open neck of the nightshirt.

"Please don't be alarmed," he said, making her laugh. "My man likes to undress me for bed at a certain time every night before he retires himself. You said you couldn't come on Sunday, so I was prepared for an evening alone. This is not," he added wryly, "part of an elaborate plan to seduce you. I mean, I *have* got an elaborate plan to seduce you, of course, but this isn't it."

"It's Monday," she pointed out, indicating the clock on the mantel. "Last night, I got here so late, it was actually Sunday. And today, it's so late, it's Monday. So I *was* here Sunday, after all. I just didn't realize it at the time."

To his disappointment, she was again clad in her green baize habit, buttoned up to the neck, with sensible shoes on her feet. What happened to the delightfully minimal gown she had been wearing the first night? "You are quite right," he said, resuming his seat as she took the sofa. "I am, of course, pleased to see you, whatever the day."

"I guess there's no real reason I can't come on Sunday," she said slowly. "It's not as though we're up to anything! We're committing no sin."

"Certainly not," he agreed heartily.

She sat down on the sofa and opened the book, setting aside the ribbon marking her place. "Chapter Eight," she read aloud, "in which the Baron arrives unintentionally in the regions of heat and darkness, from which he is extricated by dancing a hornpipe."

Benedict joined her on the sofa and placed his arm across her shoulders.

Somehow, the fact that he was sitting there in his dressing gown, rather than fully clothed, made the situation embarrassing for her. Her cheeks flamed. "You're fine in the chair," she said quickly. "I think I can trust you now. I'm sure you've learned your lesson."

Benedict frowned. "Certainly, you can trust me. However, I *hear* so much better when I am close to you. Your voice is so soft, just like Miss O'Hara's. Of course," he added, "Miss O'Hara *always* took me on her lap and cuddled me."

"Don't even think about it," she warned, laughing.

Extending one long leg, he pulled the ottoman over to them with his foot. He put his feet up and invited her to do the same.

She did so, but immediately wished she hadn't. Her ugly black shoes were just the thing for walking through parks on dark wintry nights, but they looked embarrassingly mannish on an ottoman in a gentleman's study. "Nice slippers," she sniffed. "Did your mother embroider them for you?"

"My sister," he answered.

She felt an odd stinging sensation in the tips of her breasts. It seemed connected somehow to the timber of his voice. "'I was once in danger of being lost,'" she read loudly, "'in a most singular manner in the Mediterranean—'"

"Aren't you going to rest your head against me?" he interrupted her. "I hear so much better when you do."

She realized she was sitting up very straight. With her feet on the ottoman it was a posture both ridiculous and uncomfortable. She forced herself to relax. He had already laid his arm along the back of the sofa, and as she leaned back he was able to clasp her shoulder with his left hand, pulling her closer still. She leaned her head against him and closed her eyes for a moment. She was so tired, and he smelled so good. He felt good, too. The silk of his dressing gown caressed her cheek. She drifted toward sleep.

"Lost in the Mediterranean," he prompted her, making her jump.

Chapter Eight was a very short chapter, only three pages, but she had to struggle to concentrate on the words. Not only did her mind wander to the man sitting close beside her, but her eyes frequently left the page she was reading to stray over his body. His chest, in particular, fascinated her. The thick hair showing at the opening of his nightshirt moved gently when she breathed, like a meadow moving on a windy day. Her fingers itched to touch it. Would it be coarse or soft to the touch? What would he do if she touched him?

He would want to touch her, of course. He was not a green young man. He would expect her to give him everything, and he would be angry when she would not.

She didn't dare touch him. She could only look at him and wish and wonder.

"You're not doing the funny accent tonight," he complained, breaking into her thoughts, and his voice stung her breasts again. "Is it because you found out in the last chapter that the Baron is Dutch?" he went on, as though unaware of the unsettling effect he was having on her body and her nerves.

"Please, don't be angry with me!" she burst out.

He looked puzzled. "Why should I be angry with you?"

"I can't concentrate on my reading," she said, turning to look at him. "You're just so hairy!" she said helplessly.

Benedict was taken aback. "I am sorry if it offends you, my dear," he said. "I am as God made me—well, almost as God made me. There *has* been a *slight* alteration—"

"No, it doesn't offend me," she said quickly. "Oh, you *are* angry!"

"No," he said tightly. "Why should I be angry? You find me physically repulsive. Naturally, I am overjoyed. Couldn't be happier!"

"But I don't find you physically repulsive," she answered. "I think you're nice."

"Nice?" Now he was seriously annoyed with her. "You use that word quite a lot, I've noticed. You use it for everything! This is, for example, a nice room. That is a nice book. These are nice slippers. Strawberries are nice. You use it so much, in fact, that it has become meaningless. Tell me, Miss Cherry, in what sense of the word do you find me *nice?*"

His arm tightened around her, pulling her against him. She put out her hand as if to stop him, and encountered the hard reality of his chest. As if of their own accord, her fingers raked through the hairs on his chest. They were not as soft as the hairs on her head, but neither were they as coarse as they appeared. They were short, crisp, and clean, and as her hand moved, they sprang up and tickled her fingers. Fascinating. She couldn't seem to stop touching him.

The book fell to the rug, and with it, all pretense seemed to fall away. She touched his mouth blindly, and in the next moment they were kissing, attacking one another with lips and tongues. Her hand slipped inside his nightshirt, exploring his body as her tongue strained to explore his mouth. He was as hairy as a hound, and she couldn't stop touching him.

"You are so nice to touch," she panted as his lips sought the tender skin of her neck. "You are so nice to kiss. You're so nice to me! I just think you're so nice!"

He laughed softly. "I think you're very nice, too."

"I *am* a nice girl," she said, as if he had argued the reverse.

"You are the nicest girl I ever met," he agreed, kissing her.

This time when his hand sought her breast, she did not immediately push him away. She could hardly deny that she wanted this caress in particular when her entire body arched against him. She moaned softly in the back of her throat and went on kissing him, her eyes closed. "We shouldn't be doing this," she whispered. "It's not nice."

This rejection stung him. He moved away from her so quickly that she felt like the one being rejected. She was burning alive. What on earth had made him stop?

Puzzled, she sat up, propping herself up on her elbows.

"I see," he said coolly. "You can touch *me,* but I can't touch you. Madam, I appeal to your sense of fairness, if indeed you possess such a thing!"

She sighed. It was just as she feared. He hated her. "Life isn't always fair, Ben," she said sadly.

"Clearly!" He got up and poured himself a drink. Brandy. The man was a brandy fiend.

"Please don't be angry with me," she pleaded softly.

"I am not angry."

"You sound angry, Ben."

"Well, I'm not!" he snapped. He finished his drink and slammed down the glass.

"Do you want me to leave?" she whispered.

"No," he said, but he had to think about it first.

She lifted her eyes to his face. "Do you want me to read to you?"

"No." He sat down in his chair and sulked.

She bit her lip. "I like you, Ben. But I'm not going to go bed with you. If that's what you're after with me, then you're wasting your time. I mean, I *know* you want to go to bed with me. And I suppose I want you to want to go to bed with me. And I can certainly see how you might think that I *might* go to bed with you because I haven't exactly been standoffish, but I'm here to tell you, I'm *not* going to go to bed with you, and that's that!"

His mouth twitched. "So you're saying you won't go to bed with me?"

"I'd *like* to go to bed with you," she confessed. "I mean, I *think* I might like to go to bed with you, but I guess I'll never know, because I'm *not* going to go to bed with you."

"Fair enough," he said gently.

She winced as if he had shouted. "You want me to go now, don't you?"

"No."

"You hate me," she accused.

"Not at all."

"I suppose," she said bitterly, "you've had a lot of women."

He frowned. "Why do you say that?"

"I know what men are like," she answered, shrugging. "Rapacious bastards, all."

"You do not know *me*," he said flatly. "I have enjoyed carnal relations with only one woman in the entire course of my life."

"Well, if you don't like it, why do you keep doing it?"

He chuckled. "That's not what I meant. I've only had one woman in my life."

"You're lying!" she said. She laughed, it was so unbelievable.

"Why would I tell such a lie?" he asked.

She thought about it. In her experience, men usually lied in the direction of *more*, rather than *fewer*. At least, her brothers always did. "I don't know," she was forced to admit.

"It's perfectly true. It might have been otherwise if I had not lost my arm when I was so young, but, as it is, I have had only one lover. She was governess to my sister."

"Miss O'Hara!" she gasped.

He looked shocked. "No, this was another governess. I hold Miss O'Hara sacred forever. No, this one was English."

"It figures," Miss Cherry said primly.

"My father and his second wife died when I was but eighteen, leaving their two children on my hands. Miss Smith entered the house some two years before they died."

"And that's when you entered her?" she said politely.

"I did not pursue her, Miss Cherry. She wasn't a pretty woman. She wasn't even young. She must have been forty then, about the age I am now. As far as I was concerned, she was a fixture. I never paid the slightest attention to her before my father died. But afterward, well, I was the master. She began to pay a great deal of attention to *me*."

"Slut!" said Miss Cherry.

He looked faintly surprised by this venomous comment, but went on. "I thought at first that she was afraid the new master would dismiss her from her post. I told her I had no intention of doing so. Her attentions increased; I mistook them for gratitude. Then, one night, she came to my bed."

"You should have turfed her out!"

"Alas, I was not then as wise as I am now," he said with a faint smile.

"Was she a virgin?"

He nearly choked. "Good Lord, no!"

"I thought not," Miss Cherry said contemptuously. "Personally, I'd be ashamed to offer myself to a gentleman if I were not a pure virgin."

"She was not as scrupulous as you are, Miss Cherry," he said. "She was surprisingly experienced, as I recall. Quite an abandoned woman. She frightened me."

"You *liked* it," she accused him.

"I did," he admitted. "I behaved quite shamefully. I wish I could go back and change it, but I can't. The disgraceful affair went on for two years. She always visited me; I never visited her. Of course, unbeknownst to me, everyone in the house knew of it, with the exception, I hope, of my brother and sister."

"Did you love her, Ben?"

"No, indeed."

"Not at *all*?"

"Less than that. She began to behave as if she were the mistress of my house. She began to sleep in my stepmother's room, and wear her clothes and jewelry. She began to—playfully, of course—ask me when I was going to make an honest woman of her."

"Whatever did you tell her?"

"The truth. That I never intended to marry at all. When I lost my arm, I decided that my brother would be my heir."

"But I thought you came to Bath to find a wife," she said, puzzled.

"I did. My circumstances have changed. My brother can no longer be my heir."

"Oh, no!" she cried softly. "Did he die, your brother?"

"No, no. He married a very wealthy girl. His father-in-law bought him an earldom. Now, if I die without a son to carry on, the baronetcy will be completely consumed by the new title. I have no choice but to marry."

"I see," she said, even though she did not see at all. "And *that* was the only woman you've ever had?"

"Yes."

She shook her head. "Sorry. I don't believe you."

He chuckled ruefully. "If you had seen the embarrassing way in which the affair ended, you *would* believe. No sane person would ever put himself in such a position again."

"She made a scene, did she?"

"Rather," he said dryly. "She threatened to accuse me of assaulting her, if you please, unless I married her. Naturally, I refused. She made good on her threat. She went straight to the vicar with her sordid tale. She even tore her own clothes and put scratches all over herself. Fortunately, for me, she had made enemies of all my servants. One and all, they refuted her fantastic lies. I was exonerated. But I never forgot, and I never forgave."

"And you've been a saint ever since?"

He sighed. "I may have visited a brothel or two," he admitted. "But I never—I never had carnal knowledge of any of the inmates."

She laughed in sheer disbelief. "You did, of course!"

"No," he insisted. "I was afraid I might contract a disease."

"I don't understand," she said. "If you weren't doing the deed, what *were* you doing?"

"I would allow them to palate me," he said, "but that's all."

"I have no idea what that means. Sounds awful."

"Not at all. I used their mouths," he said.

She stared at him in amazement. He wasn't even blushing. "That's disgusting!"

"I suppose that depends on your point of view," he said coldly. "Some of these young ladies are very skilled."

"*I* would never do anything like that," she declared. "It's indecent."

"That," he said, "is the whole point."

"Those poor girls! I hope you paid them well."

"I did. But enough about me," he went on airily. "What about you?"

"Me!"

"I've told *you* everything," he insisted. "It's only fair that you tell *me* everything."

"For your information, I am a pure virgin," she said hotly.

"I never said you weren't. I know I am not the first to kiss you."

"Oh, that," she said, blushing. "That's only kissing."

"You must have had offers," he said. "A beautiful girl like you."

"Well, I've been pawed at, if that's what you mean." She looked uncomfortable, but forged ahead. "There was a man who got his hand inside my dress once, but I got free of him."

"Are you referring to me?" he asked sharply.

"Oh, no," she hastened to assure him. "He wasn't a nice man like you."

A nerve twitched in his jaw. "Did he hurt you?"

She shrugged. "I told my brothers. I'm not exactly sure *what* they did to him in Phoenix Park, but he was a changed man after that. You never heard of him bothering the lasses again."

"Good."

"And then, when I was about sixteen, there was a boy at a dance who got a bit carried away. He was a nice boy, though. I could tell he was really trying to control himself. He danced me outside and shed tears on my best dress—except it wasn't *tears,* if you know what I mean. I told my brothers, and no one ever saw him alive again. I didn't mean for that to happen."

"You mean they—? They *killed him*?"

"I suppose they did. Two weeks later, they found him, when they were dragging the bog for Connery's mule. He was only seventeen. The boy, not the mule. It was really awful. If I'd known they were going to kill him, I never would have breathed a word. After that, I was the most respected girl in Ireland."

"So I would imagine!" said Benedict. "I wonder what your brothers would do to *me* if they were here."

"I wouldn't let them hurt you," she said fiercely. "They'd have to throw me in the bog with you. That's the truth of it. Anyway, my brothers are gone. I've no one at all to defend me."

"You have me," he said firmly.

She laughed. "But 'tis yourself I need protection from the most!"

"No," he said, frowning. "I will never harm you. You have my word."

The grim story of the boy in the bog had cast a pall over the evening.

"It's late," she said, closing the book. "I'd better go."

"You only read three pages," he protested.

"Oh, bollocks!" she said. "That's only sixpence."

She looked at him, shame-faced. "Could I ask you to give me a bit more?"

"We agreed on tuppence a page, Miss Cherry. If you want more money, you will just have to stay and read."

She shook her head. "I can't stay. Please, Ben! I hate to ask you, but I really need it. You've no idea!"

His manner changed instantly as he saw how distressed she was. "Are you so badly in debt?" he asked, thinking about the thousand pounds he had given her just days before. "Of course! How much do you need?"

"I don't know. Maybe three shillings? That's what I earned last night."

"Three shillings?" He almost laughed. "Are you seriously this worried about *three shillings*?"

"You don't understand," she said. "If I show up with nothing but sixpence in my fist, Nora will think we're up to something! She already *does* think we're up to something. It's no laughing matter," she assured him.

"Who, exactly, is Nora? And why do we care what she thinks?"

"Nora is . . . Well, I suppose you'd call her a servant."

He laughed. "For heaven's sake. Tell her to go boil her head. It's none of her business."

She frowned at him. "Well, let me put it to you this way, Ben. If Nora thinks I'm sleeping with you, she'll raise holy hell before she ever lets me out of the house again, and I won't be able to come here anymore and *read* to you, if that matters!"

He went to his desk immediately and retrieved a gold sovereign from the money tray.

"That's too much," she complained. "She'd *know* we were

up to no good if I started bringing home gold! She's very suspicious-minded. She'd go straight to Father Mallone and blab. He'd call me out in Mass. I'd be shamed beyond all shame."

"Three shillings," he said, counting out the correct amount.

"And the sixpence I earned," she said quickly. "I *did* read three pages."

"And sixpence," he agreed, wondering if things could get any more ridiculous.

She pocketed the sixpence, then held up the three shillings. "*This* is only to show Nora," she said so seriously he didn't dare laugh. "I didn't earn it. I'll bring it back to you tomorrow."

It rained hard the following night. He would not have blamed her if she had decided not to make the cold, wet journey to his house. But in the morning, he woke up with three shillings on his pillow.

Chapter 9

Anyone would have thought that Tuesday evening was the most important night of Cosy Vaughn's life. She spent most of the day bathing, washing and drying her long blond hair, and fussing over her clothes like a nervous bride.

"It's only a stupid concert," Allie reminded her brutally as she watched her sister at her dressing table. Cosy was in her slip and petticoats. She planned to put her dress on at the last possible moment to avoid wrinkling it.

Cosy held up two different earrings to her ears and looked in the mirror, trying to decide between them. "Which ones do you think, Allie? Me rubies or me sapphires?"

Neither matched the gown she had bought especially for this night, and both were glaring fakes. Her mother's jewels were long gone now. One by one, they had all been sold to help pay her father's debts. Without them, she felt like a knight going into battle without armor.

The gown she had bought was all wrong. She had known that even as she bought it, but it was half price, and she could not bring herself to spend more when she could spend less. Last year's model, it was a bilious, unflattering shade of green, and the shop girl had been so eager to unload it, it was practically a gift. The new models were being cut to resemble a woman's natural curves, with a nipped-in waist and a full, bell-like skirt, but the new models were costly. The green gown was in the old style, with the waist immediately under the breasts. Not only was it ugly and out of style but it emphasized that Cosima had no bosom.

The only nice thing about it was how little it cost.

"I should have learned to sew." She sighed.

"You were not to know the colonel would gamble his fortune away," Nora said soothingly, as she fussed ineffectually over the artificial flowers in the young lady's hair.

Ben always looked impeccable, Cosima thought miserably, *and he had such beautiful clothes.* Nothing garish, of course. His style was understated, but he had the best of everything. He was sure to be embarrassed to be seen with her in the ugly green dress, in last year's model. She kept putting off the moment when she had to put it on.

"Let this be a lesson to you, Allie: learn to sew."

"It's not fair," Allie said sullenly. "You get to go to concerts in the Upper Rooms, and I have to go to school all day, and then sit at home all night with Mama."

"Aye," Nora said darkly, "but your sister has to go with the *ciotog.*"

"I think he's nice," Allie protested. "He gave me sixpence when he came yesterday."

Cosima frowned. "What's he giving you money for?" she demanded, standing up to insert her stockinged feet into her high-heeled evening slippers.

Allie shrugged. "He said all the other young ladies at school would have pocket money."

"I don't want you taking money from him," said Cosima.

"Why not?"

"Why not? We've already taken a thousand pounds from him, that's why," Cosy snapped. "Sixpence, indeed! When I was your age threepenny was the most I ever got—and that on Christmas morning! And we had money then, lashes of it!" she exaggerated. "Now, where are me pearls, Nora?" she murmured, rummaging in her dressing table.

"*Your* pearls!" Allie said belligerently. "They're as much mine as they are yours. Granny Vaughn left them to whichever one of us marries first."

Cosy laughed as Nora opened the black velvet box containing her one piece of good jewelry. "And I suppose you think you'll marry before I do, Miss Allie?"

"I might!" Allie cried, snatching the pearls from her sister's hand and sprinting for the door. "I'm prettier than you are, and I'm nicer, too."

"You get back here!"

It was a ridiculous command, and not to be heeded. The chase was on.

Lady Agatha gasped in fright as her younger daughter ran through the drawing-room, followed by her furious elder daughter. Hindered by her long petticoats and her high-heeled shoes, Cosima had no choice but to leap over the sofa and tackle the younger girl. Older and stronger, she had no difficulty pinning her sister to the floor.

"It's not fair!" Allie screamed from the floor as her sister pried her chubby fingers from the necklace. "You get *everything!* Mama!"

Lady Agatha fluttered helplessly on the sofa as her eldest daughter stood up, victorious. Cosy was in the act of clasping the pearl necklace around her throat when she noticed that her mother had not been sitting in the drawing-room alone.

Benedict rose from his chair and cleared his throat apologetically. Resplendent in evening dress, he was carrying a nosegay of white hothouse roses. "Good evening, Miss Vaughn," he said gravely.

"Oh, God!" Cosy resisted the urge to cover her exposed upper body with both hands. "You should have made your presence known," she said crossly. Allie climbed to her feet, gleefully observing the spectacle of her sister curtseying to a male visitor in her underclothing.

If Benedict realized that Cosima was standing there in her petticoats and slip he gave no sign. But then, they were very

nice undergarments. She had bargained for them quite fero-
ciously. "These are for you," he said, holding out the nosegay.

"He brought you roses in March," Lady Agatha cried.
"They must have cost a fortune."

Reluctantly, Cosima went forward to take the flowers.

Benedict looked at her steadily. He could not decide if he
preferred her as a redhead or a blonde. Fortunately, he did not
have to decide. "I've hired a chair. Shall we go, Miss Vaughn?"

"Do I look ready to go to you?" she asked incredulously.

"I think you look very . . . nice," he replied. "Is that a new
ensemble?"

It was, in fact, the ensemble that "Miss Cherry" had worn
at her debut. Cosima would die of shame if he ever knew she
had traipsed across the park in her underwear.

Allie collapsed into giggles. Benedict, being under the impression that all young females giggle almost unceasingly
and without provocation, saw nothing amiss. Determined to
keep him in ignorance, Cosima said simply, "Yes; very new.
But I'm not squeezing up into a chair with you," she added
belligerently. "I'll walk."

"It rained last night. You'll ruin your shoes," he told her.

"You let me worry about my shoes," she said crossly.

"As you wish," he said stiffly. "I will dismiss the chairman,
and we will walk."

"You expect me to go to a concert with you? Like this?"

"Of course not. Fetch your cloak." He took out his watch
and looked at it.

"I'll get my cloak," she said.

She ran down the hall to her room and studied herself anxiously in the mirror. To her relief, she looked pristine and
not slatternly in her white silk undergarments. In this case,
being thin and flat-chested was a blessing; nothing untoward
wobbled to attract unwelcome attention. No unsightly rolls of
flesh lay exposed. She had good shoulders, and a nice, long
neck. The pearls helped, too.

Nora picked up the green dress.

"No," said Cosy. "Just my cloak, Nora."

"You can't go out in your shift, Miss Cosy!" Nora cried, shocked.

"I have to, Nora. I will not have the *ciotog* thinking he's seen me in my underwear!"

"But he *has* seen you in your underwear, Miss Cosy," Nora said, puzzled.

"Not if I wear it out, he hasn't!" Cosima answered with indisputable logic.

She held his arm tightly as they entered the Upper Rooms. "You're not nervous, are you?" He sounded amused.

Cosy was used to people staring at her. People had stared at her all her life. Even when she was a child, complete strangers would come up to her, pat her cheeks, and tell her what a pretty girl she was. But now she was terrified that, at any moment, someone would point out that she was wearing only a petticoat. "I don't know anyone here," she said.

"You know Lady Dalrymple and her son and daughter, I believe."

Her fingers dug into his arm. "They're going to snub me."

"No, indeed," he said, and, to her amazement, he was right. Lady Dalrymple greeted her warmly. Freddie Carteret kissed her hand. And Millie Carteret, dressed in a very daring gown of ultramarine taffeta, kissed the air next to her cheek.

Benedict was enjoying himself immensely. The pleasure of escorting a beautiful girl into a room breathlessly waiting to see her had never been his before. He swept through the crowd into the Octagon Room, where he presented her to the first lady of Bath.

Lady Matlock, herself warmly dressed in blue velvet, snapped her fan angrily as she looked at the Irish girl. That young ass, Lord Ludham, had not exaggerated; Miss Vaughn had the face of an angel. The countess would have preferred to give the Irish upstart the Cut Direct, but when Sir Benedict

Wayborn made such a point of bringing the girl over, what could one do? One was trapped into civility. "You are Irish, my dear?" she said with a faint sniff.

"I am."

"Do you play the harp? Of course, you do. All Irish girls do. You must come and play for me in the Crescent. I am excessively fond of music, but, alas, my poor health did not permit me to learn. My daughter, Rose."

With a calculating eye, she watched Miss Vaughn shake hands with her daughter. It was most irritating not to be able to detect a flaw in the Irish girl. Her face was perfection. Her creamy, radiant skin was undeniable. Even her teeth were good; small, straight, and unstained. While not quite as décolleté as Rose's wisp of lace, her white dress showed off a light, pleasing figure. Rose, even though she was endowed with a larger bosom and a respectable dowry, had her work cut out for her. Many gentlemen preferred the virginal look to the outright sensuality offered by a figure like Rose's. Lady Matlock made a mental note that her daughter needed more rigorous corseting.

"So you are Westlands's cousin, the famous Miss Vaughn!" cried Rose.

"Didn't know I was famous, but yes," Cosima answered, a little puzzled by the young lady's apparent delight in making her acquaintance.

Lady Matlock glowered at her. "I suppose you are secretly engaged to him, miss! You have a quiet little understanding, I daresay."

Benedict frowned.

Cosima was startled. "Engaged to Westlands?" She laughed. "No, indeed, ma'am. I've not seen Marcus in more than five years. In any case, my uncle, Lord Wayborn, does not approve of cousins marrying. He was always going on about that, even when we were children. Believe me, ma'am, we got the hint."

"Oh!" cried Lady Matlock, pleased. "That was very wise of his lordship. I know of nothing so abominable as cousins marrying cousins! Except of course, when a young man inherits an uncle's property. In that case, honor dictates that the young man should marry his uncle's daughter at once, if possible. Otherwise, he has been the means of injuring his cousin. But that would not apply in *your* case."

"No, indeed, ma'am."

Reluctantly, Lady Matlock acquitted the Irish girl of ruining all her daughter's hopes. Her thoughts turned toward making this pretty young person useful. "All the same! Your cousin has used my daughter very ill! He has treated her infamously, and has made her the laughingstock of the whole world!"

"I am sorry to hear that," said Cosima sincerely. "What's he done?"

"Nothing," Rose said quickly.

"Nothing!" shrieked Lady Matlock. "He has most cruelly raised all our hopes and expectations, only to dash them. In London, he danced with my daughter at every ball. And no one else! He called on her every day. He was always at her side. In short, he did everything a young man ought to do. Everything *except* propose. You call that nothing?"

"I'm sure Marcus meant no mischief, ma'am."

"And I am sure he did!" replied her ladyship very stoutly.

"I could write to him, I suppose, and ask him to explain himself," Cosy said doubtfully.

"Yes!" cried Lady Matlock, while at the same time her daughter cried, "No!"

Rose's hand jerked suddenly, spilling her punch down the front of Miss Vaughn's white silk slip. Cosima gasped in shock. Benedict instantly offered his handkerchief, but he was not as fast as Rose. "Come with me quick!" she cried, seizing Cosima by the hand almost before the other girl knew what was happening.

Rose insisted on sponging the punch stain from Miss Vaughn's dress herself, overriding the protests of both Miss Vaughn and the attendant in the ladies' retiring room. The worst of the stain was at the waist of the gown, but Rose solved the problem by tearing apart Cosima's nosegay and pinning the white roses over the pink stain. Satisfied with her handiwork, Rose led her new acquaintance into a private alcove, where they sat fanning Miss Vaughn's skirt dry.

"Forgive me, Miss Vaughn! I could think of no other way to speak to you alone."

Cosima's temper flared. "You did that on purpose!"

"I needed to talk to you," Rose explained. "Alone," she added mysteriously.

"You could have asked me," said Cosima. "This is my best petticoat! I mean, dress."

Rose's pretty face crumpled as she burst into tears. "Oh, no! You hate me!"

Cosy looked in astonishment at the chestnut-haired English girl. "Of course I don't hate you," she said impatiently. "But even if I did, why would you care? I'm hardly one of the leading lights of Bath society."

"I care nothing for Bath society," Rose declared. "Dante will have written to you by now, I am sure, so you must know who I am. Oh, Miss Vaughn, do you think you could ever love me like a sister? Indeed, Miss Vaughn, I love *you* already."

"Dante!" Cosy exclaimed. Hastily, she lowered her voice. "Dante, my brother?"

"Yes, of course." Rose laughed giddily. "Who else?"

Cosy's heart sank. Dante was just eighteen, but already he was following in the footsteps of the Vaughn men; drinking, gambling, and womanizing with reckless abandon.

"He hasn't written to you?" Rose asked anxiously. "But he promised me so faithfully!"

"Oh, God," Cosima groaned. "What else did he promise you?"

The entire story tumbled out of Rose in less than a minute. Lieutenant Dante Vaughn was the most wonderful young man in the world. She loved him. Happily, the most wonderful young man in the world returned her feelings, and, to make a long story short, the lovely couple were engaged. Owing to the disparity of rank and fortune that existed between them, the engagement was to be kept a dark secret.

Cosy sighed. Although she was only a few years older than Rose Fitzwilliam, she could not look at the other girl's pretty, innocent face without feeling old and jaded. This was not the first time she had been called upon to console one of her brothers' abandoned conquests. What the fair sex saw in the guilty, malodorous creatures was quite beyond her power to understand.

"Let me see if I have this right," she said gently. "You met Dan at a ball—once. You became secretly engaged to him at that time. Two days later, he left for India, where he will be stationed for the next ten years at least. Don't you think that might be a shade unrealistic?"

She was trying to be kind.

"It was love at first sight," Rose explained. "You'll see when you get Dante's letter. But we won't have to wait ten years. In four years, when I come of age, I shall have my money."

Cosima winced. This just kept getting worse. "You've got a fortune, have you?"

"Thirty thousand pounds," Rose said proudly. "Money is not the problem. Right now, the problem is Westlands! You see, when Dante left England, Westlands promised to look after me, to keep me cheerful, and to keep the other gentlemen away from me. Which he did, of course. Only he did it too well."

Cosima smiled in relief. "And you and Marcus fell in love?"

Rose stared at her, horrified. "No! Nothing like that! Marcus and I are good friends, that's all. But his attentions were so marked that he was obliged to leave London or else become engaged to me! Some say he trifled with me! Others say that I trifled with him! My situation became so intolerable that I was shipped back to my mother in disgrace."

Tears began to flow from Rose's large, dark eyes. Blindly, she reached for the other girl's hand. "Oh, Miss Vaughn! Mama means to force me to marry anyone she can, and be rid of me as soon as possible. And I do mean *anyone*. Why, she even threatened me with that old stick, Sir Benedict Wayborn!"

Cosima hid a smile. "Oh, no. Fate worse than death."

"Yes! She makes me dance with him at every ball. Odious man! He has not left me alone since I came to Bath. I do believe he followed me here!" she added with a shiver. "I would not be surprised if it turned out he fiddled with the wheels of my carriage so that I would be stranded in the road. You must admit, it was very suspicious that he came along right when he did and rescued me. Obviously, it was all a plot."

"Did Sir Benedict rescue you?"

"It was no great thing," Rose explained. "He is no hero, I assure you. My carriage sank in the mud, and he brought me the rest of the way to Bath in his. Now he seems to think he is owed my hand in marriage, only in exchange for a seat in his carriage! I expect, if my uncle had not been with me, I should have been compromised, and so *forced* to marry him. But, as it is, I would have none of his suit, and so I told him. Why, he's old enough to be my father! I told him plainly that I would rather die than marry him."

Cosima gasped. "He asked you to marry him? When?"

Rose's bosom swelled dangerously. "I put paid to his disgusting application right away, I can assure you. Marry him? I would as soon marry a candlestick!"

"He *is* a little stiff, I suppose."

"Stiff! A resurrection man wouldn't take him," Rose declared. "He is such a bore! He is well-respected, of course, but no one really likes him. So sour and sarcastic!"

If you only knew him, Cosy thought, as Rose rambled on. Then she realized she didn't want anyone else to know Ben, not the way she knew him.

"*You* must be careful of him, Miss Vaughn. From what I hear, he's desperate for a wife. He couldn't find anyone stupid

enough to take him in London, so he had to come here, to
Bath, looking for fresh victims. I think it very likely he will
ask *you* next. I wouldn't put it past him!"

Cosima's eyes twinkled. "Do you think me stupid enough
to take him?"

"Of course not," said Rose. "But he may try to persuade
you. He is rich, to be sure, and a baronet, but he's only Number
Fifty-six on my Aunt Maria's list of eligible bachelors, and *so
old!* Positively ancient! You *know* he dyes his hair."

Cosima screamed with laughter. "He does not!"

"He does!" Rose insisted. "You could do *much* better. You
really are a beauty, you know. Lord Ludham doesn't dye his
hair, and he's madly in love with you, too, which helps."

Cosima wiped the tears from her eyes. "Who?"

"Lord Ludham. Don't worry; you'll meet him. All he ever
talks about is you, and now that his divorce has been granted,
he's free."

"Divorce!" said Cosima, shocked.

"Yes, of course. How can you not know these things?" said
Rose, jumping to her feet. "We had better go down or we will
miss the concert."

As the two young ladies walked back down the stairs, they
were not without admirers. A waggish gentleman instantly
christened them "The Face" and "The Body," respectively.

"Ignore them," Rose advised her companion. "You know
what men are like when we pay them the least bit of attention.
They are so conceited!" She caught sight of Sir Benedict
coming toward them. "*Why* are you pursuing me?" she demanded, holding tightly to Cosima for support. "I do not love
you, sir. I will never marry you."

Benedict was unruffled. "Your mother sent me to find you,
Lady Rose."

Returning to the concert hall, they discovered that the
evening's entertainment was in danger of being canceled. The
pianist had taken ill.

"What no one seems to realize, Mr. King," Lady Matlock

said indignantly, "is that *I* am seriously ill! Have I dragged my weary body from my deathbed, only to be obliged to struggle home again, without so much as a song to show for all my effort? Why can't the bloody woman sing a cappella?" she wanted to know.

"I can play the piano," Cosima said. "I'll do it."

"There!" said Lady Matlock, pleased. "*Now* we shall have some music."

"My lady! I could not possibly ask Miss Vaughn to make an exhibition of herself," stammered Mr. King in shock.

"Why not?" cried the countess belligerently.

Cosima shrugged a shoulder. "I don't mind."

Benedict was aghast. "I am persuaded, Miss Vaughn, that your mother would not approve. You must cancel the concert, Mr. King," he said in a commanding voice.

"You will *not* cancel the concert," said Lady Matlock, just as stoutly. "I was promised a musicale and I shall have it, by God, or I will cancel my subscription! I will go to the Lower Rooms," she threatened. "And I shall take all of Bath society with me."

She glared at Benedict. "You are not at home, Sir Benedict. You can not order us all about like servants. Music, King, and be quick about it."

"I've seen the libretto, Mr. King," Cosima said calmly. "I know most of the songs already. It's simple stuff. A child could do it."

"Let her play, Sir Benedict!" Lady Rose urged him.

"I don't need his permission," Cosima said, annoyed.

Benedict could only bow to the ladies. The alternative was an ugly, degrading scene.

"Never mind *him*, Miss Vaughn," Lady Matlock said with a sneer at the gentleman. "I, Lady Matlock, will give you a note for your mother. I would never permit Rose to exhibit in the Upper Rooms, of course, but there is nothing improper in it, I am persuaded. The society in Bath is exclusive enough,

I daresay. It is not as though she would be playing in *public,* Sir Benedict. This ain't London, after all."

"I think Miss Vaughn is very brave," declared Rose. "Lord Ludham! Do you not agree?"

She could not have applied to anyone more willing to support Miss Vaughn in her scheme. "I think Miss Vaughn is splen-splen-splendid!" stammered his lordship.

"Perhaps Miss Vaughn would like to sing as well?" inquired Lady Serena. She was seated in one of the front chairs, and looked impeccable in a gown of sapphire blue satin.

"My voice is too small for that, I'm sorry to say," Cosima replied. "It would never fill a concert hall. I'd sound like a tiny bird crying out in the wilderness. But thanks for asking."

Ludham was determined not to stutter this time. "I am sure you sing beautifully, Miss Vaughn," he said.

Cosima rewarded his effort with a benevolent smile. Then, for some reason, she seemed to think it necessary to address the company at large. There was really nothing to say, but she seemed determined. "I'll just have a word with the signora," she announced, spreading her hands. "I'll be back in a squeeze, and you won't be disappointed. Sit tight!"

She followed the master of ceremonies into the anteroom, and everyone began to talk at once. Shielded by her fan, Serena whispered to Benedict, who had taken the chair next to her. "Will this be a disaster, do you think?" she asked him.

"Undoubtedly."

"How exactly does one sit tight?" Serena laughed.

Lady Dalrymple angrily declared that her Millicent played far better than Miss Vaughn, but that modesty had prevented her from putting herself forward. Miss Carteret, ever the dutiful daughter, agreed with her mother vehemently. Overhearing them, Lady Matlock said derisively, "You forget, dear; some of us have actually heard your Millie play."

Lady Dalrymple pretended not to hear the countess. "There is Mr. Fitzwilliam, Millie," she whispered to her child. "Make sure you tell him how much you like the Church."

Serena spoke again to Benedict from behind her fan. "To imagine that she could take the place of a professional concert pianist—! Evidently, her conceit knows no bounds. I only hope that you are right, and that her behavior will give Felix a disgust for her. So immodest in putting herself forward, and so disrespectful to her elders, too."

"Elders?" he said sharply.

"Why, she treated you with scorn, Sir Benedict, just now, when you tried to advise her."

Benedict did not like being thought of as one of Miss Vaughn's elders. He was only thirty-eight. "I should never have presumed to advise her," he said. "I am not her guardian."

Miss Vaughn returned in a few minutes, followed by the soloist who was a wide, sallow woman swathed in rustling burnt-orange silk. Cosima looked wild, Benedict thought with despair, if there was such a thing as an angel that had escaped cultivation. Her hair was coming down. Her cheeks were flushed. By tomorrow, everyone in Bath would have a disgust for her. Why could she not simply do as she was told?

"Hullo again," she greeted her audience cheerfully. "Thanks for coming."

The attempt at humor only seemed to puzzle her English audience.

Without further ado, she sat down at the instrument. At a signal from the soprano, she began to play. The melody was pure and simple, almost completely unadorned. Its simplicity was meant to showcase the voice of the singer, and not the skill of the pianist. Any competent student of the pianoforte could have managed to play it reasonably well. And Cosima, Benedict was relieved to discover, was at least competent. He had had his doubts.

Serena tittered over her libretto. "She is out of order already. This song should be last, according to the libretto. Will you translate, Sir Benedict?"

He did not need to glance at the libretto. Miss Vaughn was playing "Caro mio Ben."

"I don't speak Italian," he said curtly.

In the course of playing the quiet melody, Cosima's slim body rocked back and forth slightly, and her small breasts swelled creamily against the top of her white gown. Her face was sublime. She had sung this simple song to him the night they met. She was playing it now to bewitch him. He was bewitched. Without looking around, he knew that every other man in the room had fallen under her spell, too, but that was their tough luck.

The ladies were not so easily enchanted.

Serena was tone-deaf. For her, the greatest pleasure of a concert was the pleasure of being seen, admired, and envied by those less endowed than herself in taste, beauty, and breeding. "Pray," she whispered to her companion, "is she disgracing herself?"

She was delighted when he quietly explained that the music was simple enough for any good student of music to play. At least she need not fear that Miss Vaughn was a virtuoso. A plan formed in her head. If she could lure Miss Vaughn into playing something beyond her skill, then the Irish girl would be exposed as a fraud. Her admirers would begin to laugh at her. They would ridicule her failure, and forget about her success. That was the way of the polite world.

Lord Ludham adored little Miss Vaughn now, but he was an impressionable young man, always eager to do what was pleasing and right in the eyes of the world. It had been quite easy, in fact, to convince him to divorce his wife, once her betrayal was made known to him. *If the world turns against Miss Vaughn, so will Felix,* Serena thought confidently. *Then Felix will return to* me, *as he always does when his ego suffers a blow. I will send Sir Benedict to the rightabout; and everyone will be happy.* By everyone, she meant herself, of course.

At the interval, when the party went into the tea room, Serena insisted on being introduced to the heroine, the very thing she had avoided for weeks. Benedict obliged her, and did not even cringe when Miss Vaughn explained, once again, that she was Italian in her heart.

Serena inclined her head like a queen receiving homage. "Why, Sir Benedict, she is charming!" She smiled, laying her hand on Benedict's arm possessively. "You *must* bring her to my card party on Friday, Sir Benedict."

"I would be happy to do so," Benedict replied.

Cosima's back stiffened. She did not care for Lady Serena's patronizing tone. The other woman also seemed to be having a little trouble keeping her hands to herself. "Thank you! But I do not play cards," she said coldly.

"Do come, Miss Vaughn!" Lord Ludham pleaded. "If you do not play cards, I will be happy to partner you and teach you the game."

She turned her green eyes full on him, and he was struck dumb. It was as if he had suddenly come face to face with a tiger. "I do not approve of gambling," said Miss Vaughn. "Gambling has been the ruin of my family."

"Felix!" Serena chided him. "Not everyone can afford to play deep, you know."

Lord Ludham regrouped and attacked Miss Vaughn from another angle. "There will be dinner, as well, at Serena's party. You eat, don't you?"

Serena frowned. She had not thought to put herself to the trouble and expense of feeding her guests a formal dinner. "Perhaps Miss Vaughn does not approve of eating," she said, eyeing the other woman's slim figure. "Perhaps that is why she is so thin in her person."

Cosima was the only one at the table not eating. Benedict had supplied her with a plate of rich food and a glass of punch, but she hadn't touched them.

"Is the food not to your liking?" Rose asked, concerned. "Is there something else you would like? The pâté is very good."

"I'm not very hungry," Cosima said.

"I know!" said Ludham. "Serena has a pianoforte, don't you,

Serena? You could play for us, Miss Vaughn. *Do* say you'll come. It will be so flat without you. We'll be bored to sobs."

"Thank you, Felix," Serena said dryly.

"Miss Vaughn has already declined the invitation," said Benedict. "Twice."

"Is there nothing I can say to persuade you to come and entertain us, Miss Vaughn?" Serena asked. "I think you will find a *private* exhibition more pleasant than a public one."

Cosima suddenly blinded them with a smile. "I should be delighted to come and play for your guests, Lady Serena," she said in a startling reversal. "I confess, now that I no longer have an instrument of my own, I'm always eager for the opportunity to practice."

"So we have observed," Serena said.

"I won't even charge you a fee, I'm that rusty," said Miss Vaughn.

"You don't have a pianoforte, Miss Vaughn?" Ludham exclaimed. "I call that tragic."

"Perhaps we should take up a collection," Serena drawled.

"I'm sort of between pianos at the moment," Cosima said. "I have my heart set on the most beautiful new Clementi. My old Erard just wasn't cutting it anymore."

"Cutting what, Miss Vaughn?" Ludham asked, confused.

She laughed. "I just mean it wasn't fast enough for the new music. I saw a piece the other day marked '*prestissimo*'! I can barely manage 'allegro' as it is."

"I find that very hard to believe," Serena said coolly.

From her end of the table, Lady Matlock looked up from her platter of lobster patties and cream puffs. "You may come to me in the Crescent any time you like, Miss Vaughn, and play on my pianoforte. Have you brought your harp with you, Miss Vaughn?"

Cosima looked at her blankly. "My harp?"

"You're Irish, aren't you? You must have a harp."

"I left my harp in Ireland, Lady Matlock."

"You must send for it, my dear."

Cosima only smiled.

"Do come and see us tomorrow, Miss Vaughn!" Rose urged her. "We'll play duets and be so merry. Not that my talent is anything to yours," she added prettily. "But I could do with the practice."

The second half of the concert began in a flurry of Scarlatti love songs, and nearly ended in a most shocking scandal. Glancing at her audience at the top of "O cessate di pia-garmi," Miss Vaughn struck a false note, and winced. "I beg your pardon!" she cried, red in the face. She started again, but her nerves seemed unable to recover, and she stumbled on with clumsy fingers.

"The facade crumbles," Serena murmured complacently to Benedict. "Her lack of skill is beginning to show."

Benedict did not think so. Miss Vaughn seemed to be trying to catch Lady Rose Fitzwilliam's eye. Glancing over, he saw the problem instantly. The child's left breast, too large to be contained by a mere wisp of lace, had made an unsched-uled appearance in the Upper Rooms. So far, no one but Miss Vaughn and himself seemed to have noticed.

Benedict did what any gentleman would have done in his place.

He summoned the waiter.

Chapter 10

When he had obtained the necessary implement, Benedict rose from his chair and made his way across the front row. As he passed Lady Matlock, who mercifully had her eyes closed, his foot caught against Rose's chair. He stumbled convincingly, waking Lady Matlock, and temporarily blocking Rose's view of the performance.

"For heaven's sake!" Rose snapped angrily, looking over his shoulder. "Why must you be so stupid?"

"Really, Sir Benedict!" said Lady Matlock.

Benedict begged their ladyships' pardon profusely, and when he straightened up again, Rose's breast, as if by magic, was again shielded from view by its scrap of lace. Cosima had no idea how he had managed it, but he *had* managed it, and, apparently, with no one but herself being the wiser.

"Down in front," Lord Ludham said angrily as the baronet temporarily blocked his view. Like his cousin, he was also tone-deaf. Miss Vaughn could have hammered out anything she liked on the pianoforte, and he would have thought it splendid.

Benedict made his way slowly to the back of the room. By degrees, he returned to his chair, adopting a circuitous route that avoided both Rose and her mother.

Miss Vaughn recovered her confidence, and the rest of the

concert passed without incident. At its conclusion, none but the most mean-spirited made any reference to the one song that had given the pianist so much difficulty. Everyone sang her praises—to her face, at any rate. She had a smile for everyone. Lord Ludham remained fixed at her side like a guard dog.

Rather than fight his way through her admirers, Benedict remained seated with Serena.

"I don't see what all the fuss is about," Serena sniffed. "She is as thin a broomstick, and wild as a mushroom. Felix is more infatuated with her than ever," she added angrily. "You told me twenty minutes would do the trick. I think you are on *her* side," she accused him.

"Miss Vaughn will never marry Lord Ludham," he replied with simple confidence.

"And those pearls! The size of hazelnuts! They must be fake. Do you think she bleaches her hair? She must. Outside of a newborn babe or a ninety-year-old woman, I have never seen hair so white. And it doesn't hold a curl very well," she added maliciously.

Benedict thought idly that Miss Vaughn's hair would spread very nicely on a pillow, but said nothing. How could he have been so foolish as to ask this mean and petty woman to be his wife? He longed to withdraw his offer of marriage. But that would not be the act of a gentleman. Serena might even drag him to court with a breach of promise suit. Under oath, he would not be able to deny that he had made the offer.

"Her gown, Sir Benedict!" Serena went on. "It looks like a slip tossed over a petticoat. And she is too tall to wear high-heeled shoes. Why, she quite towers over Felix."

Miss Vaughn happened to glance their way at just that moment. She was still engaged in conversation with one of her conquests, but she smiled at Benedict with her eyes.

For one heart-stopping moment, they were the only two people in the room, in the world. He loved her, and she loved him. Then something Ludham said distracted her, and made her laugh. "Are you listening to me?" Serena demanded.

"Harpy," he said.

Serena gasped. "I beg your pardon?"

Benedict cleared his throat. "I was just wondering about the lady's harp."

Serena frowned. "Why?" Then her violet eyes lit up as a possibility occurred to her. "Oh, I see! You suspect she is lying about her harp. Left her harp in Ireland, indeed! Along with her carriage, her *castle,* and her golden crown, I suppose!"

A few moments later, Cosima extricated herself from the crowd and made her way to him, trailing her most persistent admirer, Lord Ludham.

Benedict climbed to his feet. "I promised your mother I would have you home by eleven o'clock. Perhaps you would like a chair, after all?" he added, glancing down at her feet.

"I'll walk, thank you," she replied coolly.

"Walk!" cried Ludham. "Let me summon you a chair!"

"No, indeed," she told him, laughing. "If I get tired, I can always climb on Cousin Ben's back and let him carry me home. He's an excellent walker. Legs like carved marble."

Lord Ludham made a mental note to begin a regimen of daily exercise.

Benedict took his leave of Serena, bending over her hand. Cosima frowned. She could not quite puzzle out Benedict's relationship to this cold, superior female. Serena was beautiful, but rather like a sculpture. They made a handsome couple. The sight of them together disturbed her. She retaliated, giving Lord Ludham her hand to kiss.

"Good night, Miss Vaughn," Serena said coldly, tucking her hand into the crook of Lord Ludham's arm.

Cosima took Benedict firmly by the arm. "Good night!"

They walked out of the concert hall into Beaufort Square. She decided to say nothing about Lady Serena. She did not want him to think she was jealous.

"Do you think I should tell Lady Rose what you did for her

tonight?" she asked instead. "She's putting it about that you were stumbling drunk!"

He shrugged.

"You don't mind?"

"I did what had to be done," he said piously. "I do not expect to be thanked."

"But the damage to your spotless reputation!" she protested, laughing.

He glanced at her. "Perhaps I do not deserve my reputation."

"I'm glad to hear it," she said. "Well, they say a good deed is its own reward. And you *did* get to feel a young girl's breast, after all. How was it?"

"You wrong me. I never touched her. I used a spoon."

"A spoon!"

"Yes. Given the enormity of the—"

"Breast?" she suggested.

"Task," he coldly corrected, "I felt a soup spoon would be best. For the lady's comfort, naturally, I warmed the metal with my breath. I shudder to think what would have happened if I had used a cold spoon."

"Aye!" she said, laughing. "If I am ever so unfortunate as to come out of my clothes, I can only hope that you'll be there to help."

"Don't worry, Miss Vaughn," he assured her. "I will be. There is something about a woman's breast that awakens all my protective instincts."

"That's quite as it should be. I realize you were busy and all," she began anew, after a brief silence, "but did you happen to notice the concert at all? Other people seemed to enjoy it."

"Yes, they did. The signora sang well, I think. There was even a song about me."

"Was there?"

"*Caro mio ben, credimi almen* . . . Something like that."

"Oh, that. Shall I translate? There once was an old man

named Ben. He wasn't the smartest of men. He forgot where he was; took off all of his clothes; and couldn't get them back on again. The second verse is a bit insulting, so I'll stop there."

"Very amusing," said the gentleman. "I especially like the way you forced a rhyme between 'was' and 'clothes.'"

As Lansdown Road became increasingly steep, she could no longer keep up the pace in her high-heeled shoes. "Stop a minute. My feet are killing me," she said. Leaning down, she pulled off her shoes. "Much better," she breathed, picking them up with two fingers.

"I did warn you," he said, slowing down. "And now we've come too far to get a chair. Do you think you can manage?"

"I can manage very well, thank you," she said primly. "It's not Dublin, after all, where the streets are paved in broken glass. Sure, Bath is as neat as a pin. You'd think it was licked clean by the angels every night."

"I have been to Dublin, Miss Vaughn," he said severely. "The streets are *not* paved in broken glass, as I'm sure you know. It is a very pretty little town."

"I'm sure it is, from your hotel window!" she retorted. "When were *you* ever in Dublin?"

"I have business at Dublin Castle from time to time."

"Oh, they're very refined at Dublin Castle. They *always* take the trouble to tidy up after their drunken routs at Dublin Castle. How is it I never saw you there?"

"At Dublin Castle?" he asked blankly.

She nodded. "Aye, at Dublin Castle! Or don't those feet of yours know how to dance?"

Belatedly, he comprehended that she was talking about balls given by the lady-lieutenant, while he had been speaking of official business with the lord-lieutenant. "I do not go to Ireland to attend balls, Miss Vaughn," he explained.

"Why not?" she demanded. "Don't you like Irish girls?"

"Some of them are quite nice," he admitted. "But others are heartless and cruel."

"Ah, so you do like us!"

He smiled. "There is a lecture tomorrow night on Merovingian Art," he said presently. "Perhaps you would care to give it?"

She shook her head. "I only lecture on the evils of drink and gambling."

"Thursday, of course, is the dreaded Cotillion. Now, *that* actually is a participatory event. No one will be amazed if you join in."

"Not I! I've no intention of turning into a social butterfly." She laughed. "I said I'd go to your lady friend's party, but that's it. Allie would have a fit if I started going out every night."

"She is back in school," he said. "How does she like it?"

She came to a stop. "You can ask her yourself," she said.

Benedict looked around in amazement. It seemed to him that they had just left the Upper Rooms, but already they were in Camden Place, standing outside her door. Allegra Vaughn was sitting on the steps huddled in a shawl.

"What are you doing out of bed?" Cosima demanded angrily. "You have school tomorrow!"

"For your information," Allie replied importantly, "it's dire!"

"What's dire?" Cosima demanded. "What's happened?"

She ran up the steps, but stopped in front of her sister, as if afraid to go any farther. "I *told* you I couldn't go out," she said angrily, turning on Benedict. "Now look what's happened!"

He walked up the steps quietly. "What *has* happened, Miss Allegra?"

"Well," said Allie, enjoying her moment, "he's been here for hours, waiting to see you, Cosy, and he says he won't go away until he gets his money."

"Is that all?" Cosima cried in relief. "I thought it was Mother's health! Dire indeed!"

"Who is here, Miss Allegra?" Benedict asked.

Wincing, Cosima hazarded a guess. "The landlord?"

"No! Not the landlord," Allie replied scornfully. "The collier! He was *not* pleased when Mama told him you'd gone out to the concert. Well, actually, *I* told him. He said young ladies ought to pay their bills before they go out to fancy concerts and such."

"Did he?" Benedict said coldly.

Allie's eyes lit up. She wasn't used to generating so much interest from gentlemen. They usually only paid attention to her elder sister. "He did! He said we owe so much money that Cosy will have to marry him to get out from under it, even if she is the granddaughter of an earl. I thought Mama would faint! However, she did not. She said she'd never survive debtor's prison, and that *of course* Cosy would marry him."

"I will bollocks," said Miss Vaughn, with feeling. "Where's Jackson?"

"You didn't pay the collier's bill?" Benedict said incredulously. "I gave you a thousand pounds! What did you do with it?"

"I am not wasting my hard-earned money on coal!" Cosy said, starting into the house.

"Are you sure you want your future husband to see you in your underwear?" Allie asked.

Cosima skidded to a stop. "Oh, God, you're right! I'll have to put some clothes on."

"*What?*" said Benedict. "Miss Vaughn! Is that a slip, thrown over a petticoat?"

"No," she answered.

"Go and put some clothes on," he said grimly. "I will deal with the collier."

Cosima opened her mouth to protest, but closed it again. He looked different, somehow. Sort of scary. "Come, Allie," she said. Taking her sister by the hand, she entered the house with her head held high.

"There you are, you little slut," said a burly man at the top of the stairs. Nora ran after him and caught his arm, but he shook her off easily.

"That's him!" Allie said, quite unnecessarily.

The man waved a bill at them. "You owe me twenty

pounds, Miss Vaughn," he said, charging down the stairs like an angry bull, "and you'll pay me now, my beauty, or I'll take it out of your hide."

"You can try," said Miss Vaughn with magnificent calm. "Who do you think you are coming here and bothering my mother? I'll have the law on you."

"The law! On me! That's rich, coming from you," replied her tormentor. "Oh, you've plenty of money to go out on the town, I see," he panted angrily. "In your pretty white dress! Hoping to catch yourself a rich husband, I daresay! And who will marry you, pretty as you are, with nothing but debt for a dowry? You're lucky I'm an honest man and marriage-minded, that's all I have to say. Some others might not be so nice."

Cosima calmly picked up an umbrella from the stand and brandished it. "You have two choices now. You can leave quietly, or you can leave *very* quietly, with your brain leaking out of your skull. It doesn't matter to me, but it might matter to you."

The burly man swelled up with righteous indignation. "How dare you threaten me! I'll throw you in prison until you are ready to listen to reason!" He roared in pain as Nora Murphy suddenly jumped on his back and ripped at his greasy hair.

Benedict slammed the door, startling everyone. He had seen enough of this tedious, farcical melodrama. What troubled him the most was that Miss Vaughn seemed quite used to dealing with impertinent tradesmen. "You!" he said, pointing at the most egregious offender.

"Me?" cried Nora, trembling.

"You," he affirmed. "Get down from there. This is not a circus, I trust."

Nora obediently hopped down.

"Thank you, sir," the collier said gratefully, rubbing his head.

Benedict smiled at him thinly. "Did you say this young lady owes you twenty pounds?"

The collier realized at once that he was dealing with a gentleman of means. He eyed Benedict warily. "That's right, sir. She's been taking advantage of my generous nature. Of course, if you'd care to pay the debt yourself, sir, I've no objection."

"You have not yet established to my satisfaction that there *is* a debt," Benedict pointed out. "Thus far we have only established that you are a bully."

The collier looked astonished. "A bully? Me?"

"You."

"Well, I never—! Who the devil are you, sir?" the tradesman demanded angrily.

"Who am I?" Benedict repeated, getting into the dramatic spirit. "I am Wrath, collier. Wrath. Perhaps you have heard of me?"

The collier shook his head.

"That's because I had neither father nor mother," Benedict explained. "I leapt out of a lion's mouth when I was scarce an hour old; and ever since have run up and down the world with a case of rapiers, wounding myself when I could get none to fight withal. That's how I lost my arm, as a matter of fact. I was born in Hell, collier! Does that clear it all up for you?"

"Oh God!" said Nora, her eyes starting from her head.

"I thought you said he was our cousin," Allie whispered to Cosy.

"Well, Mr. Wrath," puffed the collier, blinking at Benedict in confusion, "be that as it may! I have business with this young lady—"

"Not half as much business as you have with me," said Benedict very quietly.

The collier began to stammer. "Sir! I don't know what this Irish hussy has told you, but she owes money all over town. Did she tell you that?"

"No, she didn't," Benedict said.

"Well, it's none of your business!" said Cosima.

"None whatsoever," he agreed. "Collier! You say she owes you *twenty* pounds?"

"She ordered a great deal of coal, Mr. Wrath."

Benedict raised a brow. "Did she? Where is it?"

"She must have used it," the other man replied stubbornly.

Benedict's eyes narrowed. "Twenty pounds' worth? She's only been here two months. Tell me, collier. Do you cheat *all* your female customers, or just the pretty ones?"

"I *told* you everything was exorbitant!" Cosima triumphantly declared.

"Forgive me," said Benedict. "I thought you were exaggerating. May I see the bill?"

"It would seem I accidentally brought the wrong bill with me," said the collier, stuffing papers into his coat.

"Indeed," said Benedict. "I suggest you go home and find the correct bill! When you have found it, kindly present it to *me* at Number Six, Lower Camden Place, and I will be happy to take a look at it. My name is Sir Benedict Wayborn. I will tell my man to expect you tomorrow at eight o'clock."

"I thought you said you was Mr. Wrath!" the collier protested.

"That was a little joke," Benedict explained.

The collier laughed weakly. "Very funny, sir."

"You may go, collier," said Benedict. "You may exit stage left while I continue the scene with these young ladies. And thank you for laughing at my joke. Not everyone appreciates my sense of humor."

"What was all that?" Cosima demanded, closing the door on the collier. "Mr. Wrath!"

"That was a speech from a play we did in school," he said modestly. "*Doctor Faustus*. Do you know it? No? The title character sells his soul to the devil in exchange for knowledge, power, and, of course, Helen of Troy for a paramour."

"Gracious!" said Nora.

"What's a paramour?" Allie demanded.

"I don't know," said Benedict.

"So you're not Wrath at all?" Allie said disappointed. "You're only Cousin Ben?"

"To you, I am Cousin Ben. To your enemies, Miss Allegra, I am Mr. Wrath."

"What about the butcher?" Allie asked excitedly. "And the greengrocer? We owe *them* lots of money, too!"

Exasperated, Benedict glanced at the elder girl. "Perhaps Miss Vaughn would be so kind as to provide me with a list of her creditors," he said.

"I will," Cosima said, herding Allie up the stairs. "Tomorrow! Right now, I have to check on my mother, and get this girl into bed. Nora will let you out."

"Until tomorrow then," he said quietly. "Good night."

As he watched the two sisters go upstairs, he wondered how many men had tried to take advantage of Miss Vaughn in this shabby way. As he went out, he glanced at the stooped woman holding the door for him. "Good night, Nora."

"How do you know my name?" she cried in terror.

"I'm clairvoyant," he said dryly. He bit his lip, remembering that he needed to stay in Nora's good graces. Otherwise she might raise "holy hell," and prevent her young lady from leaving the house. Perhaps sarcasm was not the best way to endear himself to the Irishwoman.

Nora plucked up her courage. "She's a good lass, and you're a bad man!"

Benedict saw that they would never be friends. In any case, it was better to be feared than loved. He smiled at her coldly. "If you ever try to keep her from me, I will show you, Nora, what a bad man I can be."

"Oh God!" Nora breathed, closing the door on him as quickly as she could.

Benedict used his key to enter the park. He waited for her there, lingering just inside the gate for what seemed like hours, looking out through the iron bars like a prisoner. Twice he saw the constable of the Watch pass. The man was unpleasantly conscientious.

Finally, the lights in the Vaughns' house began to go out, one by one. The Watchman passed by once more, whistling. A few minutes later, Benedict's heart jumped as a figure in a dark cloak came out of the house and ran toward the park. She was in her stockinged feet. Her feet made no sound on the cold cobbles.

She gasped in surprise when he opened the gate for her.

"Hurry," he whispered, pulling her inside the park. "The Watchman has been unusually diligent this evening."

"Anyone would think we were committing a crime the way we have to sneak around," she said, locking the gate. She turned to look at him. *He always looked perfect,* she thought enviously. She always looked thrown together. She had been in such a hurry to go to him that she had done little more than tuck her own hair under her mother's wig and throw a cloak over her petticoats. She ran with him across the park in her bare feet, her teeth chattering.

As they reached the gate on the other side, she caught his arm.

"The constable," she said softly.

It was so perfectly quiet that he was moved to quote Macbeth. "'Now o'er the one half-world Nature seems dead, and wicked dreams abuse the curtained sleep.' All the good people of Bath are in their beds, sleeping."

She reached for his face. "It's just you, and me, and the bloody constable makes three," she whispered, pressing her mouth to his. Her mouth and hands were cold.

"Come," he said. "Let's get you warm."

He unlocked the gate, and together they went up the steps to his door. She slipped inside the warm house first. Benedict was in the act of following her, when a voice startled him.

"You, there!"

He turned. The busy constable was running up the street

with his lantern. Cosima stood just inside the door, holding her breath.

"Yes, Watchman?" Benedict said pleasantly.

The constable stopped to catch his breath. "I beg your pardon, sir!" he panted. "I thought I saw a woman, sir!"

"Do I look like a woman to you?" Benedict asked sternly.

"No, sir!" stammered the watchman. "I think she went into the park."

"Only residents of Camden Place are given keys to the park," Benedict said sternly. "You must have been hallucinating."

"Yes, sir," said the constable, unwilling to openly disagree with one of his betters. "But we've had reports, sir, of a woman thief. Only last week a gentleman was stripped, robbed, and left tied to a tree in that park. You'll want to be careful, sir."

"He had it coming," said Benedict.

"Sir?"

"Nothing. Thank you, Constable."

He entered the house and closed the door. "I'm a very bad man," he said sadly. "Lying to a constable of the Watch."

"I think you're nice," she said, opening the door to the study.

"I can't let you do this anymore," Benedict told her sternly when they were safely in his study. "It's too dangerous. I shudder to think what might have happened if that brute managed to get his hands on you."

She sat down on the ottoman in front of the fire and peeled off her wet stockings, stuffing them into the pocket of her cloak. She put her cold feet up on the fender. The warmth of the fire felt lovely. She unclasped her cloak and let it fall, stretching out her bare arms toward the fire. She fully expected him to try to ravish her, and she was not quite sure she wanted to continue resisting. It was a moot point, however. The gentleman made no attempt to ravish her.

Instead, Benedict poured her a brandy, and insisted that she accept it. She took a cautious sip. He poured one for himself and looked at her: "Miss Cherry" in her white "dress" with her red "hair" spilling down her back was a beautiful sight.

"If I were a man, he wouldn't bother me," she said resentfully.

"If you were a *gentleman,* he wouldn't bother you," he corrected her.

She looked at him shyly. "It was nice of you to walk me through the park, though."

He finished his drink all in one. "Come," he said, going out of the room through the side door. She followed him, but stopped on the threshold of his fire-lit bedroom. The big bed of carved oak dominated the space. With its dark, half-closed curtains it looked like a small stage. The threshold was cold marble. She gulped down the rest of her brandy and took one small step onto the plush rug. She was in a man's bedroom. A *gentleman's* bedroom, she corrected herself.

"I don't know, Ben," she called to him nervously. "I don't think I'm ready for this."

He appeared in a doorway on the other side of the room. "Get in here, you fool," he said impatiently. He disappeared again.

She walked slowly past the bed, as if fearing that someone might jump out and attack her. His black robe and white nightshirt had been neatly laid out on the coverlet—by his valet, no doubt. The master's slippers were on the floor waiting for him.

In the next chamber, he was lighting the candles in the sconces on either side of a huge, floor-length mirror. The other walls were shrouded in black crepe. Cosima shivered. "What are you doing, Ben?" she asked fearfully. "What is this place?"

He looked at her, candlelight dancing in his eyes. "This? This is my dressing room," he said, tugging at her hand.

She resisted him. "What's behind the black curtains?" she asked fearfully.

"What? Mirrors, I'm sorry to say. For a gouty old man, Skeldings certainly was vain."

Superstitious dread took hold of her. "Mirrors! Why did you cover them up?" she cried. "Are you practicing black magic or something?"

"Black magic?" he scoffed. "Don't be silly. Unlike Skeldings, I am essentially a modest man. I don't need to see myself from every angle. In fact, I prefer not to. Now, get in here."

He dragged her inside, and closed the door. Turning around, she saw that even the back of the door was shrouded in black crepe. She gasped as his hand touched her shoulder and whirled around to face him. "Why have you brought me in here?" she asked, trembling.

"Clothes make the man," he said enigmatically, pressing against the frame of the only mirror that had been left uncovered. To her astonishment, a door opened.

"How did you do that?" she whispered in awe of his supernatural powers.

"There's a spring mechanism," he replied, making her feel foolish. "This is my closet. I thought I might lend you some of my clothes. From a distance, you would look like a gentleman, and the constable would leave you alone. Trousers or breeches?"

She gaped at him.

"Trousers or breeches, girl?"

"I like what you're wearing now," she finally volunteered. "You always look so nice."

"I see. You want the clothes from my back," he said. "Very well."

He pushed her behind the mirrored door. The cool, dark closet smelled strongly of cedar.

"You can change in there," he explained, overriding her protests.

It took her but a few seconds to slip out of her petticoats. He handed her his clothing piece by piece, but instead of putting them on, she stood numb and mute as she watched him undress. She had seen him nude before, but she had not thought him attractive. Now the sight of him fascinated her.

His manhood was not in retreat now as it had been in her

cold kitchen. Almost scarlet, it stood up proudly. Looking at it, she could not help but think of how he had used the women in the brothels. Had they liked it?

"Everything all right in there?" he called.

"Aye!" She picked up his clothes, still warm from his body, and began to put them on. They smelled of him. He had even unpinned the sleeve of his coat for her. She found this simple act of thoughtfulness ridiculously touching.

When she stepped out of the closet in her new clothes, he was just returning from the bedroom. The nightshirt and robe that had been waiting on the bed had found their way onto the master's body. The slippers that had been waiting for him were on his feet. If he knew she had been spying on him, he gave no sign.

He studied her critically. The coat was big in the shoulders. The trousers were a little too long, and too big in the waist, but her womanly hips held them up. *Who knew I had womanly hips?* she thought, looking at herself in the mirror. She even had a bottom, apparently.

She assured him that, although she was no seamstress, she would be able to take the breeches in at the waist. Instead of stockings and shoes, he gave her a pair of boots. There was a padded bench in the dressing room. She sat down and pulled the boots on. They were too big. She would have to stuff the toes with newspaper.

Benedict guided her through the process of tying a neck-cloth. The result was lopsided. "It will do, I suppose," he said finally. "It's just for show. Like Nora's three shillings."

Nora was, in fact, laying in wait for her young lady when she came home. Her dark eyes started when she saw Cosima's male attire. He had even given her his best silk hat, beneath which she had tucked as much hair as she could.

"What's the bad man done to you now, Miss Cosy?" she cried.

"Nothing!" replied the young lady, promptly bursting into sobs.

Chapter 11

Serena cared about as much for Merovingian art as she did for Italian love songs, but she enjoyed any social gathering that Lady Matlock did not attend. When the countess was not underfoot, Serena was the highest ranking lady in Bath, a privilege she greatly enjoyed.

As Serena's escort, Benedict was fortunate enough to be allowed to fetch her ladyship's lemonade, fan, and shawl. Long ago, he had accepted the yoke of social obligation, but never before had he been forced to take the cold metal bit of it into his mouth. He didn't like the taste.

"How is little Miss Vaughn?" Serena asked him, but, fortunately, she could not be bothered to wait for a reply. "Lady Dalrymple has been telling me such interesting stories about Miss Vaughn and no less a personage than *the Duke of Kellynch*."

Serena intoned the name of this notorious philanderer in a keen whisper.

"Apparently, His Grace visited Miss Vaughn several times when the Dalrymples were staying at this place of hers in Ireland, this so-called castle. But, curiously, none of the Kellynch *ladies* ever did. It would seem our wild Irish girl is not as pure as she would have us believe."

"What utter nonsense," Benedict snapped. "The Duke of Kellynch is the patron of her father's regiment. It is only natural that His Grace should take an interest in the welfare of the colonel's wife and children."

Serena laughed gaily, drawing looks from the lecturer, a small, dry man, who evidently took his Merovingian art very seriously. "His Grace has but one interest in my sex. You and I both know the name Kellynch is a byword for debauchery. Same as his father before him." She glanced at him archly. "Oh, I *am* sorry. I had forgotten that the lady is a distant cousin of yours. But, perhaps, the relationship is closer than we had thought?"

Benedict silently cursed himself. His attempt to defend Miss Vaughn was only making Serena suspicious. "I would hate to see any lady's reputation diminished by vicious gossip," he said. "That is all."

"A lady must live a life above reproach to deserve being called so."

"If Kellynch *did* have designs on the girl, it would appear she has eluded him in coming to Bath. That must be to her credit."

"Perhaps he has grown tired of her," Serena suggested.

Something almost like a snort escaped the gentleman.

Serena read him like a book. "You do not think it possible that any man could grow tired of the beautiful Miss Vaughn, I collect. Indeed, sir, you are discomposed! I seem to have stumbled upon a secret. Now that I think of it, Miss Vaughn *does* look at you a great deal."

"Nonsense."

She laughed. "I am not accusing you of anything. I am well aware that you have no intention of marrying *her*. You need someone to preside at your table, a consummate hostess. Someone who can further your political ambitions. That is decidedly not Miss Vaughn."

"Exactly so."

"But this could be to our advantage," she said. "You forget how fascinating an older man like yourself can be to an ignorant young female. No doubt, she sees you as a sophisticated

man of the world, which you are, of course," she added
hastily. "She dreams of being sophisticated herself, and so she
is drawn to you like a moth to the flame. If you could but use
your influence with your pretty cousin to keep her away from
poor, stupid Felix, I should be very well pleased indeed." She
laid her closed fan on his arm, stroking him. "Perhaps pleased
enough to accept your offer of marriage," she suggested.

Benedict suppressed a shudder of revulsion.

"You are asking me to seduce Miss Vaughn? You, a woman,
ask me this?"

"You need not ruin her, of course, unless you want to, for
some mischievous reason of your own. Just keep her away
from Felix. The poor boy has been through enough."

"I'm afraid I must ask you to release me from my offer
of marriage," he said stiffly. "I had no idea you were so unprincipled."

Serena made rapid calculations.

Despite appearances, she was not a wealthy woman. Her
inheritance had run out. She was thirty and not getting any
younger. If she released Sir Benedict, it was by no means certain that she would ever receive another offer of marriage.
The only reason she had not seized on his offer immediately
was that she hoped her cousin Felix might one day turn to her
with love in his eyes. But if she could not bring Felix up to
scratch soon, she would have to marry Sir Benedict after all,
and she knew it.

"No," she said, when she had finished her meditation. "I
don't think I *will* release you. You made me an offer of marriage. It is hardly the act of a gentleman to withdraw it!" She
smiled coldly. "And if you *dare* to jilt me, and marry another,
I assure you, all of society will take *my* part against the lady's.
No respectable woman would ever be at home to your wife.
Your political career would be ruined."

Benedict stared at her. He did not care three straws for his
political career, but the thought of his innocent wife being re-
viled for his own error in judgement sickened him.

Serena laughed suddenly. "I was only teasing you anyway about Miss Vaughn. It was a little test, and, I'm happy to say, you passed. Of course, I am not asking you to seduce her."

After the lecture, it was his privilege to hand her into her sedan chair.

He walked home. His mind was full of ugly thoughts. As he entered Camden Place, he passed a well-dressed gentleman dragging his umbrella along the palings of the park.

"Good evening, sir!" said the stranger.

"Good evening," he answered without thinking.

The gentleman struck him on the rear end with his umbrella.

Benedict stopped. He suddenly felt ten years younger. "Good evening, Miss Cherry."

"That's *Mr.* Cherry to you," she said, taking his arm.

Pickering opened the door for his master. He could not help but notice that Sir Benedict looked unusually pleased with himself. "Good evening, Sir Benedict."

"Pickering, this is Mr. Cherry."

Pickering took the young man's umbrella.

Mr. Cherry began to giggle uncontrollably.

"You may go to bed, Pickering," Benedict said quickly, pushing his young friend into the study. "I shan't need you anymore tonight."

"Very good, Sir Benedict," said Pickering.

Benedict closed the door, but Pickering could still hear the young man giggling like a schoolgirl. Why, he must be drunk! His master was not in the habit of entertaining drunken young men after hours, and "Cherry" was hardly a surname of distinction. Pickering was worried that Sir Benedict had fallen into low company. When, in the next moment, he heard a loud crash from the study, he did not hesitate. He threw open the study door, and stood staring.

His master and the giggling young man had removed their coats and were on the floor wrestling in their shirt sleeves. In their noble exertions, they had inadvertently overset a small table. The branch of candles on it had been toppled, but fortunately the candles had guttered out. Pickering had never suspected that his master had an interest in the ancient Greek sport, but he had evidently pinned the young man down without much trouble. Although younger than his opponent, and blessed with two arms besides, Mr. Cherry was panting and moaning piteously beneath the superior athlete. The baronet was winning handily. Caught up in the excitement, Pickering fought the urge to applaud; he did not want to break Sir Benedict's concentration.

The young man seemed to realize he could not break free by fair means, and to Pickering's indignation, proceeded to violate the rules of the sport. Pickering's eyes narrowed in disgust as the young man's arms encircled Sir Benedict's neck in a python-like hold, while his slender legs, encased in black breeches and boots, stealthily began to slide over his master's hips. This was a blatantly illegal and treacherous move. One's very soul recoiled at the thought of such unsportsmanlike conduct.

"Foul!" Pickering roared. "Look out, Sir Benedict! The dirty bugger is cheating!"

"What the devil—!" Benedict leaped to his feet, his eyes blazing. At the same time, his opponent dove behind the sofa, out of sight. "Pickering, how *dare* you!"

Pickering had never seen his master so angry. He cleared his throat nervously. "I beg your pardon, Sir Benedict, but the young man was clearly cheating! He might have broken your back, heaving about like that!"

"Broken my—! Pickering, what exactly did you think we were doing?"

"Wrestling, of course," said Pickering, wide-eyed. "Isn't that what you were doing?"

From his hiding place, Mr. Cherry shrieked with laughter.

The baronet's mouth twitched. "Yes, of course, that is what we were doing. We were wrestling. Go to bed, Pickering, and do not come near this room again tonight, no matter what you hear. Leave it," he added sharply, as Pickering began picking up the overturned table.

"Very good, Sir Benedict," Pickering sniffed.

He stiffened as he heard the sharp click of the door being locked after him. There had never been locked doors between him and his master before.

"Now then!" said Benedict. "Where were we?"

She climbed to her feet. Her masculine clothes had become disheveled in the wrestling match. Her hat was gone. Her red hair was coming loose from the neat bun she had skewered at the nape of her neck. She had not bothered with the waistcoat, the neckcloth was a muddle, and his lawn shirt was so fine she might as well have been wearing a shirt made of water. Her little breasts pointed provocatively. She was still panting from her exertions and her cheeks were uncommonly rosy.

"That was close," she said breathlessly.

"I apologize for the interruption," he said courteously. "It won't happen again."

"I should go," she said softly.

"You just got here," he pointed out. "You haven't even read to me."

"I'm thinking," she said slowly, "it was a good thing your man came in when he did."

"We were only kissing," he said impatiently. "No one ever went to hell for kissing."

She thought about it. He was perfectly correct. They *had* only been kissing. She felt hot and sweaty. The tips of her breasts were stinging, and there was an uncomfortable ache between her legs, but they had only been kissing. She had never heard of anyone going to hell for that.

"That's true," she said. Her knees were shaking like a newborn fawn's and she needed to sit down. She stumbled around the sofa like a drunkard and half-fell. "But we were lying down and wriggling, too."

"It's not a sin to lie down. Nor to wriggle, if it comes to that. Though I strenuously deny that I wriggled."

"No, that was me," she admitted. But—"

"My dear girl," he said softly, "I am not some rutting beast of the field. I am nothing like that mountebank who frightened you. And I am certainly not like that young idiot who spoiled your dress with his . . . enthusiasm. You made your feelings on the subject plain. I respect your wishes. You have my word I will make no attempt on your virtue. You're perfectly safe with me. You can trust me completely."

She looked crestfallen. "I'm glad to hear it."

He sat down on the ottoman and looked at her gravely. "There are any number of things we might do that are quite pleasurable and not in the least sinful."

Her eyes began to sparkle, but she did not want to seem too eager. "Oh?" she asked faintly. "Like what, for example?"

He pulled off one of the boots she had borrowed from him. She had stuffed newspaper in the toe, but it came off easily. "Kissing, of course," he said, pulling off the other boot. She was not wearing stockings. He began kissing her feet as passionately as he had kissed her lips.

She shrieked in protest and kicked him in the face. He looked at her in surprise.

"Tickles," she explained, her face flaming.

"You must accustom yourself to the idea," he said reproachfully. "I am going to kiss your entire body, and I don't like being kicked in the face."

She caught her breath. As he continued to kiss and fondle her feet and ankles, she licked her lips nervously. "You're joking," she said.

"No, indeed," he said, pausing to feel his nose. "I really don't like being kicked in the face." He returned to her feet, caressing first one and then the other, nibbling her toes while she squirmed and gritted her teeth. He kissed her legs, brushing his fingertips and lips lightly over the tingling flesh, raining tiny goose bumps as he went.

"You're prickling me," she complained. "You need to shave."

"So do you," he retorted, tickling the hair on her legs. It was fine as silk, and so light and sparse it was almost invisible. He was only teasing her, but she took him seriously.

"I suppose," she said contemptuously, "your dirty governess was smooth as glass."

Actually, his governess had been inordinately hairy. He had almost balked when she rolled down her stockings for the first time. And the hair in her armpits had been as thick as the spreading black bush between her stout thighs. Hers was a body only a desperate virgin male could enjoy. There was no comparison between that distant, nightmarish memory and the present reality of these lovely legs.

"You're beautiful," he assured her. "I was only joking."

He opened her breeches at the knee band and began kissing her kneecaps as if he were in love with them. This, obviously, was no sin. It didn't even feel good. Her feet were on either side of him, resting on the ottoman, her shoulders were flat on the sofa, her bottom was resting on his knees, and, as he nuzzled her knees like a madman, his face was directly in line with her womanhood. In fact, he was completely ignoring the parts of her body in which other men showed the most interest. She felt ridiculous and annoyed in this absurd position.

She began to question his sanity. *Just my luck. The only man ever to set my skin on fire, and he's a madman.* Then he began running his tongue along the back of her knees, and she thought, *I must be mad, too.* When he licked her behind the knees, for some strange reason she felt warm all over. Parts of her he hadn't even touched began to prickle and sting. She began to squirm with pleasure. She couldn't help it.

He lifted her shirt—his shirt—and kissed her belly as if she were a baby. Except that, instead of making a raspberry, he kissed her navel. Hers was an odd little button of flesh, rather than a divot. She had always thought it shamefully unattractive. She was horrified and embarrassed when he suddenly took it between his lips. He tickled it keenly with the tip of his tongue, making her giggle as helplessly as a baby. He sucked it and bit it until she screamed at him to stop. He said it was like a baroque pearl, whatever that was. "Very tasty," he murmured. "I wonder what other little buttons you are hiding."

Instinctively, she crossed both arms over her breasts, but he began unbuttoning her breeches. "Ben!" she shrieked, trying to push him away.

"Do not be alarmed, madam," he said. "I am simply removing your breeches. As I have no intention of removing mine, you are perfectly safe."

Her green eyes were enormous. "You're not going to touch me *there!*"

"My dear innocent, I am going to kiss you there."

"Ben!"

He had the flap at the front of the breeches completely unbuttoned, but he had not yet uncovered her. "Why not?" he asked, softly. "It is as much a part of you as your feet or this sweet little button here." He swooped down like a hawk and kissed her belly button again. "If it's all right for me to kiss you here, why not here?"

It was like trying to argue with a Jesuit.

He snuck the breeches down over her hips as he was tickling her navel. Typical male trickery. She felt his hand move between her legs, and, instinctively, her thighs closed around it like iron, trapping him. She moistened her lips nervously. "Ben," she protested faintly.

"Only a caress," he promised softly. "Let me in, sweetheart. Trust me."

His soft, deep voice had the power to melt her bones. He pushed her unresisting legs apart. She squeezed her eyes closed and braced herself, as if for a violent attack. Benedict caught his breath as he looked at her. Tucked between her creamy, slender thighs was the neatest, prettiest little nest he had ever seen. The fine, silky hair was golden-rose in the firelight. It moved delicately as he breathed. He couldn't resist nudging the soft thighs farther apart to reveal the lips, pink and glistening as the inside of a seashell. She was so tiny he could not imagine making love to her without causing her great pain.

"You expect me to trust you," she whispered, "when you behave like this?"

"Yes, I do."

With the utmost care, he parted the delicate folds of silk, skimming his fingertips lightly along the fine, soft hair. He caressed her softly as if she were as fragile as a butterfly, and in the softness, he found the tiny pearl protected by its hood of silky flesh. When he touched her there, she whimpered in the back of her throat. Soon she was so warm, so silky, and so wet, that he couldn't resist tasting her with his mouth. He had never tasted woman flesh before.

"You taste like honey," he told her, wild-eyed.

"I think you're crazy," she said, squirming in an obvious effort to bring his mouth to her again. He took the hint.

With his tongue he parted the innermost, most delicate furrow of her body. It would have been churlish to used his fingers in such a fragile place, of course, but the intimacy was excruciating. Pinned like a butterfly between his mouth and his knees, she quivered helplessly. "Please," she begged. Then he found the little button that seemed connected to every nerve in her body, and she began to moan for release in earnest. Her slender haunches moved up and down luxuriously as if she were bobbing in a gentle ocean. Her hands went to his hair.

The first crisis stole over her little by little, in tiny, lapping waves. She hardly knew what was happening. A second climax, more powerful than the first, wrested a moan from her lips. The third shattered her into pieces. She collapsed, crying out shamelessly.

While she was still dazed and helpless, he laid her back gently on the sofa, then climbed up next to her. They were squeezed close together on the narrow couch. He lay on his right side and gently explored her with his left hand. He caressed her face and neck and shoulders like a blind man. Finally, he untied the strings of her shirt and eased it down over her breasts. She hated her breasts, but she was too warm and lazy to resist him.

Benedict was enchanted by the pale cups, each topped by a tiny, impossibly pink nipple. These were not the perfectly rounded breasts of statues. They had a shape all their own, and the fact that he was the only man in the world who would ever be allowed to see them made him very happy. The breastbone between them was as delicate as a birds. He walked his fingers down the miniature staircase, then back up again.

"They're small," she apologized.

Tiny would have been the accurate word, but she had her pride.

He played with her breasts for a long time, making the nipples erect, then feasting on them. They tasted as tart as wild strawberries. Finally, he settled down on top of her. She felt something massive and too hard to be flesh trapped against her belly.

"Are you not going to undress?" she whispered.

"No," he said.

He must have known she could no longer resist him, but he seemed to take a perverse sort of pleasure in denying himself. He laid on top of her, fully clothed. She could even feel his shoes hard against her naked feet. Her thighs were parted for him. She took him in her arms and he rested his head in the nook of her neck and shoulder.

He didn't kiss her.

After an eternity, he got up and went to pour them both some brandy.

She was suddenly furious with him. She sat up and pulled his shirt back up over her shoulders. It barely covered the soft triangle between her legs, but, at the moment, she didn't know where the rest of her clothes were.

"I suppose," she said, "that nasty governess taught you that dirty little trick!"

"What trick?" he asked innocently.

Innocently!

She refused to answer him. He knew perfectly well what she meant. She was obviously not the first woman he had ravished with his mouth.

"Oh, that trick." Smugly, he settled down on the sofa next to her with his brandy. He put his feet up on the ottoman as if he were putting the harmless piece of furniture back in its place. It really annoyed her that he hadn't even taken his shoes off. "Actually," he said airily, "I learned that at Eton. We practiced on fruit. Why do you think it's called Eton?"

She frowned at him.

"What's Eton?" she demanded, imagining a nightmarish place of unrestrained and unremitting debauchery.

He laughed until he choked. Becoming frightened, she set down her glass and pounded him on the back, forgetting that she was naked. "Oh, my dearest girl," he said fondly, when he had recovered. "I do adore you."

"But what's Eton?" she insisted, snatching up a cushion to cover herself. "What the hell kind of a place is it?"

"Eton," he said gravely, "is where great men send their sons to be educated."

"You learned that *at school?*" she cried, appalled.

"We of Eton carry on a tradition of excellence going back for centuries," he explained.

He laughed. He was a young man when he laughed.

Nora took one look at her young lady's flushed face and sparkling eyes. "He's done for you then," she said grimly.

"You have a dirty mind, Nora Murphy," she said primly, walking up the stairs with her head held high.

"Where's the money, then?" Nora demanded. "If it's only reading you are?"

Cosima paused on the stairs. She had forgotten to get her three shillings.

"Go boil your head, Nora," she said.

The next morning Pickering pretended he had seen and heard nothing the night before. The new day was a tabula rasa as far as he was concerned. He counted his blessings that the mysterious and rather noisy Mr. Cherry had not been invited to stay on as a guest.

Benedict ate his breakfast with a hearty appetite. He read his newspapers and correspondence as usual. He bathed and dressed, and was on the verge of leaving the house when a Dr. Grantham called.

White-haired and handsome, Dr. Grantham was a society physician. Most of his patients were females, and his suave and sympathetic air inspired the fair sex to confide their most delicate issues to him. To Benedict he looked like the typical sort of leech that makes most of his money catering to rich females who fancy themselves nervous.

Dr. Grantham came straight to the point. He wanted Sir Benedict to commit Lady Agatha Vaughn to the Royal Mineral Water Hospital for treatment. As Lady Agatha refused to go, and "the daughter"—presumably Miss Vaughn—refused to make her ladyship go, Dr. Grantham had no choice but to apply to a higher power. He hoped that Sir Benedict Wayborn might use his natural authority over the ladies to bring them into compliance.

Benedict looked at him in amazement. "I have no such authority, I assure you."

The doctor's amazement was equal. "Are you not a relative, Sir Benedict?"

"I am very distant cousin, Dr. Grantham," Benedict replied. The doctor smiled again. "Excellent! If you will just sign these papers, I will be able to remove Lady Agatha to the hospital at once."

"I'm not signing anything," said Benedict. "If Lady Agatha doesn't want to go to the hospital, I certainly will not make her."

"But you must understand, Sir Benedict. Her ladyship is in no condition to make these decisions. Her wits are fragile. She is actually afraid of the hospital—a quite irrational fear, I assure you! As for Miss Vaughn . . ."

"What about Miss Vaughn?" Benedict said sharply.

"I'm afraid the young lady becomes dangerously excited on the subject. I sometimes think Miss Vaughn would benefit from a few months of quiet serenity in my private asylum in Wiltshire." He shrugged. "But, then, she is half-Irish, and breeding will tell."

Benedict decided he did not like Dr. Grantham. "Lady Agatha is frail, to be sure," he conceded. "But that doesn't mean she is incompetent."

"All women are incompetent," said the doctor. "We men must think for them. If there were a man in the picture, Lady Agatha would be hospitalized. And, then, there is the matter of my fee," he went on with a delicate cough. "I can not be expected to treat Lady Agatha indefinitely without being paid."

Benedict sighed. What was the girl doing with the money he had given her?

"Send me the bill," he said. "It will be your final bill."

Dr. Grantham gaped at him. "I beg your pardon?"

"I believe my relative should be in the care of a specialist," Benedict said tactfully. "In any case, I would like a second opinion."

The doctor seemed thunderstruck. "Second opinion! I never heard of such a thing."

He went off in a huff.

Later in the day, when Benedict returned home, Pickering informed him that a Miss Vaughn had called while he was out. Pickering did not approve of young ladies who called on single gentlemen. It was not respectable, in his opinion. Benedict was not interested in his opinion. He walked through the park to Lady Agatha's house.

Cosima was furious with him. She had hired Dr. Grantham back, and she made it plain that Sir Benedict's interference was unwelcome.

"The man is a quack," he said angrily. "Your mother needs a real physician, not some spa practitioner. Dr. Grantham is a charlatan."

"Dr. Grantham," Cosima replied angrily, "is the best doctor in Bath. All the high-born ladies use him. I want my mother to have the best. And, anyway, it's none of your business. She's *my* mother, and *I* will decide what is best for her. You stay out of it!" She hissed and spluttered at him like an angry house cat. "I'm perfectly capable of looking after my mother!"

"Of course," he said stiffly. "But have you considered hiring a private nurse?"

Cosima would have loved to hire a nurse to help her mother, but Lady Agatha did not like strangers looking at her raddled face. They made Lady Agatha feel freakish and ugly. But Cosima could not betray her mother by revealing these weaknesses to *him*. Instead, she shouted at Benedict, "I'm perfectly capable of looking after my own mother!"

"You are quite right," he said coldly. "I was high-handed. Please excuse my interference. I was only trying to help."

"I don't need your help," she said fiercely and showed him the door.

"I don't suppose you are going to the cotillion tonight?" he said, lingering in the doorway.

"No, and I don't want to," she retorted.

"I shall be attending," he said. "But I shall be home at eleven-thirty."

"Good for you," she replied coldly, slamming the door in his face.

* * *

She was late. It was well after midnight when he looked up from his book and said, "Good evening, Miss Cherry."

She looked angry and flustered. "I almost didn't come," she said, flopping down on the sofa and pulling his boots off to expose her pretty white feet.

"I'm sorry," he began. "The doctor came to me—"

She interrupted. "But then I thought: that's between you and Miss Vaughn. It's nothing to do with ourselves."

"Quite," he said, closing his book.

She looked at him expectantly. He must not have thought she was coming, for he was again in his nightshirt and dressing gown. He looked like some pagan prince drawn starkly in black and white. A heat warmer than brandy coursed through her veins as she thought of what he had done to her the night before. As angry as she had been with him for interfering with the doctor, she had come here because she wanted him to do it again.

"Would you like me to read to you?" she asked when he did not attack her immediately.

"No," he said. He just sat in his chair and looked at her, kingly and remote. "I have been thinking about you all day, Miss Cherry," he said finally.

Her breasts began to tingle. "You have?"

"This isn't exactly how I pictured you, however," he said dryly.

She frowned.

"When I am with a woman, I like her to look like a woman. I lent you those clothes so that you could slip past the constable, but, I think, while you are here, we must institute a sort of dress code. You left your clothes on the floor of my closet the other night. Go into the bedroom and put them on. If you are wearing drawers, remove them."

"Who died and made you king?" she grumbled, but it was no good. She was tingling all over and they both knew it.

"Do as you're told," he said imperiously, "and I might be nice to you."

"Brute," she said. "That's blackmail."

"Fair play, madam," he corrected her. "Off you go."

She scooted to the door, her cheeks pink.

Chapter 12

"I do hope my pianoforte is *fast* enough for you, Miss Vaughn," Lady Serena said archly. Much struck by her ladyship's wit, Lady Dalrymple and her daughter tittered appreciatively. Benedict, who had the honor of aiding Serena in fleecing her good friends, studied his cards and pretended not to hear.

At the next card table, Mr. Freddie Carteret whispered to Lady Matlock, "It would have to be *very fast* indeed to be fast enough for Miss Vaughn, from what I hear."

Lady Rose glowered at him silently.

"What are trumps?" asked Roger Fitzwilliam, wondering why his hostess had placed him at a table with the only two women in the room whom he could not possibly marry.

Serena had not invited Mr. Fitzwilliam. He had arrived unexpectedly with his sister-in-law, spoiling Serena's plan of having two card tables, with Miss Vaughn odd man out. To Serena's annoyance, Lord Ludham had given up his seat to the clergyman. Lord Ludham was drooling over Miss Vaughn in the alcove where the pianoforte had been set up. And, despite all the speaking glances she had cast to Sir Benedict, the baronet had done nothing about it. Since their little tiff at the lecture on Wednesday, he seemed determined to be unhelpful.

Cosima answered her hostess's comment seriously.

"I like the Broadwood, my lady," she called back to Serena from the alcove. "But I like the Clementi better. It takes a lighter touch, and the tone is brighter, I'm thinking. The Broadwood is more of a man's instrument. You have to pound it with all your might to get anywhere, and then it mumbles at you. The Clementi is nice and crisp."

Mr. Roger Fitzwilliam turned pale. "Did she say it was a man's instrument?" he gasped.

"She's talking about the tone of the piano, Uncle," Rose snapped.

"Try the prestissimo, Miss Vaughn," Serena invited. "I got it especially for you."

"I've been admiring it," Cosima replied. It was difficult to concentrate on the music, however, with Lord Ludham breathing down her neck. She began to play the second movement of the concerto. The painful stops and starts as she wrestled with the unfamiliar composition were as difficult to listen to as Serena could have wished.

"Holy fly!" said Miss Vaughn, breaking off. "Who does this Beethoven fellow think he is? I'll need a month of bed rest after this."

"It is a poor musician, Miss Vaughn," said Serena, "who blames the composer."

"I think it's your pianoforte, Serena," said Lord Ludham.

"I'm very lazy, I'm afraid," said Miss Vaughn. "I don't like to work this hard. The Clementi, now, is light as a feather. Playing it is all but effortless."

Lord Ludham and Miss Vaughn began to speak intimately, and Serena could no longer follow the conversation. Felix, Serena noted with exasperation, did not seem to notice that Miss Vaughn was wearing last year's model in a very unattractive shade of green.

"Your cousin has made another conquest," Lady Dalrymple trilled at Sir Benedict. "Have you heard the rumor about her and Kellynch? I, for one, don't believe it."

Benedict's lip curled. "Could your ladyship mean the

rumor you started? I am glad you do not believe your own malicious falsehoods."

Lady Dalrymple blinked her kohl-blackened eyelids rapidly. "You are in love with her, I see. Naturally, you defend her."

"You are nonsensical," said Benedict. "I am too old for such foolishness, I assure you."

"They say there's no fool like an old fool," Lady Dalrymple said maliciously. "You men all fall like ninepins for a pretty face! When I think of how she used poor Freddie's finer feelings against him—! But he is much better off where he is now."

At the moment, her youngest son seemed to be lodged in the bosom of Lady Matlock.

"Theirs will be a long and happy marriage," the proud mama predicted. "For she is rich and he is handsome."

"Lord Matlock might object to the marriage," Benedict said dryly, as Freddie Carteret fawned over Lady Matlock at the next table.

"Object to the marriage!" Lady Dalrymple cried indignantly. "No, indeed. After her disgraceful behavior in London, Lady Rose is lucky to get anyone."

"Oh, I see," said Benedict. "It is the *daughter* who is to be the bride."

Lady Dalrymple giggled. "Oh, Sir Benedict! What a rattle you are! *Lady Rose* is the bride. Whom did you think I meant? Of course," she confided, leaning closer in a blatant attempt to look at the gentleman's cards, "there is a great deal left to be done. Old Matlock will insist on a marriage settlement." She sighed heavily. "Who knows how many fine romances have been destroyed by these greedy lawyers?"

"My trick, I think," said Lady Serena, sweeping up the cards.

"Lord Ludham! Do come and advise poor Millicent, or we shall all be ruined!"

"It is not my fault we are losing, Mama!" Millicent said indignantly.

"Do you *want* him to spend all evening with Miss

Vaughn?" Lady Dalrymple hissed back. "You must use your head, Millie!"

Lord Ludham pleaded that he had no skill at whist. He had no skill at music either, as Serena dryly observed, but that did not keep him from advising Miss Vaughn.

"If *I* were advising Miss Vaughn," Miss Carteret said viciously, "I would tell her to cut her hair." Her own mousy locks had been artfully clipped into a fringe that circled her entire head, leaving a towering topknot of looping braids in the middle.

"And if I were advising her," said Lady Dalrymple, "I would tell her to stay away from libertines like the Duke of Kellynch. Dear Serena, did I tell you that, while we were obliged to put up at Castle Argent, His Grace visited Miss Vaughn quite five times? He even sent her grapes and nectarines from his succession houses. Nectarines!"

"If poor Miss Vaughn has caught the eyes of James Kellynch, then she is a lost woman indeed." Serena clucked her tongue sadly. "But, perhaps, things are different amongst the Irish savages, and we must not judge them by our English standards of conduct."

"Is it any wonder she is so vain," Millicent sniffed, "when great men make such fools of themselves for her. His Grace, and now poor Lord Ludham."

"And even our Sir Benedict is not immune to her charms," said Lady Dalrymple. "Poor Sir Benedict. She will never look at you when she has an earl on her hook."

It was empty, offhand malice. Benedict was determined not to show that Lady Dalrymple had drawn blood.

"I think we must acquit her of vanity, Miss Carteret," said Serena. "If she were vain, she would take more care of her appearance. One would think she doesn't even own a mirror!"

Benedict flinched at this well-deserved criticism. Miss Vaughn's dress was a green disaster. Her hair, as usual, was slipping its pins. It irritated him that she had not spent a farthing of the thousand pounds he had given her on herself.

"Are we playing cards, ladies?" he growled.

The ladies ignored him.

"She has no taste," Millicent said, preening. Her own gown was so embellished with embroidered ribbons, braid, swags, buttons, and rosettes that one could barely discern that there was a gown of puce satin underneath it all. She had taken to wearing the new busk as well and, forced apart by this odd device, her breasts jutted to the east and to the west, respectively.

"It appears she is vain enough to aspire to become a countess," said Lady Dalrymple, pausing to cram a cream puff into her greedy wet mouth. "Poor Ludham! After all he endured with that opera girl! But at least Pamela was English! My dear Serena, how will you bear the humiliation of presenting your *Irish* cousin to the Queen? And Lady Ludham will outrank you, too!" she added gleefully.

"I am not worried about Felix in the least," Serena said coldly.

"Oh, Miss Vaughn, do play us one of your *Irish* songs," Lady Dalrymple called to the musician. "Serena has not yet had the pleasure of hearing you sing."

"Yes, do sing, Miss Vaughn," cried Lady Matlock. "Something authentic."

Cosima ran her fingers over the keys and, after a few moments, chose a completely inappropriate song to sing.

"Wherever I'm going, and all the day long,
At home and abroad or alone in a throng,
I find that my passion's so lively and strong,
That your name when I'm silent still runs in my song.

"Since the first time I saw you, I take no repose.
I sleep all the day to forget half my woes;
So strong is the flame in my bosom that glows,
By St. Patrick, I fear it will burn through my clothes!

"By my soul, I'm afraid I shall die in my grave
Unless you comply and poor Phelim save;

Then grant the petition your lover doth crave,
Who never was free till you made him your slave."

She had been quite correct in saying that her voice was not
big enough to fill a concert hall, but it was a fine, creamy
contralto, and it filled the drawing-room. The lyrics, however,
were a little too coarse for the drawing-room. To the refined
English ears of her audience, it sounded quite bawdy. Benedict was furious. She must have known dozens of perfectly
lovely Irish songs, but, perversely, she had chosen this one.

"That's not Thomas Moore," said Lady Serena, shocked.

Cosima laughed. "It is not. 'Tis a bold song, perhaps, but I
like it. I first heard it sung in *The Brave Irishman* by Mr.
Sheridan in the Smock Alley Theater in Dublin. Of course,
it's meant to be sung by a man."

Lady Matlock's voice suddenly rose from the next table. "I
wish you had a harp, Serena. I long to hear Miss Vaughn play
the harp. There's something so *authentic* about an Irish girl
playing an Irish harp, don't you agree, Mr. Carteret?"

"Oh, Miss Vaughn doesn't play the harp," Millicent
sniffed. "We were with her in Ireland three months. She
played the piano every day—very badly, too! But she never
played the harp. I don't recall even *seeing* a harp in the music
room."

"Maybe it was hiding from you," said Miss Vaughn,
laughing.

"Music room?" Serena inquired. "But I thought you lived
in a farmhouse with battlements, Miss Vaughn?"

"'Tis a farmhouse with battlements *and* a music room."

"That is how it is in these Irish houses," Lady Matlock said
knowledgeably. "The Irish are such a happy, carefree race.
There is singing and dancing from the humblest to the highest. Give us a song in Irish, Miss Vaughn! Nothing from the
playhouse. Something *really* authentic."

Cosima was startled. "You want me to sing to you in the
Irish language, my lady?"

"You *do* know your own language, I trust," Lady Matlock said severely.

"I'm afraid only peasants in the Irish countryside speak Irish these days, Lady Matlock," said Benedict. "It is no longer taught in schools."

"In the Penal Days," said Miss Vaughn, "there were people burned alive by the English only for the crime of speaking Irish. Sure Cromwell thought we were criticizing his funny haircut! I'll sing to you in Irish, Lady Matlock."

She played a plaintive, bittersweet melody on the Broadwood. She sang, her soft voice lingering in the air like perfume.

"Rop tú mo baile
a Choimdin cride:
ní ní nech aile
acht Rí secht nime."

"How strange," Serena murmured. "How primitive and pagan!"

"Is it a rebel song, Miss Vaughn?" asked Lady Rose.

"It's a hymn," said Cosima, laughing. "We sing it in chapel."

Mr. Fitzwilliam was scandalized. "In Irish? I had no idea the Church of Ireland was in such disarray. I shall write a letter to the Archbishop of Dublin at once," he added importantly.

"Miss Vaughn," Lady Dalrymple sniffed, "is a Papist, Mr. Fitzwilliam."

Mr. Fitzwilliam wrinkled his nose as if he had encountered a very bad smell. "Good heavens," he said. "I had no idea."

"There's a Catholic chapel in Bath, on Orchard Street," said Lord Ludham. "Did you know that, Miss Vaughn?"

"I did, yes," Cosima said mildly.

"I came upon it by mistake. Used to be a theater, you know, before the new one was built in Beaufort Square."

"That I *didn't* know," said Miss Vaughn.

"I paid my shilling at the door and went in, expecting quite a *different* performance!"

"I hope you got your shilling back, at least," said Serena. "With so many Irish in service nowadays, I'm afraid Bath is becoming quite a hotbed of Papism. Personally, *I* don't care to employ them. We had some, years ago. They were always going to funerals." She rose from the card table as her butler entered the room. "I see dinner is served. Shall we go in?"

A thin, dry, graying woman appeared in the dining room, but Serena waved her away. "No, Peacham, we don't need you to make us an even number for dinner. We have Mr. Fitzwilliam to complete us."

"I am very happy to complete you, my lady," said the gallant clergyman.

"Your place is there, sir," his hostess answered coldly. "Next to Miss Carteret."

"You are a younger son, are you not?" Lady Dalrymple asked him.

"I am," he admitted. "But my brother, the Earl of Matlock, has many livings in his gift, and, what's more, I am assured of a bishopric, whenever one in Derbyshire should become available."

"Ah!" said the viscountess, blinking rapidly.

"I wonder we don't have suppers at all our card parties," Lady Matlock said, draining her soup like a castaway. "The company is so much more *select* at a small dinner party."

At her end of the table, Miss Vaughn looked intently at her soup. Long, thin, white worms appeared to be floating in it. She thought Lady Serena must be playing a mean trick on her. "What is it?" she quietly asked the footman waiting on her.

"Vermicelli, miss," said the footman, confirming her worst fears.

"Is there something wrong, Miss Vaughn?" Serena inquired crossly.

Benedict, who was seated at Serena's right, said quickly,

"Don't look so worried, Miss Vaughn. Those are noodles, not worms."

"Worms!" exclaimed Rose, dropping her spoon.

"Worms!" cried Miss Carteret.

"They only look like worms," Benedict said helpfully. "Hence the name: *vermicelli,* from the Latin, meaning 'little worms.'"

"I don't want to eat anything that looks like worms!" declared Lord Ludham decisively. "Take it away, Morris."

Morris took it away.

The duck fared no better with Miss Vaughn.

Watching Mr. Fitzwilliam devour his portion with an expression of shock, she presently inquired, "Does the Church of England not observe the Lenten fast?"

"Hmmm?" he said absently. "Oh, yes, of course." Reluctantly, he pushed his plate away. His stomach growled in protest. "The Lenten fast. Thank you, Miss Vaughn. I almost forgot."

"Take it all away, Morris," urged Ludham. "It is overcooked, anyway. Serena, you should dismiss your cook at once! Worm soup, and now overcooked duck in the middle of the Lenten fast! Has the world gone mad?" He flung down his napkin in disgust.

Serena was livid with rage, but could only watch helplessly as a small fortune in fowl was removed from her table. She did not want anyone to think she was not a devout Christian.

"I am not finished," said Benedict coldly when the footman came for his plate. He was still angry with Miss Vaughn for playing that vulgar song, and he certainly was not going to forego his dinner because she was observing some silly fast. He was not religious at all, and he was not going to pretend.

No one else had thought to rebel against Miss Vaughn. They were all obliged to sit quietly while the baronet enjoyed his duck. "There," he said at last, setting aside his knife. "Now you may take it, Morris. And, by the way, it was not overcooked. It was perfectly, scrumptiously, rare."

They all groaned involuntarily, except for Miss Vaughn, who sniffed angrily.

Still smarting, despite the relative success of a dish of asparagus, Lady Serena withdrew with the ladies at the first opportunity, leaving the gentlemen to their port. While they dined, the servants had transformed the card room back into a drawing-room. Coffee was served, along with a tower of beautiful little cakes iced in pink and blue, which no one dared to eat because of Miss Vaughn. Tight-lipped, Serena ordered Peacham to take them out of sight. The thin, gray woman complied with alacrity.

"Are we allowed to have tea at least?" Lady Rose sulked.

"Who is that lady?" Cosima asked her hostess curiously. "She looks so sad."

"What lady? Oh, Peacham!" Serena laughed. "That is my paid companion: a dear, sweet thing. I don't know what I'd do without her." Despite this accolade, however, Peacham's sudden reappearance seemed to annoy her ladyship. "What is it *now?*" she snapped. "Well? Stop quivering and come out with it!"

Peacham came out with it. "It's the nurserymaid, ma'am. Lady Amelia put a frog in her best bonnet, and, well, that was that. She is gone! Lady Caroline won't stop *crying,* and Lady Imogen won't go to bed. And I can't find Lady Elizabeth anywhere!" she wailed.

Serena was embarrassed. "For heaven's sake, Peacham!" she said crossly. "You must manage the children, or you must find somewhere else to live."

Peacham departed in tears. Lady Dalrymple opened her mouth, but Serena was too quick for her. "What an interesting dress, Miss Vaughn."

"Do you like it?" Cosima said doubtfully. "Would you believe it was half-price?"

"Yes, I would," said Serena.

Millicent Carteret sniffed derisively. "I have all my clothes made *especially* for me," she said. She had to. She was far too plump to fit into any of the floor models on display in the shops, which were always made up using the least possible amount of material. "I can afford it," she added. "*I* am an heiress."

"You're lucky," Cosima said. "Everything's so exorbitant in the shops, it's no wonder most ladies can't afford nice underwear. They spend all their money on silks and velvets for the world to see, but, underneath, it's all tatty, itchy, ugly brown homespun."

Lady Serena, Lady Dalrymple, and Miss Carteret all began to itch violently under their clothes. Rose scratched herself surreptitiously.

"Personally," said Miss Vaughn serenely, "I never skimp on underwear. I always have the very finest next to my skin, and the cost be damned."

Lady Dalrymple quickly changed the subject. "Dear Serena! I didn't realize that your sister's children were with you in Bath. Poor Lady Redfyle," she added perfunctorily. "She died so young. Childbed fever, wasn't it?"

"I'm so sorry," said Cosima.

Serena glared at her. "Caroline was delicate. The doctor warned her, but she was determined to give her husband a son or else die trying. She died trying. "

"Very noble, I'm sure," said Lady Dalrymple. "But, my dear, however do you manage *four* children?"

"It *is* a burden," said Serena. "But what else can one do? They are my sister's children. I could not leave them with their father. What do men know of raising daughters?"

"I suppose Lord Redfylde comes often to visit them," Lady Dalrymple said eagerly.

"Oh!" said Millicent. "I hear he's very handsome! But I have never seen him."

"He *is* handsome," said Rose. "I have danced with him. He is like a tall, proud Viking warrior. His hair is silver, and his eyes are a piercing pale blue. His physique is incredible, too, for he boxes every day in Gentleman Jackson's saloon.

All the girls were wild for him in London. I daresay he is engaged by now."

"Lord Redfylde is a most attentive father," replied Lady Serena coldly.

Peacham returned as she had departed, in tears. "I believe, my lady," she cried, "that we must have the doctor. Lady Caroline's face is *very* red, and my nerves cannot take it!"

"For heaven's sake, Peacham! You interrupted."

"I'm sorry, my lady," said Peacham wearily.

"Lady Caroline is a baby," said Serena. "Babies have red faces. It is a fact of life."

"She won't go to sleep, my lady," Peacham moaned.

"Give her some gin," Lady Dalrymple advised haughtily. "She'll go to sleep."

"Why don't I have a go at the baby?" said Cosima, jumping up. "I love babies. I practically raised Allie, my sister. It's no trouble!"

Serena gave a shrug and Miss Vaughn went off with Peacham.

"Do you think," Lady Rose asked quietly, "we could have the cakes back now?"

When the gentlemen rejoined the ladies a few minutes later, Miss Vaughn was still upstairs, playing nursemaid, as Millicent so contemptuously put it.

Ludham was shocked. "You mean Caroline's children are all here? What? Under this roof? Serena! When did they arrive?"

Serena looked aloof. "Arrive? They came with me from London, Felix."

His blue eyes widened. "You mean they've been here all this time? They are *living* here? Why have I never seen them?"

"They are perfectly content in the nursery, Felix. Peacham looks after them."

"*I* would like to see them," he said angrily. "They are my cousin's children after all. Did you ever think of that?" He strode for the door. "Where is the nursery?"

"In the vicinity of the attic, one supposes," said Serena.

After obtaining more specific directions to the nursery from a passing servant, Ludham ascended to find Miss Vaughn soothing Lady Caroline's gums with a piece of ice wrapped in a handkerchief. Three more little ladies were in the immediate vicinity watching the operation doubtfully. The eldest, Lady Amelia, was dark-haired and violet-eyed like her aunt. Peacham had a firm grip on the other two girls, two fair-haired little angels in rose-colored muslin.

"Hullo," said Ludham, strolling forth. "I am your uncle, Lord Ludham."

"No, you're not," said Lady Amelia, a plump, haughty girl of some nine years. "You're my mother's first cousin. That makes you my second cousin, not my uncle."

Ludham was taken aback by her perspicacity. "Cheeky madam!"

Lady Amelia glared at him.

"How is little Caroline, Miss Vaughn?"

"She's cutting her teeth, my lord," said Cosima, showing him the baby's mouth, into which he peered knowledgeably so as not to disappoint her. "That's why she's so fussy, poor darling. Don't you think Lady Serena would like to see it; the tooth? Miss Peacham says no."

"Yes, of course," cried Ludham. "Bring her down; show her off! Come, children."

Lady Amelia stared in amazement. "You mean . . . go *out there*? We're not allowed to leave the nursery. Aunt Serena says we are too noisy and we make a mess."

"Not allowed to leave the nursery!" Ludham scowled. "We'll see about that!" He grabbed Lady Amelia by the hand, and they all marched downstairs.

Confronted by her cruelty, Lady Serena spluttered. "Peacham must have misunderstood my instructions! Of course, they are not *confined* to the nursery. They are not prisoners!"

She glared at Lady Amelia.

"Have a look in little Caroline's mouth," Ludham encouraged her. "She has cut her first tooth, the clever girl!"

Serena looked at the child in Miss Vaughn's arms. "How sweet."

"I've a sister about Lady Amelia's age," said Cosima. "She's a day pupil at Miss Bulstrode's Seminary for Young Ladies, right here in Bath."

"Day pupil!" To Lady Amelia Redfylde, this sounded like the glamorous life.

"I don't see why Amelia can't go to school with Miss Vaughn's sister," said Ludham. "You can't keep them locked in the attic all day, Serena! They need fresh air, and sunshine, and exercise. And just because they are girls doesn't mean they can't be educated."

"I must speak to Lord Redfylde," Serena said coldly. "His lordship is very particular about his daughters appearing in public."

"Of course," said Ludham.

Peacham came into the room wringing her hands.

"Yes, Peacham?" Serena cried impatiently. "What is it now?"

"There is a message for Miss Vaughn, my lady," Peacham said. "Miss Vaughn, you are needed at home. Your mother has had a bad fall on the stairs!"

Lord Ludham could only watch enviously as Sir Benedict left with the distraught young lady. Neither a husband or a relative, Ludham could do nothing for her, but Sir Benedict was her cousin. *He* got to place her cloak around her shoulders and order up a carriage to take her home and reassure her that everything would be all right.

Dr. Grantham was with Lady Agatha when Cosima and Benedict arrived. He came out of her ladyship's room and met them on the landing of the stairs. "I warned you this might happen, Miss Vaughn," he said, almost gloating.

Cosima's eyes were squeezed shut. "How bad is it?"

"It might have been much worse," Dr. Grantham said, as if disappointed. "As it is, she has broken her wrist."

"Oh!" She made as if to dart into her mother's bedroom, but the doctor caught her arm.

"Now perhaps you will listen to me, Miss Vaughn!" he said, giving her a shake. "Lady Agatha should be in a hospital. At the very least, your mother ought to be locked in her room at night, to prevent accidents such as these."

Cosima pulled away from him angrily. "I am not going to lock my mother in her room like a prisoner! And she doesn't want to go to your hospital."

Dr. Grantham turned to Sir Benedict and sighed. "You see how irrational this young lady is on the subject? Lady Agatha became quite dizzy on the stairs and fainted. She might very well have been killed. She ought to be locked up at night for her own safety. Sir Benedict, I implore you. Reason with this headstrong, foolish child. Put your foot down."

Cosima glared at Benedict, as though daring him to put his foot down.

"Perhaps, Miss Vaughn, you might consider—"

"I am *not*," she shouted, "putting my mother in some damned hospital, and that's final! I am not locking her in her room! And I'm not going to keep her in a state of oblivion with laudanum and God-knows-what!"

"I was going to suggest," Benedict said mildly, "that you move her ladyship's bedroom downstairs. That way, she at least need not negotiate the stairs."

"Oh," she said, embarrassed that she had interrupted him so fiercely.

"That would be most improper," said the doctor. "A lady's bedroom, on the ground floor? I never heard of such a thing. Even in cases of ill health, the proprieties must be observed, Sir Benedict. In any case, her ladyship ought not to be moved just yet."

"I don't think the man was suggesting we do it *now*," Cosima said irritably.

She went in to see her mother. Lady Agatha was in bed. Nora was covering her ladyship's pitted face with cold cream. Lady Agatha's white hair, badly thinned from years of dyeing, barely covered her spotted head. She held out her right hand to her daughter. Her left wrist was immobilized by a splint.

"Oh, Mother!" said Cosima, kneeling next to the bed. "What were you doing out of bed? Where did you think you were going?"

"I lost another tooth," Lady Agatha sobbed. Opening her mouth, she showed her daughter the small, black wound in her gum. "I didn't want to tell you, my dear. I wanted you to go to your party and enjoy yourself. You deserve your night out. I'm so sorry I spoiled it."

Cosima was awash in guilt. "I shouldn't have left you. I don't even play cards!"

"There is nothing you could have done if you had been here," said Lady Agatha.

"Where were you, Nora?" Cosima demanded of the servant.

"It is not Nora's fault," Lady Agatha said quickly. "She was with me all night. She fell asleep, right in that chair. I woke up overheated. It was very silly, I know, but I went downstairs for my fan, and the next thing I knew, the doctor was here."

"You ought to have woken me up, my lady," Nora moaned softly.

Lady Agatha could barely keep her eyes open.

"The doctor gave her something," Nora explained.

Cosima frowned slightly. "Allie?" she asked Nora. "Is she sleeping in my room?"

"Aye." Nora pressed her lips together. "The doctor gave *her* something, too."

"Oh, he did, did he?" Cosima snapped.

Lady Agatha squeezed her hand. "Will you sit with me until I fall asleep, dearest? I want to hear all about your party! I'm sure you were the prettiest girl there. Did everyone admire you? Did you enjoy yourself?"

"Oh, yes, Mother," Cosima assured her. "The ladies were

all so beautiful and kind. They paid me so many compliments, my head swelled up like a balloon full of hot air."

Lady Agatha smiled. "And was there dancing?"

"There was, of course," Cosima lied, smiling. "And I danced every dance. The gentlemen were all so handsome, I couldn't decide which one I liked the best."

Lady Agatha drifted off to sleep happily.

Cosima planted a kiss on her mother's forehead, then went to find the doctor.

He was in the drawing-room, in conference with Benedict. "—completely irrational on the subject," the doctor was saying.

"What did you give my sister?" Cosima demanded, interrupting.

Dr. Grantham blinked at her. "Miss Allegra was frightened and distraught. She became hysterical. I gave her something to help her sleep."

"That's your answer for everything, isn't it? Knock the daylights out of them!"

Dr. Grantham smiled thinly. "Do you see what I mean, Sir Benedict? Something must be done. I shall write again to Lord Wayborn. His lordship is by far the most proper person to make decisions about his sister's health."

"My uncle could care less about his sister's health," Cosima informed the man.

Dr. Grantham placed a tiny bottle on the table near Benedict. "Miss Vaughn is hysterical. Give her three of these drops, Sir Benedict, and it will relax her overwrought nerves so that she can sleep."

"You can take your drops and you can stick them where—" Miss Vaughn began hotly.

"Thank you, doctor," Benedict said. "You may see yourself out."

"The young lady has a wicked and unruly tongue," the doctor warned him in a very low voice. "I fear that stress may have caused her reason to give way. The first indication of madness in females is very often unfeminine, disobedient, and even violent speech. To be followed, I'm sorry to say, by unfeminine, disobedient, and violent behavior! You would do well to keep an eye on the young lady, Sir Benedict. If her condition worsens—!"

He broke off as Miss Vaughn suddenly sank into a chair and began to laugh hysterically. "Three drops," Dr. Grantham whispered. "Just three drops and she'll be right as rain."

Miss Vaughn began to sob like an abandoned child.

"Quite," said Benedict, showing the physician the door.

Silently, he walked over to the girl and handed her a clean handkerchief.

"He's right," she moaned, blowing her nose. "It *is* my fault. I should have been with her, instead of—! I don't even like those people!"

"It is not your fault," he said firmly. "I think you should go to bed. I'll sit with your mother for an hour or two while you rest."

"Oh, no!" she said, starting up. Her mother would die of shame and embarrassment if a gentleman were to see her without her makeup and wig, her face slathered in cold cream. "Mother wouldn't like that at all! Nora and I will take turns. Really," she insisted, wiping her eyes. "It's very kind of you to offer, but we'll manage. I'm just thankful it was no worse."

Benedict did not feel he had the right to insist. "Then I will leave you," he said quietly. "I will call tomorrow to see how the patient is doing."

"Oh, yes," she said. "Tomorrow."

It suddenly occurred to her that Miss Cherry would not be able to keep her appointment tonight, and she felt a sudden burst of anger against her mother. Why hadn't she sent Nora downstairs for her stupid fan if she was hot?

Almost in the same instant, she was wracked with horrified guilt. Her own selfishness took her breath away. Her mother might very easily have broken her neck on the stairs, and all she could think about was sneaking out of the house to spend a few hours in the company of a man she hardly knew!

What a loathsome, undutiful daughter I am, she thought, her face flaming.

"Please don't trouble yourself," he said. "I'll see myself out."

"It's no trouble," she insisted. Pride forced her to add: "I have to lock the door, after all."

"Yes, of course," he murmured, following her down.

She couldn't resist taunting him. "I'd kiss you good night," she said, as they shook hands in the doorway, "but you had the duck."

Chapter 13

Lady Rose Fitzwilliam was the first to call on the Vaughns the following morning. Cosima came halfway down the stairs to meet her. Lady Rose ran up and seized both of Miss Vaughn's hands in her own. "Oh, Miss Vaughn! How is your dear mama?"

"She must take laudanum for the pain, but her bones will mend," Cosima reported, leading the younger girl to the drawing room. "When she is better, I intend to move her downstairs into the Book room. She simply can't manage the stairs anymore."

Lady Rose listened politely, and said everything that is proper to say when one's mother-in-law-to-be takes a bad fall on the stairs. Then she burst into tears. "Oh, Miss Vaughn! I am engaged! Mother put the announcement in the paper this morning!"

"But that's good, isn't it?" Cosima said, puzzled.

Rose stared at her in amazement. "Good!"

"Aye. Now everyone will know you're engaged."

"To Freddie Carteret!" cried Rose. "Mama said she would marry me off to the first man who asked for me, and she means to do it! What am I going to do?"

"You can't marry Freddie," Cosima declared stoutly. "The man is a fortune hunter! You should have seen him sniffing around when he thought I was an heiress."

"It won't make any difference to Mama," Rose said. "She just wants to be rid of me. Her only daughter! She doesn't care who I marry. Papa is in France. The only person in the world who can help me now is Westlands! Please, Miss Vaughn! He will come to Bath if you send for him! You *will* send for him, won't you?"

Cosima was taken aback. "I don't have the power to send for him or anyone else."

"You do," Rose insisted. "You're his favorite cousin! He told me so."

"That was a long time ago, Lady Rose," Cosy said gravely. "We were children then. But, I'm sure, if *you* summoned him, and explained the situation—"

Rose snorted. "If I summoned him, he'd run as fast as he could—in the opposite direction! It's not as though I'm asking a lot. It would only be a sham engagement."

"Sham engagement!"

"Of course," said Rose. "If I'm engaged to Westlands, Mama can hardly expect me to marry Freddie! Tell Westlands I promise to jilt him the exact moment I turn twenty-one. Then, when I have my money, I shall fly to Dante in India on the wings of love. It's only four years, Miss Vaughn! Westlands won't mind waiting four years to marry. He's only twenty-five, and he's got lots of wild oats to sow. He is not a *sincere* young man like my beloved Dante."

"Oh, my God," Cosima murmured. As much as she loved her younger brother, she would never have described him as sincere.

"If you don't send for Westlands, Mama will make me marry the odious Freddie. Time is of the essence! In fact, I'm supposed to be at a fitting with the modiste now." She hopped nimbly to her feet and ran to the door. "At least I'm getting some new clothes. Oh, help me, Miss Vaughn! If you don't, I fear my wedding dress will be my shroud!"

Miss Vaughn had just put pen to paper when she heard Jackson admitting a visitor at the front door. She ran to the top of the stairs. To her disappointment, it wasn't Ben. "Hush, can't you?" she whispered furiously. "Mother's sleeping!"

"It's a delivery, Miss Cosy," Jackson said. "A pianoforte!"

Ben must have sent it, she thought. He must have missed her company last night as much as she had missed his. She ran outside to stare at the beautiful instrument on the delivery cart. "It's the exact one I wanted," she breathed, beginning to blush. "The Clementi. Is there a note?" she asked one of the delivery men.

"No, miss. Where do you want it?"

Benedict waited until after ten o'clock to call on Miss Vaughn. By this time, he knew better than to ring the bell. He knocked.

"Is it yourself, Sir Benedict?" Jackson asked pleasantly.

"Yes, Jackson. It is I," Benedict replied. "Is that a pianoforte I hear?"

He went up unannounced.

Cosima was seated at the instrument. He guessed it was the Clementi she had been speaking of in such glowing terms at Serena's card party. The manufacturer, Signor Muzio Clementi, was also a famed musician and composer of the day, and Cosima was playing one of his more intricate and lively concertos. Unlike the prestissimo she had attempted at Lady Serena's party, she obviously knew this piece well. She played it perhaps a little too fast in her excitement, but otherwise quite flawlessly. He waited for her to finish the movement.

"You got the Clementi," he said.

She looked at him glowing eyes.

"It's a beautiful instrument," she said. "It's exactly what I wanted. Thank you."

Benedict frowned, taken aback. He had assumed that she had used some of the money he had given her to buy the instrument herself. "Why are you thanking me?"

She blinked at him. "Did you not send it?"

"No," he said. "Of course not. That would not have been proper at all."

"There wasn't a note," she said. "If not you, who?"

"Ludham, of course," he said, annoyed. "You practically begged him to buy it for you."

She jumped up from the seat. "I did no such shameless thing!"

"Perhaps not," he said. "In any case, you cannot accept such an expensive present from his lordship. To accept such a gift would be tantamount to a promise of marriage. Send it back."

She scowled at him. "Why? Because you say so? You're not my father. You're certainly not my husband! You have no right to tell me what to do."

"You cannot marry him," he said calmly. "You know you cannot. You are a Roman Catholic. You cannot marry a divorced man. As far as Rome is concerned, the Earl of Ludham already has a wife. If you marry him, you would be guilty of adultery."

"I never said I was going to marry him," she said sullenly. She closed the instrument.

"You look tired, Miss Vaughn," he said.

"Why, thank you!"

"How is you mother?"

"She's going to be all right. She's resting. She's not well enough for visitors, but I'll tell her you were here. Won't you sit down?"

"No, I can't stay. I have come to take my leave of you. I am called to London."

Her eyes flickered. "London, is it? How nice for you."

"There is a debate in Parliament I cannot miss. The vote is set for Thursday. I will be gone at least two weeks, I'm afraid."

Cosima did not believe for an instant this nonsense about a debate in Parliament. London was a den of iniquity, and men went there to be iniquitous. Because of Lady Agatha's accident, Miss Cherry would not be able to visit him for the foreseeable future, and so, of course, being a man, he needed to explore other avenues. London had lots of avenues. One night alone, and he was off to London like a shot, the faithless hound. He probably kept a mistress there. If not, there was a brothel on every corner, she was sure.

She burned with jealousy when she thought of him bedding another woman.

"Well," she sniffed. "Don't let me keep you."

"Have you any commission for me while I am in London? Is there anything I might get for your mother to make her recuperation less unpleasant?"

"You could bring her an ice from Gunter's," said Miss Vaughn. "She used to go there when she was a girl. Mulberry was her favorite flavor."

"I can hardly bring an ice all the way from London," he pointed out.

She glared at him. "Of course you can. Put it in your coat, next to your cold heart. That way, it won't melt!"

"I don't know," he said coldly, "what I have done to deserve this acrimony."

"Oh, you haven't done anything," she said bitterly.

And that was no more than the truth. He never did anything but kiss her. He kissed her like a lunatic, of course, but it was still only kissing. Probably, he was tired of playing these pointless virgin games. Lady Agatha's fall was just the last straw that broke the camel's back. He was off to shag the dirty fanny off some London slut.

As far as she was concerned, it was over. He needn't come back from London at all.

"I was only joking about the ice," she sniffed.

"I think," he said quietly, "when I get back from London, we should see less of one another."

Her heart began to beat in wild panic. *Oh, my God!* she thought. *He's breaking up with me! Who does he think he is? He didn't even shag me!*

She looked down at her hands. "Is that what you think?" she said coldly.

"People are beginning to talk about us," he explained.

"Who is talking about us?" she demanded.

"Lady Serena has mentioned something. Lady Dalrymple. The very people who pressed me into escorting you to the Upper Rooms now tease me about it."

Cosima was mortified to hear that he had been "pressed." She had been vain enough to think he had wanted to take her here and there. She hadn't realized it was an act of charity on his part. "Well, no good deed goes unpunished," she said coolly.

"Even Dr. Grantham, I'm afraid, seems to think that I— That you and I—Well, he behaves as though I am your intended husband."

"Who cares what they think?"

"I care," he said quietly.

She tossed her head. "Well, maybe you shouldn't be here now!" she said.

"Yes, I must take my leave of you," he said instantly, to her chagrin. "Please give my warmest regards to your mother, and my best wishes for her recovery."

"Wait!" she said, as he started for the door.

"Yes, Miss Vaughn?"

"There *is* something you can do for me in London, *if* you're not too busy, that is."

He stood at attention. "Willingly."

"I have a letter for my cousin, Lord Westlands. He's young and incredibly handsome, but I don't know his address in London. His club is in St. James's Street, though. Would you carry my letter to him?"

"Which club?" he asked.

Cosima frowned. She had hoped to make him jealous, but he looked quite unperturbed. Probably he was already thinking of the acrobat who was waiting for him in London. "Is there more than one club in St. James's Street? I didn't realize."

"I'll find him," he promised.

* * *

Benedict had no intention of wearing himself out searching for one Marcus Wayborn, Lord Westlands. Instead, when he reached London three days later, he went to two clubs in St. James's Street, White's and Brooks's, and left word with the staff that he was looking for the young man. Rather unscrupulously, he dropped hints that something of value might be transferred from the baronet to his lordship, if only his lordship could be found.

Chronically short on funds, Lord Westlands did not waste any time finding Sir Benedict. As soon as he heard the baronet was looking for him, he walked to Parliament and was fortunate enough to catch the last half of the day's debate.

Benedict summed the young man up with a penetrating glance. Neither better nor worse in character than most young men of his class and age, Marcus Wayborn was extraordinarily good-looking. His thick, wavy chestnut hair was liberally streaked with gold, and his eyes were a deep, almost black, blue. But if one looked closer, one saw that his eyes were puffy from too many nights on the town, and his generous, red mouth fell naturally into a childish pout.

Benedict had been afraid, just a little, that the young man might be a rival. Now that he had met Westlands, however, he knew he was secure.

When he courteously offered Westlands dinner, the young man did not refuse. Benedict's carriage conveyed them to back to St. James's Street.

"You said you had some money for me, Sir Benedict?" Westlands was too pressed by creditors to stand on ceremony.

"I have a letter for you," Benedict replied, handing it over. "It is from your cousin, Miss Cosima Vaughn."

Although obviously disappointed that there was no money, Westlands chuckled. "Little Cosy?" he said with a curve to his lips that Benedict did not like. "Pretty little thing. I've not seen her in years. I suppose she's all grown up now. A child no more!"

Benedict silently contemplated his fingernails.

"I saw Dante, of course, when he was in London, shortly before he left for India. Capital fellow. Her brother, you know. At first, when he looked me up, I thought he was going to touch me for money. But he was flush! I ended up touching *him* for a fiver. However, I did take him to Lady Arbuthnot's ball." He leaned forward. "Between you and me, Sir Benedict, I shagged Lady Arbuthnot. Her ladyship is fond of a good ramming, as it turns out."

Benedict had been raised to believe it was the height of nastiness to brag about one's conquests. He forgot the lady's name immediately. "Are you going to read your letter?"

For a moment, the viscount seemed content to *smell* his letter. "She's changed her tobacco. My God, that's good leaf!"

"It's been in my pocket for a while," Benedict explained.

"Do you know Lady Maria Fitzwilliam? She always passes her paper between her legs before she writes to me," said Westlands.

"I am glad to hear it. Your letter, my lord."

"Stop coach!" When the driver had obeyed, Westlands opened his letter and read it in silence, holding it up to the window. "I cannot read in a moving carriage," he explained when he was done. Smiling, he put the letter in his pocket.

"If there is a reply," said Benedict, "I will be happy to take it with me when I return to Bath, but I fear that will not be for some time. I shall be in London all next week, and then I must attend to some matters at my estate in Surrey. You may prefer to send your reply by messenger or by post."

"Tell me something," said Westlands thoughtfully. "Did she ever grow into those enormous green eyes of hers?"

"Yes," Benedict replied. "I rather think she did."

"They used to come to us every year at Christmas," Westlands said wistfully. "The Irish Savages, my mother used to call them. It was the only time we had any *fun* at that old mausoleum in Derbyshire. Now Sandy's dead. Larry's dead. Dan's in India. And Cosy's in bloody Bath. Why the devil is she there?"

"Your Aunt Agatha is rather ill. She's in Bath seeking treatment."

He snorted. "Quackery! Spa medicine. Bath never cured anybody. Poor old Aunt Aggie. She was always sick and queer. She had smallpox when she was a baby, you know, and she was never right after that. I think all that stuff she puts on her face has leaked into her brain. I hate to think of little Cosy stuck in Bath with Aunt Ag. Can't be too jolly. Must be bored to sobs. Maybe I should go and cheer her up."

They arrived in St. James's Street and entered White's. Benedict ordered an excellent dinner accompanied by very good claret, followed by port. They ended the meal with brandy and cigars. The conversation turned to politics. Lord Westlands's title was a courtesy; he could cast no vote in the House of Lords, but his father, Lord Wayborn, was a Tory and a staunch supporter of Lord Liverpool. Westlands felt the need to apologize to his host, who was one of the leading lights of the Opposition.

"My father says you are going to lose this debate, Sir Benedict. You do not have the votes, and you cannot spin them out of the air. What's the debate about anyway?"

"It's about an apple," Benedict replied. "A rotten apple, to be exact."

"An apple! You're not serious."

"Indeed I am. Someone threw a rotten apple at His Highness, the Prince Regent, as he was driving to Parliament in his carriage. His Highness was convinced it was a bomb, and nothing could persuade him otherwise."

"Perhaps it *was* a bomb," Westlands suggested. Suddenly, he felt very important, sitting in the smoking room at White's talking politics with Sir Benedict Wayborn, the man all blue-blooded Tories loved to hate. From time to time, there had even been cartoons of Sir Benedict Wayborn in *Punch* magazine.

"It was demonstrably an apple," said Benedict. "It had seeds and a stem."

Westlands laughed. "And that's the debate? Bomb or apple?"

"The debate is whether or not this regrettable incident justifies Lord Liverpool's proposal to suspend habeas corpus in the British Isles."

"In English."

"If his proposal passes, the British government would be within its rights to arrest anyone, anywhere, without showing cause, without right to counsel, and without a trial. I see no reason for my government to treat my fellow citizens like a defeated enemy, simply because some fool bunged an apple at Prinny's head!"

"But the Tories have it all wrapped up."

"They control both Houses, Lords by right of law, and Commons by right of pocket."

Westlands laughed nervously. "You make it sound like a criminal enterprise!"

"And not by accident," said Benedict. "Is there a reply to your letter?"

Westlands hesitated. "She wants me to go there, to Bath," he said. "The thing is . . . I'm a bit short on funds at the moment . . . Nothing from the governor until Easter-tide, I'm afraid."

Benedict took out his wallet. "Would, say, twenty pounds be of any use to you?"

"I say!" said Westlands. "You're not such a bad fellow, after all."

The vote, when it took place on Thursday evening, went exactly as Benedict feared: straight down party lines. And since the Tories outnumbered the Whigs ten to one in Lords and three to one in Commons, the motion passed and the writ of habeas corpus was suspended. This meant that the government no longer had to show cause before making an arrest. Warrants were strictly unnecessary, and the accused could be locked up indefinitely without a trial or even an indictment. The Opposition had been able to wrest only one important concession from the Tories: no one could be put to death without a trial. Parliament broke up, about half of its members retiring to the clubs of St. James's Street for a well-earned drink.

Benedict would have preferred to lick his wounds in private, but as he left Parliament he was accosted by a footman in bright pink livery. The footman was standing beside a large carriage with a gaudy crest painted on the door. "Sir Benedict Wayborn?" said the footman.

Benedict eyed him warily. "Yes?"

The footman opened the door to the carriage. Inside was a corpulent, aging gentleman with a mottled face and a diamond ring on every finger. On either side of him sat a scantily clad female, and on the seat opposite him were two more. "Get in," said the footman.

"I think not," said Benedict.

The gentleman with the mottled face leaned out. Resplendent in a pink brocade dressing gown, he barked, "I am Kellynch! Get in."

Benedict stood his ground. "Perhaps Your Grace would care to get out."

"I forgot my breeches," the duke explained. "Really, it would be much better if you got in. We have a mutual friend in Bath, I think. Cosy Vaughn!"

Benedict glared at him.

"I dismissed your carriage," Kellynch went on impatiently. "Unless you want to walk home from the City, get in! Squash up, ladies," he commanded his harem.

Benedict climbed in and took his place between two of the women. The lady to his right showed him her rouged nipples. The lady to his left was snorting snuff. The inside of the carriage was rose-pink. The smell of perfumed flesh was overpowering. The attendant closed the door and the carriage swept off into the night.

Kellynch performed hasty introductions. "This is my nurse," he said, squeezing the lady to his left. "And the redhead is her sister. *That* is her other sister, and, believe it or not, *that* is her brother."

"How do you do," Benedict said.

Kellynch roared with laughter. "Oh, I do love the English. They are so polite."

"Do you wish to speak to me, Your Grace?"

Kellynch shook his finger at Benedict coyly. "You have been giving that girl money," he said, chuckling. "You are quite the benefactor, I understand."

"I fail to see how this concerns Your Grace."

"Of course it concerns me," Kellynch replied. "I am her guardian, after all."

"*You* are Miss Vaughn's guardian?" Benedict repeated in disbelief, staring at the aging lech in disgust. "I do not believe you. No one would be stupid enough to think that *you* were an appropriate guardian for an innocent young female."

"By that remark I deduce you have not met my brother, Colonel Vaughn!" the duke retorted. "*He* is quite stupid enough for anything, I assure you."

Benedict was frankly astonished. "Colonel Vaughn is your brother?"

"My father's bastard. *One* of my father's bastards, I should say, for he had many. Vaughn was the worst of them so, naturally, my father loved him the best. Scum always rises to the top. Isn't that right, ladies?"

His ladies only looked bored. "Pass the snuff, Basil," said the duke's "nurse."

"Then you are uncle to the Miss Vaughns," Benedict said quietly.

"That's right. Uncle Jimmy, they call me, with great affection." Reaching for his silk handkerchief, which he had placed in the bosom of his nurse for convenience, he coughed up phlegm. "Now, then, Sir Benedict! We come to it. I know that *I* am too nice to ravish my own brother's child, but are *you* too nice to ravish your *sister's*? That is the question."

"What? My sister? My sister has no child."

Kellynch looked confused. "You *are* one of Aggie's brothers, aren't you?"

Benedict was aghast at the suggestion. "I most certainly am not!"

The duke scowled. "You're not Cosy's uncle?"

"No, indeed!"

"No? I beg your pardon. I heard your name was Wayborn, and I naturally assumed you must be one of Aggie's brothers. Aggie has more brothers than my father had bastards, I sometimes think."

"I am not one of them, however. I am only a distant cousin. *Very* distant."

"Then what the devil are you doing giving her money?" Kellynch demanded.

"Someone had to," said Benedict. "You claim to be their guardian. Yet, when I met them in Bath, they had no credit, and nothing to live on. I helped them."

Kellynch snorted. "And you got nothing in return, I suppose?"

"I resent that disgusting insinuation."

"What's disgusting about it?" the duke wanted to know.

"Miss Vaughn was being dunned by a collier," Benedict said angrily. "A collier who had the temerity to aspire to her hand! I paid her bills. Anyone would have done the same in my place."

The Duke of Kellynch laughed. "A collier! That'll teach her."

Benedict glared at the man. "Teach her? Teach her what?"

Kellynch shifted his bulk on the cushions. "You seem like a reasonable man, Sir Benedict. I'll tell you the whole maudlin tale. When that girl Cosy, as she calls herself, was twelve years old, she got a maggot in her head about going to a ball. Her father said he would take her, on one condition: if she drove the cows to market in Dublin all the way from Ballyvaughn. He underestimated the young lady's determination. By God, didn't she do it!"

"Do what?" Benedict asked, startled.

"Weren't you listening? She drove the cows to market. From Ballyvaughn to Dublin on foot in the mud and in the rain. She put on her best dress and drove the beasts to Dublin; left them wandering in the streets for anyone to take; and made her way to Dublin Castle, nice as you please, her skirts wet to the knee and her white hair hanging down her back."

"She must have been heartbroken when they wouldn't let her in," said Benedict.

"Not let her in?" the duke repeated incredulously. "*Not let her in?* This is Dublin Castle we're talking about, not the fecking Court of St. James's! Every man in the place had his dance with her, including my old lech of a father. Guess his surprise when he found out she was his very own granddaughter! He was so pleased with her that he gave her one of his houses."

"Castle Argent."

"Now we come to the maudlin part. The house was built for my mother, the Duchess, but, at the last moment, Her Grace decided she didn't like it. A farmhouse with battlements, she called it, and vowed never to set foot in it. So to spite her, my father decided to give it to Cosy Vaughn. Since he died, my mother has been nagging me day and night about that house. She's forced me out of Ireland with her nagging. Until Cosy Vaughn agrees to see reason, and fork over Castle Argent, she will not get another penny from me."

"You expect Miss Vaughn to give you *her* house?"

"I've offered her fifty thousand pounds," Kellynch protested. "But that girl is stubborn as a mule! She flatly refused, so I cut off her funds. She'll sell if she gets hungry enough. I was making good progress, too, until *you* came along with your moneybags."

"You're withholding their money in order to pressure Miss Vaughn into selling her house? That, Your Grace, is a despicable manipulation."

"There *is* no money," Kellynch answered impatiently. "What little they had left, the talented Colonel Vaughn took with him to India. The Vaughn ladies have been existing on my largesse for the past three years. But no more! Either Miss Vaughn sells me Castle Argent or that's it. There's no income attached to the house. No land. No tenants to pay her rent. She can't keep up the house as it is. If she had a brain in her head, she would sell."

"Perhaps she is afraid Colonel Vaughn will run off with the money," Benedict suggested dryly. "A not unreasonable fear, apparently."

"She'll be twenty-one in six months. She'll have her independence then. With fifty thousand pounds, she could live anywhere. She could be queen of Ireland."

Benedict bit his lip. "She is not yet twenty-one?" he said sharply.

"No, but soon. She'll be her own woman then. Besides, her father's in India now, and will be for the rest of his life, if *I* have anything to say about it. She's just stubborn, that's all. Too proud to give up Castle Argent. But she expects *me* to give her the money she needs to keep the place up. Meanwhile, my mother never shuts up about her humiliation, as she calls it. These women! I'm caught in a leaky boat between Scylla and Charybdis." He picked up the hand of his nurse and kissed it. "Is it any wonder I crave pleasant company?"

Benedict was silent.

"I tried to get her married to any number of gentlemen who would have been happy to sell me that house for considerably less than fifty thousand pounds," Kellynch said wistfully. "But she has a suspicious nature where men are concerned."

"No wonder she has no interest in marriage," said Benedict. "You think she should keep the house? A house she cannot afford?"

"No," said Benedict. "I think she should sell it."

"And so she will—if *you* stop giving her free money!" said Kellynch. "Oh, this is ridiculous. I will give you a thousand pounds if you will promise me never to give her money again. Two thousand?"

"I can not be bribed, Your Grace."

"Every man has his price."

"And every dog his day," Benedict retorted.

"Do you gamble? Dice? Cards? What is your game?"

"You may set me down here, Your Grace," Benedict said coldly.

Kellynch's lip curled contemptuously. "You don't gamble?"

"No."

"Why not? Did you lose your liver when you lost your arm?"

"No, but thank you for your kind inquiry."

Kellynch looked at him shrewdly. "What can I do to tempt you?" he mused. "You seem to like rescuing silly little girls from naughty tradesmen. Was Cosy grateful when you sorted her collier? I'll just bet she was. Do you like being a hero to women, is that it?"

"I would like to be set down, Your Grace."

"As luck will have it," said Kellynch, smirking, "I have recently come into possession of some bills belonging to a certain lady who is currently residing in Bath."

Benedict clenched his jaw.

Kellynch saw the weakness and did not hesitate to exploit it. "Ten thousand pounds' worth of naughty tradesmen's bills! Just imagine how grateful she will be! She'll throw her legs around your neck." He laughed immoderately.

Benedict regarded him in stony silence.

"Ladies, I think I have secured the gentleman's interest at last. Shall we play for the lady's bills, Sir Benedict? No! Let us remove skill from the equation. Let it be by luck alone that her fate is decided. Let us draw cards. Have we a new pack, Kitty?" he asked his nurse.

Kitty made a fan of the cards.

Benedict drew a queen.

The Duke of Kellynch flung his deuce down in disgust.

"You win," he said angrily.

Chapter 14

On the morning Lord Redfylde came to Bath, Serena awoke with a cold hand pressed over her mouth. For a confused moment, she thought she was only having the nightmare again. She often dreamed of the first time her brother-in-law had come to her bed. She often woke up, screaming. She would scream until Peacham came running to comfort her.

But this time it was not a dream. Redfylde was in Bath. Redfylde was in her bed, his smooth naked body as powerful as a panther's. When she was sixteen, she had fancied herself in love with her sister's husband. How wonderfully kind he had been, opening his home to her when her father died. For years, he treated her with nothing but brotherly affection. He managed her financial affairs, supplying her with pocket money, and paying all her bills. In return, she had adored him. How she had envied her elder sister Caroline!

Then, when Serena turned twenty-one, Redfylde informed her that her debts were heavy. She had spent her inheritance twice over, and there was nothing left for her to live on.

Not once had her brother-in-law ever warned her that she had been living beyond her means. Not once had he warned her that she was running low on funds. Indeed, quite the opposite. He had encouraged her in extravagance, and allowed her to throw elaborate parties at his elegant London mansion. "Why did you not tell me?" she had cried, shocked, humiliated, and angry. "I could have retrenched!"

By then, it was too late to retrench. She owed thousands of pounds. She was in danger of being sent to a debtor's prison. Redfylde agreed to pay her debts. He even agreed to continue keeping her in the style to which she was accustomed. All he wanted in return was one little thing.

He still wanted it. Pushing up her nightgown, he turned her onto her stomach. Pressing her head down into the pillow, he ordered her to kneel with her bottom in the air. Without a word, she obeyed him. She was never permitted to speak on these occasions, and if she broke this supreme commandment, her punishment would be swift and severe. She could feel his hands prying her buttocks apart. She sank her teeth into the pillow, squeezed her eyes shut, and prayed that it would be over soon as he forced the smaller of the two portals. She did not know if he preferred the infertile place, or if he merely feared making her pregnant, but in moments of reflection, she found it oddly amusing that, after all these years, she was as much a virgin now as when she had first entered his house at sixteen. Slowly retreating, he instructed her to open her legs wider. Again, she silently obeyed. She had long ago ceased to fight him. It was easier this way. She tried to think of other things as he did his beastly work.

"Did you think you were free of me?" he asked, biting into her shoulder.

She knew better than to answer, but she had thought just that. When Caroline died, he had given her a choice. She could either remain in London and become his mistress, or she could move to Bath where she would raise his four daughters. She had chosen Bath. She had thought he would stay in London, and leave her in peace. She had been wrong. As he plunged into her bowels, she mulled over what dress to wear to the Upper Rooms that evening; she would have to rethink her wardrobe now, because the bastard had bitten her shoulder, leaving a mark.

"I own you," he murmured. His contempt and loathing made her burn, but she could not have argued, even if she had been permitted to speak. He *did* own her. He had bought up all her debts, and he still held them. He was now her only source of income. All she had, and all she would ever have, flowed from him. This was the price she paid to keep up appearances.

Afterward, she helped him dress. She was allowed to speak then, but only to thank his lordship for the "honor" he had bestowed upon her unworthy body. He left her. She summoned her maid, bathed and dressed as usual, then went down to greet her brother-in-law formally in the drawing-room. Although well past forty, he was a well-preserved, handsome man. The silver rinse in his hair, she was obliged to admit, made him appear almost god-like. His buff-colored pantaloons fit him like a second skin, and his coat, rather unusually, was made of yellow kid leather and must have cost a small fortune.

The picture of aristocratic elegance, she served him coffee.

"What brings you to Bath, my lord?"

"London," he said, "was a bore. Every girl I met reminded me of my pathetic, mewling wife. Fawning, stupid, sickly creatures, all. Just like Caroline. Someone ought to teach these people a lesson," he grumbled. "They can't keep bringing out these boring, pasty-faced girls year after year, and expect men of my exalted rank to stoop to marrying them. I was so bloody bored, I decided to pay you a visit."

"My lord," she said, "you flatter me."

"How do you like being a nursemaid to my brats?" he asked her when the servants had all departed. "Has it made you rethink your curious decision *not* to become my mistress? Would you like to come to London with me now?"

Serena bowed her head. The bastard actually believed that she *liked* what he did to her. Because she no longer fought him. Because she acquiesced to his brutal commands. She feared what he might do if he ever guessed how much she loathed him. "You know I can never be your mistress, my lord," she said calmly. "You are my sister's husband. I could bear the humiliation for myself, but I could never live with the guilt if I damaged *your* reputation."

She could taste the bile and vomit rising in her throat as she flattered him with these lies.

"In that case," he said, eating one of the cakes left over from her dinner party, "I think it is only fair to tell you that I lost your bills in a card game last week. You have a new protector now, and I doubt he will be willing to defer payment. I expect he will visit you soon."

"You bastard," she gasped, struggling to breathe.

He smiled, pleased with himself. "You will like him, I think."

Serena was on her feet, her fists clenched at her sides. "Who is he?" she demanded.

"Are you going to hit me with your little fist?" he asked, amused. "Remember that time you fell down the stairs? That was the last time you made a fist at me."

Serena forced herself to sit down. "Who is it, my lord?" she asked calmly.

Redfylde laughed. "It is the Duke of Kellynch. You're in for a treat, from what I hear."

Serena snatched up the coffeepot, just as the door opened. "Lord Ludham," the butler intoned, and Felix Calverstock breezed in.

Serena had a fantasy in which she told Felix everything. In her fantasy, Felix killed Redfylde in a duel. Then he took her in his arms and asked her to be his wife. Of course, this was absurd. If she ever told Felix her dark secret, he would look at her with disgust and horror. And if he challenged Redfylde to a duel, it would be Redfylde who left the field alive, not Felix. Either way, Felix would never, ever marry Serena if he knew.

"My lord!" Ludham cried, striding up to the marquess and thrusting out his hand. That he admired the older man was blatantly obvious. "I saw your gig outside. Did you drive from London? What magnificent bays! Where did you get them?"

Redfylde gave the earl two fingers to shake. "Tattersall's, of course," he replied easily, "but they were bred in Ireland. The Duke of Kellynch's Red Rogue was their sire. Their dam can be traced back to the Barb."

"Miss Vaughn says the best horses in the world come from Ireland," Ludham said, enthusiastically joining his two favorite subjects: horses and Miss Vaughn. "She's convinced me I must visit something called the Dublin Horse Fair. Hullo, Serena," he added carelessly. "You are looking flushed. Are you feeling quite the thing?"

"I am perfectly well, Felix," she answered, smiling. "Coffee?"

Redfylde crossed his long legs and yawned. "Who," he asked, "is Miss Vaughn?"

Ludham blinked at him as if such ignorance were incredible. "Who is Miss Vaughn?" he repeated in astonishment. "Only the prettiest girl in Bath!"

Redfylde glanced at Serena in amusement. "Indeed. You are not very chivalrous to your cousin, Felix. Surely, there are other ladies in Bath who at least *share* the title."

"I think not!"

Serena said severely, "Rose Fitzwilliam is a very pretty girl, Felix!"

Redfylde interrupted her. "Matlock's daughter? Or, should I say: Westlands's little castoff?" he sneered. "I met the Fitzwilliam chit in London. She is pretty, I grant you, but nothing out of the common way. Westlands must have had some reason for crying off. Some scandal in the girl's past has come to light, no doubt."

"Past?" said Serena. "The child is but seventeen."

He only smiled. "I did not come to Bath in pursuit of young ladies who have been thrown away by other men. All in all, it was a most disappointing crop of debutantes this year. Perhaps I will go to the continent and choose a little French wife. A little marquise."

"You would not disgrace Caroline's memory with a French wife," said Serena hotly.

He smiled at her. "Would I not?"

"Serena," Ludham said urgently. "Tell him how beautiful Miss Vaughn is, and he will not go to the continent. Words fail me anymore. I can't do her justice. I wish I were an artist. She makes me wish I were an artist, that is all I can say."

Redfylde laughed. "Matchmaking, Felix? Why don't you marry her yourself, if she is such a beauty?"

"She won't marry me," the younger man replied.

"Felix!" cried Serena. "You didn't ask her?"

"Yesterday," he replied mournfully. "She won't marry me because of the divorce. I can't say I blame her. The scandal has been dreadful. What woman would want to be touched by it?"

"She refused you, a British earl? Only because of a little scandal?" Redfylde snickered in disbelief. "She must be a very prim and proper miss."

"Quite the contrary," Serena snapped. "She is the most shocking flirt!"

Redfylde quirked a brow. "I am not easily shocked," he drawled.

The word that Lord Redfylde had come to Bath spread through the town like wildfire. Mr. King was beside himself with joy. If Lord Redfylde had left London for Bath, surely the fashionable crowd would soon follow. The master of cere-monies visited Redfylde as soon as possible and personally begged the honor of his lordship's presence in the Upper Rooms for the Monday dress-ball. Rather too ambitiously, he promised the marquess lively conversation in the Octagon Room, brisk play in the card room, a hearty tea, and, of course, pretty dancing partners. Redfylde thought it would be amusing to rattle the cages of the local virgins before he returned to London for the more sophisticated pleasures he preferred.

It was as though a royal visit had been announced. All of Bath dressed itself in its finest clothes and assembled in the Upper Rooms, breathless with anticipation. The marquess was late, and Mr. King broke his own rule and did not begin the ball precisely at nine o'clock. His lordship arrived thirty minutes later, with Lady Serena at his side.

The crowd parted for them, bowing and scraping. The gentlemen bowed, the ladies curtseyed. The silver-haired marquess looked devastatingly attractive in the stark black and white of his formal evening dress. His noble countenance was undeniable, his expression haughty, and his smile cruel. The ladies shivered to see him, and the men gnashed their teeth in envy. There was no competing with such an aristocrat.

He took his place at the top of the room, and all of Bath lined up to meet him. His pale eyes flicked away hopefuls as if they were mere fleas as Mr. King made the introductions. Lord Redfylde spoke only once during this reception. Glancing across the room at a girl of modest good looks who was staring at him, wide-eyed as a frightened doe, he said contemptuously, "I suppose *that* is the famous Miss Vaughn, of whose beauty I have heard so much."

The gentleman who was being presented to the marquess at that moment, looked up, startled, from the bow he was performing. "My lord?"

Redfylde waved him away. "Who gave you permission to address me? King!"

Mr. King had never left the marquess's side. "My lord?"

Redfylde yawned. "No more of these insipid people. Bring Miss Vaughn to me now. Let me have a look at the famous beauty."

Mr. King could not conceal his dismay. "Miss Vaughn does not attend balls, my lord. Her mother, Lady Agatha, is too ill to chaperone her, you understand, and her relative, Sir Benedict Wayborn, has been called away to London."

Lord Redfylde looked annoyed. He turned to Serena. "My dear, I think you had better invite this girl to tea for a private showing. Would tomorrow suit you?"

Serena inclined her head. "Yes, my lord."

* * *

As little as she wanted to entertain the Irish girl, Serena was unprepared for the humiliation of receiving Miss Vaughn's regrets, hastily scrawled on the back of an old laundry list. Her hand shook with rage as she revealed the message to her brother-in-law. "Who does she think she is?" Serena cried.

"Who, indeed?" Redfylde said thoughtfully. "She is poor and unmarried. You tell me her father is a rogue, and her mother is an old fright in a red wig. Yet she does not attend balls, and she does not jump at the chance to take tea with Lady Serena Calverstock. One might almost think the lady has no interest in securing a husband or a place in society."

It was inconceivable to him that Miss Vaughn might be wholly unaware of his presence in Bath. It was in the newspapers, and on everyone's lips. *She must be avoiding me,* he thought. *She must be trying to intrigue me by playing hard to get.*

"Is she truly a beauty?" he asked.

Serena looked at him. It would be useless to deny it. "Ask the Duke of Kellynch if she is beautiful," she answered. "He knows her. Some would say he knows her rather *too* well."

Redfylde looked startled. "Good lord! Is she *Kellynch's* Miss Vaughn?" He began to laugh. "The heiress of Castle Argent? Here in Bath? What a joke! Now I *must* meet her."

"Kellynch's cast-off mistress?" Serena sneered.

"She ain't his mistress, you fool. She's his niece. Her father's one of old Kellynch's bastards. Now tell me," he added, his pale blue eyes narrowing, "how can I meet her? I have no intention of applying at her door like a supplicant. Let it appear to be an accidental meeting of some kind."

They were alone in the drawing-room of her house, the house he paid for. He walked over to Serena, curled his middle finger behind his thumb, and filliped her hard on the end of her patrician nose. "Think of something!" he instructed her angrily.

The following afternoon, Lord Redfylde and his eldest daughter paid a visit to Miss Bulstrode's exclusive Seminary for Young Ladies, conveniently located in the heart of Bath, just steps away from Queen's Square. For nearly half an hour, father and daughter stood outside the edifice waiting for Miss Vaughn to come to collect her sister. She was late.

Surreptitiously, Redfylde looked at every female that passed through the gates. Not one in five met his idea of a tolerable woman, let alone a beautiful one. Most of them were obviously servants. They went into the school alone, and they came out with one or two female children. They dribbled away, and did not interest him in the least.

"Is that her?" he occasionally inquired of his child.

Of his four daughters, black-haired Amelia resembled her dead mother the most and her father the least. Redfylde had no use for any of his children, as they were all useless females, but he had a special distaste of his eldest. From a young age, the child had been taught by her mother and her aunt to be cold and aloof to him. The result of their interference was that Lady Amelia had no natural affection for the man who had created her.

At last he saw Miss Vaughn hurrying up the street. There was no need to ask the question "Is that her?" Even before she was close enough for him to see her face, he could perceive from her effect on the people around her that she was a beautiful girl. Heads, both male and female, turned to watch her as she passed. One young man actually ran into a lamp-post.

Her dress was striped in blue and white, like mattress ticking, Redfylde thought with all the contempt of a man of fashion, but her figure was just what he liked: slim and virginal. This was not the ideal body type for breeding, of course, but his lordship had never been attracted to ample women. Although tall and muscular, he was not very well-endowed in his manhood, and large women made him feel inadequate. A bully by nature, he instinctively was attracted to women whom he could physically overpower with ease.

"Don't just stand there," he urged his daughter impatiently as Miss Vaughn drew near the school gates. "Go and say hello."

Miss Vaughn rang the bell on the gate and stood waiting.

"I can't," Amelia cried in soft dismay. "I don't know her very well."

Infuriated by her disobedience, Redfylde gave her an encouraging, fatherly shove in the back. Lady Amelia went sprawling. He had forgotten what a mewling weakling she was, like all of Caroline's children. Not for the first time, he wondered if she was really his flesh and blood.

"You clumsy little fool," he hissed, gritting his teeth. "Get up! You are embarrassing your father. Get up, or you will be punished. I shall thrash you within an inch of your life."

Amelia looked up at him, terrified. "Please, Papa." She began to whimper.

It was the absolute worst thing she could have done. Pleas for mercy always awakened the worst cruelty in him. He bent over her, his lip curled, his walking stick in his hand.

Overcome by her fears, Amelia fainted, but, just before she lost consciousness, a beautiful angel appeared, an angel with green eyes, white hair, and a golden halo. Miraculously, the angel came between Amelia and her father, and Amelia was saved. She felt herself being lifted up and carried away to a beautiful place.

When she woke up, she was lying on the big horsehair sofa in Miss Bulstrode's private sitting room. Her head was in Miss Vaughn's lap. Miss Vaughn was quietly stroking her hair. Lady Amelia's father was there, too, but he was different. Miss Vaughn had transformed him somehow. It took Amelia a moment to realize that her father was *smiling*. He was no longer angry with her. She had escaped certain death. Miss Vaughn had rescued her.

Her mother in heaven must have sent Miss Vaughn to rescue her. It was the only possible explanation that Lady Amelia could conceive. No one else had ever loved her, and people were always telling her that her dear mama was in heaven watching over her.

"Hello," said Miss Vaughn, smiling down at her. What Amelia had thought was a golden halo was actually her round bonnet of golden straw. "You gave us all a bad scare, my lady! Do you think you can sit up now? Will you try for me?"

"Of course she can," Redfylde said. "There's a good girl." Even though he wasn't angry any longer, his voice sent a shiver through his daughter's body.

"Are you cold, *mavourneen*?" asked Miss Vaughn, her voice soft and creamy. "Would you toss me the bit of a blanket there, my lord?"

To Amelia's amazement, her father obeyed. Incredibly, he seemed ready and willing to do anything Miss Vaughn told him to. "There, now," said Miss Vaughn, when she had wrapped Lady Amelia up. "You're gonna be just fine. Your father's here to look after you. He's very anxious about you, you know."

Miss Vaughn got to her feet. Amelia whimpered and clung to her, but Miss Vaughn gently disentangled herself and went to Amelia's father. Amelia could no longer hear what they were saying, but the soft murmur of Miss Vaughn's voice made her feel safe. She knew instinctively that her father would not harm her as long as Miss Vaughn was there.

Lord Redfylde was doing his best to make a good impression. Right from the start, he was fascinated by the Irish girl. It was not just that she was beautiful; he had known and possessed many beautiful women in his time. She was different. She spoke to him with perfect ease, as if she had known him all her life. Her green eyes never evaded his. She made no attempt to disguise her Irish accent, and, if she was ashamed of her shabby clothes, she gave no sign of it. He was cynical enough to think she might be trying to get to his heart by way of his fatherly affections, but he was fascinated by her all the same.

The door opened, and a severely dressed female of some fifty summers stepped inside, leading a fair-haired girl firmly by the hand. "Late again, Miss Vaughn!" said Miss Bulstrode. "I am going to have to charge you a late fee!"

Cosima began to make excuses.

Miss Bulstrode's eyes widened as she saw Lord Redfylde. He was an imposing specimen of the nobility. He wore his tight-fitting mulberry coat and buff-colored pantaloons with distinction. "Oh!" she said. "Were you waiting to see me, sir?"

"I am Lord Redfylde," he said haughtily.

"My lord!" Miss Bulstrode made him a very deep, unsteady curtsey.

"This is my eldest daughter." To him, Lady Amelia looked disgustingly insignificant. It seemed to him that, if she could not be male, Lady Amelia might at least have been an *attractive* female. Instead, she was a fat, listless drab.

Redfylde much preferred the rosy-cheeked, fair-haired girl who had entered the room with the headmistress. The younger Miss Vaughn was tall and slim and healthy. In her time, she would be as beautiful as her sister.

Miss Bulstrode sank into another curtsey. "My lady," she murmured. "This is a great honor. Curtsey, child," she commanded Miss Allegra.

Allie's curtsey was a mere sketch.

"I'm sorry I was a bit late fetching Allie, Miss Bulstrode," said Cosima, twisting her hands together. "But Lady Amelia was feeling ill, and so . . ."

"Heavens!" cried Miss Bulstrode. "I will fetch the doctor at once!"

"She doesn't need a doctor," Redfylde said curtly. "She's had more cake than is good for her, that is all. She is fat and lazy. She needs exercise. I am determined, Miss Bulstrode," said Redfylde, "that my children receive only the finest possible education. Perhaps you would give me a tour of your seminary?"

Cosima took her sister by the hand. "I'll leave you to it," she said quickly, hoping that Miss Bulstrode would forget all about collecting her exorbitant late fee.

"You're not going?" said Redfylde.

"Please, don't leave me," said Amelia, her terror returning.

"I must," Miss Vaughn said apologetically. "I'm so dreadfully late, my mother will think I ran off with the gypsies again, like I did when I was eight."

Redfylde took a step toward her. "Perhaps you will be so kind as to look in on Lady Amelia tomorrow, Miss Vaughn? She will want to thank you properly for your kindness to her."

Cosima looked at Amelia's desperate little face and could not refuse. "I'll make time," she promised. "I'll bring Allie to see your ladyship after school tomorrow, shall I?"

She bent over Lady Amelia and kissed the child's forehead.

The visit was paid the following day. The Miss Vaughns arrived breathless, the elder wearing the same striped dress from the day before, and the younger bearing the small gift of a puzzle for the recovering Amelia.

Serena gave them tea. The elder Miss Vaughn ate nothing, but the younger ate her fill of sandwiches and cakes.

Lady Serena had not bothered to show his lordship Lady Caroline's new tooth, Cosima was shocked to discover. She was sure the proud father must be dying to see it. In fact, Redfylde had seen nothing of any of his children besides Amelia. He had only used Amelia as an excuse to meet Miss Vaughn; otherwise, he would not have seen her either. He had no desire to see them, but to indulge Miss Vaughn, he had them brought down from the nursery.

"Well, children?" Cosima said, taking Lady Caroline from the arms of her nurse. "Aren't you going to give your father a kiss?"

Amelia and Imogen and Elizabeth stared, thunderstruck by the concept.

Redfylde was annoyed. *Anyone would think the ugly little brats were terrified of me,* he thought angrily. Miss Vaughn would think he was a monster.

In fact, it never occurred to Miss Vaughn that the children might be afraid. Her own father, she was persuaded, was the worst blackguard who ever lived, but she had never in her life been afraid of him. For all his faults, Colonel Vaughn had never been violent. She decided the girls must be shy, and still grieving over the loss of their mother.

"Go on," she said, laughing. "Give him a kiss! He won't bite you!"

Pale as death, Lady Amelia stepped forward. Redfylde bent a little, Amelia put her arms around his neck and kissed her father's cheek. Reluctantly, Lady Imogen and Lady Elizabeth followed her lead. "That's better," Cosima said warmly.

"You have let them all grow fat, Serena," Redfylde said in distaste.

"Ah, sure, 'tis only puppy fat," Cosima said quickly. "All they need is a bit of exercise and fresh air, as I keep trying to tell Lady Serena. Oh, but listen to me, ganching on like a magpie, when your lordship is dying to see the tooth!"

Redfylde stared at her blankly. "The tooth?"

Without warning, Miss Vaughn brought the babe closer to him. Redfylde was startled to say the least. The babe opened its sticky pink mouth and gurgled. Reddylde had never been this close to the child before and its open mouth was as disgusting to him as an open sore. At birth, all the children had been taken from their mother and placed in the nursery.

"Take her," said Miss Vaughn.

He cringed. "I couldn't possibly," he said quickly.

Miss Vaughn ignored his protests, and placed Lady Caroline in her father's arms.

Lady Caroline began to scream the instant she felt her father's arms around her.

"There it is," Cosima exclaimed in triumph. "See? Lady Caroline has cut her first tooth! Don't cry, little baby. Papa has you now," she cooed. She gave the bewildered marquess a dazzling smile. "I just love babies, don't you? If there's a baby within a square mile of me, you can bet I'll be the one holding him."

Redfylde held Lady Caroline at arm's length.

"They do not seem to like me, however," he sniffed.

Cosima took the baby from him. Lady Caroline stopped crying as if by magic. "It's hard for them," Cosy said softly, rocking the baby from side to side. "It's not been so very long since they lost their mother. I know it's hard on you, too, my lord," she added kindly, "but you can see how much the children need you. I hope you'll be staying a while?"

He smiled at her. "I hope to stay in Bath for quite some time," he said. "After all, the children do need me."

Cosima beamed at him. "And *you* need *them,* of course," she said softly.

She felt quite proud of herself for bringing together this shattered family.

On the first day of spring, Lord Westlands arrived in Bath. Cosima saw him from the drawing-room window, and flew downstairs to the door, feather duster in hand, and opened it just as he was touching the bell.

Marcus Wayborn, Lord Westlands, peered into the interior of the house. He saw a brown Holland pinafore worn over green baize and looked no further. He held out his card with a gloved hand. "Lord Westlands to see Lady Agatha," he said.

His voice and manner were so supercilious that for a moment, Cosima debated meekly taking the card like the servant he evidently thought she was. But she was too happy to see him.

"Hello, Marcus. I wasn't sure you would come."

His eyes flew up to her face. "Cosy! Good God! What *are* you doing? Is it a masquerade?"

Her hair was wrapped in a cloth and there was a smudge of dirt on the side of her nose, but she was the same pretty little cousin he had been caught kissing behind the stables of his father's estate when she was eleven and he was fourteen. With one very intriguing difference. She had soft little breasts now.

"Spring cleaning," she explained, flicking the turkey feathers over his handsome face as if it were a knick-knack in need of cleaning. She pulled him inside the house and closed the door.

"Why are *you* doing it?" he demanded. "Where are the servants?"

"I gave them the year off," she said dryly. "Not everyone is stinking rich like yourself, Marcus! Some of us have to do our own cleaning."

"I wish I *were* stinking rich," he muttered darkly, "but I'm afraid my father keeps me on a tight rein, allowance-wise."

"Mother's sleeping, and Allie's at school, so I'm afraid you're stuck with me." She led him upstairs to the drawing-room. "I take it you got my letter," she said, returning to dusting the mantelpiece.

"I did. Interesting choice of a messenger," he observed, looking around the room. "Sir Benedict Wayborn. My father thinks he's a dangerous radical."

"Dangerous radical?"

"The man's a born troublemaker." He grinned at her affectionately. "But I suppose that comes with the territory, eh?"

The feather duster paused. "What do you mean?"

"Well, he's half-Irish, isn't he? Just like you."

Cosima looked at him in astonishment. "Who?" she said blankly.

"The stiff, Sir Benedict. His mother was Irish. Didn't you know? Lord Oranmore's daughter. Lady Angela Redmund that was."

Cosima's legs suddenly felt weak. "I think I'm gonna have to sit down," she said faintly.

"You've been working too hard," Westlands complained, putting her into a chair and kneeling at her feet. He took a deep breath. "I was wondering if you ever grew into those big, green eyes of yours," he said softly.

Holding her hands, he looked at her like a lovesick goose.

"Oh, Marcus," she said, howling with laughter. "You haven't changed a bit!"

Chapter 15

"Where is she?" the Marquess of Redfylde demanded of Serena.

The Monday dress-ball was in full bloom in the Upper Rooms, but Miss Vaughn was again a truant. Her elusiveness, which had tantalized and amused Lord Redfylde at first, was beginning to wear thin with his lordship. Redfylde could not bear to be denied anything he wanted even a little, and he wanted Miss Vaughn more and more every day.

Unwisely, Serena chose to be obtuse. "Who are you looking for, my lord?"

Her brother-in-law's hand bit into her arm. "Did you not send the carriage to Camden Place for her?" he demanded. "I told you to send the carriage."

Serena unfurled her fan. "I sent the carriage, my lord, with my compliments, but, short of instructing my footmen to abduct the girl, I could not *make* her get in."

Redfylde bit back his frustration. The situation was becoming intolerable. Miss Vaughn, it seemed, would go out of her way to visit his children, but she wouldn't lift a finger to be with their father. He supposed this was her way of bringing him to the point of marriage.

"What excuse did she give for her rudeness?" he wanted to know.

"Miss Vaughn has but one excuse," Serena replied. "The claims of her sick mama. She cannot leave poor Lady Agatha even for the space of an evening. Apparently, the woman is just sick enough to keep her daughter at home, but not sick enough to die."

"Have you sent a doctor?"

Serena laughed in astonishment. "Have *I* sent a doctor? Why should I?"

"Perhaps," he said coldly, "Miss Vaughn has reason to think Lady Serena's affection for her is not sincere, and that is why she will not make use of your carriage! You must try to make yourself agreeable, my dear. Take the poor girl under your wing."

Serena was speechless.

"I think perhaps I will use you in the carriage on the way home," he said very quietly, even as he smiled and nodded to Mr. King. "I shall open the roof so that the driver and the footmen can hear your cries of ecstasy. Or, perhaps, I shall invite one of the footmen to take my place. Would you like that, my dear?"

Serena shuddered. "I shall send Dr. Grantham to Lady Agatha at once, my lord."

By this time, Mr. King had made his way to them. The master of ceremonies was in a state of euphoria. The continued residence in Bath of the Earl of Ludham had been a blessing. The sudden appearance of the Marquess of Redylde had been like a miracle. With the arrival of Lord Wayborn's son and heir, Mr. King's cup was running over. When word got out that gentlemen of such exalted rank were disdaining London in favor of little Bath, the Upper Rooms would again be filled to capacity. Or so he hoped.

"My dear Lady Serena!" he cried, bowing. "My Lord Redfylde! Have you heard the news? Lord Westlands has come to Bath. He is here tonight with his fiancee, Lady Rose."

Serena was sufficiently surprised. She raised a well-groomed brow. "I had thought Lady Rose was engaged to Mr. Freddie Carteret?" she drawled. "I read it in the papers."

"A mistake," Mr. King confidently declared. "A mistake which I am laboring to correct for poor Lady Matlock's sake. The notice was put in wrong. Ah! Here is Lady Matlock now, with Mr. Carteret. She will tell you all about it herself. I must have a word with the musicians."

Lady Matlock seemed to have borrowed one of her daughter's filmy, low-cut gowns for the occasion. "It was the stupid man at the newspaper," she explained. "He put it in wrong. *Of course* Rose is engaged to *Westlands*. How could it be otherwise when his lordship was so attentive to her in London? He only went home to ask for his father's blessing first."

Bored, Lord Redfylde left them without a word, and strode in the direction of the card room. "How could the man at the newspaper be so stupid?" Serena murmured.

Freddie Carteret stepped into the breach wearing an obsequious smile. "It will, perhaps, become understandable when I tell your ladyship that it was *I* who placed the notice in the newspaper. The stupid fellow wrote my name down by mistake."

Serena blinked at him. "*You* put the notice in, Mr. Carteret?"

"In my capacity as Personal Private Secretary to Lady Matlock," he explained.

Lady Matlock swayed on her feet. Her new secretary took her by the arm and lead her gently to a chair. Attending to Lady Matlock when she had one of her "spells" would comprise the bulk of Mr. Carteret's new duties, but he did not mind. The countess was paying him so well that he did not feel it necessary to threaten Lady Rose with a breach of promise suit. "Dear Freddie," she murmured, patting his cheek. "When that girl is finally married, I shall take to my bed for a week. I am quite exhausted."

"Allow me," Freddie smiled, "to make your burdens my own."

Lady Matlock quivered. It would be so nice, she mused, to

have a gentleman to turn to in a time of crisis. Footmen were all very well when there was nothing better to be had, but nothing could compare to comfort of a gentleman.

Serena was surprised when her brother-in-law reappeared at the tea interval. Her surprise turned to alarm when she realized that he had lost a great deal of money at the card table. Redfylde was a wealthy man, but he hated to lose even a trifle. Serena knew from bitter experience that he would vent his anger on her if he could. She was filled with such dread that she could scarcely focus on the conversation.

Lady Rose Fitzwilliam was chattering happily about her forthcoming marriage, and, in particular, about the design of her wedding gown. The prospective bridegroom looked bored until his bride-to-be suddenly exclaimed, "I wish Miss Vaughn were here. She could describe the skirt to you so much better. What was the word she used?"

"Meringue," Westlands said, laughing. "Cousin Cosy has a definite way with words. The Irish gift of gab, you know."

Lord Redfylde swung his pale blue eyes in Westlands's direction. "Cousin?" he said sharply. "Miss Vaughn is your cousin, is she?"

Westlands glanced at him. Redfylde was an intimidating figure, and he outranked the viscount, but Westlands had the invincible arrogance of youth on his side. "I said so, didn't I?" he replied rudely. "Are you hard of hearing?"

"If she is so," Redfylde said coldly, "why do you allow her to be held prisoner to her mother's illness? Lady Agatha is your aunt, I suppose?"

Rose said quickly, "Indeed, my lord! Westlands sent a chair for Miss Vaughn, but she could not leave her mother."

"Is the woman so sick?" Redfylde demanded.

"Who is sick?" Lady Matlock demanded, panting indignantly. "Agatha Vaughn? Pshaw! I am persuaded she is not half as sick as I am, but I do my duty. I chaperone Rose to all these events, in spite of my wretched health. I *extend* myself for my daughter's sake."

"I think," said Miss Millicent Carteret, "that it is a matter of clothes! Everyone knows the Vaughns are poor. It is not Miss Vaughn's fault, of course, but there it is. You saw that hideous green affair she wore to Lady Serena's card party! It has been a year, if not longer, since we saw a lady's waistline under her armpits! Not a very flattering look when one is as small-bosomed as Miss Vaughn."

"I did not realize that Miss Vaughn had attended a party at your house, Serena," Redfylde said angrily. "You did not tell me."

"She also attended a concert, my lord," Serena murmured, "so, you see, her concern for dear mama comes and goes."

Lady Matlock recalled that it had been Miss Vaughn who had brought Lord Westlands to Bath. Due to her influence, the young man had lost no time in engaging himself to Rose. Lady Matlock's ordeal was almost at an end, thanks to Miss Vaughn. Lady Matlock saw an opportunity to do the Irish girl a good turn.

"Such a pretty girl, my lord!" she said. "She plays and sings like an angel. I can't recall when I heard anything that gave me more pleasure than hearing her play. How I would love to present Miss Vaughn to Society! Sally Jersey would eat her pink pearls if she had to receive Miss Vaughn at Almack's. With the right clothes and hair, I think she would do very well."

Redfylde smiled to himself. The idea of spurning all the unworthy London debutantes in favor of Miss Vaughn appealed to him. Cramming her down the throats of jealous mavens like that Jersey cow would be a rare pleasure.

Westlands frowned at his fiancée. "If it is only a matter of clothes, Rose, why do you not give her something? You have more dresses than you can ever wear as it is, and you will be getting all new things for your trousseau, anyway."

"With all my heart," cried Rose. "I would do anything to help Miss Vaughn. But she is so slim, I doubt my clothes would fit her. Westlands can span her waist with his hands!

And that is without *any* corseting!" she added in amazement. "I could not believe my eyes."

"Indeed," said Lord Redfylde severely. "Do you *often* have occasion to span your cousin's waist with your hands, sir?"

"Only when my fiancée bids me to do so," the young man replied. "Why do you ask, sir? Are you acquainted with my cousin?"

Redfylde was annoyed with himself. He had not meant to betray his interest in the young woman until he was certain that interest would do him credit. "Hardly," he replied. "But I believe my children are fond of her. Are they not, Serena?"

"They are indeed," Serena answered dryly.

Lady Amelia regarded Miss Vaughn as a heaven-sent protector, and the younger girls followed her lead. They would have adored the Irish girl even if she didn't help them with their lessons, comb out their tangles without pulling, and sing them to sleep. When she was around, their father was almost kind to them.

Westlands said, "Cosy's always had a soft spot for brats."

"I wonder, Serena," said Redfylde coldly, "that you do not give Miss Vaughn some of your dresses. You are still slender. They would fit her better."

Serena smiled thinly. She had been starving herself for years in order to fit into the floor models of her favorite dressmakers. "Perhaps I should give her my jewels as well," she sniffed.

"A little generosity," Redfylde snapped, "would not go amiss."

Serena heard the threat in his voice. She forced a smile. "Perhaps Lady Rose would be kind enough to help me go through my wardrobe?" she suggested. "As Miss Vaughn is such a good friend of yours, you will be a better judge than I of what she likes."

"Of course!" said Rose instantly. "I should love to."

"Then why not come and stay with me for a few days?" Serena suggested. "Give your mama a well-deserved rest," she added persuasively. "Why don't you let me take Rose home with me tonight, ma'am? You can send her clothes along in the morning with her maid. I am only three doors down from you, after all."

Lady Matlock seized the moment, and was soon on her way home in the care of her Personal Private Secretary. Serena smiled at Redfylde, knowing full well that he was anything but pleased by this development. With Lord Matlock's daughter in the house, he would not dare molest his sister-in-law. Redfylde gnashed his teeth in frustration, but he had no one to blame but himself. Giving away Serena's dresses had been his own magnificent idea.

"Come, come," said Lord Ludham, starting up from the table. "Are we not dancing?"

"You are late, Felix," Serena chided him. "The set is already forming. You must find your partner at once and apologize. Who is she?"

He grinned at her suddenly. "Why, you, if you will have me," he said.

Serena found herself, at the age of thirty, blushing like a schoolgirl. Rose had to help her pin up her skirts. She didn't even know which dance it was until they were in line, and the boulangere was struck up.

Dr. Grantham was dispatched to Camden Place the next day, and, armed with orders from Lady Serena to make Lady Agatha better, he recommended daily vapor baths to the patient. The baths were located in Stall Street, and had been recommended to Lady Agatha before, but she refused to be carried anywhere in a sedan chair, and the Vaughns did not keep a carriage. Carriages, in fact, were not used in Bath as often as they were in other places, owing to the extreme steepness of the streets.

Lady Agatha was terrified of the chairs. They reminded her of coffins, she said.

It was ruinously expensive to keep a carriage, of course, but it was an important outward and visible sign of one's place in the world. A carriage separated the upper echelons from the hoi polloi. Despite her poverty, Serena insisted on keeping a carriage, and this she sent to take Lady Agatha to the baths. It made Lady Agatha weep with joy to think that, when she was gone, her daughter would have the assistance of good friends like Lady Serena Calverstock.

With the carriage coming every morning, it seemed silly to walk Allegra to school. The Miss Vaughns simply rode with their mother to Stall Street, then walked the short distance from the baths to Miss Bulstrode's Seminary.

As Dr. Grantham employed a private nurse to attend his patients in the bath, there was nothing for Miss Vaughn to do while her mother was undergoing the treatment. The carriage brought her to Serena's house in the Royal Crescent. The offer of clothes caught her by surprise. She did not think that Serena liked her. She felt instantly ashamed of herself for not liking the English lady. At first she refused, but Serena and Rose quickly overwhelmed her scruples. Besides, it was against her nature to resist anything as tempting as free, beautiful dresses.

She gave in, and the three women went up to Serena's dressing room.

Serena's maid brought out dress after dress, each more exquisite than the last. None of these, Cosima was sure, had been bought off the floor model at half cost.

Serena left them to it, saying, "Take anything you like, Miss Vaughn. I've a feeling you will be going places."

"What does she mean by that?" Cosima asked suspiciously. Perhaps it was ungrateful, but she couldn't help but wonder why Serena was being so nice to her.

Rose had selected a peacock blue walking dress for her friend to try on. It would need to be taken in a little at the waist and bosom, but, after that, it would be perfect for a picnic in the country. "You have made a conquest of Lord Redfylde," she told Cosima, giggling. "The poor man was beside himself at the ball because you were not there. He danced with no one. He's a little old for you, of course. He has a married daughter my age, you know. But he's still handsome, don't you think?"

Cosima snorted. "Right!" she said sarcastically. "A Big Lord like that, interested in the likes of me. He'd be too proud."

"I think he is going to propose to you," said Rose, smiling. "No; I'm sure of it."

Cosima laughed it off. "You're mistaken, Lady Rose. It's not been seven months since his wife died, and he is so devoted to his children."

"He needs a son," Rose said simply.

Cosima was horrified. "If people think I'm trying to take advantage of a grieving widower—! Oh, my God, I'll die of shame!" She began to take off the peacock blue walking dress. "Help me out of this. Indeed, 'tis very kind of Lady Serena, but I can't accept charity!"

"Don't be silly," Rose chided. "*She* can't be seen in public wearing these again. Try this ballgown. Are there dancing shoes to go with it?" she asked the maid.

The maid went to search the shelves in the huge, cedarlined closet.

"Let me tell you about Serena," said Rose, when the maid had gone. "She hated you until you refused Lord Ludham's offer of marriage. Now she's absolutely delighted with you. Poor thing, she's so obviously hoping Ludham will ask *her*. Of course, he never will. She's so old! I daresay, he thinks of her as his old maiden aunt."

"Does Serena want to marry Lord Ludham?" Cosima asked in astonishment. The idea of anyone actually wanting to marry a divorced fellow was beyond her power to understand.

"Of course she does, silly," said Rose. "He inherited the earldom from her father, you know. If she'd been born a man, she'd be the Earl of Ludham, not he."

Lady Serena's maid returned with a pair of silver kid dancing pumps, ending this topic of conversation. Cosima tried the shoes doubtfully, but to her amazement, they fit. In the end, she walked away with five new costumes, five pairs of shoes, and three spectacular hats. She had a dress for the morning, a dress for promenading outdoors, a dress for promenading indoors, a ball gown, and a dinner dress. It was nowhere near enough, but, as Rose told Lady Serena, she could not make Miss Vaughn take any more. A seamstress was engaged to make the minor alterations, and Miss Vaughn went down to thank Lady Serena.

Lord Redfylde was there listening to poor Amelia with a pained expression as the child practiced at her aunt's pianoforte. Cosima was too nervous to look at him.

Rose chattered happily. "We've chosen the peacock blue for the picnic. You wouldn't believe what it does to Miss Vaughn's eyes! It makes them look blue."

"I can't possibly go on a picnic!" Cosima said too loudly. "My mother's just starting the new treatments, and we don't know yet how she'll like it."

"It's only one day, Miss Vaughn," Lord Redfylde said. "Your mother will have the private nurse to sit with her. Lady Serena has made all the arrangements."

Poor little thing, he thought kindly as he looked at her. She looked adorably flustered. *She must be in love with me,* he decided.

Cosima gnawed at her bottom lip. "Mother's very shy around strangers, my lord. I can't leave her at home with a stranger."

"But you deserve a day out," cried Rose. "And so does Miss Allegra! Lady Agatha would be the first to say so. If it comes to it, *I'll* sit with her, while you and Allie go."

"I can't ask you to do that," Cosima said firmly. "My mother would be the first to tell me to go, that's true. But I couldn't enjoy myself out in the country if I thought she was unhappy or sick or hurt. Honestly, Lady Serena, I'm so grateful to you for inviting me, and I thank you most kindly for the clothes, but if my mother's not well, I won't be going, and neither will Allie."

"It would be so good," said Lord Redfylde, "for the children."

Cosima smiled at him in relief. She had forgotten that Rose was only a foolish, romantic young girl. Of course, Lord Redfylde was only thinking of his children. Probably his heart was so tender and sore from the shock and grief of his wife's death that he couldn't even look at another woman. Silly Rose.

Lady Amelia jumped up from the pianoforte. Her father was never more cross than when he did not get his way with Miss Vaughn. "But you must come to the picnic!" she pleaded. "We need you there."

Cosima winced. She did not want to believe that Lord Redfylde was contemplating marriage, but she worried that the marquess's children were becoming too attached to her. It wasn't healthy. "I'm sorry, Lady Amelia," she said softly. "It's just too far, darling. If something were to happen when I was halfway to Blaize Castle, I'd never forgive myself."

She glanced at the clock, unable to bear Lady Amelia's pleading eyes. "I'd better be going. Mother will be getting out of the baths any minute. She'll worry if I'm not there. Thank you again."

She bobbed a hasty curtsey and practically ran from the room.

"Poor Miss Vaughn." Rose sighed. "Poor Miss Allegra. Poor Lady Agatha. There must be something we can do to make their lives better."

"If Miss Vaughn can't go to the picnic," Amelia said timidly, "could we not bring the picnic to her?"

Her father looked at her with scorn. "Go to the nursery at once," he said. "I believe you have tortured your aunt's pianoforte enough for one day."

"Stay a moment," said Rose, as Amelia's eyes filled with tears. "That's not a bad idea. There's a park running through the middle of Camden Place, you know. We could have the picnic there. The servants can carry Lady Agatha out on a sofa, if need be. We could put up a tent. Hire a string quartet. Do the thing properly."

"If Miss Vaughn should still refuse?" Serena asked.

"We won't tell her," Rose said smugly. "We'll kidnap her, and take her to the park whether she wants to go or not."

Redfylde considered the idea, and approved. "Well done, Amelia," he said, giving his eldest daughter two fingers to shake.

Benedict returned to Bath on the afternoon of the picnic. It was nearly three weeks since he had last been seen or heard from in Bath. "What is all the commotion in the park?" he asked Pickering wearily as Pickering helped him out of his coat.

"Lord Redfylde has taken over the park for a picnic. The entire neighborhood is invited, servants included." Pickering was worried that he was going to be stuck indoors unpacking the master's trunk while others enjoyed themselves in the park on this beautiful spring day.

"Lord Redfylde!" Benedict exclaimed. "Has he taken a house in Camden Place?"

"No, sir," Pickering replied. "He has taken an interest in the Miss Vaughns."

Benedict was quiet for a moment.

"Ah," he said. "I believe I will go and pay my respects to Lady Agatha."

"You will find her in the park reclining upon a sofa," said Pickering. "Lord Redfylde has put up a silk pavilion to keep the sun off of her."

"Has he indeed," Benedict murmured. "You may go to the picnic, if you like, Pickering. Leave the unpacking until tomorrow."

He made a beeline for the park.

When he had left Bath the trees were just beginning to bud with new life. Now they were laden with new green growth and the lilacs were in bloom. Children were flying kites and sailing model boats on the pond. On the green lawn were banquet tables laden with platters of roast fowl, ham, and beef. Fruits and cakes were piled onto huge silver epergnes. Crystal goblets and silver cutlery sparkled in the sunlight. Liveried servants were variously employed carrying plates to and fro, shooing away flies, fanning ladies, and getting unruly children down from trees. Their liveries were in every color of the rainbow. He saw Serena's pale lavender livery and Lady Matlock's pea-green among the many colors.

A small orchestra was playing Haydn near the Italian fountain.

Allegra Vaughn was among the children sailing model boats on the pond. Benedict walked over to her. "That is a beautiful boat, Miss Allegra."

"You're back!" she shrieked. "What did you bring me from London?"

He smiled at her. "A marionette and a puzzle map of the world. How is your mother?"

Allie dragged him over to the white silk tent. Underneath it, laid out on the grass, was what appeared to be an elegant drawing-room. Lady Agatha, painted like a doll, sat at length on the sofa, a fur over her knees. Lady Matlock and Lady Dalrymple sat near her, enjoying the shade. Dr. Grantham was timing Lady Matlock's pulse against his pocket watch.

Lord Redfylde, resplendent in tight yellow pantaloons and a scarlet coat, stood a little apart from the ladies, drinking champagne. He looked vigilant, as if he were waiting for something. Looking almost girlish in her white muslin gown, Serena Calverstock was flying a kite with Lord Ludham's assistance.

"Excuse me," said Mr. Freddie Carteret, stepping past Allegra and Benedict to supply Lady Matlock with a fresh glass of iced champagne and a plate of lobster patties.

Miss Vaughn was notable by her absence.

"Sir Benedict!" Serena greeted him in surprise. Her heart began to pound. The only way she would ever be free of Redfylde was to marry. But how could she bring herself to accept Sir Benedict's proposal *now,* when Felix was being so attentive?

"I was beginning to think you were never going to return," she said glumly.

Redfylde glanced at Benedict. He had once rented the estate neighboring Sir Benedict's in Surrey, but the two men never enjoyed anything more than a nodding acquaintance.

"Some business at Wayborn Hall delayed me longer than expected," Benedict explained, paying his respects to each lady in turn. "I did not have the opportunity to congratulate you, Mr. Carteret," he added civilly to that young man. "Pray, allow me to do so now. I wish you and Lady Rose much happiness."

Lady Matlock laughed gaily. "You are sadly behind the times, Sir Benedict. Rose is engaged to marry Lord Westlands. They are playing badminton over there," she said, fluttering her fingers in no particular direction, "with Miss Carteret and my brother-in-law. Mr. Carteret is now my personal private secretary."

"Good heavens," Benedict murmured. "Was I gone so long?"

Lady Agatha had been staring at him in puzzled silence ever since he bent over her hand. "Who is he?" she finally whispered in desperation to Dr. Grantham. "He looks familiar."

"She's only funning!" Allegra assured him. "It's Cousin Ben, Mama." She grabbed Benedict's hand. "Come on! You must be hungry."

"Where is your sister?" he asked as she led him over to the banquet table.

"I don't know," she answered, shrugging. "She was here a moment ago."

"Miss Vaughn has gone to change Lady Caroline," one of the footmen cutting fresh pineapple at the table volunteered.

"Who is Lady Caroline?" Benedict asked Allie, "and what is she being changed into?"

Allie grinned her changeling's grin at him. "I'll show you."

* * *

Cosima was changing the baby on Lady Agatha's bed in what was once the Book room. Benedict was pleased that she had taken his advice.

"You're back!" she said breathlessly as Allie dragged him in. All the cool and aloof things she had practiced to say to him when he returned ("Look what the cat dragged in," "The prodigal returns!" or "Have we met before? You look vaguely familiar.") simply did not occur to her, and she was left standing there, grinning at him like a fool.

Hastily, she drew the curtain that separated her mother's bed from the rest of the room, affording a little privacy for two sets of very pink cheeks, hers and Lady Caroline's. Her heart began to pound in her chest. She felt as if she had been dead for three weeks and was just now coming alive. In her haste to finish with the baby, she drove the diaper pin into her finger and gasped in pain.

"I see you took my advice," he said.

"The curtain was my idea," she said.

Benedict examined her minutely when she at last opened the curtain. She looked beautiful, of course, but she had changed in three weeks. Short creamy-blonde curls framed her heart-shaped face in the Grecian style. She was wearing a striking ensemble of brilliant blue superfine peacock. It looked fashionable and new and there was not a wrinkle on it anywhere. The strong color made her eyes look more blue than green.

The changes made him nervous. He had only been gone three weeks!

"You cut your hair," he said stupidly.

"It's only a fringe," she said, touching a hand to the curls over her eyes.

She picked up the baby, and, now clean and dry, Lady Caroline cooed as they left the "bedroom." On this side of the curtain there was a little sitting room so that her mother could receive visitors in situ, if she felt up to it. There was a lady's escritoire, two dainty gilded chairs, and a number of tiny tables and footstools. On one of the tables was a bowl of fresh lilacs. Its lemony perfume filled the air.

Cosima covertly examined him for some sign that he had been womanizing his way through London for the last three weeks. There was none, which just went to show what deceivers men were.

"Do you know where my jumping rope is?" Allegra demanded.

"Under your bed, I should think," Cosima replied. "Everything else is!"

Allie ran out of the room.

"No running in the house!" Cosy called after her uselessly.

She smiled at him, but it was a cool smile. After the initial surprise of seeing him, she was now recovered. "How was London, then?" she inquired politely. "Did all the girls cry when you left?"

"On the contrary," he said. "I distinctly heard cheering."

"Oh? Then what kept you away from Bath so long? I was sure it was a woman."

It pleased him to think she might be jealous. "I had business on my estate."

"Business? Oh, you mean with the governess?"

Anyone else would have received a sharp set down for this impertinence. But he merely smiled and answered, "One of my neighbors was intent on selling a strip of land that lies between my estate and his. I don't care to have a stranger for a neighbor, so I was obliged to buy it myself. Paid too much for it, too."

"You're a rich bastard," she said cheerfully. "You can afford it."

He reached into his coat for the packet of bills he had won from the Duke of Kellynch on the turn of a card. "I have obtained your bills," he said. "They will trouble you no more."

He held them out, looking forward to receiving her gratitude.

Cosima only laughed and jiggled the baby. "When did they ever trouble me?" she wanted to know. "Put them in the desk there, if you will. What do I owe you for them?"

The key was in the lock. He opened the little desk and placed the bills inside. "I've no intention of paying you back, of course," she added. "I'm only curious."

"You owe me nothing. I won them from the Duke of Kellynch on the turn of a card."

"The Duke of Kellynch?" She stared at him blankly. "Jimmy?"

"*Uncle* Jimmy," he corrected.

She scowled. "Uncle Jimmy has a big mouth," she observed.

"He certainly does," Benedict agreed. "He told me all about Castle Argent. Fifty thousand pounds is a lot of money, Miss Vaughn. You ought to take it."

"If my grandfather had wanted to give me money, I would have been pleased to take it. But he didn't. He gave me that house. It's mine, and I intend to keep it."

"Think of what you could do for Miss Allegra and your mother with fifty thousand pounds," he urged her. "You could live anywhere you wanted."

Her eyes flashed. "I can see," she said coldly, "that three weeks in London haven't changed you a bit! You're still the same interfering, nosy, high-handed—"

"There you are, my dear," Lord Redfylde said, striding into the room. He looked singularly out of place among the little tables and chairs. "Where is the new nursemaid?" he demanded angrily when he saw that she was holding his youngest child.

"I sent her down to the kitchen for a basket," Cosima replied, just as the girl came running into the room swinging a basket by the handle.

Cosima went to work, wrapping the baby up and laying her in the basket. Lady Caroline went to sleep instantly. "Put her in the shade, mind," she warned the girl. "I won't have her ladyship boiling in the hot sun like a lobster."

"No, indeed, Miss Vaughn," replied the nursemaid, whisking Lady Caroline away.

"Are you acquainted with Sir Benedict, my lord?" Cosima asked.

"Yes, of course." Lord Redfylde gave the baronet two fingers to shake. Oddly enough, Benedict did not avail himself of them. "Come, my dear," he went on, turning to Miss Vaughn. "Everyone is asking for you." Redfylde held out his hand, and she took it without hesitation.

"Did you hear that, Cousin Ben? Everyone is asking for me."

She went out on Redfylde's arm, laughing.

Benedict stood by, forgotten.

"I was only gone three weeks," he muttered angrily.

Chapter 16

The evening finished with a fine display of fireworks. Benedict thought it would never end. Finally, the musicians had packed up, and the guests departed little by little. Lady Agatha was carried home in her chair. Lord Redfylde was the last to leave. He kissed Miss Vaughn's hand. The servants he left behind worked like demons in the dark park, packing everything up and carrying it away.

Lady Agatha slept soundly as Cosy and Nora got her undressed and into bed. Allie, on the other hand, announced her intention of staying up all night, and Cosima was seriously tempted to give her some of Dr. Grantham's sleeping drops. A glass of warm milk did the trick, however, and, just a little after midnight, Cosima was finally able to disguise herself as Mr. Cherry and slip out of the house.

All that remained of the festivities in the park were a child's toy boat and a few ribbons streaming from the trees. She used the key he had given her to enter the house. "Three weeks," she said angrily, throwing open the door to the study. "Three weeks, and not so much as a dirty look from your direction! Who do you think you are?"

Benedict was seated at the fire reading one of his edifying books. "Pickering, you may go," he said calmly as his manservant emerged from the dressing room.

"Good evening, Mr. Cherry," the manservant said pleasantly.

"You may finish unpacking in the morning, Pickering," Benedict said.

She pulled the brim of the top hat down over her eyes as Pickering went past her. "Good night, Sir Benedict. Good night, Mr. Cherry."

"I did not expect you this evening," said Benedict when Pickering had gone.

"I suppose," she said angrily, "you had a different girl every night in London, *reading* to you. You faithless hound!"

He couldn't help but laugh. "You flatter me. Believe me, my life is not that interesting. Besides, something tells me you weren't exactly lonely without me. Lord Redfylde seemed very attentive." His voice, sharp with jealousy, thrilled her. He was jealous and did not even try to conceal it.

"I don't know what you're talking about," she said. "I've never met Lord Redfylde."

"Never met—!" He became angry. "You were laughing and flirting with him all afternoon," he accused her, climbing to his feet. His snowy white nightshirt hung loosely from his spare frame. "You had him eating out of your hand. He *kissed* you good night."

"Oh, that. That wasn't me, Ben. That was Miss Vaughn. And he only kissed her hand."

"Don't," he said curtly. "I'm too tired for games. You are Miss Vaughn. There is no Cherry. Ridiculous! I've known all along, my girl. You didn't fool me for a minute."

Walking up to her, he tore the hat from her head.

And stared.

"What have you done to yourself?" he demanded.

Her hand went up to her hair. She had cut it to an inch and dyed it bright red with henna. During the day, she had been wearing a wig made of her own pale hair.

"Why? What's the matter?"

Benedict's heart was pounding. He had seen Miss Vaughn— the real Miss Vaughn—only a few hours before. Her hair had been blonde, as always, and, while it had been cut in the Grecian style, it certainly had not been cropped or red.

"I cut it," she helpfully explained. "Don't look so stricken, Ben. It will grow back."

With her short red hair, white skin, and huge green eyes, she looked more feminine and vulnerable than ever. Even the man's clothes she was wearing seemed to emphasis her delicate bone structure. She didn't look like Miss Vaughn at all, he realized. Not when one looked closely and critically at her. Cosima was hard-eyed and tough as nails. She teased men and laughed at them. She always had to have the upper hand. Cherry was soft and kind.

And real.

He cupped her chin with his hand. The happiness in her green eyes nearly unmade him.

"Are you real?" he asked softly.

She smiled at him. "I'm as real as you are, Ben."

"You were not at the picnic?"

"No, Ben. Miss Vaughn doesn't want me showing my face to the world. Not while a big lord like himself is sniffing around. Of course, nothing will ever come of it, but—"

She was not allowed to finish. His mouth closed over hers possessively.

"I suppose," she said shrewishly, turning her face away, "you had your fun with that mouth while you were in London! And I've been here breaking my heart for you."

"I was only gone three weeks."

"Three weeks is an eternity!"

"I suppose it is, for a woman," he said.

He smiled at her warmly. He looked so young and handsome when he smiled that she felt her knees turn to butter. "There is no one else," he said. "There is only you. Cherry."

It was a ridiculous, adorable name, the name of a girl in a play.

"Oh?" she said, catching her breath. "I'm sorry, Ben. You

said you wanted to see less of me. So I bought my ticket to America. I only came to say good-bye."

"You're not going to America," he said.

His gray eyes gleamed, and suddenly she no longer wondered what it was about this man that had so captivated her. "Am I not?" she asked.

"Not in my clothes, you're not," he said. "Go and take them off at once."

She gasped. "But I can't go to America naked!"

"You're not going to America," he replied. "You're going to bed. Take off all your things, and wait for me in the bedroom. I'll be with you very soon."

She frowned slightly. "Wait for you? Where are you going?"

He touched her mouth. "Trust me," he said.

"What are you going to do to me?" she asked.

His mouth curved. "If you don't do as you're told? Nothing."

If she had run away from him, he would not have stopped her from leaving.

"Well," she said, "they are your clothes. I don't want to be accused of stealing from you."

She slipped into the bedroom, quick and silent as a thief.

Left alone in the study, Benedict groaned. He had denied himself the pleasure of watching Cherry undress, not out of concern for her modesty, and certainly not due to any reticence on his part, but because he knew he would not be able to control himself as her delicate female body emerged from the masculine clothing. His self-restraint had already been pushed to the limit, but he forced himself to think about the consequences of making love to the girl. He had nothing to use to prevent conception, and he refused to risk making the girl pregnant. He was not the sort of man to leave a girl with ten pounds and a babe in her belly; he despised that sort of selfish, thoughtless man.

And yet, not making love to her was equally unthinkable. She was willing, and he had a painful erection. This desire was no mere impulse that could be shaken off. This was a deep, driving need, as powerful as hunger or hatred, and it could not be denied. He could not deceive himself. His desire was so strong there was no way he would be able to withdraw from her body before she carried him to a climax. If she became pregnant through his carelessness, he feared she would hate him.

There was only one feeble thing he could do to protect her. It was distasteful to him, but he did it anyway. Taking off his dressing gown and his nightshirt, he masturbated into the nightshirt, catching his seed in the fine white linen. The first emission scarcely interfered with his arousal, but, he felt, the danger of conception had been diminished significantly, and, relieved of at least some of its burden, his body would be better able to withdraw at the critical moment.

Belting his robe on again, he entered the bedroom.

He had not specified where she was to wait for him in the bedroom, but she had chosen to sit on the edge of his bed. He was going to bed her. She knew it, and so she waited for him on the bed, her feet flat on the floor, her knees clamped together, her white arms crossed over her breasts. Her white skin gleamed in the firelight. She looked quiet and submissive, more proof that she was not Miss Vaughn, if any more were needed.

Sheer, masculine power surged through him as he looked at her, enjoying her as he might enjoy a painting he had recently acquired. Finally, he spoke. It was a simple command and she obediently moved her arms, and placed her hands at her sides. She was trembling, and despite the warmth of the fire, the small pink nipples of her breasts stood out in keen points. Without speaking, he looked at her for a long time. She tried to raise her eyes to his, but her courage failed her. It dawned on him slowly that she was not merely overcome with desire for him. She was a virgin and she was terrified.

"Would you be more comfortable in a nightshirt?" he asked her gently.

Her green eyes flickered up to his and he was amazed to

see that she was hurt, hurt that he would even consider allowing her to cover herself. "It makes no difference," she said.

It was true. Whether clothed or naked, she was equally vulnerable to him.

He approached the bed. Her lips fell open as she realized that under the black brocade, he was already naked. Thick black hair bristled on his chest. Her eyes fell to the embroidered belt. It was loosely tied, and beneath it the gown parted on either side of his member. The foreskin was pushed back and the constricted head was scarlet and engorged. Benedict presented himself to her without a trace of embarrassment.

"Ben!" she said helplessly, color surging back into her cheeks.

"It's just another part of my body," he replied, apparently unconcerned by her embarrassment. He did not touch her. He did not kiss her. He seemed to be in no hurry. He just stood there waiting.

She suddenly realized what he expected of her and a panic she could not fight welled up within her. "You wish me to— to palate you—like the whores in the brothels?" she whispered, her cheeks burning with shame.

He looked surprised. In fact, he had just been giving her a little time to get used to his appearance before forging ahead. But if the lady was offering . . . "If you wish."

"No!" she said, shaking her head vehemently. "I won't do it."

He shrugged. "Then don't."

She shivered. The thought of pleasing him excited her, but the thought of taking him into her mouth filled her with disgust. Even worse, what if she did it wrong and it gave him no pleasure at all? "I couldn't. It's not nice."

"Then we had best leave it."

Quite unreasonably, his reasonable attitude annoyed her.

Cosima had never been so desperately nervous in her life. She had expected him to do everything. He had always taken charge before. Now he seemed to expect something of her beyond quiet acquiescence. "I'm not one of your whores," she snapped.

She realized, of course, that her evil genius—or, as Nora would have it, her Christian conscience—was doing its best to ruin everything, but she couldn't seem to help it.

For the first time, he looked angry. "I said: leave it."

To his complete astonishment, she burst into tears. The last vestiges of doubt vanished completely. Miss Vaughn, he knew, would never, ever cry in front of a man. She would rather die first. "How long are you going to make me wait?" she demanded in a broken voice.

He tried to make her laugh. "Perhaps an hour. Maybe two."

Her mouth fell open. "Ben!" she said angrily.

He laughed softly as he bent to kiss her mouth. "I was just looking at you. I enjoy looking at you. You're very beautiful, you know. I don't often get the chance to admire such a beautiful girl."

Her nerves were raw and her temper frayed.

"There's no need," she said, "to coddle me. You don't have to pay me pretty compliments, and you don't have to kiss me, either! I'm not a baby. I've made up my mind to let you have me. So there's no need to be kissing me now. All I ask, is that you be quick about it." She glanced at him. "I'd like to get it over with, if you don't mind. I'm not going to cry, if that's what you're thinking!"

She seemed quite unaware that tears were rolling down her cheeks as she spoke.

He looked at her as if she had sprouted a second head. "You want me to—"

"For God's sake!" she said. "If you don't do it now, I'm leaving."

"All right," he said. "Lay down for me. I'll be as quick as I can."

"Finally!" Without question, she obeyed, falling straight back on the bed.

"No; don't cover yourself," he said, as her hands automatically sought to hide her nakedness from him. "I want to look at you." Obediently, she held her arms at her sides, her fists clenched. The embarrassment of being totally open to his gaze was too much; she closed her eyes and waited for him with as much anticipation as dread.

"Could you hurry, please?" she snapped, braced for the ultimate in unpleasantness. "I'm getting cold."

Her knees had parted a little and he was able to stand between her legs. The soft furrow between her legs lay exposed, and, as he nudged her thighs farther apart, he could not resist parting her completely. She was small and tight like a little apricot. The flesh was cool to the touch and dry, as if she had no desire for him. "You're not ready for this," he said, withdrawing his hand.

Cosima was insulted. "I am ready," she protested, opening her eyes.

He had moved away from her.

"No," he said gently. "You're not."

"I am," she insisted. "Ben, I love you. I'm ready. I swear it."

"You are not ready, my girl," he said firmly. "Not yet."

He slipped to his knees between her thighs. Her hips jerked in protest as his breath caressed her inner thighs.

"Why don't you just take me?"

He replied with a caress. It was like the first time all over again. She did not mean to squirm; she could not seem to control her own body. Even as he caressed the soft lips, her body closed against him in a tight ring, as if determined to keep its virginity forever. He tried to enter her with a finger, but even that her body would not permit. There seemed no possible way to enter her without rending the tender flesh. Her thighs tightened convulsively at his every approach, and her hands tugged at his hair. She wanted him, she swore she wanted him, but her body betrayed nothing but fear and anxiety.

"I'm sorry, Ben," she said, tearfully. "I don't know what's the matter with me."

"Don't be sorry," he answered, lowering his head until it

rested on her belly. "You're perfect." He caressed her gently, stroking the soft hair until she would at least allow him this without tensing up. He was patient. Little by little, the muscles relaxed, and finally, her defenses collapsed utterly. He could go anywhere, touch anything. She bit back her moans, biting her lip to keep her mouth locked. She was ashamed that he was having to work so hard.

Probably his other women had never made him work so hard.

She covered her face with her hands as he probed her gently, then slid his tongue between the soft lips.

The first trickle of honey was the sweetest. Salty and fragrant, it penetrated the buds of his tongue and whet his appetite. He caressed her with his mouth until she moaned. Her hands fell away from her eyes, and blindly her fingers caught at his hair. Her body began to move in rhythm with him. The warm, silky wetness that lay deep within her began to flow at last as he carried her slowly and deliberately up the heights of pleasure. As she peaked, sighing softly, he tried to enter her again with his finger. Her flesh quivered in response but did not defend itself.

"Please . . ." she murmured, still hiding behind her hands. "I can't take any more."

He stood, unbelted his robe, and placed himself at the soft entrance between her thighs. His own body was clamoring for release, but he took her gently, by degrees, giving her time to become accustomed to his size before he inconvenienced her with his entire length. "Wrap your legs around me," he told her as he prepared for the first real thrust.

Almost in disbelief, she felt her body part for him. The momentary discomfort was nothing compared to the pain she had feared, and the pleasure of having him inside her was incredible. She had not expected to feel any pleasure for herself at all. Sexual intercourse, as far as she knew, was something that men took from women for their own pleasure. Women endured it for love of the man, but for no other reason. To hear her brothers describe it, it was a crude and violent act. Not so, she was discovering. It was another caress, deeper and more binding than any other caress, more serious and frightening, but no other touch compared to the pleasure of this full, unfettered possession. As he touched the final barrier between them, she began to weep with emotion, not pain, and as he broke through her maidenhead, she came undone, clasping him as close to her as she could. He lay within her, rigid.

"Are you all right, my darling?" he whispered.

"Yes, I think I'm all right," she answered. Unbelievable but true. She was fine.

Pinned to the bed, she felt suddenly free. His dressing gown served as a blanket, and under its cover she felt bold enough to slide her hands along his slim body, her fingers combing through the thick hair on his torso. Propping himself up on the stump of his right arm, he filled her completely, his left hand on her breast. Together they looked down at where their bodies had joined. He kissed her lips then, plundering her mouth with his tongue as he had plundered her body with his manhood. "I can feel you inside me," she said in wonder as he broke the kiss. "Why do men think they possess women?" she asked him very seriously. "It's so obvious that women possess men. You're mine now."

He groaned softly.

At first, she did not understand that he moved away from her merely for the pleasure of possessing her again, but she learned quickly. It was like a dance; they moved apart only for the pleasure of drawing deeper together. Faster and faster it went, until she felt herself on the very keenest edge of pleasure again. But before she went over the edge, he suddenly left her completely. He got up from the bed and went into his dressing room.

Cold air slapped her body. Stunned and dismayed, she rolled herself up in the coverlet of his bed and wept. He returned shortly, his robe belted neatly. He was smiling at her.

"Did I do something wrong?" she asked, confused.

"You were perfect," he assured her. "You make me wish I had two hands."

Relief flooded through her veins. She smiled back at him, proud and shy at the same time. "Aren't you glad you have one, though?"

He laughed, throwing himself down beside her on the bed. He wondered if it would be too selfish of him to take her again. He had not observed any blood on his member when he went to relieve himself, but her thin body must be bruised and sore. It would be unkind to abuse her generosity. Another time, when she was used to such exercise, he would take her repeatedly, or, at least, as much as pleased them both. For now, he was content caressing her little breasts, coaxing the bright pink nipples erect between his fingers. She snuggled up against him, warm, contented, and drowsy.

"Ben?" she asked him suddenly. "Why didn't you tell me you were Irish? I'd not have made you wait so long."

"I'm not Irish," he answered, sounding puzzled.

She lifted her head to look at him. "But I thought—! Your mother—?"

"My mother? My mother was *born* in Ireland, but she never considered herself Irish."

She frowned. "What part of Ireland?" she wanted to know.

"Oranmore. Her father was Lord Oranmore."

She had to sit up. "Oh, God!" she said staring. "It's true, then! You're one of those black-hearted Redmunds from County Oranmore, aren't you? They do say that the father of the first Redmund was the devil himself."

"My mother was a lovely woman," he protested.

"If I had known you were a Redmund," she said, shaking her head, "I would have conquered my lust and abstained entirely!"

She looked at him thoughtfully. "Too late now, I suppose."

"Yes," he agreed. "Much. The die is cast. The deed is done."

"The dirty deed," she corrected him. "Will we do it again

sometime, do you think?" she asked, tangling her fingers in the soft hair of his chest.

"Yes. When you're feeling up to it, of course," he added chivalrously.

Her eyebrows shot up. "Feeling up to it? You think you've worn me out? Is that it?"

He smiled smugly. "Haven't I?"

"Devil a bit!" she said, pushing him onto his back. "If anybody's worn out, 'tis yourself."

He laughed. "Nonsense, my girl. I went easy on you, because it was your first time."

"Is that so?" she said, pinning him down. "Well, it's not my first time *now*."

In a trice, he reversed their positions on the bed and took full possession of her loins in one stroke. "You're going to regret this in the morning," he murmured.

"Not me," she answered recklessly. "I could go all night."

This time, he made no attempt to withdraw from her body to avoid conception. He had no seed left to spill. He was utterly drained. "Come to London with me," he panted as they came to rest. "Come to London, and I will give you anything you want."

"And do what there?" she asked gently. "Be your mistress?"

"You already are," he pointed out.

She became angry. "Mistress, indeed! We're lovers now, Ben. I'm not your mistress, and you're not my keeper. I won't be going to London with you. Understand that."

"Why not? We can be together there."

She began looking for her clothes. "Aye! When it suits you. The rest of the time, I'd be— Well, what exactly *would* I be doing while you're making speeches in Parliament and making love to your wife?"

"I'm not married."

"You will be," she answered. "That's what you came to Bath for, isn't it? And you couldn't marry me, of course. You'd be a laughingstock if you married a girl like me."

"No," he said slowly. "Not a laughingstock."

"But you can't marry me." She laughed suddenly. "Don't worry! I'm not going to make a scene like your crazy governess."

"Thank you," he said. "I do love you, you know. It's the way of the world."

"Right," she said. "Besides, what makes you think I want to marry you anyway? Sure I don't even like you. I'll be your lover until the day you marry another. Hopefully, by then, I'll have you out of my system."

"I have to marry," he said. "It needn't change anything between us."

She pulled away from him. "I won't be your partner in adultery, Ben," she said coldly. "It's a terrible sin, and I won't do it."

"Sin!" For a moment, he looked contemptuous. He was not religious, and he did not believe in sin. "You don't seem to mind fornicating with me. Is that not a sin?"

"I know it is!" she said angrily. "I can't help making a fool of *myself,* but I'll be damned if I help you make a fool of your wife. God will forgive me for the sins I can't help. I'm young! I've plenty of time to repent from a youthful indiscretion. Adultery is another matter entirely."

"You're babbling. Come to London with me," he commanded.

She smiled at him sadly. "No. I can't leave my family, Ben."

"Even though they lock you in the attic and make you cut your hair?"

"Don't spoil it," she begged. "I've been in love with you for weeks, and for weeks I've been a virgin in my body only, for thinking of you. I'm not sorry for what I've done, but I won't go to London with you, so don't ask."

She left the room to finish dressing.

Benedict sat down on the edge of the bed with his back to her. He was still sitting there when she returned dressed in his clothes. "Shall I come tomorrow?" she asked softly.

"If you wish," he said stiffly.

"I *do* wish. I love you. You believe me, don't you?"

He got up from the bed. "Do you need money?"

The color drained from her face. "Ben! How can you even—"

"To show Nora, of course," he said quickly.

"Oh!" She shook her head. "There will be no hiding it from Nora," she said ruefully.

Chapter 17

She was right. Nora was waiting in the hall to confront her when she got home. "So you've done it, then?" the Irishwoman said in a harsh whisper.

"I have," Cosima said calmly.

"And you, with your mother dying in this house! Cavorting with himself like a trollop!"

Cosima felt the first stab of guilt. "Is Mother all right?" she cried.

"She's fine," said Nora, relenting. "Sleeping like a baby."

Cosy turned on her savagely. "You scared the life out of me, Nora!"

"You deserve to have the life scared out of you," Nora replied. "Out fornicating all night while your mother—"

"Is sleeping like a baby!" said Cosima. "You know where I am, if I'm needed. You know where I am, and you know who I'm with, and you know what I'm doing, and I don't care!"

Nora gaped at her. "You're not going back?"

Nora had no inkling that intercourse with a man might be even vaguely pleasant, let alone worth risking one's immortal soul.

Cosima lifted her chin. "I am, woman, and if you try to stop me, woe betide you. I love him, Nora, and he loves me."

"You love him? He loves you?" Nora was bewildered.

"I didn't think you'd understand," Cosima said coldly. "Good night, Nora."

By Thursday, the word had spread throughout Bath that Miss Vaughn would at last be attending a ball. As there were only two cotillions to be danced, competition for her hand was fierce among the gentlemen. Lord Redfylde, having claimed the right to open the ball with the Irish beauty, withdrew discreetly to watch the melee.

Every man in Bath wanted to dance with her, and, as Lord Redfylde gazed at her through his quizzing glass, it was not difficult for him to see why. In her white gauze dress, she was the closest thing to an angel he had ever seen. It fitted her slender body to perfection; no one would ever have guessed it had originally been made for another woman. The sight pierced even his wicked heart, something he had not thought possible. His mind was quite made up.She would be envied by all women, and he would be envied by all men.

They were perfect for one another.

"Behold, your new sister," he told Serena almost giddily. "How will you like curtseying to the former Miss Vaughn?"

Serena stiffened. "She is *Irish,* my lord. Have you thought of that?"

He shrugged. "What of it? They are prodigious breeders, I believe. She will give me strong, healthy sons. Your sister," he added maliciously, "never managed that, for all she was a fine English lady. Caroline was weak. Only seven pregnancies in ten years."

His three eldest children, all female, were either dead or married.

"Think of your children, my lord," Serena urged him.

He sneered. "I would give my daughters, all, back to God in exchange for one healthy son. Besides, the little ones adore her."

Serena struggled to keep calm. The depth of her hatred

for the man would only amuse his lordship, and make her humiliation taste the sweeter. "In that case, I wish you happy."

He smiled, watching his future marchioness as she deftly kept all her would-be lovers at arm's length. She did it so graciously, too, without making enemies of them. "I shall be the envy of every man I know," he said happily.

"She is thin! What makes you think she will give you children?"

"Blood," he answered simply.

"Blood!" Serena protested. "Look at her mother! The woman is a fright!"

Lady Agatha was seated at some distance away, looking around her with feverishly bright eyes. Dr. Grantham was again attending to her ladyship; his bill was going to be enormous. Redfylde did not need to look at Lady Agatha. Her heavily painted face, her red wig, her wizened body, were all as repellent to Lord Redfylde as they were to Serena.

"It is unfortunate that Lady Agatha suffered the pox as a child," he said. "However, it is very telling that, despite her frailty, she managed to bear three sons, all of whom grew up to be soldiers. When I marry the daughter, I will put the mother out of the way, perhaps at my Lincolnshire estate. She will never be seen again." He smiled at her. "I did not realize you disliked Miss Vaughn so much."

Serena looked away. She knew that smile. Redfylde enjoyed causing her any kind of discomfort. He reveled in her humiliation. And she would be humiliated if Cosima took her sister's place as Marchioness of Redfylde. "I am only trying to spare your lordship the embarrassment of having such a wife," she sniffed.

Redfylde yawned. "If only you had been so conscientious before I married Caroline!"

"I was a child when you married Caroline," she said.

"But such an eager child," he said. "You remind me of Miss Allegra Vaughn."

Having made sure that Lady Agatha was supplied with a

glass of punch, Benedict approached Serena just as Lord Redfylde excused himself to claim his partner for the first cotillion. "You are not dancing this evening, Sir Benedict?" she said, fanning herself.

She was caught, she realized, between a rock and a hard place.

And there was not a hero in sight.

"How very observant you are," he replied curtly, then regretted it. It was not Serena's fault he had been so unwise as to fall in love with a girl who did not exist in the eyes of the world. Rather than invigorating him, the affair seemed to be draining his strength little by little. He was hollow-eyed and exhausted. He could not marry Cherry, and she stubbornly refused to become his mistress. She called it being lovers, for she was young and foolish. He was older and wiser. To him it was hell.

But it was not Serena's fault, and it was un-gentlemanlike to take it out on her.

"I beg your pardon," he said. "Would you care to dance?"

"I am content to watch the others," she replied.

"I see Ludham has not quite given up on Miss Vaughn," the gentleman observed presently. "Did she grant him the second cotillion, do you think?"

"That I do not know," Serena said. "But he *will* give up on her after tonight. They all will. My foolish brother-in-law has decided to marry her. There's no stopping it, I'm afraid. He knows she is Kellynch's niece, not his mistress. He is rich enough not to care that she is portionless. Her beauty is to be her dowry. Her beauty and her womb. He is persuaded that she will bear him strong, healthy sons. There's no reasoning with him."

"I see." Benedict was thinking rapidly. How would this development in Miss Vaughn's life affect his own relationship with Cherry? That was his only concern. Would Cherry be more likely to accept his offer of a home in London when her half-sister became Lady Redfylde? Surely Miss Vaughn would not want such a beautiful girl living with her and her new husband?

Lord Redfylde, meanwhile, was enjoying the beauty of his partner almost as much as he was enjoying the envious stares of the other men. "To whom did you grant the second cotillion, my dear?" he asked Cosima. "They all looked so eager. Who is the lucky man?"

Cosima had a fair view of her mother, though it varied as the movement of the dance changed her position. No one was talking to Lady Agatha, not even Dr. Grantham, who was standing behind her ladyship's chair.

"I trust you will not dance with Ludham," Redfylde went on. "He may be next to me in rank, but he has an unsightly harelip."

Cosima glanced at her partner. Occasionally, Lord Redfylde made comments that she thought beneath him, and she had to remind herself of his many kindnesses to her family. "I'd rather have a harelip than a hare-brain, wouldn't you?" she reproached him gently.

"Poor Ludham! He seems to have both."

"Lord Ludham has been very kind to me," said Cosima stiffly.

Redfylde frowned at her; she seemed almost to be arguing with him.

Looking back at her mother, Cosima saw to her dismay that Lady Agatha had spilled her punch. Dr. Grantham, who was standing behind Lady Agatha's chair, did not seem to be aware of the small mishap. Cosima was about to leave her partner and dash over to her mother when, suddenly, Sir Benedict appeared at her mother's side, his handkerchief at the ready.

Cosima relaxed. "I'm sorry," she said, returning her attention to her partner. "What were you saying, my lord?"

The Marquess of Redfylde was not used to being ignored. Quite the opposite, in fact. If this sort of thing continued to happen, he would be obliged to discipline Miss Vaughn—

after they were married, of course. "I simply wondered whom you selected for the second cotillion, my dear," he said, smiling pleasantly.

"I was thinking I'd dance with . . . Sir Benedict Wayborn," she said, her green eyes twinkling with mischief, "if he'll have me."

Lord Redfylde looked at her in disbelief.

"Sir Benedict Wayborn?" he repeated. "The cripple?"

He began to laugh.

Cosima glared at him until he stopped.

"I beg your pardon, Miss Vaughn. I did not mean to offend you. But you have *two* cousins in Bath, I believe. I would rather see you dance with Westlands. *He* will do you credit."

"Marcus is engaged to Lady Rose," she said primly. "They make a charming couple, don't you think?"

"When do they marry?"

"I don't believe there's a date certain as yet," she said vaguely.

"I don't approve of long engagements," said his lordship. "What is the delay, if a man knows what he wants? Will you be going to London for the wedding?"

"I shouldn't think so," said Cosima. "Mother's health . . ."

"I would prefer to be married from Westminster, of course," he said, "but I daresay Bath Abbey will do in a pinch."

"Oh?" said Cosima. "Are you getting married?"

He smiled magnanimously. "Yes, I have decided to marry you, Miss Vaughn. You are a very fortunate young woman, indeed. You will be the envy of all your sex. Cosima," he added softly. "Cosima, Marchioness of Redfylde. Redfylde's marchioness. Lady Redfylde. How do you like the sound of that, my dear?"

"Oh, God," Cosima breathed. Her face was the color of ashes. Rose had warned her that the lonely widower was falling in love, but she hadn't listened.

Redfylde was pleased by her reaction. It showed the

proper humility, he thought. The other couples assembled for the dance were staring at them. He welcomed their stares as his due.

"I would like to be married as soon as possible," he said, perhaps a little too loudly. "I have already obtained the special license. I've spoken to the Bishop of Bath and Wells. We can be married tomorrow, if you like."

"I'm going to have to stop you right there," Cosy whispered rapid-fire. She was acutely aware that they were now the center of all attention in the room. "I'm so sorry! I can't marry you, my lord. Oh, God! I should have listened to Rose, of all people."

"Rose?" he said sharply, turning to eye that young lady, who was standing but two feet from Cosima. Rose looked back at him wide-eyed. "What has she to do with this?"

Cosima's ashen face slowly turned red. She hung her head contritely. "She tried to warn me. But I thought you were too high-and-mighty to ever bother yourself about me! I vow to God, I hadn't a clue your intentions were honorable! I thought you were only flirting with me, my lord." She bit her lip. "I'm truly and deeply honored that you would even think of me in that way, and I really love your children. I know you've been kind to us, and Allie just adores you, but . . . I can't marry you. I don't love you. I'm sorry. Sorrier than I can ever tell."

She actually means to refuse me, Redfylde thought in disbelief. *A penniless Irish nobody!* Only a fool would refuse such an advantageous offer. *She must be insane,* he decided.

Twelve couples had lined up for the set, men on one side, ladies on the other. Redfylde sensed that they were all laughing at him, that they could hardly wait to go forth to all the nations and spread the word of his humiliation. Redfylde's disbelief turned to blind rage.

Rose had not overheard everything, but she had heard enough. She began to giggle. "She won't have him," she communicated to Miss Carteret, who had not been able to quite hear. "Redfylde has asked Miss Vaughn to marry him, but she won't have him!"

"Good heavens!" cried Miss Carteret. "She must be mad."

Rose's partner began to laugh, too. "Marcus, for God's sake," Cosima hissed at him, but that only seemed to make the young man laugh harder.

"Serves him right," Westlands said, unfeelingly. "The man's old enough to be your father, Cosy! He had the insufferable conceit to presume that you would have him just because he's rich and he has a title! She don't love you, Redfylde! She can't stand the sight of you. She only felt sorry for you because you're a widower with four little brats with runny noses and dirty nappies. It was pity, my lord. Pity!"

"Marcus!" cried Cosima, but she might as well have been admonishing a rabid dog.

Lord Redfylde glared at everyone. "This isn't over, Miss Vaughn," he rasped.

"I'm so sorry," she said again.

The Marquess of Redfylde turned on his heel and left the dance floor. The spectators parted for him. In his rage, Redfylde saw Serena's lips curve in a sardonic smile. He saw Lady Agatha, pockmarked in her red wig, her childish eyes delighted with everything around her. He saw Mr. King fluttering helplessly. Lady Dalrymple's lorgnette dazzled in the candlelight. All the nameless little people who had lined up to meet him when he first came to Bath now were laughing at him. The unthinkable had happened. The Marquess of Redfylde had lowered himself to ask for the hand of Miss Vaughn, and the ungrateful young woman had refused him.

Only one person dared to speak to him as he left the room. "You must forgive her, my lord," Sir Benedict Wayborn said quietly. "She is very young. I'm sure she did not mean to encourage your attentions."

Redfylde's cold blue eyes flickered. "She has humiliated me," he complained.

"She did not mean to, my lord."

"You are her relative. Speak to the ignorant chit," Redfylde said angrily. "If she is contrite, I will not be too severe on her. When people see we are married, they will forget this . . . unfortunate incident. I shall bring her to heel."

"Bring her to heel?" Benedict quirked a brow. "This is England, my lord. We do not compel women to marry against their will."

Redfylde's rage exploded. "What do you know of England, sir? You are Irish."

Without another word to anyone, the Marquess of Redfylde quit Bath.

Everyone in the ballroom began talking at once.

"What an ass!" Lord Westlands said.

"My word!" said Rose Fitzwilliam. "Are you all right, Miss Vaughn?"

Cosima was white as a sheet. She nodded. "Shouldn't someone go after him?"

"Screw him," said Westlands. "He'll marry someone else within a fortnight, I'll wager."

"I asked Miss Vaughn to marry me weeks ago," said Lord Ludham. "When she refused, naturally, I was disappointed. But, I trust, I behaved better than *that!* I was never angry with you, Miss Vaughn. I hope you know that."

"Indeed, my lord," Cosima said faintly. "You were very gentlemanlike."

Mr. King bustled up to her. "Your partner has deserted you, Miss Vaughn. Perhaps you would care to select another?"

"I think I must sit down," she said. Suddenly, she did not feel like dancing. But then everyone in the set, even Millicent Carteret, offered at once to sit down with her, which would have left the dance floor bare. "Please, don't let me spoil the entire dance for everyone."

"Finish it out with me," Lord Ludham urged her. "Serena won't mind sitting down."

Serena looked stricken, but she gave up her place to Miss Vaughn with a cool smile.

"There, you see?" Ludham smiled. "*My* partner has deserted me, too, Miss Vaughn. You would be saving me from an embarrassing situation."

Cosima allowed herself to be persuaded, but, as the music resumed, she thought guiltily of the small fortune Lord Redfylde must have spent on that absurd, grandiose picnic. She thought guiltily of how kind he had been to her mother and to her sister. She thought guiltily of his motherless children. At least she had not accepted any gifts from the man.

"Lord Ludham," she said quickly. "You really must allow me to send the pianoforte back. It was wrong of me to keep it. I can see that now."

He looked astonished. "Nonsense! I gave you that pianoforte because you are my friend. You're still my friend, I hope?"

"Yes, of course," she said quickly. "But—"

"Then keep it, for God's sake," he urged her. "I didn't give you that piano to guilt you into marrying me. I just wanted you to have it. Of course, I *did* want you to marry me," he admitted, blushing.

She gave an involuntary laugh.

"But it's not why I gave you a present," he went on quickly, "and I'd be ashamed to take it back now. Never again will I ask you to marry me, rest assured. Unless, of course, you've changed your mind?"

She shook her head rapidly. "I'm sorry. No."

"Fair enough," he said cheerfully. "You see? I'm not going to throw a tantrum. We're not all like Redfylde, you know."

She did not smile back. "I wish people would stop staring at me," she said. "I'm sure they blame me for flirting with the poor man. Honestly, I didn't mean to stir him up."

"Oh, don't mind them," said Ludham. "They're just trying to figure out who he is."

"Who who is?" she asked, confused.

"The man you're in love with, of course."

"What!" she exclaimed, startled.

He chuckled. "You've refused an earl, and now a marquess. Either you're a madwoman or you must be in love with someone else. They just want to know who he is, that's all. Who has captured Miss Vaughn's heart?"

"That's ridiculous!" she said, her cheeks burning.

They finished out the dance and went in to tea. When the orchestra struck up the second cotillion, it was Ludham who noticed that Miss Vaughn had no partner. "Thank you," she said gratefully in response to his attention. "I believe I will sit quietly with my mother."

"But you mustn't be a wallflower, my dear!" Lady Agatha pleaded. "It would pain me to see you sitting down. I long to see you dance. This may be . . . This may be my last opportunity to do so." She dabbed tears from her eyes.

"Will you dance again with me, Miss Vaughn?" Ludham promptly asked. "It will set tongues wagging, but I don't care."

"They'll be wagging anyway after this night," Cosima replied grimly. "But you should dance with your cousin. I've taken you away from her long enough."

"Serena? I can dance with her any time."

"Then you can dance with her now," Cosima said.

"All right. I will. But first I must find you a partner." He lifted his voice, saying, "Who will dance the next with Miss Vaughn?"

Cosima was horrified by the sudden rush of eager young men.

"Please!" she said, catching Ludham's arm. "I already have a partner, my lord. He'll be collecting me in a moment. Go and dance with Lady Serena."

"I will wait with you," declared Ludham. "It is ridiculous that your partner is not here. Stop the orchestra!" he called to Mr. King. "Miss Vaughn's partner is not here. Who is he, Miss Vaughn? He ought to be drawn and quartered!"

* * *

Lord Ludham found his quarry outside smoking a thin cigar. "Sir Benedict!" he cried angrily. "What are you doing? Miss Vaughn is waiting for you to claim her."

Benedict frowned at him in confusion. All he wanted to do was go home and be with Cherry. Every moment spent in other pursuits was to him wasted time. "What?"

"Have you forgotten?" Ludham insisted. "You promised to dance the second cotillion with Miss Vaughn. You had better hurry, or she will give your dance to someone else!"

"There must be some mistake," said Benedict. "I did not—"

"It is no mistake. Hurry!"

Not satisfied with publicly humiliating Lord Redfylde, Miss Vaughn evidently had decided to play a mean trick on him, Benedict thought. But he was too much of a gentleman to accuse the lady of lying. There was nothing to do but present himself with a correct bow.

"Miss Vaughn," he said coolly. "I understand this is our dance."

He did not even frown at her, but she knew instinctively that he was furious. "I thought you'd gone," she said quickly, giving him her hand.

"How could you think so," he responded acidly, "when I am engaged to dance the second cotillion with you?"

As he led her onto the floor, she tried to explain. "I didn't want to dance, so I said I was engaged to someone else. I thought you'd gone already, so I said it was you. I didn't think you would mind."

He did not lose his temper, but he did yield to sarcasm. "No, indeed. Why should I mind if people think I do not honor my commitments?"

She tried to make him smile. Cherry could always make him smile. Miss Vaughn, evidently, was another matter. "You don't care all that much for your reputation, surely," she said, faltering.

The gentleman was not amused. "What are you up to?" he demanded.

"Nothing! I hear," she went on airily, "that you're a wonderful lover."

They were at the bottom of the set, and not yet dancing, although the music had begun already. They stood opposite one another, an arm's length apart. At the top of the set, Lord Ludham was dancing with Serena. Serena looked young and radiant.

"What?" Benedict said sharply. "*What* did you say?"

He was looking daggers at her. He had no idea how attractive he was when he was furious. "Mind you, I don't believe a word of it," she said. "When a girl is in love, she tends to exaggerate her lover's capabilities."

"How dare you!" he whispered. "She *told* you?"

Cosima widened her eyes at him. "We're sisters," she said innocently. "Remember? We have no secrets between us. I know all about you and your odd little ways." She clucked her tongue. "What she sees in you, I don't know. There's no accounting for taste, I suppose, if taste it can be called."

"I suppose," he said grimly, "*you* want me to end it."

"That would be one way of rectifying the situation," she observed dryly. "Of course, she'd be very unhappy, if that matters to you. She imagines herself in love with you, you know."

"You may find this hard to believe, Miss Vaughn," he said stiffly, "but I love her, too."

"Oh, you love her?" said Miss Vaughn, after a moment. She touched the pearls at her throat. "That's nice. Here I thought you were just slaking your lust. I didn't realize it was love. That makes it all so much nicer, don't you think? The fornicating, I mean."

Benedict flinched. "I would marry her if I could, but I can't. You know I can't."

"You'd be a laughingstock," she agreed. "Your career in Parliament would be over."

He smiled at her grimly. "I don't expect you to believe me. You've never been in love. You are beautiful, but you are cold and heartless. One sympathizes with Lord Redfylde."

The insinuation that she had wronged Lord Redfylde stung, but she smiled.

"You're wrong, Ben. I do believe you," she said. "I'd like to help you. I've a soft spot for lovebirds."

He snorted.

"I really would like to help," she insisted. "I want the poor girl to be happy, after all, and, for some strange reason, your hairy, bony self is what makes her happy."

"Do you expect me to believe that her happiness matters to *you,* Miss Vaughn? I am not so naive. You are making a game of me."

The dance had reached them at the bottom of the set. They began the steps automatically.

"Her happiness matters to me as much as my own," she replied. "Tell me, Ben. Do you think you could make us *both* happy?"

"What do you mean?" he asked suspiciously.

The dance brought her close to him. "Marry me," she said, departing.

He had no opportunity to answer until they drew together again. She was too quick for him. "You can't marry *her.* She's a nobody. But you could marry me, couldn't you? I'm somebody. I'm Lord Wayborn's niece. My grandfather was an earl. I'm bona fide."

They drew apart again.

"Are you making sport of me?" he demanded.

"I am not," she answered. "You asked me to marry you before," she pointed out. "If I had said yes, we might be married right now. Lady Wayborn! Sort of rolls off the tongue, doesn't it?"

"What about Cherry?" he asked quietly. "I couldn't do that to her. Marry her sister? No." He shook his head in distaste. "It would kill her."

"Trust me," she said dryly. "She'd much rather you marry *me* than someone else. And, of course, if you marry me, I'll let you keep her. She could even live with us. I wouldn't object."

Benedict could hardly trust his ears.

"For all intents and purposes, *Cherry* would be your wife, not I. I'd be a sort of a figurehead, if you like. Of course," she added in a minatory tone, "you could have no *other* mistresses. Just her."

"Are you perfectly serious?" he asked quietly.

"I am."

"Ha! What's in it for you?"

"I'm not greedy," she assured him. "I want to keep what I have, that's all."

He looked at her thoughtfully. "Castle Argent?"

She nodded. "You must give me your word never to sell it when you are my husband."

"Agreed."

"And my mother and my sister are my concern," she went on. "I will make all decisions regarding them, and you will not interfere."

Benedict was beginning to see the simple beauty of the plan. "Your sister, *Allegra*," he clarified. "Your other sister would be *my* concern, and my responsibility."

"Agreed."

"You'll need money, as well, of course," he said. "If you won't sell Castle Argent, you must have money for its upkeep. I understand there's no income from the property."

"I'll trust you to be generous."

He hesitated. "There is one thing you might not have considered," he murmured to her. "I will need a son and heir. As my wife—"

She laughed lightly. "Think again! Did you imagine you'd be taking the pair of us to bed with you? That won't be possible, I'm sorry to say."

He actually blushed. "The thought never crossed my mind."

"Of course not," she said dryly. "I'd be willing to raise her

children as my own. Sure, won't they look like me anyway?
My little nieces and nephews."

He thought about it. "You would really do all this? Does
Castle Argent mean so much to you?" He frowned, puzzled.
"Is that why you refused Lord Redfylde? Because you feared
he would sell your house?"

"I refused him because I don't love him. As you know, I'm
cold and heartless. Are we agreed, then? You'll marry *me,* and
live happily ever after, with *her?*"

"I will have to think about it," he said.

She frowned. "What is there to think about?" she said
sharply.

"I will have to speak with—with Cherry, of course."

"Of course," said Miss Vaughn.

Chapter 18

Miss Cherry was late in arriving, but, as always, her lover was happy to see her.

"Good evening, Miss Cherry," he said, setting aside his book as she took off her hat and tossed it onto the sofa. "We need to talk."

"Hush!" she commanded.

Kneeling before him, she placed her palms on his thighs. The submissive posture aroused him instantly, but he wished that she was not dressed as a man. "I have been thinking about you all day, Ben," she said, her voice unsteady, her green eyes wide with longing. "I want to do it. I want to do it now. I want to do all the dirty things you like," she said, sliding her hands underneath his nightshirt, along his hairy thighs. "I can't bear the thought of some other woman pleasing you in ways that I have not."

He stared down at her. "You mean you . . . you wish to palate me?"

"You'll think you've died and gone to a brothel," she promised.

His mouth went dry. Never had the green eyes looked so far from innocent; never had her small mouth looked so luscious. Yet his first instinct was to deny himself. "I thought—It seemed to disgust you."

"Nothing about you could ever disgust me, Ben," she said softly. "Did you not do the same for me? Without my asking? It didn't disgust you to kiss me down there."

"No."

"Well, then. I can't believe I was so selfish. Can you ever forgive me?"

"I'll try," he promised as she rolled his nightshirt up.

"It's just another part of your body," she murmured.

As she took the aroused member gently in both hands and brought it to her lips, he shivered, groaned, and sank lower in his chair, his eyes falling closed. His left hand clasped her behind the neck as he inched into her clinging mouth.

His self control was not equal to the pleasure. She fell back as he suddenly pushed her away. "Did I do something wrong?" she asked him.

"That was perfect," he said warmly. "Really, you were very, very good."

"Better than the whores in the brothel?" she demanded.

"Without a doubt," he said, almost in pain. "Now, go get undressed for me, there's a good girl. Wait for me in the bed. I will be with you soon, I promise."

She took his hand. "Come with me now, darling Ben," she said playfully. "You could be my maid and undress me."

"No," he said harshly. "I hate seeing you dressed as a man. Now, go."

She was taken aback by his tone. "Are you angry?"

"I will be," he snapped, "if you don't do as you are told."

"Fine!" she snapped, departing for the bedroom just before he disgraced himself.

Her anger melted when he presented himself to her a few minutes later, smiling warmly. "You're a difficult man to love," she complained softly as he came to bed.

"I know," he said, softly kissing the nipples of her breasts. They were soft and warm, but they soon stiffened as he played with them. "It's not fair on you. Forgive me?"

He eased his hand gently between her legs, opening her. He

was always gentle with her. He always entered her as if she were still virgin. She sighed softly.

"There's nothing to forgive."

"I think it's a wonderful idea," she said when he told her about Miss Vaughn's surprising offer. "I wish I'd thought of it," she added, tracing idle patterns across his torso with a lazy hand. "The woman is a genius, I'm thinking. I stand in awe of her unmitigated brilliance. She must frighten herself at times, with all that massive brainpower."

They were lying together in bed, as naked as newborn babies. He pulled her as close to him as he could. "I don't want to lose you, Cherry. I don't know what I'd do if I lost you. I do believe my heart would stop."

She laughed softly. "Marry Miss Vaughn, and you won't lose me."

He frowned suddenly. "I wish you would not tell Miss Vaughn *everything,* Cherry," he admonished her. "I'm a private man. What happens between us when we are intimate should remain between us. You should not have told her we were lovers."

"I never said a word to Miss Vaughn," she assured him. "She's only pulling your leg. Godsakes, I'd be too scarlet to tell anyone what we do with our bodies like a pair of beasts. I'm shameless, I know, but I'm not *completely* shameless."

"Good," he said, relieved.

"That's settled, then?" she said happily. "You'll marry Miss Vaughn?"

He kissed the top of her head, ruffled her short hair with his fingers. "That's what I want to talk to you about," he said. "I've done a very foolish thing. I've made a horrible mistake."

She sat up straight. "In London?" she cried. "I knew there was someone! I could smell it on you!" She jumped out of bed and started to dress.

"No!" he said, trying to catch her. "It's not what you think.

I asked someone else to marry me. It was very stupid, and I'm sorry for it now, but there it is."

She stared at him. "Miss Vaughn, you mean."

"No. Someone else. It was the same day, in fact. Your sister made me so angry that I asked someone else. You don't know her. Her name is Serena Calverstock."

"That black-haired bitch!" She picked up a boot and threw it at him.

He dodged it. "I've asked her to release me, but she won't."

"*You're engaged?*" she howled.

"No," he said violently. "Absolutely not."

She took a deep breath. "What's the problem then?"

"She won't give me an answer. Look, she obviously means to refuse me. She just wants me to take her to the theater and partner her at cards. She wants an escort, not a husband. She can't keep me dangling forever. I promise you, I'll be free in a month. Maybe two."

"*Two months!* We could all be dead by then."

She sat down on the edge of the bed. He put his arm around her shoulders, and she made only a half-hearted attempt to shake him off. "I knew I couldn't trust you," she said bitterly.

"You can," he said, kissing her neck the way she liked. "She will refuse me in the end. I can be very disagreeable when I choose to be."

"Aye!" she said.

His slipped his hand between her arm and her ribs and claimed her breast.

"Two months?" she whispered, undone by his touch. "Then you'll marry me? I mean, us? Miss Vaughn?"

"Of course, my darling," he said, his warm voice sending shivers down her spine. "I ought to have told Miss Vaughn, but I wanted to tell you first."

She nodded wearily. Disentangling herself, she began to dress.

"Don't go," he said, admiring her slender body as it disappeared into his clothes.

"It's late, Ben."

A sudden panic seized him. "Darling, you do realize that she means nothing to me? You are the one I love."

She shrugged. "If you say so."

"You will come tomorrow night, won't you?"

Her shoulders slumped. She wished she had the strength to tell him no. "I'll come," she said. "It's not as though you're married to her, or even engaged. I'll come."

"Ten o'clock? I've a wretched card party, at Lady Dalrymple's, but I'll leave early."

She nodded again.

"I've a present for you," he said the moment she arrived the following night.

She frowned at him as she took off her coat. He was still in his evening dress. He looked splendid, a picture in stark black and glittering white. "We discussed this, Ben. No presents. I'm not a whore. I just like being with you, that's all. You don't have to buy me presents."

He shook his head impatiently. "It's not that sort of present. To be perfectly honest, it's a present for me. It's in the dressing room. I want you to put it on. Then we will have a little supper, and then, who knows?" He grinned at her like a wolf, making her laugh.

They both knew what would come after, but she looked in dismay at the covered dishes on the big ottoman. "Oh, Ben, I'm sorry. I can't—"

He glanced at the clock. "Only eleven-thirty. And it's Friday, I know."

He smiled at her. He thought it was perfectly absurd that she insisted on abstaining from eating meat on Friday, but he knew better than to tax her about it. She would sleep with him every night, and in bed deny him nothing, but she would not eat meat on Friday. "It's only scallops, I promise. And lobster, and smoked oysters, and a little caviar. Nothing whatever to interfere with your firm religious beliefs."

She was moved that he had taken such trouble for her.

"Go and get dressed, darling," he urged. He did not have to ask again.

She found the box on the bench in his dressing room. Inside was a black satin gown. Puzzled, she put it on. Black was the color of mourning, but widows did not wear satin. Nor was the style appropriate for a woman in mourning. The low-cut bodice laced at the back. It had no sleeves and was held up by nothing more than black satin ribbons. The skirt was flat and straight at the front, but gathered into pleats down the center of the back, emphasizing the rounded cheeks of her bottom. Without the pleats in the back, she would not have been able to walk, the skirt fit her so snugly across the hips. Decidedly it was an indecent dress, but there was nothing slattern about it. Its simple lines, and the rich sheen of the satin made it seem quite elegant.

"How does it fit?"

She jumped at the sound of his voice. Even more foolishly, she trembled as he approached her. This was her lover. She was not afraid of him in the least. And yet she trembled like a deer at the approach of the wolf. His hand clasped her shoulder and his lips touched her neck. His eyes, when she met them in the mirror, were warm with approval. She felt like a woman. A little too much like a woman for comfort. Honey began to flow between her legs, and she blushed.

"Who died?" she asked, trying to shake off the odd anxiety that had seized her.

He laughed softly in her ear, and she shivered, biting her lip. "I think I did. Black is my favorite color," he added by way of explanation, slipping his hand across her breasts, which were barely covered by the black dress. "I knew it would set off your beautiful white skin to perfection, and I was right."

"I can't wear this, Ben," she protested weakly. "It's not decent!"

She stood trembling as he slipped his hand into the bodice and cupped one breast. "You should tighten the laces," he said reproachfully. "I would not be able to do this, if you had dressed yourself properly."

She giggled nervously. "Properly!" she said. "There is *nothing* proper about this dress."

He withdrew his hand and looked at her in the mirror. "Do it," he commanded softly and urgently. "Tighten the laces." When she had pulled the laces as tight as she could, he helped her tie them. She could barely breathe, but her bosom looked magnificent. With the waist cinched in, her breasts and hips appeared fuller, and between her breasts was a rich, deep groove that had never been there before. He grunted in satisfaction. "Now," he said, catching her roughly around the waist, "you are properly dressed."

He seemed unable to prevent himself from caressing her. He ran his hands over the satin dress, the satin skin. It was all a single piece to him, the one black as sin, the other white as snow. The stark contrast excited him, and drawing on his excitement, she became excited, too. *I can always breathe tomorrow,* she thought madly as he began to stroke her bottom through the dress. The warmth of his hand penetrated the cool, smooth satin, and, involuntarily, a moan escaped her lips. She had never been so wet, so aroused, by so little. It was as if he had been caressing her with his mouth for hours. She wanted to be taken violently until her body could bear no more.

Her legs could no longer sustain her and she fell forward, breaking her fall on the padded bench. The warm smell of the cool leather filled her nostrils. In the morning he would sit down on this leather bench while his valet tied his shoes for him, but tonight it had a different purpose. With a catch in his voice, he forbade her to rise and she remained kneeling, waiting. He knelt over her and lifted her skirts, watching himself in the mirror as he caressed her bare bottom. He soaked his fingers in the soft wetness between her thighs. In this position, the damage to his right arm remained out of view, and he enjoyed the illusion that he was a whole man. He dropped his dressing gown and peeled off his nightshirt. He wanted to watch himself as he made love to her.

Her eyes were half closed, a lazy smile on her lips as he rubbed the swollen head of his member between the lips of her body. He mounted her as the stallion mounts the mare, his thighs hard against hers. Retreating until only the very tip remained between her lips, he brought his hand around her body, caressing her from the front until she came undone, moaning incoherently, her body tossing. The sensation of her body tightening around him, the irresistible music of her cries, the vision of her face panting with pleasure, awakened a beast in him, and his first thrust was so violent that she was forced to cling to the leather bench with both hands.

She cried out in surprise. He had always been gentle with her before. She realized now that he had been holding back his passion, harnessing it on a tight lead, hoping to spare her. She did not want to be spared. She wanted him to lose all control.

He paused because she had cried out.

"Please," she begged. She looked at him in the mirror and deliberately pushed her backside against him. After that, he took no notice of her cries. The more violent he became, the more excited she was. More than once he watched her face melt in pleasure as he drove into her. After the initial gasp of surprise, not one word of protest did she utter. Quite the reverse. She pleaded, she begged, she beseeched him to rend her. He would never have dreamed she could be so strong. Wrapped tightly in the black satin dress, her slender body seemed invincible. He was the more vulnerable, completely naked, completely a slave to his desires.

"I love you," she gasped as he drove into her for the last time. He looked at her beautiful face in the mirror. Her smile was serene. Then he could no longer see. His climax blinded him. He made no attempt to pull out this time, instead filling the furrow with his seed.

It no longer mattered if there was a child. In two months

or less, he would marry Miss Vaughn and Cherry's children would have a secure place in the world. He wanted a child. He wanted dozens, as many as her unbelievable body could give him.

They collapsed to the floor tangled together. As he slowly returned to himself, he was ashamed, ashamed that he had used her so violently on the floor of his dressing room. The sight of her in that black dress had driven him almost insane with desire, but that was no excuse for battering her so cruelly.

"I was a beast. Forgive me," he murmured despondently.

"I don't think I can," she responded. "You should have taken me like that weeks ago, you cruel bastard." To his amazement, she laughed.

As they lay on the floor, she began to stroke his arm. Not his left arm, but his right arm, even the seam at the base of the elbow, where the surgeons had done their work. She stroked it as if it were any other part of him, and it felt good. This was acceptance, love, untainted by pity. Cherry loved him, and desired him, too, just as he was.

He would never let her go. He would die first.

"I will be so beastly to Serena that she refuses me within a week, I swear," he said.

He could feel her mouth moving over him, but he was too sated to even open his eyes. "Are you going to be beastly to me as well?" she asked, laughing softly.

But she was too sore for him to be beastly. When he tried to enter her again, she howled like a wounded animal. "Come," he said simply, helping her up from the floor.

He opened a door, and showed her the big, steaming Roman bath on the other side. It hissed like the devil. He had to go in first to demonstrate that it was safe before she would commit so much as a toe, but finally she pulled off the black dress and followed him into what looked to her like the mouth of hell. The hot water burned her skin all over, especially the wound between her legs. In a little while, though, it burned away all the pain.

They sat together on the bottom step, water up to their shoulders, and burned.

"I love you," she said.

"I love you, too," he answered.

"I think," said Lady Rose Fitzwilliam to her partner as they were waltzing in her mother's drawing-room, "that Miss Vaughn must be in love with you, Marcus. Why else would she refuse an offer from the Marquess of Redfylde?"

It was a week after Lord Redfylde's abrupt departure from Bath.

Westlands looked smug. He suspected as much himself, and he rather enjoyed hearing the words spoken aloud. "Of course, she is in love with me," he said proudly. "She has been in love with me since she was a child, poor girl. I gave her her first kiss."

Rose shivered. She could still feel her first kiss. Dante Vaughn, the blond god of love, had given it to her, behind a curtain at Lady Arbuthnot's ball.

A few feet away, Lord Ludham was patiently teaching Miss Vaughn the waltz. Miss Vaughn had never waltzed before, and she needed the practice for the ball Lady Matlock was giving in honor of her daughter's betrothal. They had only been practicing a few days, but already poor Miss Vaughn was limping. It was as if she had been engaged for hours in some extreme activity that had left her body painfully sore. She could scarcely move.

Millicent glided by in the arms of Roger Fitzwilliam. She had persuaded him to change his scent and he had promised to quit smoking. At first Miss Carteret had balked at attending the waltzing sessions at Lady Matlock's. "I already know how to waltz," she had protested, pouting. "I waltz very well."

"You must pretend not to," her mama instructed. "Men love teaching women how to do this and that. It makes them feel masterful. So you must always pretend to be ignorant, Millie."

"I think," Millicent sniffed now, "Miss Vaughn is only pretending to be ignorant in order to keep dancing with his lordship."

"I think," Lord Westlands said, "she needs a better partner."

He wondered if it would be thought odd if he left Rose to teach his cousin the waltz. Ludham was obviously making balls of it.

As he was just deciding against it Sir Benedict Wayborn suddenly left his partner, Lady Serena, and cut Lord Ludham out.

Rather than pretend he was holding her left hand in his nonexistent right, Cosima simply placed both her hands on his shoulders. "There," Benedict said, pleased with himself. "That ought to make her ladyship angry enough to refuse me."

The tips of her breasts tingled as always at the sound of his voice.

"I have been a perfect beast to her for the last week, and still she won't give me an answer. Stop fighting me, Miss Vaughn," he added crossly as she stumbled against him. "Yield when I advance."

It took her a moment to realize he was referring to the dance. "In your dreams," she said. "You must have me confused with that redhead of yours."

"Believe me, Miss Vaughn, there is no confusion. The one is sweet and generous, and the other is cold and heartless."

She raised a brow. "If that's how you feel, maybe you should marry *her*, instead of me."

"We both know that is not possible."

She watched Serena whirling around the room in the arms of Lord Ludham. "Have you said at least *three* beastly things to her today?" she asked sullenly.

"Certainly I did. I told her I despise women who dye their hair. I told her her maid is prettier than she is. And I declared my intention of waltzing with every *young* woman at Lady Matlock's ball."

"You're a cold hard bastard," said Miss Vaughn. "No wonder she loves you so much."

The butler drifted into the room and spoke quietly to Lady Matlock, who was languidly fanning herself on a sofa as her guests danced. "What!" she cried, jumping up like a young gazelle and clapping her hands for the musicians to stop.

The butler then addressed the company at large. "His Grace, the Duke of Kellynch."

"Bollocks," Cosima whispered, her grip tightening on Benedict's shoulders as her father's half-brother lumbered into the room. Kellynch's dark eyes widened appreciatively in his puffy, red face, then narrowed, as he saw the partner she was still embracing.

Benedict calmly disentangled himself.

Lady Matlock ran forward to greet her caller. "James! This is an unexpected pleasure."

"Emma," he said, kissing her on both cheeks in the continental manner. "You're looking ravishing, as usual. Sorry to interrupt," he added carelessly.

"Not at all," she assured him. "These young people are just practicing the waltz," she explained, "for a little ball I am giving in honor of my daughter's engagement. It's at the end of the month. The ball, not the engagement. I hope you will attend, now you are in Bath."

He leered at her. "Tempting," he said. "Very tempting. But, I'm afraid, I have pressing concerns in Ireland. I shan't be staying in Bath more than a day or two."

Miss Vaughn snorted audibly, drawing His Grace's attention. "Perhaps you will introduce me to your company, my dear Emma?" he suggested. "Which of these charming young ladies is your daughter?"

Rose came forward shyly and curtseyed.

"Lovely," the duke said greedily. "Charming."

"I didn't realize you knew the Duke of Kellynch, Mama!" Rose said, staring at the infamous duke in fascination. She had heard that he was a rake and a libertine, but, she supposed, that must have been in his younger days. He was far too fat and old now to chase women. But he had Dante's cool green eyes, so she could not help liking him.

Kellynch chuckled. "I knew your mother when she was your age, my pretty. And she was just as luscious then as you are now. Tell me: who is the lucky man you have chosen for your husband?"

"I have the honor of being engaged to Lady Rose," said Westlands.

Kellynch ignored him. "Come, my lovely," he said to Rose. "Introduce me to your friends. But first, give your Uncle Jimmy a kiss. A little jealousy will do your young man good."

Giggling, Rose obliged him with a peck on the cheek. Rather unconventionally, she brought the duke to her guests, rather than the reverse, which would have been more proper. "Miss Vaughn, you know, of course," she said when they reached Cosima.

"Of course," he said, kissing his niece's hand extravagantly. "The beautiful and talented Cosy Vaughn. You have made quite a fool of poor Lord Redfylde, from what I hear, Cosy. It is all over London. I hope you will not live to regret your choice."

"Thank you for your concern, Uncle James," she answered tartly. "I believe you know Sir Benedict Wayborn."

Kellynch looked amused. "Sir Benedict Wayborn?" he echoed, smiling. "I think not."

"I beg your pardon," said Benedict, frowning. "We did meet. Your Grace has forgotten."

"Oh, we've met, I grant you," Kellynch replied. "But you're not Sir Benedict Wayborn. You have been deceiving your company most shamefully."

He rocked on his heels, enjoying the sensation he had touched off in the room.

"An imposter!" cried Lady Matlock. "How can this be?"

"Ben?" said Cosima.

Rose's eyes were starting from her head.

"What nonsense," said Benedict. "Of *course* I am Sir Benedict Wayborn."

"No, you're not," Kellynch insisted. "You're the Marquess of Oranmore."

"Oh, God!" said Cosima.

"I am no such thing," Benedict said firmly. "My maternal grandfather is still very much alive, I can assure you."

"Kenneth Redmund has been dead four months," Kellynch declared. "May God rest his black and tarnished soul."

"It's true," Cosima said suddenly. "It was in the *Times* of Ireland, about the time we were leaving for England. Your grandfather's dead, Ben. I'm sorry."

Benedict was taken aback. "It was not in the English papers," he said. "My grandmother sent me no word."

"Well, she wouldn't, would she?" Kellynch snorted. "Your grandmother never forgave your mother for marrying against her wishes. She'll cut you out of the succession, if she can."

Benedict scoffed. "This is all nonsense. Even if my grandfather *is* dead, I am not Lord Oranmore. There are at least four, possibly five, people who stand between the title and me."

Kellynch looked disappointed. "Too bad. I thought I was onto something there."

The small gathering in Lady Matlock's drawing-room sighed in disappointment.

Cosima exclaimed in disgust. "Very funny, Uncle James!"

Kellynch laughed. "Had you going, didn't I?"

"Bastard," she muttered.

"And this is Lord Ludham," Rose said quickly, leading the duke away. "And this is Lady Serena Calverstock. By Order of Precedence, I ought to have introduced *them* to you first," she said ruefully. "Then Lady Dalrymple, then . . . But in all the excitement, I'm afraid I forgot all about the Order of Precedence."

"I have that effect on women," Kellynch said modestly. He looked at Serena, smiling.

"It's quite all right," Ludham assured Rose. "We are all

friends here. We do not stand on ceremony. Serena is not offended, are you, old thing?"

Serena could scarcely breathe, let alone speak. She stared at Kellynch in silent horror. He might have been a handsome rake in his youth, but he was a loathsome, bloated beast now. Redfylde had lost her bills to *this* man? For a moment, she feared she was going to faint.

Ludham was concerned. "Serena? Are you quite all right?"

Serena forced herself to smile. "Yes, of course, Felix. Perfectly all right. What brings you to Bath, Your Grace, if you have pressing concerns in Ireland?" she inquired politely.

"I was feeling a little gouty," Kellynch replied. "I decided to stop in Bath to sample the local cure. I'm a little acquainted with your brother-in-law, my dear," he went on, his eyes resting on her powdered bosom. "Redfylde and I play cards whenever we are both in London with nothing else to do. From time to time, I sell him some horses."

"Yes, I know," she said coolly.

"May I just say, you are more beautiful than your portrait in the National Gallery."

"I was but sixteen when that was painted, Your Grace," Serena replied.

He shrugged. "It sometimes happens that a woman is handsomer at thirty than she is at twenty. You make the case for it. Redfylde told me you were a beauty, but he did not do you justice. A man could drown in your eyes, eh, Lord Ludham?"

The lady flinched, wondering what else Redfylde had told the old degenerate.

"They are striking up the waltz again," said Kellynch, looking at her greedily. "Will you dance with me?"

Serena curtseyed. She had no choice but to dance with him, and he knew it, she thought bitterly. There was no doubt in her mind that he had come to Bath to take possession of her. Unless she wanted to go to debtor's prison, she would have to give him what he wanted. *A private humiliation,* she thought, *must be easier to bear than a public one.*

"You dance beautifully," the old lech murmured, closing his eyes as he turned her. "You make me wish I were twenty years younger."

Serena struggled to maintain her composure. "What do you want of me, Your Grace?"

He raised his brows. "Want of you?"

"I am not a child, Your Grace," she said impatiently. "I know you have my bills. I cannot buy them back from you, as I'm sure you must know. I know that you can throw me into debtor's prison any time you like. What are your terms?"

He drew in his breath wistfully. "I don't have your bills, my beauty. I wish I did, but I lost them on the turn of a card, I'm *very* sorry to say."

"No, Your Grace," she said. "You *won* them from Redfylde on the turn of a card!"

"I did," he agreed, "but then I lost them again. Perhaps I gamble too much."

"What?" she gasped.

"I'm sorry, my dear. When I found out you were thirty, I'm afraid I lost interest. How was I to know the years had been so very kind to you? God knows they have not been kind to me," he complained.

"Who?" she demanded. "Who has my bills?"

"Frankly, I'm surprised he hasn't tried to use them to get you into bed," said Kellynch. "But I daresay he has been preoccupied with the beautiful Miss Vaughn."

Serena gave a faint cry of distress. "*Felix?*" she hissed. "Felix holds my debts?"

Kellynch was surprised. "Ludham? No! It is Sir Benedict Wayborn I mean."

Serena's stricken violet eyes swung across the room and came to rest on that gentleman. He was dancing with Miss Vaughn. They seemed to be enjoying each other's company.

* * *

"It really is too bad," Miss Vaughn was saying to her partner. "I've always wanted to be a marchioness. Ever since I was a little girl."

He smiled at her. "Then you should have married Redfylde," he said.

She shook her head. "He'd sell my house to Kellynch in a heartbeat, put my mother in a private hospital, and send Allie away to some cold English school where I'd never see her. No, thanks. Besides, you must know I could only marry with an Irishman."

"I'm not an Irishman."

Her green eyes sparkled. "No! You're Protestant Ascendency scum. But that's close enough for me. I'm sorry about your grandfather," she added softly.

"I never knew him. Shall we change partners?" he asked at the end of the dance. "It will appear conspicuous if we do not."

"You should dance with Serena," she suggested impishly. "It will give you the opportunity to say three *more* beastly things to her. And step on her feet."

He did not wait long to take advantage of that opportunity.

"You are looking very tired today, Serena," he said. "Are you ill?"

Serena looked at him coldly. She was fortunate, in a way, that marriage had always been Sir Benedict's objective. Other men were not so "honorable."

"I've decided to accept your offer, Sir Benedict," she calmly announced.

He looked relieved.

"I quite understand," he said. "I don't know what's come over me the last few days. I've been beastly to you, I know. I do apologize, and I absolutely wish you the best."

She stared at him in angry astonishment. "Are you mocking me?"

He shook his head. "No! Naturally, I'm very sorry that you find you cannot marry me. I am swallowing my disappointment as we speak."

"Sir Benedict," she said severely, "I have just *agreed* to marry you. I am *accepting* your offer of marriage."

"Oh," he said, stepping on her foot again. "Sorry! Are you sure? Quite sure? You don't want to think about it a little more, perhaps?"

"Bastard."

"I beg your pardon?"

She forced a smile. "I said: of course, I'm sure. Felix!" she called to her cousin, who was dancing nearby with Miss Vaughn. "Felix, wish me happy. I have just agreed to become Sir Benedict's wife."

Chapter 19

"An interesting development," Kellynch remarked, sidling up to Miss Vaughn.

Cosima was rigid with impotent rage.

"Excuse me," she said, moving away from her uncle. "I have to go and collect my mother from the baths." She could not bear to look at Benedict and Serena. She had no intention of congratulating them. She felt sick. Quickly, she took her leave of Lady Matlock.

As she was leaving the drawing-room, Kellynch caught her by the elbow.

"I'll go with you, my dear. I have my carriage."

She tried to withdraw her arm, but he would not allow it. "What are you doing here in Bath?" she asked as they went out. "I haven't changed my mind about selling Castle Argent, if that is what you think."

"It's not always about you," he chided. "It's Allie's birthday," he reminded her. "Did you think I would forget the birthday of my favorite niece just because she happens to be the sister of my least favorite person in the whole world?"

"Oh, God!" Cosima said, horrified and guilty. Sadly, for the past week, she had gone completely shameless. If she wasn't writhing in ecstasy with the man like an abandoned harlot, she was sure to be thinking impurely about him at all other times. She had forgotten Allie's special day. Her golden birthday, too, for Allie was turning ten on the tenth of the month.

She felt exactly like the wicked hussy she was.

"Well, you've been busy pursuing your own pleasures," Kellynch said dryly. "Dancing, breaking hearts. I'm not surprised you forgot your own sister's birthday."

Cosima's face was red. "You're right! I'm the worst sister in the whole world. I've got to get her a present, Uncle Jimmy. Help me, please."

He yawned as the footman put down the steps of his big, comfortable carriage. "Don't be so hard on yourself," he said. "I daresay, Aggie did not remember either."

"No," Cosima admitted, "but I've nothing like her excuse. She's not getting any better."

"Well, she never was entirely well," he pointed out, climbing into the coach, and beckoning her to follow. After a moment's hesitation, she did. "Poor woman."

"The baths don't seem to be helping much."

"At least she's clean," he said dryly. "I thought I'd take you all to the theater tonight," he went on. "A girl only turns ten once."

She frowned. "What's the play? Some of these plays are not appropriate for children, you know. It's all smut and violence these days, everywhere you turn."

"It's *The Beaux Stratagem,* one of Sheridan's best. I took you to see it in Dublin when you were Allie's age, and look how beautifully you turned out. Do you remember?"

"No."

He looked at her in silence for a moment. "You look thin, Cosy. I thought Lent had been and gone. You're nearly as stringy as old Nora Murphy. I almost didn't recognize you."

"I'll be fat again by summer," she assured him.

He was even more shocked by Lady Agatha's appearance. Never had she been robust, but he was completely unprepared for the frail, wizened woman who looked at him in confusion.

"You remember the Duke of Kellynch, Mother," Cosima prompted her, as she spread the rug over her mother's knees.

"You remember me, don't you, Aggie?" Kellynch encouraged her.

Lady Agatha was easily persuaded. "Yes, of course."

"His Grace has come for Allie's birthday."

"Oh," said Lady Agatha. "Is today Allie's birthday?"

"It's all right, Mother. I forgot, too."

"And who is Allie?" Lady Agatha asked tentatively. "Tell me again."

"Good God," murmured Kellynch. "It must be hell for you."

"Don't talk about her like she's not here," Cosima whispered crossly.

In honor of Allie's birthday, they decided to fetch the child from school early.

"Surprise!" Cosima said weakly, when Allie at last appeared at the school gate. "Happy birthday. Did you think we forgot you?"

"Uncle Jimmy!" Allie shrieked when she saw the familiar face.

"You're looking stout as a Connemara pony," her uncle said, relieved. Cosy was so thin, and Lady Agatha so frail that he wasn't sure what to expect from Allie.

Allegra hugged her sister impulsively. "This is the best birthday surprise ever."

"If only everyone was so happy to see me," Kellynch remarked dryly as Allie snuggled against him in the carriage. "Now, then," he said, when the carriage was on its way to Camden Place, "Cosy thinks we ought to take you to the theater now that you are a grown-up, but I think we should sit at home and read a nice book of sermons. What do you think?"

"I long to see the theater again," said Lady Agatha dreamily.

"May I go really?" Allie asked, not quite believing it.

"Of course," said Cosima. "It's your birthday, darling!"

Allie hugged her again. "I knew you wouldn't forget me, Cosy."

Over her head, Cosima offered her uncle a silent thank you for letting Allie think the trip to the theater was her idea. Not all men were bastards, after all. At least, not all of the time. She absolutely refused to think about Ben. That chapter of her life was over, definitely.

"You're not crying, are you?" Allie asked her, shocked.

"You're just growing so fast, that's all," Cosima said quickly, wiping her eyes.

Benedict called in Upper Camden Place while the ladies were dressing for their night out. *He certainly took his time,* Cosy thought bitterly. Lady Agatha was using the desk in the small sitting room as a dressing table, so Miss Vaughn received him in the drawing-room. She was wearing the evening gown Serena had given her. Her flaxen hair was piled on top of her head. The fringe she had cut helped to conceal the fact that it was a wig.

She wanted him to see for one last time what he was losing forever.

He was dressed to go out as well. His black coat and snowy white waistcoat became him very well. "Miss Vaughn," he said, shaking her hand. "You left so quickly. I was hoping to catch you before you left. You are going out tonight?" he asked, noticing her dress.

"Yes. It's Allie's birth-night. Our uncle is taking us all to the theater."

"I will see you there," he said without enthusiasm. "I am escorting . . . Lady Serena."

"You must allow me to congratulate you," she said quickly. "Congratulations!"

He sighed. "I am sorry, you know. I don't know what possessed her to accept my proposal, but she did, and I must honor my commitment to her."

"Of course," she said politely. "You are a man of your word."

"She would be publicly shamed if I jilted her. No honorable man could do such a thing. I should not have asked for her hand. I made a mistake. But I cannot turn my back on it."

"I understand perfectly," she assured him. "I'm fine, really."

He smiled at her. "Of course you are. I knew you would be. You are young and beautiful. You will find someone else."

Her temper frayed. "Are you suggesting that I marry someone else?"

"Of course," he said. "It's Cherry I'm worried about. I must see her. I must explain—"

Cosima cut him off. "She already knows."

"Damn," he muttered. "Damn!" He looked at her anxiously. "Upset?"

She stared at him. "Destroyed," she whispered.

"Poor darling. May I see her?"

Suddenly, she wanted to hurt him, to deal him a deep, mortal wound. "She doesn't want to see you, Ben. You will never see her again. It's over. Understand that."

He looked blank for a moment. He did not understand her sudden hostility. "You can't keep me from seeing her, just because you didn't get what you want, Miss Vaughn."

"Yes, I can."

"Nothing has changed between Cherry and me."

She gasped. "How can you say that? You're to be married!"

"We will still be together, Cherry and I," he said firmly. "Serena is not the sort of woman to interfere in her husband's affairs. She will expect me to keep a mistress."

"How nice for you," said Miss Vaughn. "Maybe I will marry. But, when I do, I'll take her with me. Your little pet. A little present for my husband."

His face didn't change, but she could tell by his eyes that he wanted to murder her.

"You will not keep us apart, Miss Vaughn. She loves me, and I love her."

Cosima opened her mouth to shout at him, then clamped her lips shut. Shouting would change nothing. Telling him the truth, that she, Miss Vaughn, was his lover, would only add more thorns to the crown of humiliation she was already wearing. It would change nothing. He was committed to marry Serena, and there was nothing she could do about it.

"She belongs to me," said Benedict. "You will not understand this, Miss Vaughn, but she needs me. She is the sort of woman who enjoys belonging to a man completely. I am sorry she is unhappy, of course, but in the end, she will come to me, no matter what you say. I command her, not you. She will do as I wish."

"You *command* her?" she repeated in disbelief. "Aye, you like to order her around like a slave when you're in bed, don't you? But you and I both know that's just your way of begging. If anything, *she* commands *you*. You're here, begging to see her," she pointed out. "She won't be begging to see you anytime soon! I promise you that."

She turned away to fight back the tears.

"I suspect you know that no other woman is going to put up with your perverted appetites," she said scathingly. "Do you think Lady Serena would ever allow you to use her mouth like a common prostitute? Sure who could bear the taste of you but a woman in love?"

"How dare you," he breathed.

"Why don't you go and suck her belly button and see what happens?"

He stared at her in silence.

"And do you think her ladyship would ever wear that tight black dress for you, and let you take her on the floor of your closet like an animal? I highly doubt it."

He was gray around the mouth. "She told you everything, I see. I asked her not to."

She smiled. "Asked her? Maybe you should have commanded her. Sure, she wouldn't dare disobey one of your commands. You have her so well-trained."

Without a word, he left her. She stood rigid in the center of the room until she heard the front door slam. Then she collapsed in tears. Blindly, she ran to her room, and tore off her dress.

Serena's dress.

"Box them all up," she screamed at Nora. "Send them back to that black-haired bitch!"

The Duke of Kellynch was twenty minutes late. The Vaughn ladies came out wrapped in their cloaks. Allie's was scarlet. Cosima's and her mother's were dark blue. Nora's was black as a bat wing. "Sorry I'm late, ladies," Kellynch said affably as the footman helped them into the carriage. "My dinner must have disagreed with me, but I'm better now."

"Don't worry, miss," he told Allie. "They're holding the curtain for us."

As the duke had hired a private box for the evening, they were spared having to enter the theater via the thronged main entrance. Instead, they gained the theater by passing through the private residence next door. Lady Agatha had to be carried up and down a series of stairs, but she did not mind that in the least, and Kellynch's footman assured her ladyship that she was light as a feather. The ladies went into the private retiring room attached to the box, divested themselves of their cloaks, and put the finishing touches on their toilettes.

The Duke of Kellynch had not set eyes on Miss Vaughn's dress until she entered the box. Had he seen it earlier, at her mother's house, he almost certainly would have ordered her to go upstairs and change. However, it was too late now. He was not a man who shocked easily, but this was too much, even for him.

"God in heaven, woman!" he cried. "Are you trying to kill me?"

Still standing, Cosima calmly smoothed down the skirt of her black satin dress.

"What?" she asked innocently.

"Did somebody die?" Lady Agatha asked, confused. "Are you in mourning, dearest?"

"No, Mother," Cosima assured her.

"You need a bloody husband," Kellynch said grumpily. "Somebody who can lock you up and throw away the key. You are not fit to be seen in public."

"What a prude you are, Uncle Jimmy," she sniffed. "I'm beginning to think your reputation as a libertine is completely undeserved."

His Grace was not the only one to notice Miss Vaughn's costume.

"Good gracious!" exclaimed Lady Dalrymple, while still fumbling for her quizzing glass. "Kellynch has brought a vulgar widow to the play!"

Beside her, Millicent had the opera glasses. "It is Miss Vaughn."

They were guests of Mr. Fitzwilliam tonight. The clergyman was shocked speechless by Miss Vaughn's indecent attire. Never in his life had he seen anything like it. Clearly it belonged in the boudoir, yet it was the somber color of deepest mourning.

Lady Dalrymple snatched the glasses from her daughter.

The black gown set off Miss Vaughn's white skin to perfection, and its tight corseting worked wonders on her slim figure, but it was all very—

"Shocking!" she gasped.

All eyes were now trained on the gilt-latticed box the Duke of Kellynch had hired for the evening. The gentlemen stared, shocked. The ladies stared, shocked.

Then everyone began to talk at once.

Apparently oblivious to the uproar she had touched off, Miss Vaughn stood for a moment, calmly adjusting the straps of her gown. Lifting her eyes upward, she studied the four compartments of the ceiling, which featured some famous paintings by Cassalie. She studied them long and hard, supremely indifferent to the fact that she was being lecherously ogled by every man in the theater. Kellynch begged her to be seated.

"Let them look," she replied. "The creatures," she added

contemptuously. She gave them a few minutes more to enjoy the spectacle, then she sat down with her white arms folded on the edge of the box. "Let them suffer."

On his side of the theater, Benedict found it difficult to contain his rage. That dress was never meant to be worn by any woman other than Cherry, nor seen by any eyes other than his own. It was to be enjoyed by the lovers in perfect privacy, and not displayed on Miss Vaughn for the shock and amusement of all Bath.

Cherry had betrayed him.

Either she had brought the dress to Miss Vaughn or she had given Miss Vaughn the key to his house, allowing her to get it herself. He did not care very much that Miss Vaughn was making a spectacle of herself, but Cherry's betrayal was a deep and painful wound.

"You must excuse me," he informed his companions, Lady Serena and Lord Ludham. "I am feeling unwell." He left the box, then the theater, and walked, almost carried off by fury, to the heights of Camden Place.

Coward, Cosima thought contemptuously. *The least he could do is sit and look at me and suffer like a man.* "And you call yourself an Irishman," she sneered aloud.

"What did *I* do?" Kellynch asked Allie, who merely shrugged.

"Will the play never begin?" she complained. "Don't they know it's my birthday? Don't they care?"

The Duke of Kellynch signaled to the manager, who was standing nervously on the stage in front of the curtain. The crowd grew still, and the noise subsided from a roar to a murmur.

"Cosy!"

A man had found his way into the duke's private box, but it was not the man she wanted.

"Marcus!" she said, annoyed. "You should be with Rose."

His handsome face was almost white with rage as he stalked into the box. "Excuse me, Your Grace," he said, his voice tightly controlled. "I would like to have a word with my cousin in private!" Without waiting for an answer, he dragged Cosima out of the box into the elegant suite of rooms attached to it. "Are you trying to give every man in Bath an erection?" he demanded furiously, pushing her against the wall.

Cosima began to cry.

Instantly contrite, Westlands wiped her tears away. "I don't mean to be such a beast. I know you're hurt because I'm engaged to Rose, darling," he went on gently. "But it's only a sham. I love *you,* Cosy. I've always loved you. Since we were children . . . Do you remember? You thought marrying me would make you a marchioness, because I was a Marcus?"

She sighed impatiently. "That was a hundred years ago, Marcus. We were children."

"I've had my fun," he said. "I don't pretend I've been a monk, but, I swear, I always knew I'd come back to you in the end. Just be patient, my love. I *will* marry you, over my father's objections, if need be. If he cuts off my allowance, I'll borrow against my expectations. I am his heir; nothing can change that."

He began to caress her, using his right hand. The man she loved didn't have a right hand. She tried to wriggle from his grasp. "No," she murmured, catching her breath in dismay as he pushed her back against the wall and kissed her. Because she wanted to be punished, she ceased to struggle and allowed his kiss. But she could not return it, and when his lips left hers, she turned her face away and went back to the box to watch the play.

"I'm ready to sell," she whispered to Kellynch. "I'll sell you Castle Argent. I don't want it anymore. I don't want to be tied to anything anymore. I want to be free."

He looked at her in astonishment.

She must really love this boy Westlands, he thought.

For some reason, he had thought she was in love with the older, gray-eyed man.

* * *

"Is it yourself, Sir Benedict?" Jackson inquired pleasantly. He had taken advantage of the ladies' absence and reeked of whiskey. "Sure the family has all gone out this night."

"I want to see Cherry," he said, pushing his way into the hall.

Jackson looked at him in astonishment.

"Never mind," Benedict said angrily. "I'll find her myself."

He went all over the house, and looked into every room, including the attic and the kitchen. The tortoiseshell cat curled up in the chair opened one green eye and rolled lazily onto its back. Returning to the scene of his first humiliation did nothing to improve Benedict's temper.

"Where is she?" Benedict demanded of the bewildered Jackson. "Where is she hiding?"

"They've all gone to theater with himself," Jackson replied. "Even Nora, to wait on her ladyship."

"I want Cherry," Benedict said sharply. "Short red hair. The illegitimate one?"

"The what?"

"Damn it, man! The love-child!"

Jackson was offended. "Love-child, indeed!" he said with cold dignity. "And you call yourself a gentleman."

Seething, Benedict walked through the park to his own house. As he unlocked the gate on his side of the street, it occurred to him that perhaps Cherry was waiting for him in the study as usual. He ran up the steps to the house and fitted his key in the lock.

"Good evening, Sir Benedict," Pickering said smoothly. "You are home early."

"Is she here?" his master demanded.

Pickering blinked at him. "Who?"

Benedict held his temper in check and went silently into his study. She wasn't there. Nor was she in the bedroom. The note was propped against the brandy decanter. How well she knows me, he thought bitterly.

The note was simple in its cruelty, with careless, slanting dashes instead of punctuation.

Caro mio Ben—
    You once said if you lost me your heart would stop beating—
I expect you to keep your word—

　　　　　　　　　　　　　　　　　　　　—CV

Cherry Vaughn, he knew, was too generous and loving ever to have written such a note. It could only have been written by the ruthless Cosy Vaughn. He walked out of his house and back into the park. He waited for Kellynch's carriage to appear.

The evening had been too much for Lady Agatha and her youngest child. They had both fallen asleep on the way home. Kellynch carried Allegra into the house himself, while his footman carried Lady Agatha up the steps. Miss Vaughn was the last to enter the house. A few moments later, the Duke of Kellynch and his footman departed.

Cosima went up to her room, opened the window, and leaned out. The taper in her hand drenched her pale hair and creamy skin in a warm, golden orange glow. Her unsurprised face as he left the shadows told him that she had known he would come. He could have killed her.

"My mother is sleeping downstairs," she warned him. "So don't you dare shout at me."

"You have something that belongs to me," he snarled at her.

"Oh, yes, of course," she murmured, setting down her candle. It took her a moment to loosen the laces enough to free her body from the black dress. She made a ball of the satin and flung it out of the window. It landed a little short of the street, and hung on the wrought iron gate in front of her house. The cold, clean night air caressed her body, hardening the nipples of her breasts. As she lifted the candle again, he could see that she was naked.

Unless it was being eaten by dogs, Miss Vaughn's naked

body had no power to please him. "Where is she?" he demanded. "What have you done with her?"

"What are you looking at?" she suddenly demanded.

A constable of the Watch stood next to Benedict, looking up at the naked girl curiously.

"Constable, you may go," Benedict said harshly. "Nothing to see here."

The constable seemed to disagree.

"Move along, Constable," Benedict snapped, "or I'll have you arrested for eavesdropping on a private conversation."

The watchman wisely withdrew. In his line of work, it didn't pay to offend the gentry.

Miss Vaughn hadn't budged from the window.

"Tell you what," she said agreeably. "I'll sell her to you."

"What?"

"That's what you do with a whore," she said pleasantly. "You sell her, don't you?"

His mouth twisted. "Name your price."

"No," she insisted, leaning out the window. "*You* name your price. How much is the girl worth to you?"

Chapter 20

Four days later, the arrangements had been made with his bank. Benedict went to Lady Matlock's house to take his formal leave of Bath, interrupting the waltzing-lesson. "We are very sorry to see you go, Sir Benedict," said Lady Matlock, suppressing a yawn. "But, I daresay, you must go and pay your respects to your grandmama in Ireland."

"Er . . . yes, of course," he murmured. In fact, he had no thought of doing any such thing. He had no idea where he was going or how long he would be gone. Miss Vaughn had not yet told him where he could find Cherry. He murmured something about family duty.

Now I am a liar, he thought grimly. *A liar, as well as a hypocrite.*

He took his leave of Serena. "You must invite your Irish relations to our wedding, Sir Benedict," she said in a tone that suggested she hoped none of them would be able to attend.

Lord Ludham cheerfully promised to look after Serena while Benedict was gone.

Last of all, Benedict turned to Miss Vaughn.

"Miss Vaughn."

He bowed to her. She was wearing the dress that looked like mattress ticking. Her pale hair was neatly braided with pin-curls on her brow. She looked harmless and demure as she curtseyed. "Have you got my money?" she asked quietly.

"The papers have been delivered to your house," he answered in a low voice. He had signed his inheritance over to her, the princely sum of thirty thousand pounds. "All you have to do is sign. Now tell me where I'm going."

She smiled at him. "Did you not hear? You're going to Ireland to pay your respects to your grandmother. If you hurry, you just might overtake Kellynch. He left about two hours ago."

"She's gone back to Ireland then?"

"Where else?" said Miss Vaughn.

Lady Matlock's voice pierced the illusion of privacy. "What are you doing there so secretly with Miss Vaughn, Sir Benedict?"

Benedict stepped away. "I was just asking Miss Vaughn if there might be some service I could perform for her while I am visiting her native country."

"Oh, fetch her harp!" cried Lady Matlock at once. "I'm sure if you brought her harp from Castle Argent, she would play for us."

Benedict was sardonic. "I would be honored. Whereabouts *is* Castle Argent?"

She shrugged. "Oh, you know. West of Dublin, east of Galway City."

His lips thinned. "Somewhere between Malin Head and Mizen Head?"

She smiled faintly. "You can't miss it."

"Believe me, I won't," he said coldly.

To his surprise, Miss Vaughn followed him out.

"Cousin Ben?" she called.

He paused on the stairs and looked at her silently.

"You'll want to take the Grand Canal from Dublin, and get off at Ballyvaughn. That way you won't get lost," she said sheepishly. She had meant to keep herself aloof of him, and remain at the top of the stairs, but her feet, as if possessed by a will of their own, were straying toward him one step at a time. She couldn't bear to think what might happen to him in Ireland if he got lost in the countryside. Some of those bogtrotters had no manners.

"It's a short walk from Ballyvaughn to Castle Argent. And don't mind the dog," she added. "She'll knock you down and lick your face, but she'll never hurt you. Her name is Dolphin, but we call her Dolly. Take this with you," she added, now close enough to give him her handkerchief. "Keep it in your pocket, and she'll know you're a friend."

"Yes, Mother," he said rudely.

Taking the square from her, he used it to blow his nose.

"Bastard," she said dispassionately.

"Bitch," he muttered, turning away.

Sadly, his manners had sharply declined since meeting Miss Vaughn.

It was good that he was leaving Bath, Cosima told herself. By the time he returned, the fire between them would have burned itself out. When he returns, he will be just another man to me. Soon enough, a married man. Serena will take him to London and there it all would end.

But, for now, she felt like a bereaved widow.

When Benedict reached the Welsh coast the following night, the choppy Irish Sea was in no mood to be crossed, and he was forced to put up for the night at one of the local inns and wait for the morning packet to Dublin. When he went down to dinner, he found the Duke of Kellynch dining alone. "Lord Oranmore! So you decided to go to Dublin and claim your inheritance after all," the duke greeted him. "Good for you!"

"I am not Lord Oranmore," Benedict said firmly, taking his seat at a separate table.

"I see," said Kellynch. "Incognito, eh? Would you care to join me for dinner?"

Benedict studied the bill of fare studiously. "No, I thank you."

"I'm having the duck," Kellynch told him loudly. "I dare-say if it were an English title, you'd have lost no time claiming it," he went on, "but as it is only an Irish title, it is of no consequence to you. Would it interest you to know that your grandfather left behind a fortune of five hundred thousand pounds? Hmmm?"

The lady at the table next to His Grace gave an involuntary gasp.

Benedict reluctantly left his table and sat down at Kellynch's. Anything to shut the man up. "You go from nonsense to nonsense, sir. I am *not* Lord Oranmore, and my grandfather had nothing like five hundred thousand pounds. How could he? That is an absurd sum."

"It *is* an absurd sum," Kellynch agreed. "It makes me angry whenever I think of it. Of course, every landowner in Ireland was compensated for his boroughs when the Act of Union passed in oh-one. My father got his fair share of the windfall. But your grandfather was unique in that he regarded it as a bribe—flatly refused to spend a penny of it. Didn't stop him from taking it, mind you. He just wouldn't spend it. Instead, he invested it. Probably, it was looking at all those zeds that carried him off in the end. You're lucky. *My* father gambled all his boroughs money away in the first year."

"I daresay it will take my cousin Ulick more than a year to gamble away five hundred thousand pounds," Benedict said dryly.

"Ulick? He'll be doing no gambling this side of hell."

"Good Lord," Benedict said, startled. "Did Ulick die?"

"In a Barrack Street brothel with a smile on his mug. Of course, that's not *exactly* how your grandmother decided his obituary should read in the *Times* of Ireland."

"I'm sorry to hear it. His son must be, what, eleven or twelve by now? I trust he has sound guardians to watch over him."

Kellynch shook his head sadly. "Poor lad! He never saw the age of seven, let alone eleven. Fever carried him off, along with his poor mother. The two daughters were left unscathed. Sure they're fine young ladies now, your cousins. Nuala and Glorvina."

Benedict waited without comment while the waiter served the meal.

"That is very sad," he said carefully. "However, my uncle must be pleased."

"There's not a lot of pleasure to be had in the cemetery," Kellynch said. "Not below ground anyway."

"Cousin Tom?"

Kellynch shook his head. "Don't ask."

"So you're saying that *I'm* Lord Oranmore? Why was I not informed?"

"Your grandmother would move heaven and earth to cut you out of the succession, that's why. Lady Angela Redmund could have married the richest man in Ireland, but one of those Richmond girls snapped him up when your mother married that English fellow. Your grandmother never spoke to her daughter after that. Now, she's married Glorvina to some chinless wonder in the hopes the union will produce male issue before *you* come traipsing into Ireland with your greedy aspirations."

Kellynch chuckled. "Unbeknownst to her ladyship, poor Gerald had the misfortune of insulting Cosy Vaughn one night at Dublin Castle. Her brothers took him to Phoenix Park and put some manners on him. He won't be cutting the mustard any time soon."

Benedict frowned. "I suppose that sort of thing happens quite often in Ireland."

"Not to the Lord Mayor's son, it doesn't!" For a moment, the duke looked wistful. "Ah, but they were a breed apart, Larry and Sandy Vaughn. What they did to young Lord Lucan—! But his death was not entirely in vain. The creatures were more apt to be respectful of Miss Vaughn after that."

"And their other sister as well," said Benedict.

"Allie? Sure, she's too young for all that. Thank God!"

The meal was finished in silence.

"By the way," the duke went on, as they went out to the lounge to enjoy brandy and cigars. "She's agreed to sell me the house. After swearing up and down she wouldn't. But that's a woman for you. The answer's always no, until it's yes, eh? They have us by the balls from the minute we're born until the minute we die. Funny thing is, I actually have the money, for I've just sold my house in Dublin. Now all I have to do is convince my mother to move out."

Benedict stared. "Miss Vaughn agreed to sell you Castle Argent?"

"Aye. Fifty thousand pounds! 'Tis highway robbery."

Benedict pressed his lips together. Before leaving Bath, he had signed over to Miss Vaughn thirty thousand pounds. If she had agreed to sell Castle Argent to Kellynch, it was not because she desperately needed funds. The woman was a greedy, scheming bitch. The sooner he got Cherry away from her, the better.

Wouldn't Cherry be delighted when she found out that her lover was Lord Oranmore, with a staggering fortune of five hundred thousand pounds? And wouldn't Miss Vaughn gnash her teeth?

"I admit I was surprised," said Kellynch. "Cosy Vaughn is as stubborn as a mule! But, I suppose, love has made her see the light at long last."

"Love?" Benedict scoffed. "Miss Vaughn?"

Kellynch laughed. "That young lad of Lord Wayborn's. What's his name—Waylands?"

"Westlands."

"He came to the box that night at the theater and had a bit of a chat with his pretty little cousin. All of a sudden, she said she'd sell me the house. It doesn't take a genius to figure out she's reached an understanding with this Wetlands boy."

"Westlands," Benedict corrected him automatically.

"He'll be breaking it off with that poor girl Rose any minute now," Kellynch sighed. "For there's no getting between Cosy Vaughn and what she wants."

"Between ourselves, we've given her a handsome dowry, too!" Benedict said bitterly.

The next morning, the Irish Sea was smooth as glass, and the mail packet crossed without any difficulty, decanting its passengers in Dublin in time for tea. "My wife is sure to have sent a carriage for me," said Kellynch, moving with surprising speed around some bags of wool on the dock. "Come; I'll set you down at Saint Stephen's Green. Oran House is on the west side, in French Walk, in case you don't know. The three front windows are broken forward under a pediment. You can't miss it."

Benedict declined, and, leaving Pickering to deal with the luggage, he left the docks and walked into Dublin, ignoring the hordes of boisterous, dirty children who crowded around him, offering to do any mortal thing for a penny. Try as they might, they could not make themselves as pathetic as their London counterparts. Benedict could almost suspect that they were begging as a competitive sport, their tales of misery were so wildly inventive, and they told them with such sparkling eyes. Also, their dirty cheeks were suspiciously rosy. The dregs of London were too miserable to tell stories.

He walked west, following the River Liffey to the center of Dublin, where stately mansions with elegant facades faced the river, in marked contrast to the eastern limits, where the houses had their backs to the river. Turning south, he walked past the spires of Trinity College to Saint Stephen's Square. Oran House stood across from a long promenade shaded by lime trees. Its brass name plate was almost completely covered in ivy, but its distinctive architecture made it easy to find.

A very proper English butler in black livery answered the bell. Benedict took out his card, then hesitated. He was no longer Sir Benedict Wayborn, as it said on the card. The full implications of this suddenly hit him. He would be obliged to give up his seat in the House of Commons, and take his grandfather's place in the House of Lords. There he would be as the lone voice crying out in the wilderness, a reformer surrounded by Tory conservatives.

"What name shall I give her ladyship?" the butler coldly inquired.

"Lord Oranmore."

"Lord Oranmore," the butler said severely, "is dead. Perhaps you noticed the black crepe on the knocker?"

"I'm new," Benedict explained. "I've just arrived from England to take possession. I haven't had a chance to get any new cards printed up."

The butler's eyes flickered. "In that case, my lord, her ladyship will be delighted if you join the family for tea in the drawing-room."

"I doubt it, my good man, but lead the way."

The drawing-room was so large that it took him a moment to find its occupants. His maternal grandmother was seated beneath the tall windows in a gilded French armchair, tiny and frail-looking in her widow's weeds. Her lavender hair was dressed in a simple pompadour. Her small, heart-shaped face still bore traces of what must have been in her youth a remarkable beauty. Her eyes were clear and gray, rather like Benedict's own. Two young females, presumably Ulick Redmund's daughters, sat near the marchioness. Like their grandmother, they too were dressed in high-necked mourning gowns. The younger had Ulick's dark red hair, while the elder was a black-haired, blue-eyed beauty of perhaps eighteen. Behind the ladies, holding a cup and saucer of translucent Belleek, was a chinless young man, also dressed in black.

Benedict went down the length of the room and bowed. Lady Oranmore silently stretched out her hand to him, and he kissed its cold papery back dutifully. "Grandmother."

He withdrew to find two more feminine hands outstretched to him. "Cousin Glorvina, Cousin Nuala," he said, making nice. The younger girl looked terrified, while the elder had an odious self-assurance that reminded him, unpleasantly, of Miss Vaughn.

"Gerald was just leaving," said Lady Oranmore.

The chinless young man reddened, but turned in his cup like a good boy. "Glorvina?"

His wife looked at him calmly. "Yes, Gerald?"

"Are you coming with me?" he asked impatiently.

Lady Glorvina Redmund had eyes only for her English cousin. "But you are only going to your club, Gerald," she said sweetly, "where you will drink too much, and tell dirty stories to your drunken friends. I'm much better off staying here. Do please sit down, my lord," she said, smiling at Benedict with great tenderness and respect. "Phelan!" she called to the servant. "Take Mr. Napier's dirty cup away." She already had a fresh cup in hand. "Milk and sugar, my lord?"

Her husband stalked out of the room without another word.

"Thank heavens he is gone," cried Lady Oranmore when the footman had closed the double doors. "He is *such* a beast. You wouldn't think it to look at him, but he is cruel and violent. We've been living in the most dreadful fear of him since your grandfather died. I'm so glad you're here, my lord. I would have sent for you at once, but Gerald prevented us. He was *so* hoping that poor Glorvina would conceive and bear a son before you found out that you had come into the title."

"There is not the least chance of that," Glorvina hastened to assure Lord Oranmore. "I hope you do not think that *I* would ever be part of a scheme to cut you out of your inheritance? It was all Gerald's idea, and, as his wife, I am bound to obey him, or there is no telling what he will do to me when we are alone." Her beautiful dark blue eyes filled with tears. "It has been the most beastly four months of my life! I thank God you have come to free us from his tyranny."

Benedict felt ashamed of himself. Based on Kellynch's version of events, and that version alone, he had formed the idea that his grandmother was a formidable old harridan bent on wreaking an unnatural vengeance upon her only daughter's son. In fact, nothing could be further from the truth. Lady Oranmore and her granddaughters were innocent victims being held prisoner by an unscrupulous man who was beastly to his beautiful young wife.

"I am here now," he said. "I will look after you all."

Glorvina smiled. Nuala, who had not yet dared to speak, stared at him round-eyed.

"I was never frightened for myself," said Lady Oranmore. "What could he do to an old woman, after all? My concern was only for you, my lord. Gerald would do anything to cut you out. *Anything.* My dear boy, you are in grave danger. I trust you are not traveling alone?"

Her light gray eyes widened in grandmotherly concern.

"My manservant, Pickering, is with me," he assured her. "He will be here soon. I thank you for your concern, Grandmother, but I seriously doubt that Mr. Napier has any serious plan to harm me. After all, he would gain nothing by it. The title and the fortune would simply pass to my cousin Mr. Power." He smiled. "Indeed, if I have anything to fear, it is William Power. And five hundred thousand pounds is a considerable temptation."

Lady Oranmore gasped. "Who told you that?" she said, choking.

"Oh, didn't you know? The Duke of Kellynch told me. I happened to meet him at Holyhead. We made the crossing together."

"What's *he* doing back in Dublin?" Glorvina demanded.

"He's sold his house here and has come to move his mother out."

Lady Oranmore snorted. "Wild horses couldn't drag Maud Kellynch out of that house!"

"Well, perhaps she can be persuaded to assume residency of Castle Argent now that Miss Vaughn has agreed to sell it."

The three Redmund ladies stared at him in disbelief. Lady Oranmore spoke first. "Cosy Vaughn has sold Castle Argent? *Cosy Vaughn?*"

"Oh, you've heard of her," said Benedict, with a derisive sniff. "From what I can gather, she's hoping to be married soon."

Glorvina's cheeks were red. "Indeed!" she said shrilly. "And who'd marry with trash like that? She's no virgin, you know!" She gave a soft cry of sympathy as, startled by the V-word, Benedict spilled his tea over his hand.

"You've burned yourself, my lord!" Glorvina cried, fluttering over to him like a beautiful black butterfly.

"It's nothing." Handing his tea to her, he pulled a handkerchief from his pocket to mop up the spill.

Glorvina drew back as though scalded. "C.V.!" she cried, spying the monogram on the handkerchief. "Whose initials are those?"

Benedict was embarrassed. "They are not initials," he said, thinking quickly. "All my handkerchiefs are numbered in Roman numerals. This is number one hundred and five."

"I see." Glorvina smiled prettily and returned to her seat. "More tea, my lord?"

"No, thank you, Glorvina."

There was a short silence, broken by Lady Oranmore. "May I ask what your plans are? You'll stay here, of course. I will have your grandfather's compartment prepared for you. I would like to introduce you to Dublin society, such as it is, before you marry Nuala. Have I your permission to send out the invitations?"

Benedict paused in the act of folding his handkerchief. "I'm sorry. What did you say?"

"I would like to introduce you to my friends," said Lady Oranmore.

"No; after that."

Lady Oranmore had to think. "May I send out invitations?"

"No; before that. Something about marrying Nuala?"

Lady Nuala Redmund looked from her grandmother to her sister in terror.

"Of course, if you'd rather marry *me,*" said Glorvina, patting her sleek black hair, "a divorce will not be a problem.

Gerald, for all his brutality, has been an utter failure as a husband. I am *virgo intacta,* my lord. You can have a doctor's certificate, if you like."

Benedict jumped up from his chair. "I'm afraid that will not be possible, ladies," he said quickly, setting down his cup. "I'm engaged to be married already to someone else."

"Break it!" Lady Oranmore said instantly. "These are your cousin's daughters, sir! If Ulick were alive, *he* would be Lord Oranmore and not you. Marrying Nuala is the least you can do. The very least."

"I am aware of that, Grandmother," Benedict said. "Naturally, I am prepared to be generous with the girls. But I can not marry Nuala—or Glorvina, for that matter. I must keep my word to my betrothed." He went on before he could be interrupted. "As for my staying in this house, I shall be perfectly comfortable in a hotel when I return to Dublin. Believe me, I mean to intrude upon your lives as little as possible."

Lady Oranmore looked at him sharply. "When you return to Dublin?" she echoed. "You mean, you are not staying? Are you returning to England?"

"I must," he answered. "But, first, I have some business outside of Dublin."

His grandmother frowned. "Outside of Dublin? What sort of business?"

Benedict decided it would be silly not to tell the ladies where he was going. Foolish, too, for if Gerald Napier or William Power really did have designs on his life, it would be to his advantage if his family knew exactly where he was going and by what method he intended to get there. "My business is at Castle Argent, as a matter of fact."

"How extraordinary," said Glorvina, wide-eyed. "We were just talking about the place."

"Yes," he said. "When Miss Vaughn heard that I was going to Ireland, she asked me to fetch her harp."

Glorvina smiled down at her beautiful white hands.

"Her harp? How nice," sniffed Lady Oranmore.

Nuala reached for another piece of cake and got her plump fingers slapped.

"I should probably go now," said Benedict, who could see that his twenty minutes were up. "I was told the best way to go would be to take the Grand Canal to Ballyvaughn. Would you be so kind as to direct me to the terminus?"

"The Canal!" Lady Oranmore exclaimed in horror. "You'd never make it there alive! Those barges capsize every chance they get, and I'm not surprised, for they let too many people on. Let Thady take you in the carriage, my lord. You'll be much more comfortable."

Benedict was not in the least surprised to learn that Miss Vaughn had suggested a method of travel most likely to result in his death. Still, he hesitated to deprive his grandmother of her carriage. He offered to hire a hack, but her ladyship insisted. "Thady knows the way like the back of his hand, and he will keep you safe. The biggest regret of my life was not healing the breach with Angela before she died," Lady Oranmore went on, dabbing her eyes with her black silk handkerchief. "I couldn't bear it if anything happened to you, my only grandson. Do it for me, dear boy. I shall not sleep a wink until you are with me again."

"Thank you, Grandmother," he said, truly moved by his grandmother's tears. "I will be back by tomorrow evening, I hope."

As he took his leave, the ladies again extended their hands, and again he kissed them.

"Good-bye," said Nuala, speaking for the first time.

Hearse-like, her ladyship's black coach was drawn by two horses so sleek and black that Benedict wondered if they might have been dyed as a tribute to his dead grandfather. Black ostrich plumes nodded on their foreheads. Small and bandy-legged, Thady Lanyon also appeared to have been dipped in a vat of black dye. His frieze coat was black, his black hat was trimmed with a black cockade, and his shaggy black brows seemed almost to meet up with his shaggy black whiskers and beard, leaving just enough room for his big nostrils and tiny coal-black eyes.

Even the Oranmore coat of arms had been obscured on the coach door by a panel of black crepe. As Benedict climbed inside, he almost expected the upholstery within to have been dyed black as well. However, the seats were done up in a pale gold brocade, worn to a dull sheen.

The coachman turned the horses in a westerly direction, traveling on the Lucan Road. "And has your lordship ever been beyond the English Pale?" Thady asked, opening the trap in order to speak to Benedict.

Not wanting to seem like a cold, aloof aristocrat, Benedict allowed himself to be engaged in conversation. "No; but I have been to Dublin many times. Is it very far to Castle Argent?"

"Not at all, at all," he was assured. "Not fifteen miles. I'll have you there in a shake."

"A shake being three hours?" Benedict called, amused.

Thady laughed. "Two, if you're lucky."

"Is there an inn at Ballyvaughn?" he asked. He did not quite know what to expect when he got to Castle Argent, and he did not want to assume that he would be welcome to spend the night there if it should prove necessary. He wasn't even sure he would want to.

"Sure there's nothing but turf-cutters and shebeens in Ballyvaughn," Thady sneered.

Benedict grimaced. "I may have to ask you to drive back to Dublin through the night."

"Ourselves will rest this night in Lucan." Thady spoke with authority. "And I'll carry you home to Lady Oranmore in the morning. There's a respectable hotel in Lucan, in the shade of Lucan Castle, where Lady Lucan weeps for her poor murdered son, and he with his unrecognizable body hauled out of the bog like it was yesterday."

Benedict took out his watch. He estimated that he would reach Ballyvaughn by eight o'clock. His errand at nearby Castle Argent should be concluded within an hour. With any luck he would be at the respectable hotel in the village of Lucan no later than ten o'clock. Cherry would be with him, of course. He became aroused thinking about their joyful reunion. He did not expect her to be anything but thrilled to see him.

"Is there a not-so-respectable hotel in Lucan?" he asked Thady. "I'm hoping to have a young woman with me on the return."

A shocked silence fell between them. Thady's disapproval was palpable.

"A perfectly respectable young woman, of course," Benedict said hastily. "I would not be staying *with* her, of course, in the not-so-respectable hotel. I was thinking that completely separate hotels might be best. I would hate to do harm to a young lady's reputation."

"You'd not want to get yourself mixed up with any of the lasses in these parts," Thady warned. "Look what happened to Lord Lucan. Cut down in his prime."

The Irishman kept up a steady stream of idle talk as the coach rolled through the western limits of Dublin. Benedict very soon lost track of what was to his left and what was to his right. The view from his window was one of unvarying wilderness, broken only occasionally by a small clearing, and, once, by a distant view of a round tower. Finally, as night fell, he closed the curtains, and closed his eyes.

What seemed like only a few minutes later, he opened them again. The coach had stopped. The door was open and Thady was standing outside with a lantern in one hand and a pistol in the other.

"I was hoping," Thady said apologetically, "to murder your lordship at the gates of Castle Argent itself, and have your carcass fall dead at Cosy Vaughn's feet, but I'd not want to be upsetting the other young lady, so, if you don't mind, my lord, I'll be murdering you here and now, in this Godforsaken place."

Chapter 21

About three weeks after Ben had left Bath, Cosy received a small parcel from her native country. Opening it, she discovered a man's ring, a black onyx set in gold. With it was a silver watch and a note on black-edged paper. There was no need to look at the inscription on the watch. She knew perfectly well it was Ben's.

The note began, "My dear Miss Vaughn," but, as she had already glanced at the signature at the bottom, Cosy knew this to be sarcasm. *It is with great sorrow,* Lady Oranmore's note continued, *that I write to inform you of the death of my dear grandson, Sir Benedict Wayborn. You are sincerely to be pitied for your loss, my dear. To have clawed one's way out of the mud; to have climbed to the heights of Dublin society, such as it is—to have come within a hair's breadth of actually marrying Lord Oranmore—to have had a fortune of some five hundred thousand pounds almost within the grasp of your greedy fingers—only to be tossed back to the mire from which you came—is a torment I can only guess at as I sit in my beautiful mansion on St. Stephen's Green—or St. Stephens's Green, as you no doubt call it.*

Let it haunt you, Miss Vaughn, that your doomed lover died on his way to Castle Argent to fetch your harp. Let your only comfort be in knowing that his last words on this earth were—and I quote—Tell Cosy I love her.

"Ben would never say that, you lying bitch," Cosima said aloud.

She told no one of the note. She hid Benedict's watch and ring in her dressing table, next to her grandmother's pearls, and locked the drawer. She would hold them for Ben until he returned. It was only a cruel prank. Ben would explain when he got back.

But Ben did not return to explain anything. The following week, Benedict's manservant returned from Ireland without his master. Five or six couples were practicing the waltz in Lady Matlock's drawing room when Lady Dalrymple brought the news, having heard it from Mr. King. Sir Benedict Wayborn had been shot and killed, robbed by a highwayman on an Irish road.

Lady Serena gasped, "Oh, thank God!"

All eyes turned to her, and she hastily added, "Thank God he did not suffer!"

Lord Ludham had been dancing with Miss Vaughn, but when he saw Serena's agony, he left her abruptly. "My dear Serena! You are distraught."

Cosima stood quite alone, as cold and white and remote as marble.

Serena clung to him as if for strength, and even managed a few tears. She actually was distraught, but not about the sudden death of her betrothed. As soon as she could shake off the sympathy of her friends, she went by sedan chair to Camden Place in the hopes of retrieving her bills. Pickering was wrapping the knocker of No. 6 in black crepe when she arrived.

"It is only some silly letters I wrote to him," she explained as he let her into his master's study. "I would hate for my letters to fall into the wrong hands," she added, wiping her dry eyes with her lace handkerchief.

"Of course, my lady, of course," the manservant murmured.

But a thorough search of the room failed to unearth Lady

Serena's bills. "I daresay," Pickering concluded, "your lady-ship's letters were of such value to Lord Oranmore that he kept them on his person always."

Serena's eyes lit up. "Of course! Then they would be with him now at the bottom of the bog or whatever. Thank you, Pickering! That is a great comfort to me."

As she left the house, she came face to face with Miss Vaughn, who looked at her with cold green eyes. Shock and disbelief had carried Cosima this far without tears. "What are you doing here?" she demanded of the other woman.

Lady Serena sniffed. She had come out of the house almost giddy. All her debts and obligations had been swept away. She was free. She was not afraid of anyone, least of all this Irish upstart. "I have come to see Pickering," she said with icy dignity. "What are *you* doing here, Miss Vaughn?"

Cosima couldn't answer. She hadn't even realized where she was going until she had found herself face to face with Serena. *He loves me,* she wanted to scream.

Her ladyship stepped back into her chair, leaving Miss Vaughn in the street.

Pickering coldly closed the door in her face.

By the end of the week, the house in Lower Camden stood empty, as it had stood before Cosima ever knew of Benedict Wayborn's existence. Other than that, her world was merci-fully clear of visible reminders of him. She had never signed the papers granting her access to his inheritance of thirty thousand pounds, but she still had them, along with the papers memorializing the sale of her house to the Duke of Kellynch, which she had never bothered to sign either. Now, of course, there was no need to sign anything. She hid the papers, along with a few hundred pounds that remained from the "reward" she had collected for the return of the personal effects Benedict had left in her kitchen on the night they met, in an old tinderbox under the floorboards in her bedroom.

At first, Serena wore black for Lord Oranmore, and gar-nered great sympathy in Bath as the bereaved fiancée. Within weeks, however, Lady Dalrymple began to observe signs that Lady Serena had begun to allow Lord Ludham to attempt to console her. Serena lightened her mourning to purple, which suited her beautiful violet eyes to perfection, and she allowed the earl to take her on long walks in the Sydney Gardens, which, judging by the roses in her cheeks and the sparkle in her eye, proved to be a very beneficial exercise. No one could condemn her ladyship; after all, she was not a widow, and, as Serena pointed out, her dear Benedict would not have wanted her to mourn him. He would have wanted her to be happy.

In the spirit of what the dearly departed would have wanted, Lady Matlock decided that the engagement party of Lady Rose Fitzwilliam and Lord Westlands need not be postponed after all. It was to be the last great event of the Bath season, before the fashionable crowds veered off for the summer horse racing season, and, with the assistance of her now indispensable Freddie, Lady Matlock meant to make it memorable.

Of course it was very sad about poor Lord Oranmore, but . . .

Life goes on.

The last thing Cosima wanted was to attend a ball celebrating what she knew to be a sham engagement. Lord Westlands prevailed over her objections, however, by insisting that both Lady Agatha and Miss Allegra Vaughn be invited. Private balls, Lady Agatha was soon observing, were so much nicer than public ones, and she quite looked forward to it. As for Allie, the ten-year-old was over the moon at the prospect of attending her first ball. Westlands, her handsome cousin, the guest of honor, had promised to dance with her. For Allie, who would have been content to attend her first ball as a mere spectator, this was almost too much joy.

Cosima would have to be there to look after her mother and sister.

For the occasion, Mr. Carteret outdid himself. The countess's ballroom was decorated with a surfeit of artificial and real flowers; the former for unfading beauty and the latter for their rich scent. Her house in the Royal Crescent resembled the garden of Eden, only with chandeliers and a parquet floor dusted with French chalk. In addition to the main ballroom, there was to be dancing outside in the Crescent Fields. On the night of the ball, this arrangement was to cause Cosima no end of anxiety, for her mother preferred to sit indoors while Allegra ran amok outside.

"Miss Vaughn," Mr. Carteret remarked amusingly to Lady Matlock, "is like a worried sheepdog that cannot bear to have her little flock separated."

"What is she wearing?" Lady Matlock asked, wrinkling her nose.

For the occasion, both Allegra and her mother Lady Agatha had splurged on new gowns. Lady Agatha looked quite the lady of fashion in her cream and gold striped silk. Over her wispy hair she wore a golden turban with a rakish tassel that hung over one eye. Miss Allegra was equally fine in a pale pink chiffon gown that swept the floor and was trimmed with ribbons of rose-colored satin. As a special treat, Cosima had pinned up Allie's long flaxen hair and had permitted the child to wear their grandmother's pearls. Allie felt quite grown up.

But Cosy had foregone all the gowns Lady Serena had given her and was making do with the ugly green dress she had worn ages ago to Serena's card party. She sat down with her mother and refused to dance with anyone. She had to be there, but nothing could induce her to enjoy herself. And she was in no mood for a new gown.

Allie had her dance with Lord Westlands. She would have preferred to waltz with him outside in the fragrant air, beneath the moon and the stars, like a proper heroine, but Lady Agatha was too cold to venture out, and it was a spectacle her mother would wish with all her heart to see. To Allie it was a dream come true. When he returned her to her mother, she wanted to cry.

Westlands could not help but notice that Cosima was

despondent. He thought it was because she was in love with him. "It will not be long now," he whispered to her.

Cosima was watching the dancers. Radiant in a gown of lilac satin, embellished with glittering arabesques of jet, Lady Serena floated by in the arms of her cousin. They danced beautifully together, like a pair of angels. "No," she agreed. She fully expected Serena to marry Lord Ludham. Everyone did now. He was so attentive.

Westlands gave her shoulder a comforting squeeze.

"Aren't you going to dance with Cosy?" Allie demanded.

"If I do not dance with my fiancée at once," he told her with a quick smile, "I fear she will become jealous and marry someone else."

Toward the end of dinner, Cosima was asked to play. She took her place obediently at the pianoforte and played the light-hearted Mozart concerto that was on the stand in front of her.

The mint sorbet had just been removed when Fletcher, Lady Matlock's butler, descended to the dining room and announced Lord Oranmore in his stentorian voice.

Cosima's fingers froze on the keys. Had she heard that right, or was it a hallucination? Slowly, she turned her head to look.

"Who?" cried Lady Dalrymple, dropping her spoon and fumbling for her quizzing glass.

"Must be the new one," Lady Matlock remarked to Mr. Carteret. "How very good of him to come to Bath to pay his respects to me!"

"There's nothing new about *him*," Mr. Carteret remarked, looking at the new arrival with a critical eye. "Fifty, if he's a day."

Lady Serena suddenly stood up and fainted. Lord Ludham was almost too surprised to catch her.

"Ben!" shrieked Miss Allegra, getting to him in the quickest way, which meant scooting under the dining table and out the other side.

Cosima remained motionless on the piano bench. Benedict looked gaunt in his black clothes. He was sunburnt. His lustrous black hair had been cut down to an inch, and what remained was no longer black, but heavily dappled with silver. He was one of those unfortunate blue-muzzled men who must be shaved twice a day to keep them human. He needed a shave now very badly. His eyes were icy and gray as he looked around the room.

To her, he looked utterly beautiful.

"You look so old!" cried Allie.

"Good God," murmured Lord Westlands, coming forward to shake his hand. "Good God! It *is* you. We thought you were dead, sir—er—my lord. What a pleasure it is to see you."

"Congratulations, my lord," Benedict replied, "on your engagement."

Westlands flushed with embarrassment. "Everyone has been so upset about you—your—" he broke off in embarrassment. "We thought a little ball might cheer everyone up."

Benedict's face gave away nothing of what he might be feeling. Cosima tried to emulate his implacable self-possession as he finally approached her. She was shaking from head to foot.

She began to stammer like an idiot.

He bowed to her. "Please, don't allow my presence to disturb you any more than my absence, Miss Vaughn," he said dryly. "Please, finish your Mozart."

Somehow she did not faint. Somehow she resisted the urge to throw her arms around him and cover his hard, angry face with kisses. Somehow she did not burst into tears. Somehow she kept her countenance. "I won't," she said faintly.

"You missed a key change in the middle of the adagio," he said.

"You came back from the dead to tell me that?" Her voice shook.

"Play!" he urged as she sat staring at him. "You obviously need the practice."

After a moment, she obeyed.

By this time, Lord Ludham had gotten Serena into an upright position and had persuaded her to take a little wine. Now he approached Lord Oranmore like an ambassador. "Serena has been devastated, my lord, as I am sure you can imagine."

"I fear that my imagination is not as strong as your lordship's."

"Sir!" Ludham protested. "Serena has suffered a great deal. A little kindness from you would not go amiss. She has believed you to be dead for weeks."

Serena smiled at him weakly. She was trying to look on the bright side. He was now the Marquess of Oranmore, and, it was rumored, he had been left a vast fortune. "My lord," she said. "I can not tell you how h-happy I am to see you."

"Clearly," he replied. "I have arranged for us to be married next week."

Serena quivered. "So soon, my lord?"

"My recent experiences have taught me that life is short and precious," he explained. "This time next week, we shall be in Oranmore, my dear."

"Oranmore!" she cried. "You don't mean—! You do not intend to *live* in Ireland?"

"Of course," he replied. "I am Lord Oranmore. I must live amongst my people, such as they are. We'll have to stay in one of the tenant's cottages while the house is rebuilt, of course. I'm afraid the rebels burnt the original structure to the ground in Ninety-eight."

"Rebels!" Serena squeaked, turning white. "But, surely, my lord, with your vast fortune, we need not actually live in Ireland!"

He cupped his ear as if he had difficulty hearing. "Vast fortune?"

"Are you not rich?" she cried.

"I suppose I am," he replied, "by Irish standards. You will not be obliged to eat cabbage more than twice a week, I should think."

"What about the fortune you inherited from your aunt?" she demanded.

He glanced at Miss Vaughn who was murdering Mozart while listening feverishly to the conversation. "I seem to have misplaced it," he said dryly.

"Never mind all that," cried Miss Allegra Vaughn. "Where have you been all this time? What have you been doing? And why are you not dead?"

"And so, to make a long story short," said Benedict, now seated at the dining table to the right of Lady Matlock, "he fired his pistol at me, point blank."

Seated on the arm of his chair, Allie gasped in horror.

Benedict paused to take a sip of his claret. By this time, Cosima had abandoned the piano and was sitting on the arm of her mother's chair. She caught her breath as she imagined the bullet of hot iron piercing his flesh.

"*Where* were you shot, Cousin Ben?" Allie demanded. "Have you got a scar?"

"He aimed for my heart, Miss Allegra, but it was a misfire."

" 'Twas a miracle, then!" Allie breathed.

"It was not a miracle, Miss Allegra," he said impatiently. "A good assassin is conscientious. Thady wasn't. He didn't keep his powder dry, that's all. When his weapon misfired, I stood up and kicked him in the face. The pistol flew into the carriage and landed on the seat next to me."

"Good on you," said Allie, favorably impressed.

"Don't interrupt," Benedict said sternly. "Master Thady became very civil after that. He confessed all. At first, I could not believe that my grandmother could be involved in such a dastardly scheme."

"Lady Oranmore!" For a moment, Lady Dalrymple looked as if she meant to dash right out and find the nearest newspaper office, but then she seemed to think better of it. *Who,* and *what,* were not enough for newspapermen, as she knew from bitter experience. The loathsome creatures always wanted the *when, where,* and *why,* too, before they paid up.

Benedict continued. "Thady swore that, if he returned to Dublin empty-handed, my grandmother would—quote—'do him in.' I am not a vindictive man, I hope. I took pity on him. I gave him my watch and my ring to take back to Dublin in the hopes that my grandmother would be convinced he had done the job. I wanted to see what the greedy old harridan would do next."

Cosima chewed at her bottom lip savagely.

"Thady went back to Dublin to tell Lady Oranmore of my unfortunate demise. The old girl was so upset that she instantly set about marrying off my first cousin Nuala to my second cousin, Mr. Power, who, in addition to being my second cousin, is also my heir. Poor boy. He wept when I sent him and his mother packing."

"I hope you got back to Dublin in time to stop the wedding!" said Cosima. "That girl is not sixteen!"

"Yes, of course," he said impatiently. "Nuala is my ward, and she can not marry without my permission."

Cosima looked down at her hands. "So you never saw Castle Argent? You went back to Dublin, and that was the end of it?"

"*I* would have gotten your harp for you, Cosy," said Westlands. "Come hell or high water. Oh! Begging your pardon, ladies. I did not mean to use such strong language."

"I *did* go back to Dublin," said Benedict, "but not right away. The assassination attempt had merely hardened my resolve to complete my errand, Miss Vaughn. I was very eager to get my hands on your . . . harp. I had no intention of going back to Dublin with nothing."

He took a sip of wine.

"I walked on to the charming little village of Lucan. There I found a friendly tavern where none but the landlord spoke English—or so I was told. Perhaps they simply did not wish to speak to me. I don't know. But I spent the night there, and woke up next to a man with a fish; neither had been in the bed when I laid down, but I daresay that was my fault. Fortunately, the salmon was well-wrapped in what appeared to be a lady's shawl, but I don't criticize.

"I explained to the landlord that I was trying to get to Ballyvaugn on the Grand Canal. The landlord winked at me in a friendly manner and said that I had the look of a man on important government business. Naturally, I was flattered. Not supposing that my true errand, that of fetching a young lady's harp, would be of any interest to this earthy tradesman, I allowed him to think what he liked. He said he would have me there in a 'shake,' which, in Ireland, is usually, but not always, less than a fortnight. He gave me some very good directions to another charming little village from whence I found the canal. I got on the passenger boat without any difficulty, but rather surprisingly, my traveling companions were all Roman Catholic priests."

"What! All of them?" said Cosima, startled.

"Yes; all. Two dozen holy men in long black dresses and me."

"It's called a cassock, you know!"

"They were so kind. They even shared their lunches with me. I suppose I must have looked hungry to them. After lunch, we continued on our way in prayerful silence, down the length of the beautiful, leafy, green canal, until finally, my endeavors were rewarded. I saw a splendid stone building rising in the distance to my right. Charmed by this vision, I asked the young seminarian sitting next to me if we had reached Castle Argent. He looked at me as if I were mad and said, ''Tis Patrick's College.'"

Cosima gasped. "You went the wrong way entirely! You're in Maynooth!"

"Indeed! I had gone north to the *Royal* Canal, when I ought to have gone south to the *Grand* Canal. But I daresay the landlord made an honest mistake. Father Moynihan kindly suggested that I go back to Lucan, and walk to Adamstown from there."

"Right," said Miss Vaughn.

"I explained that I was rather in a hurry, had important business, et cetera, and Father Traynor, who knew the area better, suggested that I take the shortcut to Straffan. He said it might save me as much as an hour."

"Is there a road from Maynooth to Straffan?" Cosima said, puzzled.

Benedict summoned the waiter for more wine. "No," he said. "Why do you ask?"

"You walked through the bog?" Cosima asked, wide-eyed. "In your gorgeous clothes?"

Benedict waited while the waiter poured his wine, then calmly held it to the light to examine its color. "The phenomenon," he said slowly, "known as a *moving bog* is not as rare as one might think. It is caused, or so I am told, by significant amounts of water accumulating between the lighter, porous material of the bog and the hard clay that is usually to be found underneath. Water, as I'm sure you know, Miss Allegra, seeks its own level. As it does so, it carries the bog along with it, and, in this case, it carried me as well. So Father Traynor's shortcut really *did* save me an hour."

Miss Vaughn laughed. "I think Lord Oranmore is telling us a bit of a Munchausen story."

Benedict ignored this impertinent remark. "So there I was, covered in flotsam, and, for all I know, jetsam, too, in what I supposed to be Straffan."

"Was it not Straffan?" Cosima asked.

"Why not?" he replied. "If a miserable string of sod huts wants to call itself Straffan who am I to object? I explained to the lovely turf-cutters plying their trade in *Straffan* that Father Traynor of St. Patrick's College, Maynooth, had sent me to them, and that I had important business at Castle Argent. They could not have been nicer to me. One of them took me for a very educational tour of the nearby waterways in his flat-bottomed boat. At the end of the tour, he struck me on the back of the head with his—one wants to use the correct word here—*loy*. The Irish do not call a spade a spade," he explained. "They call it a loy, but, believe me, it does the work of a spade."

"Good heavens!" said Lady Dalrymple.

"I'm sure it was an accident," Benedict said mildly. "I woke up in a clump of coarse yellow grass growing, I know not how, on a stretch of otherwise barren heath. My friend had vanished with his loy. No doubt, he had gone to get help, and, had I been thinking clearly, I might have waited for him. But I was not thinking clearly. I got up and walked, using the sun to navigate, in an easterly direction. Needless to say, by this time, I no longer had the look of a man on important government business. In fact, I had been stripped of my coat, my breeches, and my boots, and, of course, my wallet. I can only suppose that the man with the loy must have taken them to convince the skeptical authorities of my existence. I must say, I miss my boots."

"What a good thing," said Miss Vaughn, "that you gave your watch and your ring to Thady for safekeeping."

"Quite. My grandmother tells me she sent them to my fiancée. Serena?"

Serena looked at him blankly. "What? I haven't seen them," she stammered.

Cosima opened her mouth to speak, and then closed it again.

Benedict mistook this false start for a yawn. "But I can see that I am boring my company," he said grimly. "Suffice it to say that, once I no longer resembled a man on important government business, the local population couldn't have been nicer, and their command of the English language was at least as good as that of any Yorkshireman. I walked to the nearest town and was conveyed to Ballyvaughn like a king on a cart piled with peat bricks."

"So you made it there all right?" Cosima said anxiously.

He smiled thinly. "I did. I walked up the lane to the gates of your demesne, Miss Vaughn, a scant twenty-four hours after I left Dublin. Unfortunately, I no longer had your hand-kerchief to show your wolfhound, having carelessly left it in the pocket of my coat, along with my wallet."

"That's quite all right," she assured him. "I've a lot of hand-kerchiefs. As for Dolly, she wouldn't hurt a fly. She's big as a horse, but gentle as a lamb."

"That is just what I told her as she came bounding down the lane to meet me," Benedict replied. "Coming at me at full speed as she was, she had only to put her paws on my shoulders, and down I went. I must have been very tired because I went to sleep immediately. I woke up sometime the next day, having been taken up to the house in my sleep by another Thady—"

"That'd be *our* Thady," Allie said knowledgeably. "Thady Jackson."

"Let us call him the 'good Thady,' Miss Allegra, to distinguish him from the 'bad Thady' who tried to kill me."

"No wonder your hair turned white," said Lord Westlands. "Personally, I would have thrashed 'bad Thady' within an inch of his life and driven him ahead of me all the way back to Dublin."

"But then," said Rose, "Lord Oranmore would not have gotten Miss Vaughn's harp."

"So you *did* get Miss Vaughn's harp, after all," said her mother. "Well done, you!"

"Oh, God!" Cosy said guiltily. "I should have told you. My harp isn't at Castle Argent!"

"No," said Benedict. "It isn't."

"You didn't get the harp?" Lady Matlock pouted. "You mean you went all that way, only to come back empty-handed?"

Cosima bristled. "None of this would have happened if he'd taken the Grand Canal like I told him to."

"You are quite right, Miss Vaughn," he drawled in reply. "I should have trusted you."

"This whole thing is ridiculous!" declared Lord Westlands.

RULES FOR BEING A MISTRESS

341

"*I* would have gone back to Ballyvaughn with a troop of soldiers. And if your harp was not there, Cosy, I would have found it, wherever it was. *I* would not have given up so easily."

"Ah, to be young again," said Benedict.

After dinner, it pleased Lord Oranmore to dance with his fiancée. Serena listened wide-eyed as he laid out his plans for his future wife. Afterward, he was waylaid by Miss Allegra Vaughn, but he coldly refused to dance with her.

"You are far too young to be at a ball, Miss Allegra," Benedict told the child sternly. "Even a private ball. You should be at home in bed."

He went off to dance with another young lady. In fact, as far as Cosima could tell, he danced with *all* the young ladies present, including Rose Fitzwilliam. He even danced the boulangere with Miss Carteret. Only then did he trouble himself to find Miss Vaughn sitting with her mother.

"Are you not dancing?" he asked. He was surprised. He had never known Miss Vaughn to want for a partner.

She shrugged. "I might, if someone asked me."

"*I* am asking you."

"In that case, Lord Oranmore," she said coldly, "I'd be delighted," and allowed him to sweep her off in a fast Viennese waltz.

"And how do you like being Lord Oranmore?" she asked him.

"I like it very well, Miss Vaughn."

"Do you find that it's easier to get a woman into bed now that you're the Big Lord?"

"Yes, Miss Vaughn," he replied. "Yes, I do."

Her eyes narrowed. "Is that so?" she snapped.

His grip on her hand tightened almost painfully. "The waltz is a very short dance," he said impatiently. "So let us come straight to the point. *Where is she?*"

She did not pretend she didn't know who he meant. "Didn't you find her?"

"She was no more at your house than your bloody harp

was," he said tightly. "As you well know! Need I remind you, Miss Vaughn, that I paid you thirty thousand pounds for her?"

"I suppose you want your money back."

"No," he said angrily. "I want what I paid for."

"Don't worry, my lord," she said coolly. "I'm sure you'll find someone to commit adultery with you. Men always do."

"Where is she, damn you?" he snarled.

"She's gone, Ben," she said quietly and firmly. "You'll never find her. Perhaps," she added, "she wasn't yours to command, after all. Perhaps you're not quite as fascinating as you seem to think. Besides, you're getting married in a week, are you not? You'll have Lady Serena to command soon enough."

"I have your harp, Miss Vaughn," he said harshly.

She stumbled, but made a quick recovery. "What? You said—"

He went on coldly, "If you don't tell me where she is, I will break it up for firewood along with your pianoforte. And don't pretend you don't care, Miss. The Dowager Duchess of Kellynch would hardly want to display your harp in a glass case in her drawing-room in Dublin if it meant nothing to you."

"How did you get it away from her at all?"

"I stole it," he explained. "That seems to be how things are done in Ireland."

"You mean you snuck in at night and—"

His lip curled. "I don't sneak anywhere. The butler announced me. They were drinking tea in the parlor. I smashed the case and walked out with it. No one said a word."

Her eyes shone with admiration. "They must have thought you were a madman."

"I am a madman," he replied. "You would do well to remember that, Miss Vaughn. If Cherry doesn't want to see me anymore let her tell me so face to face. That is all I ask. I don't want to destroy your harp, but I will."

"I have your watch and your ring," she said quickly.

"My grandmother sent them to *you*?" he said sharply. "She

told me she sent them to my betrothed. She must have thought . . ."

"Where would she get a silly idea like that?" said Cosima.

The music ended, catching them both in surprise.

Benedict grasped her arm. "I don't give a damn about my watch or my ring. I want to see her. I *must* see her. I will trade you the harp."

"Oh, Ben," she said softly. "As long as it's not in that bitch's drawing-room, I don't care a damn about that harp. Sure I never even learned to play it."

He looked utterly dejected. He had nothing left to bargain with.

Cosima couldn't bear the broken look in his eyes. "The park," she whispered. "Wait in the park after the ball tonight, and I— She'll come to you."

"She's still in Bath?" he said incredulously. "What park?"

Her eyes flickered. "Our park," she said softly. "Camden Place. She's been here the whole time, Ben."

"Are you keeping her *locked up*?" He stared at her, revolted. "I swear to God, if you have harmed her in any way, I will wring your bloody neck!"

"Cosy?"

Lord Westlands suddenly appeared at her side. "Is everything all right?" he asked, eyeing Benedict with suspicion. "You look flushed, Cosy."

"I'm just tired, that's all. Please excuse me!" she murmured, rushing away from them.

"What did you say to her?" Westlands demanded of Benedict. "Why is she so upset?"

"I imagine she is upset because you are marrying someone else, my lord," Benedict replied. "She even sold her house to provide herself with a dowry worthy of you."

Westlands flushed. "I am not going to marry someone else," he muttered. "Cosy knows that I love her. If she would only trust me a little!"

Alarmed, Benedict forced the younger man to the side of the room.

"What about Lady Rose?" he said sharply. "You made a commitment to her."

Westlands glanced around furtively, torn between the need for secrecy and the need to defend himself from the inference that he was a complete cad. "Kindly keep your voice down, my lord!" he whispered. "Rose knows all about it. We're eloping tonight, after the ball."

"Indeed," Benedict said coldly. "And what becomes of the girl you leave behind?"

Westlands scowled at him. "Rose is eloping with Dan, of course. The four of us are going together."

"Who the devil is Dan?" Benedict demanded.

"Dan," Westlands elaborated. "Dante Vaughn. You know: Cosy's brother!"

Benedict stared at him. "I thought the boy was in India."

Westlands grinned. "He had to come back for his girl, didn't he?"

Chapter 22

After putting her mother and sister to bed, Cosy went to her own room to change. Already she regretted promising Ben that she would meet him in the park. She sat down on the bed and set her candle on the table next to it. Reaching up, she unpinned her blonde wig and slipped it off, taking the close-fitting stocking cap underneath with it. Her scalp itched, and she scratched it, dragging her nails through the short red locks.

Vocabulary was by no means the strong suit of Lieutenant Dante Vaughn. "What in the bejasus have you done to yourself, woman?" he cried, stepping out of the shadows.

Cosima gasped in surprise, jumped to her feet, and whirled around to see her brother. In the next moment, she was being lifted off her feet as the young man enfolded her in a bear hug. "Faith, and you put the heart across me!" she complained when he had set her on her feet again. She took a careful inventory of him. Everything seemed to be in order. Green eyes. Shock of blond hair. Nose that had been broken at age nine. Lopsided grin with inexplicable, yet fatal charm, and a chipped front tooth. He was not in uniform.

"*What* are you doing here, Dan?" she demanded. "You're supposed to be in India with the rest of the regiment. You've been cashiered, haven't you? What did you do?"

"I made it as far as Gibraltar," he answered. "I wasn't cashiered. I got bit by a monkey. It wasn't my fault!" he added, laughing as she punched him in the arm.

"Not another Munchausen story!" she said sternly.

His green eyes widened. "A what?"

"Never mind! They shoot men for deserting, did you happen to know that, Dan?"

"I'm no fecking deserter," he said angrily. "I'm away without leave, that's all. Even if they don't believe I was bit by a monkey, I'm an officer, and they can't flog me."

"Oh, Dan!"

He frowned at her. "So what *did* you do to your hair? Are you sick or something?"

"What?" Awkwardly, her hands went to her hair. "Penance."

Dante gave a low whistle. "Are you pregnant?" he demanded. "Is that why Marcus is so fecking eager to marry you?"

"What are you talking about?" she said angrily. "Marcus is engaged."

Dante flushed darkly. "I knew how it would be when I left. That fecking aunt of hers hated the sight of me. First she said I could dance with Rose, because I was Lord Westlands's cousin, but then she changed her mind. She made Rose dance with some fecking ancient geezer and why? Because *he* had money. Well, at least I've both my fecking arms, unlike himself!"

Cosima's legs went out from under her and she sat down hard on the bed.

"It made me sick to think of that old bastard getting his cold, scabby hands on my Rose, I tell you. Well, *hand,* I should say, for he had only one, and the left one at that."

"Are you in love with her, Dan?" she asked him quietly.

He snorted. "I am feck," he answered. "You know I don't believe in all that shite. No more than yourself. She's got money, this girl. She'll be the making of me."

"Dan!"

"There I was in me hospital bed in Gibraltar," he said. "I

started thinking about the class of woman I might find in India. Girls and women, not fit to be married in England, so their parents ship them off to India in desperation. I thought to myself: Dan, you're better than that. Why not arrive in style with a rich and lovely young wife? Have you seen her, Cosy? Lady Rose Fitzwilliam? Sure, I can't wait to get my leg over all that beauty."

"You're disgusting," said his sister, but Dante only laughed.

"So we're leaving this night," he said, unperturbed. "Marcus is bringing Rose to meet us at Bath Abbey. We're going to Bristol. Marcus has found a clergyman who will marry us for five pound. Get your things, woman. You're coming with, so you are."

"Do you think for one moment that I would take part in your scheme?"

He laughed. "You will. I'm going to marry Rose and her pretty portion, and *you* are going to marry Marcus. You'll be a countess one day, you lucky bitch, when the old man dies. That boy's head over ears in love with you. It's touching, really. He thinks you're an angel, and I hadn't the heart to tell him the truth, poor sorry bastard."

"I'm not going to *elope* with Marcus," Cosima said firmly.

"Ah, come on," he said, squeezing her hand. "It'll be grand. Amazing! Fantastic! A double elopement! Are you waiting for the big society wedding in Westminster fecking Abbey? 'Tis Catholic you are, and you'll take what you can get."

"I'm not going to marry Marcus," she said. "Much less elope! I don't love him, Dan."

"You've changed more than your hair," he observed. "What's all this crazy talk about love? You're not in love with someone *else,* are you?"

"I am," she said fiercely.

"You damn fool! With that face, you could take your pick! No, I'm pleased for you, Cosy, really," he added quickly as she glared at him. "Is he a nice man?"

"He is not," she said proudly. "He's a cold, heartless bastard."

Dan grinned at her. "Sure a nice man would be no good to you. What you need is a dragon to guard you from all the snakes in this life. You, with all that beauty on your face."

"Funny," she said coldly. "I was just thinking the same thing about Lady Rose!"

He laughed easily. "I'll look after her, so I will. Are you sure you won't come?"

"Certainly not."

He shrugged. "Suit yourself. All I want, then, are Granny Vaughn's pearls to give the girl. I've nothing else to give her, and I'm the first to marry, so you'll hand them over."

"I will not," said Cosima, her green eyes narrowing.

"You will," he insisted. His green eyes narrowed too.

Benedict waited in the park with growing impatience. There was a candle burning in the room he knew to be Miss Vaughn's. Through the filmy lace inner curtains, he could see moving shadows. What the hell was she doing? Where was Cherry? Was Cherry even in the house?

He was reflecting for the hundredth time on the indignities of his position, when, abruptly, the candle in the window went out. He crept closer to the gates of the park. It had begun to rain, so there was no fear of being discovered by the Watchman, who could be relied upon to stay warm and dry in his sentry box.

The front door of No. 9, Upper Camden Place, opened silently, and a young man came out. To Benedict's astonishment, Cherry ran after him, and clutched his arm. Without speaking, the young man threw her off so violently that her head struck the door frame, and she fell down on the steps. Rage swept through Benedict's spare body like a pillar of fire.

"You there!" he shouted, frantically fitting his key into the lock of the gate.

The young man took off running in the direction of Lansdowne Road. "Come back here, you cowardly bastard!"

Benedict shouted, running out of the park to help Cherry to her feet. Blood was trickling down the side of her face.

"Ben!" she whispered, as he clasped her to his body. "Thank God, you're here. You have to stop him! He's going to do something terrible. He—"

"Hush," he commanded, dragging her into the house. Once inside, he took out his handkerchief and pressed it to the side of her head. It was dark as pitch in the hall. He moved her toward the door to the sitting room.

"Mother's asleep," she protested weakly.

He didn't question why Cherry was calling Lady Agatha Mother. He scarcely noticed it. "The kitchen," he muttered, and began dragging her in that direction. "I am going to clean that cut. Then I am going to find the man who hurt you, and I am going to—"

He paused as she stumbled on the stairs.

"Who was he?" he asked her, helping her to her feet.

"It wasn't his fault," she said quickly. "He got bit by a monkey!"

"Oh, dear God. You're delirious," he said, white-faced with concern. He pushed her into the kitchen, overriding her protests, and placed her in the chair nearest the fire. "Let's have a look at this cut," he said, sitting down in the other chair. The tortoiseshell cat hissed indignantly, and jumped down.

"There's no time, Ben," she said. "You must help—"

"Silence," he said, wiping the blood from her face. The cut was mercifully small, but it bled profusely, and a thick, hard knot had already formed around it. He stood up and got the whiskey bottle from the niche in the chimney. He felt murderous anger toward Cherry's attacker, and he had to force himself to be tender with the girl. "This may sting a little," he said, pouring a little whiskey onto his handkerchief.

"There's no time," she insisted. "That was my brother Dan. He's supposed to be in India, but he came back to England for Lady Rose."

"Ah, yes," he said, cleaning her cut.

"You have to stop him, Ben! He's going to kidnap Rose and make her marry him!"

He snorted. "From what I understand, the young lady is perfectly willing. Lord Westlands is going to marry Miss Vaughn, and Rose is going to marry what's-his-face."

"*You knew?* You knew, and you did nothing to stop it?"

Angrily, she pushed his hand away from her face.

"It is not my place," he said, "to interfere. Now hold still."

"You helped Nuala Redmund!" she pointed out.

"And from that you deduced that I intend to make a career out of stopping weddings? Nuala is my responsibility. Rose Fitzwilliam is not. As for Miss Vaughn, after the way she has treated you, and me, I don't care if Westlands takes her to Perdition."

She winced again, but this time it was his words that stung.

"I love you, Cherry," he said quietly. "You *must* come with me to London. Surely you can see that now."

She was already shaking her head. "Ben— I can't—"

"You must try to trust me a little. I will find a way to make you happy, I swear."

She lifted her eyes to his. "If you want to make me happy, stop Dan from ruining that poor girl's life. She thinks she's in love, but he's only interested in her money. And getting his leg over, of course! Like all men."

Benedict remained unmoved.

"She's only seventeen! She has her whole life ahead of her. She deserves better than my galloping eedgit of a brother! Look what he did to me! I'm bleeding! Do you want that girl's blood on your hands as well?"

"No, of course not," he said finally.

"Marcus is supposed to meet Dan at Bath Abbey with Rose and the carriage. They mean to go to Bristol tonight. He's not even going to marry her by Catholic rites! I doubt it's even legal. If you hurry, you can stop them, Ben. Please."

"Of course it's not *legal*. The girl's only seventeen," Benedict muttered. "Oh, all right! I'll do it. For *you*."

She caught his hand and pressed it to her cheek. "Thank you, Ben."

"Miss Vaughn should be ashamed of herself. I will make sure her part in this is exposed to the world. Aiding and abetting this rascal in what amounts to a rape! As a woman she should have more feeling for poor silly Rose. She deserves to be whipped at the cart's tail. As for that brother of hers—" He broke off suddenly, bent down, and kissed her mouth fiercely.

"I'm so sorry, Ben! I'm sorry for everything!"

"What?" he said sharply.

"I mean: I'm not sorry for anything, of course!"

He smiled at her. "Too right you're not. We'll talk when I get back."

The amazing, fantastic, double elopement was in desperate trouble already. "What do you mean, she's not coming?" Rose and Westlands cried in unison when Lieutenant Vaughn gave them the news outside Bath Abbey.

Dante shrugged. "I'm sorrier than I can say, Marcus, but she says she won't marry you."

Marcus jumped out of the comfortable carriage he had hired to take them all to Bristol. "What do you mean?" he demanded angrily.

"She won't have you, and that's the truth of it." Dante tried to enter the carriage where Lady Rose was sitting, almost in tears, but Westlands shoved him back. "What was I supposed to do?" Dante wanted to know. "*Force* her to marry you? Kidnap her?"

"Oh, Dan!" cried Rose. "You don't understand. If your sister doesn't come with us, I can't go either! I can't leave Bath in a closed carriage with a man who is not my husband! Not without a chaperone!"

"It's all right, love," Dante assured her. "It'll be fine. Marcus will chaperone you."

"Then I'll be with *two* men who are not my husband!" she wailed.

"If Cosy's not going, I'm not going," Westlands said with awful finality. "Why should *I* stick my neck out for you if there's nothing in it for me?"

"What?" Dante looked at them, perplexed. "Rose?"

"I'm sorry, Dan," said Rose. "It would not be respectable."

"You're fecking codding me!" said Dante, throwing up his hands.

"I am not accustomed," Rose said frostily, "to such language as this."

Westlands climbed into the carriage with Rose and closed the door.

"You said you loved me!" Dante cried, running after the coach as it raced off into the night. "I'm away without leave because of you! I gave up *everything* for you!"

As the vehicle turned the corner, he succeeded in clambering up Lady Rose's luggage on the back step. He heard Rose shriek from within the coach, and then the curtains of the back window opened, and Rose's pale face looked out.

"You bitch!" he howled. "How could you do this to me?"

The next moment, he was being dragged from the back of the carriage. He fell to the cobbles and his attackers began beating him with blackjacks. No stranger to the Law, Dante realized at once that he had run afoul of the Night Watch. He managed to get a blackjack away from one of the constables. He fought like a demon, and cracked his share of skulls, but, in the end, he was overwhelmed by their superior numbers. Blood ran into his green eyes as he fell to his knees. "Bastards," he muttered as he began to lose consciousness.

He woke up in the roundhouse. He was tied to a chair, his hands behind his back. He looked up into the face of a fat, sweating constable, and said, "What's a nice girl like you doing in a place like this?"

The constable raised his blackjack to strike.

"Not yet," said a freezing English voice.

"Yes, my lord," said the constable.

Dante did his best to sneer as a tall, slim, aristocratic-looking man approached him. Dressed all in black, the aristocrat was smoking a long, slender cigar. His close-cropped hair glinted with silver in the light provided by a single lantern hung from a hook in the ceiling. Only belatedly did Dante notice that the aristocrat's right arm had been amputated. This did nothing to lessen the man's aura of absolute, ruthless power.

"You dirty old bastard!" Dante roared, recognizing him as Lady Rose's erstwhile dancing partner. His hair had been jet black then, but Dante was sure it was the same man.

The fat constable swung his blackjack at that, striking the young man in the lower back. Dante collapsed to his knees. "Is that any way to talk to Lord Oranmore, you Irish filth!"

"Thank you, Constable," Lord Oranmore said. "That's enough, I think."

"It's no trouble, my lord," the constable assured him. "I'd just as soon kill an Irishman as look at one. Dirty buggers. Always up to something."

"Untie my hands, Mary; we'll see who kills who," Dante said.

"Constable!" Benedict said sharply as the blackjack swung across the young man's knees. "May I remind you that this man is part of a vast Irish conspiracy to bring down the government, blow up the Houses of Parliament, and assassinate the Prince of Wales!"

"What the hell are you talking about?" screamed Dante, enraged.

"You're under arrest," Lord Oranmore explained.

"Is that all, then?" Dante sneered. "Sure I thought it was serious! On what charge?"

"Charge?"

"I have the right to know the charge against me!"

"Actually," said Benedict, "you don't. Habeas corpus has been suspended. You have no rights at all. You stand accused of treason, Mr. Vaughn. I, Lord Oranmore, accuse you. And, I'm afraid, that's enough to send you to Australia for the rest of your natural life."

"*And* he's Irish, my lord!" the constable said. "Don't forget that!" He kicked Dante savagely. "Scum! You're not fit to lick the boots of an Englishman."

"You, sir, are a dirty liar," said Dante, concentrating on the real enemy, the lord with the cold gray eyes. "You can't prove shite against me."

"I don't have to prove anything," said Lord Oranmore. "There will be no trial. You'll never see a magistrate, Mr. Vaughn. They will simply lock you up and throw away the key."

"The only good Irishman is a dead Irishman," said the constable darkly.

"We need the names of his fellow conspirators, constable. They will want to interrogate him in London. Unfortunately, he'll have to be alive for that."

"Yes, my lord."

"Go and see what is taking so long," Lord Oranmore commanded. "I would like a moment alone with the prisoner." When they were alone, Benedict said simply, "You should never hit a woman, Mr. Vaughn."

Dante snickered. "I've better things to do with women."

"In particular, you should never, ever hit *my* woman."

Dante thought the bastard was talking about Rose. "She says I hit her? That lying bitch!"

The next moment, he was flat on his back, with the hot end of a cigar a quarter of an inch from his eyeball. The aristocrat's knee was pressed against his throat.

"That sort of behavior, Mr. Vaughn, simply cannot be tolerated in the civilized world."

The constable entered the room at that moment. "The wagon's here, my lord, to take the prisoner to London."

"Very good, constable." Lord Oranmore climbed to his feet

and straightened his clothes. Noticing a little blood on his shoe, he took out his handkerchief and gently wiped it away.

The sky over Bath was painted scarlet by the dawn. Nora answered the door, but Miss Vaughn came flying out of her mother's room, her blonde hair pulled back simply with a ribbon. "Ben! Thank God!" she cried throwing her arms around him. "Did you find him?"

Instinctively, he began disentangling himself from her grasp, but he paused suddenly. Tears glistened in her green eyes. She looked exhausted, and she was shaking like a leaf.

"I did."

She groaned. "Married?"

"No. It would appear that the lady changed her mind."

"Oh, thank God! Was he very angry with me?"

Benedict shrugged. "Your brother seems angry at the whole world, Miss Vaughn."

"Aye! That's him." She laughed shakily. "Where is he?"

"On his way to London. I had him arrested. That ought to teach him to hit women," he said with grim satisfaction.

Her eyes widened. "What do you mean, Ben? Dan never hit me. I hit *him*, to tell you the truth. He was trying to take my pearls, so I broke the washbasin over his head, poor lamb."

"He hit Cherry," Benedict snapped. "I saw him. He pushed her so hard she cracked her head on the door. I hope he's beaten every day for the rest of his life."

Cosima's hand crept up to her forehead. Underneath the fringe of her blond wig, a sizeable goose egg had formed. "Oh, that," she said crossly. "That was nothing."

"Nothing!" Benedict said angrily. "Cherry had a nasty cut on her head. Where *is* Cherry? I want her now. I am taking her away with me, and you will never see her again."

"Oh, Ben," she said miserably, hanging her head. "How did it ever come to this? Cherry doesn't exist. She never did."

"You little bitch," he said coldly.

She had fantasized many times about telling him the truth. This was not how she imagined it. "*I'm* Cherry, Ben. I made her up." She pulled off her wig and faced him defiantly.

He stared at her in disbelief. "Why would you do such a thing?"

"Don't flatter yourself, man," she said crossly. "I only did it to drive you mad."

"Was it worth it?" he snapped.

She winced. "It's not true, Ben. I wanted to be with you," she said simply. "I fell in love with you like an eedgit, and I just had to have you."

"Why didn't you tell me? Why play games?" he demanded. "I would have married you!"

"*I* can't just up and marry at the drop of a hat," she protested. "I've my mother and my sister to think of! Besides, I'd already turned you down. I didn't want you to think I was . . . changeable."

"Heaven forbid."

"I must look awful," she said, rubbing her hair. Her roots were growing out white. "Say something! Did you never guess? Did you not know me, in your heart of hearts?"

There was a deadly pause.

Then he touched the bruise on her forehead. "I must have wanted to believe it," he said.

"You wouldn't have taken me to bed if you knew I was Miss Vaughn," she said softly. "You're too honorable a man to ruin a well-born young lady. I'm not sorry I did it. God help me, I'm not."

"This is terrible," Benedict said grimly.

"What are you going to do now?" she asked him.

"I'm going to marry you, of course."

She shook her head impatiently. "You can't marry me. You're engaged to—to *her*. Anyway, I was talking about Dan, not ourselves. You can't leave him to rot in gaol, Ben. He never hit me, I swear!"

"I think Dan is right where he should be," Benedict said stubbornly.

"I have one brother left to me in this world," she said fiercely. "If any harm comes to him, Benedict Redmund, I'll have your hide for it! I'll never forgive you!"

"I'm sure he's fine," said Benedict.

The last time he had seen Dante Vaughn, he had been tied to a chair. Both of his eyes were swollen shut, his nose was broken, and blood was running down his chin from a split lip.

"Of course," he added reluctantly, "if it will make you feel better, I'll just go and see about getting him released."

"Thank you, Ben," she said gratefully.

She was shocked and horrified when Dante crawled into her kitchen a few hours later. He was doubled over in pain. His eyes were swollen shut. His nose was broken. His lips were split. She hardly recognized him. "Oh, my God!" she cried, running to him.

"I'm fine," he croaked. "I'm all right."

"You're not fine," she said, easing him into a chair.

He told her what had happened to him while she cleaned him up.

"I'll kill him," she said.

"You stay away from Lord Oranmore," Dante told her. "He's a desperate man altogether. I thought I was dead. Fortunately, he left me to his flunkies. I made short work of *them*."

"You didn't kill anyone?" she asked fearfully.

He laughed scornfully. "Didn't have to."

She made him something to eat. "What are you going to do now?" she asked him while he shoveled thick slabs of bacon into his mouth.

He shrugged. "I'll go to India. I'll need money," he added.

"Of course," she said instantly.

She ran upstairs to her bedroom and pulled the tinderbox from its hiding place beneath the floorboards. Grabbing the roll of bank-notes, all the cash she had, she ran back downstairs. Dante snatched it from her and began to count it.

"It's all there, what I owe you, boy!" she said with angry sarcasm.

Her brother had the grace to blush. "You always manage," he said gruffly, by way of thanks, and pocketed the money.

"What about Lady Rose?" she asked him.

"That bitch," he said impassively. "I'm off women forever." He finished his meal, kissed his sister good-bye, and left.

"Did you find him?" Cosima asked Benedict when he called later in the day.

"Oh, yes," he assured her. "He's fine. He's gone to India."

"You saw him?"

"Yes. He asked me to tell you good-bye."

She struck him across the face as hard as she could. "Liar!"

Benedict sighed. He really ought to have guessed the boy would go to his sister the moment he escaped from the roundhouse.

"I saw what you did to him!" she accused. "My own brother!"

"He's lucky it wasn't worse," Benedict grumbled.

"Get out!" she said. "I never want to see you again."

"I simply cannot understand," said Lady Matlock, as she poured out the tea for her guests, "why your son neglected to tell you he was engaged to my daughter. Young people these days!" She held out the cup and saucer for the footman to take to Lord Wayborn.

Earl Wayborn was seated only a few feet away, but he preferred to have his tea brought to him. He was a good looking, imperious man with a natural inclination to be stout.

"I daresay Marcus knew we would not approve!" Lady Wayborn said in the unpleasant, piercing shriek of a female fishmonger. One could tell at a glance that she had been married for her money. There could be no other reason.

Lord Wayborn looked at his wife with contempt. "We, madam? No one asked for your opinion." He gave Lady Matlock one of his charmless smiles. "My wife," he said, "is a stupid woman. I cannot seem to break her of the habit of speaking out of turn."

"My lord," whispered his lady, "I beg—"

"What is worse, she does not *know* she is stupid," went on his lordship. "She *will* speak, just as if she had something interesting to say."

Lady Wayborn took the hint.

"There is nothing whatever objectionable about Rose," said Lady Matlock.

"This tea is not china," Lord Wayborn snapped at the footman. "Take it away, and be damned!" He took out his snuffbox, employed the long nail of his little finger as a spoon, and sneezed manfully. "Dowry?" he said, snapping his box closed.

"Thirty thousand pounds," Lady Matlock said proudly.

"Matlock will have to do better," said Lord Wayborn coldly. "This is my son and heir we are talking about. I would not part with Westlands for less than fifty thousand pounds."

Lady Matlock snorted. "Impossible!"

"Then we have nothing more to discuss," said Lord Wayborn. "Lord Redfylde may marry a penniless girl if he wishes, but my son will marry to please me. Marcus will return to London and marry Miss Schwartz."

"Oh!" said Lady Matlock. "Is Lord Redfylde to be married at last? And to a penniless girl? He seems to have a taste for that sort of thing. He proposed to your niece only weeks ago."

"Yes; I know," said his lordship, dragging his lady up from her chair by the arm. "It was unforgivably rude of Miss Vaughn to have refused his lordship. She ought to have gotten down on her knees and kissed his feet. But I will soon set *that* to rights."

When they had gone, Lady Matlock wondered what she ought to do about Rose. She would never get a husband in England now. "What shall I do?" she asked Freddie Carteret.

"Send her to India," he answered, "with the other rejects."

"What would I do without you?" she purred.

Cosima received Lord Redfylde's second proposal as gently as she had the first. "It's so kind of you to think of me, my lord," she said. They were seated in the drawing-room in Camden Place. "I would not have hurt you for the world. You were never anything but kind to me."

Looking into her soft green eyes, Lord Redfylde quite forgot the ridicule he had endured when he left Bath. Miss Vaughn, he recalled, had been nothing but apologetic. It had been others who had ridiculed him. There would be no need whatever to punish the lovely girl after they were married. She was refusing him out of maidenly modesty, not mischief.

"I *will* be kind to you, Miss Vaughn," he said fiercely. "You'll see."

"My lord," she said sadly. "The truth of it is, I'd make you a terrible wife. And you couldn't even divorce me, for I'm a Catholic, and we'd have to be married by Catholic rites."

"I have no intention of divorcing you," he said. "You will be mine until the day you die, like Caroline. You will, of course, learn to embrace the Church of England. You will never have to wear the same dress twice to Sunday services. You will have the best of everything."

Cosima laughed nervously. "The best would be wasted on me entirely, I'm afraid."

"You do not think you are worthy," he said fondly. "If only more women were like you. My dear Miss Vaughn, the very fact that you *know* you're not worthy tells me that you are."

Her eyes widened. "Allie will be so delighted to see you,"

she said, changing the subject. "I'll go and get her; she's sulking in her room." As she spoke, she edged for the door, but Lord Redfylde forestalled her departure by seizing both her hands in his.

"My lord!" she said, a little sharply. "You go too far. I thank you for thinking of me, but I can't marry you. I'm very sorry to have caused you pain, but I'm sure you'll find someone loads better in London. A handsome nobleman like yourself! You shouldn't demean yourself with the likes of me."

She tried to pull her hands away.

As much as he adored her, Lord Redfylde was becoming impatient. "Your scruples are to your credit, Miss Vaughn! However, I did not make my choice lightly. I am fully aware that you are penniless. I am rich. You are ignorant of the ways of society. It will be my pleasure to teach you. Your clothing allowance would be very generous. You would be the envy of all other ladies. And your sister, as well, of course. The younger Miss Vaughn would have the best of everything, too."

"That's very kind of you," she said sadly. "But I'm sorry, I don't love you."

His hands tightened painfully. His pale eyes narrowed. "I will teach you to love me."

It sounded like a threat. "My lord, you are hurting me," she complained, but he did not release her hands until a sudden loud knock at the front door startled them both.

"Ah!" said Lord Redfylde complacently. "Here is someone who will overcome your ridiculous modesty with good sense."

"I'm sure it's the doctor," said Cosima, again attempting to leave the room.

"Let the servant answer the door," Redfylde said. "It is improper for a young lady to answer her own front door."

"I'll get it!" Allegra Vaughn shouted from the hall.

"Excuse me," said Cosima coldly. "But I want to speak to the doctor."

She opened the door and walked downstairs just as Allegra

was opening the front door. Lady Wayborn had grown fat since Cosima saw her last, but Lord Wayborn was unchanged.

Cosima curtseyed. "My lord. My lady. It's so good of you to visit us. Mother's a little poorly today, but I'm sure—" She jumped as she suddenly felt a hand gripping her shoulder. Lord Redfylde had followed her downstairs.

"Ah, Wayborn," he said easily. "Miss Vaughn is being very silly, I'm afraid. You are her uncle. I expect you to speak to her. Sanction her if you must, but I *will* lead her to the altar by week's end, or the deal is off."

"Deal?" said Cosima.

Lord Wayborn looked around for a servant to help him out of his coat. Finding none, he snapped his fingers for his own footman. "Your lordship is too kind," he said, eyeing Cosima with dislike. "I would not say the young woman is being silly. I would say she is being selfish and ungrateful! I will soon teach her what she owes her family. She will do her duty."

Cosima looked at him incredulously.

Lord Redfylde was smug.

"Allie," Cosima said sharply. "Go and play in the park."

"I don't want to play in the park," Allie said.

"Now, Allie!" Cosima said through gritted teeth.

"I never get to—!" she howled as her elder sister pushed her out the door and closed it behind her.

"Let me get this straight," Cosima said, looking hard at her would-be husband. "I refused your lordship, but, instead of behaving like a gentleman, you ran crying to my uncle! You child!" she sneered. "And now the pair of you have come here to strong-arm me. Well, I won't be strong-armed, gentlemen. Let me be clear," she said loudly and distinctly. "I will never, ever marry you, Lord Redfylde. Now I think you should leave," she added, opening the door for him.

"Take care, my dear," Lady Wayborn trilled. "Or his lordship will change his mind about having *you* at all."

Redfylde's pale blue eyes narrowed. "No fear of that, my

lady. I do not change my mind, once it is made up. You will be my wife," he told Cosima softly. "I will have you."

"Not," said Cosima, "in a hundred years."

"I had thought," Lord Redfylde said coldly, "that you were merely being too modest. But now I see that you are, as your uncle says, selfish and ungrateful. I will cure you of that when we are married." He stepped closer to her. "I will break you like a filly, my dear, and you will thank me for it. I will teach you obedience, and you will learn to submit to my wishes as if they were your own. You will belong to me as surely as any mare in my stable. The sooner you submit, the happier you will be. The longer you resist, the worse your punishment will be."

Cosima said angrily, "You cannot force me to marry you, sir."

"You think not?" he smiled. "Talk to her, Wayborn. Explain the facts of life to your stubborn niece. I will be waiting at my hotel."

He departed with his head high.

"That is a very ugly dress," said Lady Wayborn. "We must get you some new clothes."

"Do be quiet," her husband said irritably. "Now then, miss," he continued, turning to Cosima. "In the absence of your father, I stand as your guardian. You must obey me or suffer."

"I won't!"

Walking up to her niece, Lady Wayborn swung her plump arm, striking Cosima across the face with an open palm. One of her rings cut Cosima's cheek. Having delivered the blow, she turned to her lord, rather like a puppy that expects praise from the master. In this she was disappointed, however.

Lord Wayborn was incensed. "You fool!" he hissed. "You've cut her face. *That* is Lord Redfylde's face. If she is damaged in any way, her *value* will be affected. You stupid, stupid woman!" Drawing back his arm, he dealt his wife a blow to the face that sent her reeling.

Lady Wayborn crumpled to the ground, sobbing.

Chapter 23

Benedict had decided to give his disgruntled lover a day or two of quiet reflection, hoping that her hot Irish temper might cool. The carefully composed letter he sent to her on Tuesday was returned to him on Wednesday, unopened. This infuriated him so much that he forgot he was giving her temper time to cool. He crossed the park and pounded on her door.

To his astonishment, a supercilious manservant in a frock coat answered his knock.

Benedict had rather been looking forward to seeing Jackson's unlovely face as he asked the absurd question, "Is it yourself?" He was taken aback by the manservant's austere majesty.

"Good morning, Lord Oranmore. It is a great pleasure to see your lordship again."

This one-sided familiarity was even more of a surprise.

"Who the devil are you?" Benedict demanded, frowning. "Where is Jackson?"

"This person your lordship refers to has been dismissed," replied the man. "He drank, I believe."

"Nora?"

"Attending Lady Agatha, I believe. I am Willoughby, my lord."

"Willoughby," Benedict repeated thoughtfully. "I know you, don't I?"

"Your lordship is very good." The man smiled. He was the sort to crowd as many honorifics into his speech as he possibly could. "I attended my master, Lord Wayborn, on the auspicious occasion of your lordship's sister's marriage to His Grace, the Duke of Auckland."

"Is Lord Wayborn here?"

"Not at present, my lord. The family are all out."

"Oh," said Benedict, subdued. "His lordship is staying here, then? In this house?"

"Yes, my lord," Willoughby replied. "And Lady Wayborn as well, of course. If your lordship would care to leave a card?"

"Yes, of course." Pickering had had thousands of new cards printed up. Benedict thought with a pang how Jackson would have admired the new cards. Willoughby extended a simple silver tray upon which the card was placed. Willoughby wore pristine white gloves. He did not smell of whiskey. "When do you expect the family to return?"

"They are visiting Lady Serena Calverstock in the Royal Crescent this morning," Willoughby informed his lordship. "My lord and my lady will be delighted to know that your lordship called."

Benedict left in embarrassment. He had not known that Cosy's uncle was in town; he had not been reading his newspaper with due diligence. No wonder his letter had been sent back unopened! It was most improper for a bachelor to write a letter to a young lady to whom he was not engaged. He ought to first ask Lord Wayborn's permission to pay his addresses to her.

He could hardly do that when he was still engaged to Lady Serena Calverstock.

What a mangle.

And why the devil were they visiting Serena? As far as

Benedict knew, there was no special connection between
Serena and the Derbyshire Wayborns.

Miss Vaughn was playing a quiet, simple tune on the
Broadwood pianoforte in the alcove when Lord Oranmore
was announced. Benedict had been able to hear her playing
as Lady Serena's butler brought him up the stairs. He recognized the melody of "Caro mio ben" and smiled to himself.
So her temper had cooled, after all.

Cosima stopped playing, but did not leave her seat. Lady
Amelia was seated to her right in the alcove. Lady Elizabeth
was on her lap. Cosima began guiding Lady Elizabeth's
pudgy pink fingers on the keys.

Serena sprang up as her betrothed was announced. "My
lord! How pleased we are to see you." She curtseyed.

"Are you?" he said rudely, giving his best impersonation of
a villain. Why Serena had not broken the engagement yet was
beyond his power to understand. No woman in her right mind
would want to marry a man who snarled at her constantly. He
glared around. "When we are married, Serena, I will not have
you wear that perfume. It makes one sneeze. Have you gained
weight? You need more exercise. That dress is most unbecom-
ing. It makes you look fortyish."

Besides Lord and Lady Wayborn, Lord Redfylde and Lord
Ludham were also present. Lord Redfylde was watching his
children in the alcove with an amused expression.

Lord Ludham set down his cup of tea. "I beg your pardon!"
he said angrily.

"My lord!" Serena said quickly. "I believe you know
everyone."

Lord Wayborn's smile was oily. "Lord Oranmore. We heard
of your elevation the moment we arrived in Bath," he said. He
was standing between his wife's chair and a tower of pink and
blue iced cakes. Unaware that the cakes were weeks old, Lady

Wayborn eyed them longingly, but she did not dare reach for them. Her husband thought she was too fat already.

"How wonderful!" Lady Wayborn echoed her lord, smacking her lips as she thought of those cakes. "Even if it *is* only an Irish title. You must be thrilled. And soon to be married! To such a pretty gel, too! I call her a gel, but I daresay, she is a fine lady. A fine lady, indeed!"

Lord Wayborn glared at his gabbling wife, but he smiled unctuously at Benedict. "And how is your lovely sister, my lord?"

"Oh, the dear duchess!" cried Lady Wayborn. "I long to see her. She was such a handsome bride. But, I daresay, Lady Serena will be a handsome bride as well. And Miss Vaughn, too," she added generously.

Lord Redfylde stood up abruptly and joined Miss Vaughn and his two daughters in the alcove. He did not want the garrulous Lady Wayborn to spoil his surprise.

He placed his hand on Miss Vaughn's shoulder. "You are just in time to hear our joyous news," he said, smiling. "Miss Vaughn has at long last consented to end my agony."

Benedict started in surprise. "Agony?"

"This beautiful creature has consented to be my wife," Lord Redfylde explained. "We are to be married tomorrow."

"Tomorrow!" Serena exclaimed in surprise. "Is that not sudden, my lord?"

Redfylde looked at her coldly. "I do not believe in long engagements." He turned to his daughters. "Kiss your new mother," he commanded them. "You will call her Mama, and you will love her, as I do."

Amelia kissed her new mother's cheek obediently. Cosima enfolded both children in a warm embrace as Lord Redfylde went on. "The wedding will take place at nine o'clock tomorrow morning in Bath Abbey. I expect you all to be there." He glanced at Lord Oranmore. "You are welcome, too, my lord. You are, after all, Serena's fiancée. Serena, I expect you to have the children packed and ready to go."

Serena was frankly astonished. "You're taking the girls? What? All of them?"

"Of course," he said coolly. "Miss Vaughn adores them. After the wedding, we shall go to London for a week or two. And then we shall depart for an extended tour of the continent."

"All of you?"

"There will be servants, of course," he snapped.

Serena felt that her world was falling apart. The only income she had was that which Redfylde gave her for the upkeep of his four children. Without it, she was so poor that she would have no choice but to marry that odious monster, Lord Oranmore.

She didn't dare jilt him. He still had her bills, as far as she knew. If she jilted him, he would throw her into debtor's prison. She had never wanted him for her husband, but now she was terrified of the marriage. He was beginning to show a cruel streak she had never suspected. She did not want to live among the angry, rebellious peasants of Ireland. She did not want to marry a man who was rich only by Irish standards. She did not want to eat cabbage. As she sank into these miserable thoughts, Miss Vaughn was being congratulated.

"You are a very lucky young woman, miss," Lord Wayborn told his niece.

"Indeed, she is," cried Lady Wayborn. "Ten *thousand* a year!"

"I am happy for you, Miss Vaughn," said Lord Ludham. "Though I confess I am a little surprised."

Redfylde looked angry. "Surprised, Felix? Why so?"

"Did she not refuse you?" said Ludham. "What changed your mind, Miss Vaughn?"

"Miss Vaughn," Lord Redfylde said coldly, "believed she was undeserving of the honor. I have persuaded her that she is. That is all."

Benedict had not said a word. *She will never go through with it,* he thought. *She is only punishing me.* He had underestimated her capacity for cruelty, that was all.

Miss Vaughn suddenly laughed. "Not so, my lord!" she said, smiling at Redfylde.

Redfylde stiffened. He did not like to be contradicted.

"I was testing the strength of your love, my dear," she went on, cuddling the child in her lap. "I knew that if you truly loved me, you would come back. But, if you did not love me, you would simply go away and ask someone else and forget all about me." She reached out her hand to him and looked up at him adoringly. "I am overjoyed to say you passed the test. I only hope you won't be too disappointed in me when we are married."

Redfylde relaxed, took her hand, and kissed it. "My beauty! As though I could ever forget you. You should have known I would stop at nothing to possess you."

Benedict could bear no more of this sickening spectacle. If the heartless wretch thought she was going to make him jealous with this absurd charade . . . well, she was right.

"What was that tune you were playing when I came in, Miss Vaughn?" he said sharply. "It sounded familiar."

Her eyes swung to him. They were cold and green as the sea. Her temper had cooled, all right. It had cooled to ice. "That was nothing," she said, with a mocking smile. "Only finger exercises. That reminds me, Lord Ludham," she went on, dismissing Lord Oranmore. "I really must return the pianoforte you were so kind as to give me. Now, what would my husband think of me," she went on as he began to protest, "if he knew I was in the habit of accepting gifts from other men? Think of my reputation!"

"I am perfectly capable of buying my wife anything she desires," Redfylde added.

"Please keep it as a wedding gift," said Ludham. "I insist."

"I am so fortunate in my husband that I want no wedding gifts," said Miss Vaughn, pressing Redfylde's hand to her cheek. "But, with your lordship's kind permission, I could give it to the Church. They could raffle it off, couldn't they?"

"Of course," said Ludham, miffed.

"Won't you sit down, Lord Oranmore?" Serena said, holding out a cup of tea.

Benedict ignored her. "Where is Miss Allegra? Is she not here?"

"She is at school, of course," said Miss Vaughn coolly.

"And Lady Agatha, I suppose, is in the baths on Stall Street?"

"Yes, of course," said Lord Wayborn impatiently.

Benedict went to Miss Vaughn in the alcove. Her eyes widened, and she hugged Lady Elizabeth and Lady Amelia to her. "I fear I shall be too busy to attend your wedding, Miss Vaughn," he said coldly. "Please accept my most heartfelt congratulations. You are indeed a very lucky young woman."

He left the room without a backward glance.

"What a rude man!" cried Lady Wayborn. "No one would ever guess his sister was a duchess. He was most unkind to you, Lady Serena. If I were you, I would not marry him."

"No one asked you," Lord Wayborn said irritably.

"My betrothed is looking tired," Lord Redfylde remarked. "You should take her home, Wayborn. I want her well-rested for the morrow. You will dine with me this evening at my hotel. There will be documents to sign, and so forth."

"Oh!" said Lady Wayborn. "We should be delighted to dine with you, my lord!"

"Not you," said her husband brutally. "Why would Lord Redfylde want *you* at his table, you silly cow? The sight of you is enough to put a man off his feed for a week. *I* shall be dining with Lord Redfylde alone."

Lady Wayborn bustled to her feet. "Come, Miss Vaughn!" she said sunnily. "You must rest. Tomorrow is your big day."

Lord Redfylde departed with them, Peacham came to collect the children, and Serena was left alone with Lord Ludham. Serena covered her face with her hands and sobbed. "Oh, Felix! What am I going to do? I cannot marry that odious man!"

Lord Ludham suddenly took her in his arms. "Of course

you're not going to marry him, you fool. You're going to marry me!"

"I can't marry you," she wailed. Choking back sobs, she told him about the bills Lord Oranmore was holding over her head like the sword of Damocles. "I owe him quite ten thousand pounds! If I jilt him, he will throw me into debtor's prison! He will do it, I know, for he is quite as cruel as Redfylde."

Ludham frowned. "Has Redfylde been unkind to you?"

"Beastly," she said. "He had my bills before Lord Oranmore got them."

She did not elaborate.

"Don't be afraid," said Lord Ludham. "No one is going to throw my wife into debtor's prison." He took out his handkerchief and dried her eyes.

"Oh, Felix!" she said, sniffling happily. "I was sure you would hate me if you knew."

"Hate you? After all the mistakes I've made, I'm glad."

"Glad!"

"Yes," he said. "You've always been there for me when I've made a muddle of things. Now it's my turn to be there for you. You never seemed to need me."

"Oh, Felix!" She melted in his arms like an ecstatic school-girl, hardly daring to believe that this was really happening to her. "I do need you! You've no idea how much I need you."

Lord Oranmore headed for Stall Street to assess the situation. He soon saw that it was no good, however. It would be quite impossible to kidnap Lady Agatha from the all-female baths.

It would have to be Miss Allegra, then. Once he had Allie in his clutches, he would send Miss Vaughn a ransom note demanding that she jilt Lord Redfylde and marry him, Lord Oranmore, instead. Miss Vaughn would do absolutely anything to get her sister back, he knew.

He went to Miss Bulstrode's Seminary for Young Ladies and rang the bell.

The housekeeper showed him into a tidy office appointed with a massive desk and horsehair furniture. Miss Bulstrode rose from the desk, looking flustered.

"I am Lord Oranmore," Benedict said imperiously. "Fetch Miss Allegra Vaughn at once. I am her cousin."

"My lord!" said Miss Bulstrode. She licked her lips nervously.

"I am in a hurry, Bulstrode," he said, sneering arrogantly. "I am marrying her sister in the morning, so, you see, I am practically her guardian."

"Oh!" said Miss Bulstrode, breathlessly. "But I had understood that Miss Vaughn was to marry the marquess!"

Benedict's gray eyes sliced into the woman. "*I* am the marquess, you foolish old woman," he said harshly. "The Marquess of Oranmore. Now fetch Miss Allegra before I lose my temper."

"At once, my lord!" yelped Miss Bulstrode. She galloped out of the room.

"I should think so indeed!" he snapped, then sat down on the sofa and lit a cheroot to steady his nerves. He had never kidnapped anyone before, and the strain of being rude and menacing was getting to him. It crossed his mind briefly that he might be going mad, but he dismissed it. When one goes mad, it never crosses one's mind that one might be going mad. Only sane people think that way.

Miss Bulstrode came hurrying back with Allegra in tow, and he hastily tossed his cheroot away. "Ah, Miss Allegra," he said pompously, giving the child two fingers to shake. "I am come to take you home."

Some papers on Miss Bulstrode's desk suddenly burst into flames.

"I'm so sorry," Benedict said, forgetting to be the arrogant aristocrat. "I fear I may have tossed my cheroot onto your desk by mistake." He picked up a vase of flowers and dumped its contents over the headmistress's desk. The fire spluttered out.

"That's quite all right, my lord," said Miss Bulstrode, with a smile pasted to her face.

Benedict had hired a carriage. It was waiting outside.

"This isn't the way to Camden Place," Allegra said suspiciously.

"No," he said. "I am going to be honest with you, Miss Allegra. I am not taking you home. At least, not right away. I am kidnapping you. It is very wrong of me, I know, but it can't be helped. I simply cannot allow your sister to marry Lord Redfylde. I hope you can forgive me one day. You'll understand when you're older," he added doubtfully.

Allie threw her arms around him and squeezed. "Oh, thank God!"

"You don't like him either?" he guessed.

"I hate him!" she cried. "And so does Cosy! The only reason she agreed to marry him is because they've been holding me prisoner at the school! I've been locked in the attic for days, with nothing to eat but bread and water. I'm wasting away!"

Indeed, she did not look quite as rosy-cheeked as usual.

"That," he said, "is despicable."

"That," she answered darkly, "is my uncle. He *sold* Cosy to Lord Redfylde for ten thousand pounds! He is forcing her to marry him—in Bath Abbey!"

Benedict groaned. He had been so blinded by his feelings that he had not picked up on that important detail. Of course, Cosy would never consent to be married in Bath Abbey, by Protestant rites. She had even tried to call his attention to it, when she mentioned giving her pianoforte to the Church. And she had told him where to find Allie. And, most important, she had been playing "Caro mio ben" on the pianoforte when he arrived.

"I am such a fool," he murmured. "And your mother, Miss Allegra?" he said quickly. "Is she really in the baths?"

"We don't know where she is," Allie replied. "Uncle Wayborn

signed some papers, and the doctor took her away. He had men with him. Cosy tried to stop them, but the doctor put something on a handkerchief. He put it over her nose and mouth, and—and—"

To his horror, Allie began to cry.

"She went down so fast, I was sure she was dead! They carried her upstairs and locked her in her room. That's the last time I saw her."

Benedict took out his handkerchief.

"Don't cry, Miss Allegra," he said. "Everything's going to be just fine."

He felt quite calm, almost serene.

Lord Wayborn picked up the banknote for ten thousand pounds and put it in his pocket. He leaned back from the table in the private dining parlor of the York House Hotel and thanked his host profusely as the waiter filled his glass with a magnificent port bottled in the previous century. "A toast to the bride and groom," he said, lifting his glass.

"To me," Lord Redfylde agreed, lifting his own glass.

The door was thrown open and a fat constable burst into the room. The entire Bath Watch crammed into the room behind him, armed with pistols and blackjacks.

Lord Redfylde spilled his port all over himself.

"You're under arrest!" screamed the fat constable.

"How dare you!" said Lord Redfylde, jumping up. "I am the Marquess of Redfylde! This is the Earl of Wayborn. You are interrupting a private dinner!"

The constable sniffed, unimpressed. "You've a bloody cheek, you have! I'll teach you to impersonate a lord and an Englishman, by God, you Irish dogs! Lord Oranmore warned us you would use those *very* names."

Lord Oranmore entered the room. "*That*," he said scathingly, pointing at Lord Redfylde, "is one Patrick O'Toole, and *that*," indicating Lord Wayborn with equal scorn, "is one Seamus

O'Riley. I have it on good authority that they are plotting to assassinate the Prince Regent. Impersonating Lord Wayborn was the biggest mistake you could have made, Mr. O'Riley. Lord Wayborn happens to be my cousin."

Benedict smiled. It was not a nice smile.

"But-but-but *I* am your cousin, sir!" squawked Lord Wayborn. "I am not Irish! Do I sound Irish to you?" he appealed to the constables.

Lord Oranmore sneered. "The Irish are gifted mimics. One finds them on stage constantly, sounding just like you and I, Constable. That is what makes them so dangerous."

Lord Wayborn flung his arm out in accusation. "*He's* the one who's Irish!"

The fat constable laughed.

"I suppose," said Lord Redfylde coldly, "that Serena has been complaining about my treatment of her. Well, she asked for it, the little slut." He laughed harshly. "She begged for it. And so she will again. Once a whore, always a whore."

"Is that," said Lord Oranmore, "any way to talk about a Princess Royal?"

"Oh, no, he didn't!" screamed the fat constable without pausing to reflect that none of the Royal Princesses were named Serena. "Bring the chains!"

The fat constable was determined that these two Irishmen would not escape as the other one had. Lord Redfylde went down under a swarm of brawny constables wielding black-jacks.

"I'll get you for this," he howled as they shackled him.

"Better search them, constable," said Lord Oranmore. "They may be armed."

"Blimey!" roared the constable. "This one's carrying a bank-note for ten thousand pounds!"

"For purchasing armaments, no doubt," said Lord Oranmore. "Better let me take that. Evidence." He tucked it into his coat pocket.

"Why are you doing this to me?" wailed Lord Wayborn.

"Think of my poor wife! And poor Miss Vaughn! Tomorrow is her wedding day!"

The watchmen hauled them both away to the roundhouse.

Lord Oranmore took out his watch and clucked his tongue.

As he was leaving the York Hotel, he almost collided with Lord Ludham.

"My lord!" they both said at once.

"I came here to find Redfylde," said Lord Ludham.

"You just missed him, I'm afraid."

"Then I will deal with him later. I will deal with you now, Lord Oranmore."

Benedict looked apologetic. "I am a little pressed for time, my lord. Perhaps another time—"

"Then I shall be brief, Lord Oranmore. Serena doesn't want to marry you. I am come to get her bills back from you."

"What bills?" asked Benedict impatiently.

"Don't pretend you don't understand me, sirrah! I refer to the bills you won in a card game. You have been using them to blackmail Serena into marrying you."

Benedict opened his mouth to deny it, then closed it again.

"Oh, those bills," he said. "I didn't know they were Serena's. I thought they were another lady's."

"You what? Where are they?"

"I will get them," Benedict promised. "Really, I'm very pressed for time."

He took out the banknote the constable had found in Lord Wayborn's pocket. "Please give this to the lady as a token of my good faith. You have my word as a gentleman that Serena will never be troubled by those bills again. Good-bye."

He left Ludham staring at the banknote, open-mouthed.

Imagine, carrying that much cash around.

"Willoughby!" shrieked Lady Wayborn as the butler opened the door to the drawing-room quite unexpectedly. Her ladyship was supine on the sofa with a box of chocolates open on her ample stomach. She struggled into the sitting position, depositing the chocolate box onto the floor. "What is the meaning of this intrusion? How dare you?"

"I'm sorry to disturb you, my lady," said Benedict, striding into the room. "But I have just this minute received a letter from my sister the duchess. I thought you might like to read it."

Lady Wayborn was now on her feet, and Willoughby was disposing of the chocolate box. "Oh!" she cried in delight. "The duchess! Oh, do come in, Lord Oranmore! Willoughby! Tea!" Her small, piggish eyes lit up suddenly. "Or would you rather have a sherry, my lord? Sherry for his lordship, Willoughby."

Willoughby withdrew discreetly.

Lady Wayborn sat down. "Pray, be seated, my lord. It is so good of you to come to see me. My husband neglects me so." She fluttered her lashes coyly. "But, really, there was no need to push your way past poor Willoughby. I would never have denied you admittance. How is dear Juliet? Breeding, I trust? Why, it has been over a year since the marriage took place. *I* gave my husband a son and heir precisely nine months after the wedding," she gloated, preening. "I *do* hope Her Grace is not barren. Then the Duke will be obliged to divorce her, which would be a great shame, for I believe it was a love match.

"We are always eager to hear about our dear duchess," she went on, taking the piece of paper he offered. "Such an original! Whoever heard of honeymooning in Canada? My Lord Wayborn was persuaded it was most unwise. So perilously close to those ungrateful American savages!" She looked at the page. "'If you ever want to see your sister again—'" she read.

Benedict snatched it away from her. "Er . . . wrong letter," he muttered. "Here."

He took out his sister's letter and handed it to Lady Wayborn.

Lady Wayborn took it eagerly.

"Is Miss Vaughn at home?" he inquired presently.

"The poor girl is simply exhausted," Lady Wayborn replied, her eyes glued to the duchess's letter. "Burnt to the socket! Dr. Grantham has forbidden her to leave her bed until tomorrow morning. Oh, Her Grace does not say anything about my younger son," she pouted in disappointment.

"There's something about James on the back," he said, and the lady turned over the letter eagerly. "Two thousand a year, I believe. I do hope," he went on smoothly, "that you remembered to lock Miss Vaughn in her room. We can't have her escaping, not with the wedding tomorrow."

Lady Wayborn started up in alarm.

"It's all right," said Benedict. "Lord Wayborn and I have no secrets from one another."

She blinked in confusion. "You don't?"

"No, of course not. In fact, I have just come from the York." He smiled again. "I came here in the hopes of finding you quite alone, Lady Wayborn."

"Oh!" said the lady, blushing. "Why?"

"I want to do something shockingly indecent to you, of course," he replied. "*Did* you remember to lock Miss Vaughn in? It would be a shame if we were interrupted."

"*Of course* I remembered to lock the door, you naughty man," cried Lady Wayborn. "Here is the key, if you don't believe me."

She withdrew a large black key from between her generous breasts, showed it to him, and then put it back. "I am so relieved," he said.

"Not that it's at all necessary," said Lady Wayborn. "The doctor gave us something to help her sleep."

"Laudanum, of course," said Benedict.

Lady Wayborn selected a tall bottle from several on the small table next to her.

"We can't give her laudanum—she won't drink it. Fights like a tiger. We use ether. My maid holds her down, and I put it over her nose and mouth with my handkerchief. So easy! Of course, she *is* just a slip of a girl. It doesn't take much."

Benedict took the bottle from her ladyship and went over to the window to read the label. "Is that safe, do you think?"

"Dr. Grantham assures us it is very safe and confidential," said Lady Wayborn.

She squawked in surprise as a sodden handkerchief suddenly covered her nose and mouth. Lady Wayborn was a large woman. She did not slump over immediately, but kicked her legs and struggled. For one awful moment, Benedict feared he had murdered the woman.

Then she began to snore.

Gingerly, he reached between the woman's breasts and pulled out the key. It was greasy from her ladyship's body oil.

Benedict couldn't think of anything more shockingly indecent than that.

He rang the bell. When Willoughby appeared, he said calmly, "Her ladyship has had too much to drink. You had better put her to bed. I can show myself out."

"Not again," Willoughby muttered. He went out to fetch the footmen and Lady Wayborn's maid. Benedict went downstairs and opened the door. Then he closed it again and ran back up the stairs. He made his way to Cosima's room and unlocked the door.

The room was black as pitch. Benedict dug out his cheroot case and struck a match. Cosima was tied hand and foot to the iron bed. She was unconscious. They had not bothered to undress her completely, but her feet were bare. Her wig was gone.

"Cosima! Cosy! Wake up!"

Her eyes popped open. "Ben," she croaked.

The match burnt his fingers and he dropped it.

He lit another match and ran to her.

"Never mind about me," she hissed. "Ben, you must find Allie! Mother is in the hospital, but they won't tell me where they're keeping Allie! You—"

He found a candle and lit it. "I have Allie," he said shortly.

"*You* have Allie?" she repeated. "You have Allie, and I'm not dreaming?"

He kissed her. "You are not dreaming. Now let's get you out of here."

He took out his pocket knife and cut her bonds.

"Can you walk?"

"I think so," she said, but in this she was quite mistaken. Because of the ether, her legs were too weak to hold her. She fell back on the bed like a rag doll.

"Bastards," he snarled. "I will have to carry you."

She looked at him sadly. "You can't do it, Ben. I'll walk. I'll manage."

"Is that so?" he said coldly. He caught her behind the knees as she pulled herself to the edge of the bed, and, in the next minute, she was upside down. Her bottom was on his shoulder and his left arm was like a band of iron around the back of her thighs.

She felt dizzy. "I think I'm going to be sick," she moaned.

"Then be sick," he snapped, straightening up. With her body bent in half, she was light as a feather. He heard her retch.

"You will never manage all these stairs," she said presently. "Really, I believe I can walk. Ben, you will fall and hurt yourself. Put me down!"

"It's so nice," he said tightly, "to be with a woman who has such confidence in me! I am carrying you down these stairs, madam, and that is my final word."

He carried her down to the landing. Willoughby looked at them in surprise. Two footmen were carrying Lady Wayborn's bulk from the drawing-room. They stopped and looked at Lord Oranmore in surprise, too.

Benedict thought quickly.

"The house is on fire," he said. "Everyone should get out as quickly as possible. Don't—"

Willoughby shrieked in terror. The footmen dropped Lady Wayborn and ran off in all directions. Lady Wayborn's maid flew out of her ladyship's bedroom, screaming.

"—panic."

Benedict calmly stepped over Lady Wayborn's inert body.

"What did you do to her, Ben?" Cosima asked curiously.

"Ether," he answered briefly.

"We can't leave her, Ben. We can't let her burn up in a fire."

"Don't be silly," he snapped. "The house isn't on fire."

"It isn't? But you said—"

"I lied, my love. I lied!"

Huffing and puffing, he carried her the rest of the way down. The servants very kindly had left the door open for him. He carried her out to the waiting carriage and put her inside next to her sister. Allegra had never seen her sister without her blonde wig.

"Holy fly! What did they do to you?"

Benedict climbed up into the carriage. Cosima was white-faced, leaning against the side of the vehicle, holding herself very still, struggling not to be sick. She opened her eyes and asked quietly, "Mother?"

He smiled at her. "I'm afraid I have no authority to countermand your uncle's orders," he said apologetically, "unless, of course, you marry me."

A glint appeared in her eyes. "That's blackmail," she said weakly.

He smiled at her. "Black is my favorite color," he reminded her. "Do you think Father Mallone will marry us now, even though you are so drugged you cannot even stand?"

"He will," she assured him, "when he hears my confession."

Epilogue

Two months later, Lord Oranmore addressed the House of Lords for the first time. His beautiful young wife was seated in the gallery. "Don't you see, my lords, if this can happen to Lord Wayborn and Lord Redfylde, it can happen to any of us! Look at them: so bruised and battered, I almost didn't recognize them!"

Lord Redfylde glared around him. His face had healed, but his ears had been sliced off and were gone forever. Lord Wayborn had a look of shock permanently etched on his face.

"Looking at them, one might almost believe they had been tortured!" Benedict went on. "But, of course, Lord Liverpool assures us that the British government doesn't torture people, and, naturally, I take the word of a gentleman!"

Lord Liverpool looked decidedly liverish.

"My lords, I *did* warn you that suspending habeas corpus in the British Isles would lead to just such terrifying abuses of power, did I not? I strongly urge you, my lords, to correct Lord Liverpool's tragic lapse in judgement before some innocent person suffers as Lord Wayborn and Lord Redfylde have been made to suffer."

As he resumed his seat, Lord Oranmore looked up at his beautiful young wife in the gallery and smiled. Her ladyship was smartly dressed in a costume of ultramarine blue. On her head was a tiny blue hat with an eye veil.

"I am going to destroy that Irish bastard if it's the last thing I do," Lord Redfylde snarled.

The Prince Regent beckoned to the Prime Minister. His quizzing glass was glued to his eye as he stared at a vision in bright blue. "Who is that beautiful young woman in the gallery?"

"That is Lady Oranmore, your Highness," Lord Liverpool replied.

"Yes, but who *is* she?" His Highness said impatiently. "Where did he get her?"

"She is niece to Lord Wayborn," the Prime Minister replied. "She was going to marry the Marquess of Redfylde, but Lord Oranmore stole her."

The Prince Regent looked at Lord Oranmore through his quizzing glass.

"Interesting," he said.